Join the army of fans who LOVE Scott Mariani's Ben Hope series . . .

'Deadly conspiracies, bone-crunching action and a tormented hero with a heart . . . Scott Mariani packs a real punch'
Andy McDermott, bestselling author of *The Revelation Code*

'Slick, serpentine, sharp, and very very entertaining. If you've got a pulse, you'll love Scott Mariani; if you haven't, then maybe you crossed Ben Hope'
Simon Toyne, bestselling author of the *Sanctus* series

'Scott Mariani's latest page-turning rollercoaster of a thriller takes the sort of conspiracy theory that made Dan Brown's *The Da Vinci Code* an international hit, and gives it an injection of steroids . . . [Mariani] is a master of edge-of-the-seat suspense. A genuinely gripping thriller that holds the attention of its readers from the first page to the last'
Shots Magazine

'You know you are rooting for the guy when he does something so cool you do a mental fist punch in the air and have to bite the inside of your mouth not to shout out "YES!" in case you get arrested on the train. Awesome thrilling stuff'
My Favourite Books

'If you like Dan Brown you will like all of Scott Mariani's work – but you will like it better. This guy knows exactly how to bait his hook, cast his line and reel you in, nice and slow. The heart-stopping pace and clever, cunning, joyfully serpentine tale will have you frantic to reach the end, but reluctant to finish such a blindingly good read'
The Bookbag

D1579289

'[*The Cassandra Sanction*] is a wonderful action-loaded thriller with a witty and lovely lead in Ben Hope . . . I am well and truly hooked!'

Northern Crime Reviews

'Mariani is tipped for the top'

The Bookseller

'Authentic settings, non-stop action, backstabbing villains and rough justice – this book delivers. It's a romp of a read, each page like a tasty treat. Enjoy!'

Steve Berry, *New York Times* bestselling author

'I love the adrenalin rush that you get when reading a Ben Hope story . . . *The Martyr's Curse* is an action-packed read, relentless in its pace. Scott Mariani goes from strength to strength!'

Book Addict Shaun

'Scott Mariani seems to be like a fine red wine that gets better with maturity!'

Bestselling Crime Thrillers.com

'Mariani's novels have consistently delivered on fast-paced action and *The Armada Legacy* is no different. Short chapters and never-ending twists mean that you can't put the book down, and the high stakes of the plot make it as brilliant to read as all the previous novels in the series'

Female First

'Scott Mariani is an awesome writer'

Chris Kuzneski, bestselling author of *The Hunters*

THE DEVIL'S KINGDOM

Scott Mariani is the author of the worldwide-acclaimed action-adventure thriller series featuring ex-SAS hero Ben Hope, which has sold nearly two million copies in Scott's native UK alone and is also translated into over 20 languages. His books have been described as 'James Bond meets Jason Bourne, with a historical twist'. The first Ben Hope book, THE ALCHEMIST'S SECRET, spent six straight weeks at #1 on Amazon's Kindle chart, and all the others have been *Sunday Times* bestsellers.

Scott was born in Scotland, studied in Oxford and now lives and writes in a remote setting in rural west Wales. When not writing, he can be found bouncing about the country lanes in an ancient Land Rover, wild camping in the Brecon Beacons or engrossed in his hobbies of astronomy, photography and target shooting (no dead animals involved!).

You can find out more about Scott and his work, and sign up to his exclusive newsletter, on his official website:

www.scottmariani.com

By the same author:

Ben Hope series
The Alchemist's Secret
The Mozart Conspiracy
The Doomsday Prophecy
The Heretic's Treasure
The Shadow Project
The Lost Relic
The Sacred Sword
The Armada Legacy
The Nemesis Program
The Forgotten Holocaust
The Martyr's Curse
The Cassandra Sanction
Star of Africa

To find out more visit **www.scottmariani.com**

SCOTT MARIANI

The Devil's Kingdom

avon

AVON

A division of HarperCollins*Publishers*
1 London Bridge Street,
London SE1 9GF

www.harpercollins.co.uk

A Paperback Original 2016

2

Copyright © Scott Mariani 2016

Scott Mariani asserts the moral right to
be identified as the author of this work

A catalogue record for this book is
available from the British Library

ISBN-13: 978-0-00-748621-2

Set in Minion by Palimpsest Book Production Ltd, Falkirk, Stirlingshire

Printed and bound in Great Britain by
Clays Ltd, St Ives plc

MIX
Paper from
responsible sources
FSC **FSC C007454**
www.fsc.org

The adventure began in *Star of Africa*.

Now, in this thrilling sequel, Ben Hope is in the
most desperate situation of his life . . .

PROLOGUE

Oman

The man stood at the high, broad window and spent a few moments gazing pensively at the view. From the house, the landscaped gardens of the Al Bu Said residence sloped gently down towards the sea. Palm trees swayed in the Indian Ocean breeze. He could see the light dappling the water like liquid gold around the gleaming white hull of the family's superyacht, moored in its private marina in the distance. It was a late afternoon in November, but the sun was warm through the bulletproof glass of the window.

What a way to live, the man thought. He drank in the spectacular view for a few moments longer before dragging himself away. Dreams were all very well. But it wasn't his view, and such opulence would remain infinitely beyond his reach if he lived to be a thousand years old. Not everyone could be born into such unimaginable wealth. Maybe that was just as well.

Turning to look back at the rest of the big room, he faced the darker reality of the situation.

And what a way to die, he thought, shaking his head sadly. Their money had done them no good in the end.

Most physical signs of the brutal quadruple murder were

1

long gone, erased since the forensic team had finished their work. The bodies of Hussein Al Bu Said, his wife Najila, and their two children – Chakir, twelve, and seven-year-old Salma – had been housed in a mortuary at the family's privately owned hospital in Salalah until they had finally been laid to rest yesterday, amid scenes of unbelievable public mourning.

It had been the most shocking incident. Two weeks after the murders, all of Oman was still stunned. Not because the super-wealthy businessman had necessarily been an adored figure – but because if highly protected members of one of the oldest noble family dynasties in all of the Persian Gulf could be targeted by criminals and butchered in their own home like cattle, then who was safe?

Now all that remained was to catch the perpetrators of this terrible crime. That job belonged to the man standing in the window. His name was Zayd Qureshi, and he was one of the most senior detectives of the Royal Oman Police's Special Task Force. The ROP had pledged that they would not rest until the perpetrators were brought to justice.

The Al Bu Said residence was empty except for Qureshi and his number two, Detective Faheem Bashir, who had served in some slightly mysterious capacity in the Sultan's Armed Forces before transferring to the police. Qureshi had long ago given up quizzing Bashir about his secretive background. And at this moment, it was the last thing on his mind. He liked to revisit the scene of the crime when all had gone quiet. It helped him to still his thoughts, and get into the head of the criminal. To catch a crook, sometimes you had to think like a crook, see the world through their eyes.

Qureshi's investigation team had managed to trace certain leads. A car seen racing away from the scene of the murder had been traced to its owner, who told the police it had been stolen; his story was confirmed by CCTV footage of the theft, although the thief's identity was still unknown. So far, the police had produced no solid results. The only thing they knew for sure was that this was a highly professional robbery to order, evidenced by the fact that the thieves forced Hussein Al Bu Said to open the safe but left a fortune in cash and jewellery unmolested.

'There's only one reason why anyone would do that,' Qureshi said out loud, to nobody in particular. 'But what did they take?'

Faheem Bashir, who had no better idea of the answer than his superior, said nothing and went on looking around the desolate crime scene as though it might cough up more clues for them.

Neither Qureshi nor Bashir noticed the presence of the third man who had stepped silently into the room behind them.

'They took the Star of Africa,' the man said. 'Hussein's diamond.'

The detectives turned, startled. It was highly unusual for anyone to be able to sneak up on Bashir like that.

'Who are you?' Qureshi demanded. 'How did you get in here?'

The stranger made no reply. He was about ten years younger than Bashir and twenty years younger than Qureshi; somewhere in his early thirties, lean and compact in build. His black hair was swept back from a high brow and a chiselled face that radiated a brooding, simmering energy. His dark eyes were mournful, and yet filled with a contained fire of rage that Qureshi found unsettling.

The stranger gazed around him, apparently uninterested in the detectives, as though all he'd come for was a last look at the place. Then he turned and left the room without another word.

Qureshi went to go after him, but Bashir stepped into his path, gently pressed a hand to his boss's chest to block him, and shook his head.

'What are you doing? Get out of my way, I want to talk to that guy, find out who he is and what he's talking about. What diamond?'

Bashir let his hand drop, but he was still shaking his head.

'I could tell you who he is,' Bashir said. 'But I'd have to kill you.'

Chapter 1

The Democratic Republic of Congo

It was a rough road that the lone Toyota four-wheel-drive was trying to negotiate, and the going was agonisingly slow. One moment the worn tyres would be slithering and fighting for grip in yet another axle-deep rut of loose reddish earth, the next the creaking, grinding suspension would bump so hard over the rubble and rocks strewn everywhere that the vehicle's three occupants were bounced out of their seats with a crash that set their teeth on edge.

At this rate, it was going to be several more hours before they reached the remote strip where the light chartered plane was due to pick up the two Americans and fly them and their precious cargo to Kinshasa. Once they got to the airport, the pair intended to waste no time before jumping on the first jet heading back home and getting the hell out of here. But safety and escape still seemed a long way beyond their reach. They were still very much in the danger zone.

The battered, much-repaired old Toyota was one of the few possessions of a local man named Joseph Maheshe who now and then hired himself out as a driver and guide to tourists. Not that many tourists came here anymore, not even the thrill-seeking adventurous ones. It was a precarious place and an even more precarious trade for Joseph, but the only one he knew. He'd been a taxi driver in Kigali, back over the border in neighbouring Rwanda, when the troubles there twenty years earlier had forced him and his wife, both of them of Tutsi ethnicity, to flee their home never to return. Joseph had seen a lot in his time, and knew the dangers of this area as well as anyone. He wasn't overjoyed that the two Americans had talked him into coming out here. He was liking the grinding sounds coming from his truck's suspension even less.

While Joseph worried about what the terrible road surface was doing to his vehicle, his two backseat passengers had their own concerns to occupy their minds. They were a man and a woman, both dishevelled and travel-stained, both shining with perspiration from the baking heat inside the car, and both in a state of great excitement.

The man's name was Craig Munro, and he was a middlingly successful freelance investigative reporter based 7,000 miles from here in Chicago. In his late forties, he was twice the age of his female companion. They weren't any kind of an item; their relationship was, always had been and would remain professional, even though the lack of privacy when camping out rough for days and nights on end in this wilderness sometimes forced a degree more intimacy on them than either was comfortable with.

The woman's name was Rae Lee, and she had worked for Munro as an assistant and photographer for the last eighteen months. Rae was twenty-four, second generation Taiwanese-American, and she'd been top of her law class at Chicago University for a year before switching tracks and studying photography at the city's prestigious Art Institute. She had taken the job with Munro more for the experience, and for ideological reasons, than for the money

6

– money being something that wasn't always in good supply around her employer's shabby offices in downtown Chicago. The camera equipment inside the metal cases that jostled about in the back of the Toyota was all hers. But as expensive as it was, its true value at this moment lay in the large number of digital images Rae's long lens had captured last night and early this morning from their concealed stakeout.

It was an investigative journalist's dream; everything they could have wished to find. More than they'd dared even hope for, which was the reason for their excitement. It was also the reason for their deep anxiety to get away and home as fast as possible. The kind of information and evidence they'd travelled to the Democratic Republic of Congo to acquire was precisely the kind that could get you killed. And the Congo was a very easy place in which to disappear without a trace, never to be seen again.

The hammering and lurching of the 4x4's suspension made it impossible to have any kind of conversation, but neither Munro nor Rae Lee needed to speak their thoughts out loud. They were both thinking the same thing: when they got back to the States, their work would begin in earnest. The physical danger would be behind them, but the real grind would await them, and Munro's endless deskbound hours of writing the sensational article would be just part of it. There would be scores of calls to make, dozens more contacts to chase, many facts to verify before they could go live with this thing. It was serious business. While what they'd found would cause a substantial stir in certain quarters, not everyone would be supportive. Some very wealthy and powerful people would use every ounce of their influence to block the publication of this information in every way possible. But what they had was pure gold, and they knew it. They were going to be able to blow the lid off this whole dirty affair and open a lot of eyes to what was really happening out here.

'How much further?' Munro yelled, leaning forwards in the back and shouting close to Joseph's ear to be heard.

'It is a very bad road,' the driver replied, as if this were news to them. He was a French speaker like many Rwandans past a certain age, and spoke English with a heavy accent. 'Two hours, maybe three.' Which put them still a long way from anywhere.

'This is hopeless,' Munro complained, flopping back in his seat.

Rae's long hair, normally jet-black, looked red from all the dust. She flicked it away from her face and twisted round to throw an anxious glance over her shoulder at the camera cases behind her. The gear was getting a hell of a jolting back there, though it was well protected inside thick foam. 'We'll be okay,' she said to Munro, as much to reassure herself as him. 'Everything's fine.'

But as the Toyota bumped its way around the next corner a few moments later, they knew that everything wasn't fine at all.

Rae muttered, 'Oh, shit.'

Munro clamped his jaw tight and said nothing.

The two pickup trucks that blocked the road up ahead were the kind that were called 'technicals'. Rae had no idea where that name had come from, but she recognised them instantly. The flatbed of each truck was equipped with a heavy machine gun on a swivel mount, drooping with ammunition belts that coiled up on the floor like snakes.

The machine guns were pointed up the road straight at the oncoming Toyota. A soldier stood behind each weapon, ready to fire. Several more soldiers stood in the road, all sporting the curved-magazine Kalashnikov assault rifles that Rae had quickly learned were a ubiquitous sight just about everywhere in the Congo, across a land mass bigger than all of Europe.

'Could be government troops, maybe,' Munro said nervously as the Toyota lurched towards the waiting roadblock. In a badly decayed and impoverished state where even regular army could closely resemble the most thrown-together rebel force, sometimes it was hard to tell.

'Maybe,' Joseph Maheshe said. He looked uncertain.

There was no driving around them, and certainly no way to double back. Joseph stopped the Toyota as the soldiers marched up and surrounded them, aiming their rifles at the windows. The unit commander was a skinny kid of no more than nineteen. He was draped in cartridge belts like an urban gangsta wraps himself in gold chains and had a semiauto pistol dangling against his ribs in a shoulder holster. A marijuana reefer the size of a small banana dangled from his mouth. His eyes were glassy and his finger was hooked around the trigger of his AK-47.

'Let me handle this,' Munro said, throwing open his door.

'Be very careful, mister,' Joseph Maheshe cautioned him. Anxiety was in his eyes.

As Munro stepped from the car, two soldiers grabbed his arms and roughly hauled him away from the vehicle. Rae swallowed and emerged from the other passenger door, her heart thudding so hard she could hardly walk. She'd heard the stories. There were a lot of them, and they generally ended the same way.

The soldiers on the trucks and on the ground all spent a second or two eyeing the Oriental woman's skimpy top, the honey flesh of her bare shoulders and as much of her legs as were made visible by the khaki shorts she was wearing.

Her attractiveness was an unexpected bonus for them. A few exchanged grins and nods of appreciation, before the teen commander ordered them to search the vehicle. They swarmed around it, wrenching open the doors and tailgate and poking around inside. Munro and Rae were held at bay with rifles pointed at them. Joseph Maheshe didn't try to resist as they hauled him out from behind the wheel.

The soldiers instantly took an interest in the flight cases in the back of the Toyota. The unit commander ordered they be opened up.

'Hey, hey, hold on a minute,' Munro said, putting on a big smile and brushing past the guns to speak to the commander. 'You guys speak English, right? Listen, you really don't need to open those. It's just a bunch of cameras. What do you say, guys? We can come to an agreement. Nothing simpler, right?' As he spoke, he reached gently into the pocket of his shorts, careful to let them see he wasn't hiding a weapon in there, and slipped out a wallet from which he started drawing out banknotes marked banque centrale du congo, the blue hundred-franc ones with the elephant on them.

The commander grabbed the wallet from him, tore out all the Congolese money that was inside as well as the wad of US dollars Munro was carrying, his credit cards and American driver's licence, and stuffed it all in his combat vest. He tossed away the empty wallet.

'Hey. I didn't mean for you to take everything,' Munro protested.

'Shut up, motherfucka!' the commander barked.

'Give me back my dollars and my cards, okay? The rest you can keep. Come on, guys. Play fair.'

Rifles were pointed at Munro's head and chest. Beads of sweat were breaking out on his brow and running into his eyes. He held up his palms.

'What is your business here, American bastard?' the commander asked.

'Tourists,' Munro said, his face reddening. 'Me and my niece here. So can I have my dollars back, or what?'

Rae was thinking, *Please be quiet. Please don't make this worse.* How could she be his niece? For such a gifted investigator, he was a hopeless liar.

The commander shouted orders at his men. Two of them stepped up, grabbed Munro by the arms and flung him on the ground. Rifle muzzles jabbed and stabbed at him, like pitchforks poking hay. Rae screamed out, 'Don't shoot him! Please!'

More of the weapons turned to point at her. She closed her eyes, but they didn't shoot. Instead, all three of them were held at gunpoint while the soldiers went on ransacking the Toyota. They opened up the camera cases, spilled out Rae's gear and quickly found the Canon EOS with the long lens. The commander turned it on and flicked through the stored images, calmly puffing on his joint, until he'd seen enough to satisfy him. He shook his head gravely.

'You are not tourists. You are motherfucka spies. We will report this to General Khosa.'

At the mention of the name Khosa, Rae went very cold. That was when she knew that nothing Munro could say or do would make this situation worse. It was already as bad as it could be.

'Spies? What in hell are you talking about? I tell you we're tourists!' But it wasn't so easy for Munro to rant and protest convincingly while he was being held on the ground with a boot sole planted against his chest and a Kalashnikov to his head.

'Kill this *mkundu*,' the commander said to his soldiers. 'When you are finished with the whore, cut her throat.'

Rae felt her stomach twist. She was going to be gang-raped and left butchered at the roadside like a piece of carrion for wild animals to dismember and gnaw on her bones. She wanted to throw up.

She had to save herself somehow.

And so she said the first thing that came to her.

'Wait! My family are rich!' she yelled.

The commander turned and looked at her languidly. He took another puff from his joint. 'Rich? How rich?'

'Richer than you can even imagine.'

He showed her jagged teeth. 'Rich like Donald Trump?'

'Richer,' Rae said. That was an exaggeration, admittedly. It might have been true back in about 1971, twenty years before she was born, but the Lee family fortunes had dwindled somewhat since then. 'If you don't harm us, there will be a big, big reward for you.' She spread her arms out wide, as if to show him just how much would be in it for him.

The commander digested this for a moment, then glanced down at Munro and kicked him in the ribs. 'This mother-fucka says he is your uncle.'

Munro grimaced in pain and clutched his side where he'd been kicked.

'He's my friend,' Rae answered, fighting to keep her voice steady.

The commander seemed to find this hard to believe, but his main concern was money. 'Is his family rich too?'

'We're Americans,' she said. 'All Americans are rich. Everybody knows that, right?'

The commander laughed. 'What about him?' He pointed at Joseph Maheshe.

'He is just a stupid farmer,' another of the soldiers volunteered. 'How can he pay?'

'This man is our driver,' Rae protested. 'He has nothing to do with this. Leave him out of it.'

The commander stepped closer to Joseph and examined him. Joseph had the classic Tutsi ethnicity, with fine features and a rather narrower nose, slightly hooked, that generally, though not always, distinguished them from Bantu peoples like the Hutu. During the Rwandan genocide it had been the worst curse of the Tutsi people that they could often be recognised at a glance.

'This one looks like a cockroach,' the commander said. It wasn't the first time Joseph had heard his people described that way. Cockroach was what the Hutu death squads had called his brother and their parents, before hacking them all to death.

'Get on your knees, cockroach.'

Without protest, Joseph Maheshe sank down to his knees in the roadside grass and dirt and bowed his head. He knew what was coming, and accepted it peacefully. He knew the Americans might not be as lucky as this. He was sorry for them, but then they should not have come here.

The commander drew his pistol, pressed it to the side of Joseph's head and fired. The sound of the shot drowned out Rae's cry of horror. Joseph went down sideways and crumpled in the long grass with his knees still bent.

'We will take these American spies to General Khosa,' the commander said to his men. 'He will know what to do with them.'

The soldiers tossed the camera equipment into the back of one of the armed pickup trucks. The two prisoners were shoved roughly into the other, where they were forced to crouch low with guns pointed at them.

'You saved my life,' Munro whispered to Rae.

Eventually, that would come to be something he would

no longer thank her for. But for now they were in one piece. Rae looked back at the abandoned Toyota as the pickup trucks took off down the rough road. Joseph's body was no more than a dark, inert smudge in the grass. Just another corpse on just another roadside in Africa. The vultures would probably find him first, followed not long afterwards by the hyenas.

As for Munro's fate and her own, Rae didn't even want to think about it.

Chapter 2

At various and frequent points throughout the ups and downs of what was turning out to be an unusually eventful existence, Ben Hope was in the habit of pausing to take stock of his life. To evaluate his current situation, to consider the sequences of events – planned or not – that had got him there, to ponder what lay ahead in the immediate and longer-term future, and to reflect on how he was doing generally.

All things considered, he had always thought of himself as being a pretty normal type of guy, and so he figured that this stocktaking exercise must be something most normal folks did, even though most normal folks probably didn't tend to find themselves in the kinds of situations that invariably seemed to keep cropping up in his path. Just like most normal folks didn't have to do the kinds of things he had to do in order to get out of those situations in one piece.

In his distant past, Ben's stocktaking had involved thoughts like: *Okay, so passing selection for 22 SAS might be the toughest challenge you've ever taken on, but you will not fail. You can do this. You will be fine.*

Many years later it had been more along the lines of: *All right, so you've walked away from the military career you struggled so hard to build and the future looks uncertain. But it's a big world out there. You have skills. You will make it.*

15

Or, some years further down the line again: *So she's left you for good this time, and you feel like shit. But you won't always feel this way. You'll survive, like you always do.*

If there was one thing Ben had learned, it was this: that wherever the tide might carry him, whatever fate might throw at him, however desperate his situation, however impossible the task facing him, however dark his future prospects or slim his chances of survival, he would live to fight another day. He would not be defeated or deterred, not by anything, not by anyone. That spirit was what had driven him, bolstered him, enabled him to be the man he was. Or the man he'd thought he was.

But not now. Not anymore.

Everything had changed.

Because at this moment, as he sat there helpless and surrounded by aggressive men with guns, slumped uncomfortably on the dirty open flatbed of an old army truck with his knees drawn up in front of him and his head resting on his hands and every jolt of the big wheels and stiff suspension on this rough road somewhere in the middle of the Congo jarring through his spine, he was fighting a rising black tide of emptiness.

If there was a way out of this one, the plan had yet to come to him. And if there was a tomorrow, it wasn't one that he was sure he wanted to face.

Sitting next to Ben, staring silently into space with a pensive frown, was his trusted old friend, Jeff Dekker, with whom he'd survived so many narrow scrapes in the past and come through in one piece. Beside Jeff was the tough young Jamaican ex-British army trooper named Tuesday Fletcher, on whom Ben had quickly learned he could absolutely depend.

But Ben was barely even aware of their presence. All he

16

could think about – all that really mattered to him – was that his son Jude Arundel, just at the point in their troubled relationship where it looked as if they were finally bonding, was lost to him and there wasn't a single thing Ben could do about it. And that riding happily at the front of the irregular militia convoy speeding along this dusty road, wearing a self-satisfied grin and probably smoking another of his huge cigars in victory, was the man who had taken Jude from him.

That man's name was Jean-Pierre Khosa. Known as 'the General' to the army of heavily armed Congolese fighters who both feared and loyally served him, Khosa had every reason to be smiling. Most men would be, when they were carrying inside their pocket a stolen diamond worth countless sums of money and there was nobody to stop them from gaining every bit of power that wealth like that could afford.

Ben knew little about Khosa, but he knew enough, and had seen enough, for the seeds of doubt inside his own heart to grow into a chilling conviction that here, now, at last, was an enemy he couldn't defeat. That Khosa could beat him.

And that maybe Khosa had already won.

Khosa seemed to know it, too.

There was no telling how many miles they'd driven through this jungle, coming across no sign of human habitation for hour after bruising, spine-jarring, mind-numbing hour. Ben had lost his watch before the start of the journey, and with it all track of time, except for the position of the sun which told him it would soon be evening again. They'd been travelling like this all day, and most of the night before with only a short stop in the middle of nowhere, for the troops to rest, brew coffee and gulp down a bowl of nondescript dried meat, beans, and rice. Ben hadn't been hungry but he'd taken what

17

he was offered. Military wisdom, left over from his past. Eat when you can, sleep when you can, preserve your strength.

They'd come a long way since then, and they were still in the middle of nowhere. There was an awful lot of nowhere around these parts.

The truck in which Ben and his friends were passengers was a dozen or so vehicles back from the spearhead of the convoy. To the rear, the long procession of armoured pickup trucks and Jeeps stretched out far in their wake like a cobra winding its way between the verdant thickets of wide-bladed leaves and tangled shrubbery that overhung the track and formed a tunnel overhead, blotting out much of the harsh sunlight that would otherwise have been cooking them inside their vehicles. Ben had counted thirty-five vehicles behind them when they'd set off, but the tail end of the snake had soon become obscured by the plume of dust thrown up by so many chunky off-road tyres pounding the rutted, sunbaked surface.

The dirt road seemed to go on and on forever, hardly changing. Now and then they would cross a rickety river bridge, and now and then the endless forest would break to offer views of sweeping plains and mountain valleys and mist-shrouded peaks in the distance. The Congo was a vast territory the size of most of Western Europe's countries combined, but with barely any paved roads to connect it together and even less chance of running into any kind of major traffic, let alone a contingent of police or government troops. The authorities had the good sense to keep to the cities and give outlying areas a wide berth. Khosa's small army rode through the jungle as if they owned the place – and to all intents and purposes they did. They were making no secret of their presence as they roared along to the soundtrack of angry African rap music that was blasting from a boombox wired to PA speakers somewhere back along the line, with all the aggressive confidence of two hundred or more pepped-up and hot-blooded young men with enough military hardware to level a town and the will to deploy it at the drop of a hat.

Ben was suddenly aware that Jeff Dekker was watching him, and glanced up to meet his friend's gaze. Jeff's face, his dark hair, and the DPM combat jacket he was wearing were all caked in dust. He looked weary and careworn, but there was a twinkle in his eye and his smile was irrepressible. Jeff was like that.

'Mate, it's going to be okay. You know that, don't you?'

Ben said nothing. He tried to smile back, but his face felt numb.

'Jude'll be all right,' Jeff said. 'He's as tough as his old man. Tougher.'

Ben didn't reply. He appreciated his friend's attempt to reassure him. But he didn't believe a word he was saying.

'We'll get out of this,' Jeff said. 'We'll find him. Hear me? Wherever these bastards have taken him, we'll find him.'

Ben remained silent. Finding people was something he'd done a lot of in his time. He thought about all the kidnap victims he'd saved in the past, during the years between leaving the military and going into business with Jeff, when he'd called himself a 'crisis response consultant' – that catch-all phrase that didn't quite do justice to the things he'd had to do or the methods he'd employed to help people who needed it.

Many of those he'd rescued had been children. All of them had been someone's loved one. All of them strangers to him, and yet he'd risked his own life – and taken a good many others – to preserve theirs. And now, the victim incarcerated out there somewhere in conditions Ben didn't even want to imagine was one of only two people in the world he could call his kin, and he was utterly powerless to help.

Ben couldn't close out of his head the image of the last time he'd seen Jude, being forced at gunpoint into a black Mercedes limousine and taken away by a well-dressed African named César Masango. General Jean-Pierre Khosa called Masango his 'political attaché'. Ben could think of better terms to describe him.

Kidnapper. Gangster. Walking dead man. That was just three.

'Where we are going, you will be too busy to look after your son,' Khosa had said as Masango took Jude. *'So my friend César will be looking after him now.'*

And that had been it. Jude was gone. Where he was now, Ben had no way of knowing.

And even though it had been only a matter of hours ago, it seemed like weeks had gone by. That final image of Jude disappearing into the car was tearing Ben's mind apart. Half of him wanted to forget it, erase it, pretend it never happened. The other half of him needed to cling to it, like a fading photograph of a loved one that, once gone, would take the memory of that person with it.

'I'll come for you.' Those had been his last words before they'd parted. It was a promise that Ben did not know if he could keep.

Ben wondered whether he'd ever see Jude again.

Jeff must have been able to tell from Ben's expression that the reassurance wasn't working. The optimism seemed to drain from him. When he spoke again, his tone was sullen. 'It's all my fault this happened to Jude. Hadn't been for me, he'd never have set foot on that fucking ship in the first—'

'It's not your fault,' Ben cut in before Jeff could finish. He'd said it before, and he'd say it again. Ben knew all about the ravages of a guilty conscience from his own past. Come what may, he didn't want Jeff to bear the responsibility for what had happened. When Jeff had pulled strings with his contacts to get Jude the crewman gig with the American merchant vessel MV *Svalgaard Andromeda* on the East Africa run from Salalah in Oman to Dar es Salaam in Tanzania, he couldn't have known that the ship would be attacked. Any more than he could have known that one of its secret passengers, a crook named Pender, was carrying a stolen diamond bigger than a man's fist, which ruthless killers would do anything to acquire. Events had unfolded from there the way they had, nobody could have done anything to prevent them, and only one man still living could be held responsible for the things that had taken place.

Khosa. Ben had the man's face pinpointed in his mind like a sniper's target in the crosshairs of a rifle scope. And what a face it was. A demon's face, bearing the hideous tribal scars that you couldn't look at without a shiver of apprehension. But as evil as he looked, Khosa's lunatic mind was the thing Ben feared most.

'It's not your fault,' Ben repeated to Jeff.

One of the soldiers guarding them in the back of the truck reached across with the barrel of his AK-47 and jabbed Ben painfully in the ribs with it. Like many of Khosa's fighters he was a young guy, no more than twenty or so. He had a red bandana tied around his head and was wearing a faded Legion of the Damned T-shirt with an ammunition belt for a heavy machine gun draped around his lean shoulders like a fashion accessory.

'Quiet! No talking!' the young trooper yelled. English was taking over from French as the main European language in the Democratic Republic of Congo, and most of the militia troops spoke it, or something close to it. That made it difficult to have any kind of a private conversation; all the more so when conversation was forbidden altogether.

Ben slapped the rifle barrel away. 'Watch how you speak to me, sonny. You're addressing General Khosa's military advisor.'

Which, technically, was true. That was the essence of the blackmail deal between Ben and the General: in return for Jude's safety, whenever they got to wherever the hell they were going, Ben was to begin his new role of training Khosa's troops and impart to them his military skills, with Jeff and Tuesday as his second- and third-in-command. Train them for what purpose, exactly, Ben didn't yet know. It wasn't a prospect he relished, but right now his agreement to Khosa's terms was the only thing keeping them all alive.

'You listening, you scummy little arsemonger?' Jeff said, glaring a hole in the soldier with the full authoritative weight of a former Special Boat Service non-com officer. He'd been a Royal Marine Commando before that, and used to a slightly higher calibre of military personnel than Khosa's army had to offer. 'So point that weapon somewhere else before I stick it through your left ear and out your right, and ride you up and down this road like a fucking motorbike.'

The soldier moved back and leaned his rifle across his knees, eyeing them with wary uncertainty.

'Bloody bunch of numpties,' Tuesday said, giving the soldier a headshake and a look of contempt.

Ben had to smile then. The warmth of their camaraderie touched him like a glimmer of sunshine on a cloudy day. It wasn't much, but it was good.

Along with Ben, Jeff, and Tuesday Fletcher, there was a fourth prisoner crouched in the back of the lurching truck. Lou Gerber had served as a staff sergeant with the United States Marine Corps many years earlier, before he'd taken to the sea as a merchant mariner. Besides Jude, the white-bearded, bald-headed Gerber was the last surviving crew member of the *Svalgaard Andromeda*, out of more than twenty men who had set out from Salalah Port in Oman not two weeks earlier.

Ben had spent a lot of time thinking about the men who had died aboard that ship. Some had been killed during the storming of the vessel by Khosa's men, hired by Pender to pose as Somali pirates. More had died in the aftermath of the attack, while Jude and the other survivors rushed to lock themselves into the safety of the engine room. One, a vicious thug named Scagnetti, Ben had been forced to dispose of himself when he tried to hurt Jude. Soon after that had come the typhoon that had scuppered the ship and drowned all but a handful of the remaining crew.

In the days since the shipwreck they'd been whittled down even further, one by one. Condor, hacked to death by Khosa's men in an earth-floored hut somewhere in Somalia; Hercules, a gentle giant of a man who had loved his pet bird and his freewheeling life at sea, thrown into a pit with a hungry man-eating lion in a grotesque parody of an ancient Roman gladiatorial spectacle.

Gerber was alone now, and for the first time since Ben had met the guy, he looked all of his sixty-seven years plus a good bit more. Already hit hard by the death of his close shipmate Condor, he'd barely spoken a word since they'd all been forced to witness Hercules's cruel end. He seemed to have given up. His head was bowed and he stared at the floor of the truck with eyes that looked like holes out of which his soul had leaked away.

'Gerber,' Jeff said, trying to catch his attention. 'Hoi, Gerber, you awake?'

If Gerber could hear him, he made no sign of showing it. Jeff shrugged and sighed.

Ben closed his eyes and tried to relax his muscles into the

jarring motion of the truck. He knew how Gerber felt. But if indeed Gerber had given up, that was something Ben couldn't allow himself to do. The black feeling kept coming and going in tides, like chill surges of floodwater that threatened to overwhelm his defences and drown all the strength and resolve he had left. He clenched his fists and told himself to ride it. He willed himself to believe that he would come through. And so would Jude. Ben didn't know if he believed it. But he knew that if he didn't convince himself it was true, he'd go crazy.

Soon afterwards, the convoy arrived at its destination deep in the heart of the jungle.

And soon after that, Ben began to think he really was going crazy.

Chapter 3

Ben was slumped in the back of the truck with his eyes still shut when he sensed that the vehicle's motion had become smoother and he was no longer being shaken about. He opened his eyes and peered out of the back of the truck. Dusk was melting into evening. He must have been dozing. The headlights of the vehicles behind dazzled him; he shielded his eyes with his hand and saw that the rutted dirt track had either joined, or become, a properly surfaced road. The concrete looked newly-laid. The trees were cut back from the edges and ditches had been dug out on both sides. The clean-cut ends of sawn branches, still fresh, told him that the work must have been done not long ago.

Ben threw a quizzical look at Jeff and Tuesday.

'Seems like we're getting somewhere,' Tuesday commented. 'Wherever somewhere is.'

'I don't know, mate. Looks to me like we're still in the arsehole of the bloody jungle,' Jeff said. 'Who'd build a road like this out here?'

It wasn't too long after that, maybe twenty minutes, maybe half an hour, before the convoy rolled to a halt. Hot metal ticking, engines growling, exhaust fumes drifting in the headlights. Ignoring the soldiers and guns, Ben clambered to his feet on the flatbed and turned to gaze past the truck's cab.

His legs felt like two planks of wood and his back was aching.

In the bright glare of the convoy's lights, he saw that Khosa's Land Rover at the front of the line had stopped at a wire-mesh double perimeter fence that stretched away in both directions until it was lost in the darkness. The convoy had pulled up at a set of steel-mesh gates inset into the outer fence, ten feet high and plastered in warning KEEP OUT signs in English, French, Kituba, Lingala and Swahili, just in case the locals didn't get the message from the heavily armed guards who were manning the gates on the inside. The inner and outer fences were spaced about ten metres apart, creating a corridor between them in which Ben could see the figures of patrolling guards. In a pool of bright halogen floodlight beyond the chain-link mesh of the inner fence sat a cluster of guard huts, around which more soldiers were standing cradling automatic weapons and squinting into the procession of headlights queued up at the gates. The tall fences themselves were supported by steel posts and topped with spikes and coils of razor wire. High-perched security cameras peered down.

Ben had seen a thousand perimeter fences just like it, around army bases all over the world. More recently, Khosa's men had taken them to a rundown ex-military airfield in Somalia, another forgotten leftover from another fruitless civil war. There, the fence had been hanging in disrepair, abandoned for many years. This one, like the road leading to it, looked as if it hadn't been there long at all. Along the perimeter's length for as far as Ben could see, the trees had been severely cut back in what must have been a major clearing operation involving a large number of men and machines. Such a new and well-constructed installation was an incongruous sight in the midst of this green wilderness with its unmade roads and shambolic wooden bridges.

From this side of the wire it looked as though a large area of jungle had been cleared on the inside of the perimeter as well. Did Khosa really have that kind of manpower? Ben's initial assumption had been that the man's army was no different from any number of ragtag tinpot militia forces he'd come across during his SAS days, when his squadron would occasionally be sent to various parts of the African continent to deal with the more troublesome gangs of marauding thugs who stepped out of line by massacring and raping the locals and abducting UN aid workers. But he'd been learning from the outset that his assumption was a shaky one. General Jean-Pierre Khosa was full of surprises. Never pleasant ones.

What Ben didn't yet realise was that the biggest surprise was yet to come, one he couldn't have foreseen in a thousand years.

Jeff and Tuesday were on their feet next to him in the truck, following his gaze. Lou Gerber hadn't moved or even looked up.

'What do you reckon?' Jeff said.

Ben shook his head. 'Whatever it is, we're about to find out.'

There was a lot of activity going on at the head of the stationary convoy. Doors were opened and soldiers were milling about. Greetings were exchanged, laughter shared, backs slapped. Ben looked for Khosa but couldn't see him. The General must be still in his Land Rover, puffing on a Gran Cohiba and fondling his diamond, maybe thinking about who he was going to order hacked to death next, or whose head he might blow off on a whim using the magnum revolver he carried on his belt. Those burdensome decisions of leadership.

The soldiers inside the compound opened the outer gates

first, followed by those in the inner fence. The men outside returned to their vehicles, slammed their doors, and the convoy slowly began to roll through the gates, waved in by the grinning guards. The convoy accelerated and sped onwards, pushing a bubble of light into the darkness beyond the perimeter.

The concreted road continued for a quarter of a mile up a steep rise that had been completely shorn of vegetation, creating a barren landscape of ploughed earth and craters where countless trees had been ripped out by their roots. The more Ben looked, the more perplexed he was by this place. He could sense Jeff and Tuesday's growing sense of bewilderment, too. Far behind them, the tail end of the convoy had passed through the inner gates and the soldiers had closed up the perimeter with an air of finality that took away any doubts Ben might have had that this place, whatever it might be, was their final destination.

Ben narrowed his eyes when he saw the glow lighting up the sky from beyond the crest of the rise ahead. If it was a military camp, it was on a grand scale. The biggest he'd seen in Africa, rivalling major NATO bases in Europe. But that was impossible.

Khosa's Land Rover crested the rise and dropped out of sight. A dozen vehicles later, the truck reached the top of the hill – and then Ben saw it, and his mouth fell open at the sight.

It wasn't the biggest military camp in Africa. It wasn't a military camp at all.

The manmade valley below was illuminated across its length and breadth by thousands of lights. The single road swept down the deforested hillside into what, unbelievably and yet undeniably, appeared to be a whole city.

A city enclosed behind a militarised security perimeter.
Khosa's own city?

Ben blinked. His mouth went dry. He blinked again, tore

his gaze from the surreal sight and exchanged looks of bewilderment with Jeff and Tuesday.

The road had widened into a smooth and immaculate double carriageway by the time they reached the final security fence. Blinding halogen spotlamps blazed down from masts. The gate was heavily guarded by a unit of at least a dozen sentries and a six-wheeled armoured personnel carrier with twin machine guns swivelled their way.

'I'm not believing this,' Jeff said. 'Tell me I'm fucking dreaming, guys.'

'It's real,' Ben replied. 'Don't ask me how, but it's real.'

Once more, there were waves and happy greetings as the convoy rolled through the gates. Some three hundred yards down the single straight road that crossed what had once been a valley deep in the jungle, now transformed into a barren no-man's land, the line of vehicles rumbled past the first buildings. Side streets radiated left and right, forming a geometric grid system of two-hundred-foot-square blocks. Many of them were still empty and undeveloped patches of land; others sprouted semi-erected multi-storey buildings; others again were fully finished with high-rises and office blocks. Signs of recent construction were everywhere, cranes looming into the night sky and heavy plant equipment filling every empty corner. Street after street after empty street, all still, all silent, all lit up but eerily deserted. There were no cars. There was no movement. Not a single civilian to be seen anywhere, as if the entire population had fled or been vaporized by a hydrogen bomb leaving behind only empty buildings.

Like a vision from a post-apocalyptic world, or the most expensive movie set that had ever been built and was waiting for the film crews and herds of extras to move in.

'What in hell's name . . . ?' Jeff muttered.

Tuesday was shaking his head. 'Please don't tell me that Khosa built this place.'

'Whoever built it,' Ben said, 'I've a feeling you won't find it on any maps.'

'Khosa City,' Jeff grunted. 'Jesus Christ. Who *is* this guy?'

The deeper the convoy rolled into the city, the fewer construction sites they passed and the more finished the place appeared to be, as if it had been built from the centre outwards. The main drag had grown into a broad boulevard. The architects had planted neat avenues of maple trees down its length, and laid clipped green lawns either side, and pavements and modern street lighting that glowed off the brand-new buildings.

Here and there they passed small patrol units of militia. Any non-military personnel in the place were either locked down tight in a curfew, or there simply weren't any in the first place. The streets were lit up but almost every window of every building was dark and empty. The only other vehicle they saw was a six-wheeled APC identical to the one guarding the inner perimeter, which emerged from a side street and rumbled past them in the opposite direction.

Jeff said, shaking his head, 'Where did they get the workforce? The materials? The *money*?'

Ben could have added a thousand more questions, but there were no answers to be had. Not yet. All he could do was stare at the surreal scene. Maybe Khosa had had their coffee last night spiked with LSD.

The convoy rumbled on, past empty parks and deserted squares and block after block of high-rise apartment buildings, all giving off the same uninhabited aura. Then the line of trucks and pickups veered across an intersection and rounded a corner, and Ben's stupefaction racked up to a new level. Because the grandiose eight-storey building he could now see ahead, nestled a little way from the road next to an enormous and extravagantly illuminated plane tree, was the Dorchester Hotel in London's Park Lane.

The Dorchester, here in the Congo. Complete with its sweeping nineteen-thirties façade and grand entrance and garden frontage of sculpted shrubs, ornamental railings, stone fountains, and flower beds. Ben closed his eyes for a moment. When he reopened them, it was still there.

Not dreaming.

The hotel was the first building they'd seen thus far that showed any sign of life. Light streamed from the entrance and many upper-floor windows were aglow against the night sky. At the head of the convoy, Khosa's Land Rover turned off the street to park outside the building. The following vehicles kept on going down the street, and for a moment Ben thought the truck was going to do the same – until it too broke from the moving line and pulled to a halt directly behind Khosa's personal transport.

The soldiers in the back of the truck jumped up and stabbed and poked with their rifles to get the prisoners moving. 'Keep your panties on, girls,' Jeff growled at them. Gerber seemed to take no notice of anything much that was happening around him. Ben and Jeff helped him to his feet, and down the wooden ramp from the flatbed to the pavement.

Outside the Dorchester Hotel. In the Congo. If Gerber was having the same hard time as the other three accepting reality, he wasn't letting it show.

The night air was fresh and still, and fragrant with the scent of the hotel garden flowers whose perfume was strong enough to mask the lingering tang of exhaust fumes left by the convoy. A billion stars twinkled above the silhouetted city skyline. Khosa had stepped down from his Land Rover and paused outside the hotel, his tall bulky outline bathed

31

in golden light shining from the entrance, clasping his hands behind his back in statesmanlike fashion as he exchanged a few words with one of the men who had been riding along with him at the head of the convoy.

While his soldiers looked dusty and tired from the long journey, the General appeared as fresh and energetic as if he'd just finished a leisurely breakfast and donned a crisp new uniform to attend to the first business of the day. His combat boots gleamed as though he'd spent the whole drive polishing them, the gold Rolex on his thick wrist was resplendent under the lights, and the red beret on his head sat at a jaunty angle. If it hadn't been for the tribal scarring that distorted his face into a monstrous demon's mask, he might have seemed almost jovial.

As the soldiers prodded and shoved the four prisoners in his direction, Khosa turned to give Ben a beaming white smile that looked like the last thing a shark's dinner might see before being swallowed up in one bite. It was usual for him to ignore Jeff and Tuesday as the underlings they were. As for Gerber, Khosa viewed the 'Goat Man' with as much regard as for an inchworm. Ben had twice had to persuade him not to have the old sailor hacked to death by his men.

'Ah, it is very good to be home again,' Khosa said in his deep, resonant voice. 'Soldier, welcome to my executive head-quarters.'

Chapter 4

Khosa led the way to the entrance, a bodyguard flanking him each side and one step back, their guns ready as though they were expecting an ambush inside the grand foyer. Khosa himself seemed completely at ease, like a guy strolling in his front door and about to hang up his jacket and hat and call, 'Honey, I'm home!'

Ben followed, with Jeff and Tuesday in his wake both keeping a concerned eye on Gerber. The rest of the soldiers from the truck strutted along behind, their loaded and cocked Kalashnikovs trained on their new guests and menacing scowls on their faces. The real Dorchester didn't know how lucky it was.

'I know what you are thinking, soldier,' Khosa declared.

Ben said nothing. He was painfully aware of the man's bizarre ability to read minds, so there didn't seem any point.

'Yes, yes. You had not expected anything quite like my little camp.' Khosa chuckled. 'Even if you do not want to admit it.' He paused at the entrance and turned to admire his little camp for one last moment before stepping inside, arms spread wide.

'It is not a big city,' he said modestly. 'Big enough for eighty thousand people at the moment, but growing every week. Tomorrow I will have my Captain Xulu show you around, and you will see for yourself what we have here. The sports stadium is still under construction, to the west. So is the airport, on the other side of it. Both will be finished soon. The hydroelectric power station is to the north, where the river runs. On the other side of the river lies the industrial zone.' He grinned, obviously delighted by the bewildered expression that Ben couldn't hide. 'You are realising, at last, that you should not have underestimated me. Did I not tell you? But you would not listen. Now let us go inside.'

It had been years since Ben had last set foot in the real Dorchester, and he'd had more on his mind that day than to admire the decor. But from hazy memory the architect of this bizarre recreation seemed to have done a creditable job, right down to the marbled pillars and magnificent tiled floor. The only thing missing from the lobby was any kind of reception staff. Khosa's boots rang on the tiles as he led them briskly towards the lifts.

Behind him, Ben heard Jeff say to one of the soldiers, 'Hey, arsehole, take my luggage up to my room and see to it that everything is cleaned and pressed, okay?' If Jeff couldn't blast his way out of a tight spot, he'd joke his way through it. Tuesday was either being more restrained, or he was just too stunned to speak.

The lift glided up to the top floor. Its doors slid open to an empty corridor with Persian carpeting and artwork on the walls. A sharp-eyed visitor might have noticed the assortment of automatic weaponry propped along one wall, but as far as Ben could tell the rest was authentic.

Ben was understanding less and less. His confused thoughts whirled back to the events in which Jude had been caught up aboard the cargo ship, the *Andromeda* of the Svalgaard Line. Jude had described it all in detail afterwards. His take on the situation was that the jewel thief called

34

Pender, travelling in secret under the assumed name Carter, had hired Khosa and his crew to intercept the vessel in the guise of Somali pirates as a means of smuggling off the ship the enormous diamond he had in his possession. Pender had sensibly attempted to conceal the true nature of his precious package from Khosa, until things had started to go badly wrong for him and he quickly ended up as fish bait. In retrospect, he'd made a serious error of judgement in choosing Khosa for the task. That had probably been Pender's own final thought, too, as the machetes came out.

Ben hadn't doubted his son's account of those events for a moment. But if Jude was right, then Khosa's discovery of the diamond had been no more than a lucky accident – lucky for him, less so for Pender. Which in turn meant that, up to that point, all that Khosa had stood to gain from the deal was whatever Pender was paying him by way of a cash fee.

That was where it all stopped making sense, as far as Ben could see. Why would this brutal, sadistic warlord, apparently endowed with the limitless resources needed to build his own private city in the middle of the jungle on such an unbelievably lavish scale, bother to travel all the way to the Indian Ocean to take on a mercenary job for the likes of Pender? If Khosa was already so fabulously rich and powerful, he wouldn't even have been on that ship to begin with. Especially if he hadn't known about the diamond in advance.

Ben thought about the motley assortment of aircraft that had brought them here in stages from where Khosa had found them drifting in the Indian Ocean. The air-sea 'rescue' had been carried out with an ancient Puma helicopter the best part of fifty years of age, even more battered and worn out than the two Bell Iroquois choppers, relics from the Vietnam War, that made up the rest of Khosa's helicopter fleet. Then there had been the prehistoric DC-3 Dakota that had taken them almost to the Congolese–Rwandan border when it ran out of fuel and almost killed them. If Khosa could afford to build a city in the jungle, what was he doing flying around in piles of scrap metal?

None of it added up.

Khosa strode along the corridor and threw open a gleaming set of double doors to reveal a suite of palatial proportions. 'This is my command post,' he declared proudly, sweeping an arm to usher them inside.

Ben's confusion deepened when he stepped into the suite. He'd never set foot inside the White House, or been invited into the Oval Office. But this was the nearest thing. The vast room was decked out in sumptuous style, dominated by a carved hardwood desk the size of a Buick. Its gleaming surface was bare, apart from an old-fashioned dial telephone in red plastic, and a scale model of a Napoleonic-era field cannon.

Seated at the desk was a small, slender African man of about sixty, with thick spectacles and silvery hair buzzed to a stubble. He wore a crisp short-sleeved khaki shirt that hung on his reedy frame, with a mass of colourful military decorations over his heart and epaulettes studded with regalia. The man rose with a delighted smile as Khosa entered the room. Ignoring the motley crew of prisoners and soldiers who had filed through the doorway, he hurried from the desk and rushed over to greet his commander. They shook hands warmly. 'It is good to see you again, Your Excellency. I believe the mission was a great success.'

Ben had never heard a lower-ranking officer refer to a general as 'Your Excellency'. But this was hardly a normal kind of army.

'Oh, yes. A very great success,' Khosa replied, patting the lump in his hip pocket that made it look as though he was carrying an apple in there. He removed his beret and skimmed it into the nearest antique armchair, threw his bulk into a silk-upholstered sofa with a deep sigh of satisfaction, drew another of his trademark Cuban cigars from a breast pocket and took his time lighting it. Through a dragon's breath of pungent smoke, he turned to Ben.

'Soldier, allow me to introduce my second-in-command, Colonel Raphael Dizolele. Colonel, I would like you to meet Major Hope of the SAS, our new military advisor. He is going to help train the army for us.'

Dizolele turned the smile on Ben, but it wasn't long before he realised that the new military advisor wasn't inclined to shake hands.

'This is Captain Dekker,' Khosa said, motioning at Jeff, who scowled back at him as if he wanted to twist his head off and punt it out of the window. 'Also a celebrated warrior in his own country. And this young man' – pointing at Tuesday – 'is the finest marksman in the British army. I am told he can kill a man from two miles away with a rifle.'

Or so Ben had claimed on Tuesday's behalf, mainly as a way to prevent Khosa from having him diced into pieces. Ben worried that his strategy might have worked too well.

'Wonderful news, Excellency,' said the beaming Dizolele. 'And this old man is what?'

Khosa threw a sour look at Gerber, who was just staring at the floor as if he'd fallen into a state of senility. 'A sergeant of the United States Marine Corps. Major Hope believes he is of use to us. We will see. I have not decided yet.'

The dismal introductions over with, the colonel updated Khosa on events during his absence. Neither seemed to have any problem discussing business in front of the underlings. 'There was an incident with some of the workers,' Dizolele reported. 'A minor revolt in which three guards were killed, but the disturbance was soon brought back under control and the instigators have been punished.'

Khosa nodded, his face blank. 'Good. Anything else?'

'I am happy to report that the payment we expected from America has been received in full, by wire transfer to one of our offshore accounts.'

Khosa seemed mildly pleased by this. 'Is the package still intact?'

'In perfect condition, Excellency. Should we return it?'

'It would be a mistake to return it too quickly. Issue another demand instead.'

Ben wondered what they were talking about. A faint alarm bell was ringing in his mind, but he couldn't be certain.

'The same again?' Dizolele asked with a smile.

'No, this time double it to two million. Remind them of what will happen if they do not pay. If they are slow, give them a warning.'

'A warning, by which I take it his Excellency means . . . ?'

Khosa made a casual gesture, indicating his growing boredom with the conversation. 'The usual. Whatever does not spoil the goods too badly. I leave such details to your judgement, Raphael.'

That alarm bell in Ben's mind was ringing a little more loudly now.

Dizolele clasped his hands and bowed his head, like a sycophantic mouse. 'Thank you, Excellency. It will be done exactly as you say.'

'Is there anything else, Raphael?'

'I am also pleased to report that the shipment from our friends in the east arrived safely while you were away. The items are awaiting your approval.'

This seemed the most welcome news of all. Khosa's horror mask of a face crinkled with contentment. 'I will inspect them shortly. Thank you, Raphael. If that is all, you are excused.'

Once the little colonel had left the room, Khosa stood and paced the deep-pile carpet for a moment or two before seating himself importantly at his desk. He leaned back in the leather chair, laid his big hands flat on the shining desktop and fixed his implacable wide-angle gaze on Ben and the others. His eyes were so far apart that it was impossible to stare back at both of them at once. He seldom blinked, and his breathing was that of a man in the deepest state of tranquillity. He drew another long puff from the Cuban, exhaled a huge cloud of smoke and said, 'Well, soldier. What do you think?'

'I think you know what I think,' Ben said.

'I do, soldier. I do. But I would like to hear it from you.'

'I think that whatever dirty little business you're up to in this luxury rathole of yours, it's obviously paying off pretty well so far.'

Khosa smiled. 'Is this your way of telling me that you are impressed, Major Hope?'

Ben had known this man less than a week and already he had seen him order scores of brutal executions, lay waste to an African village and personally blow out the brains of one of his own men. Whatever Khosa proved himself capable of, 'impressed' wasn't the word to describe Ben's reaction.

'It's my way of telling you that all good things come to an end, *General*. I wouldn't get too complacent.'

Khosa reached out a lazy arm and swivelled the model field cannon on his desk so that its barrel pointed towards Ben. 'I see. And what else do you think?'

'I think that nothing bad had better have happened to my son,' Ben replied. 'Because if it has, all good things might come to an end that bit sooner.'

'You think I should let him go?'

'That would be the smartest move you've ever made in your life.'

Khosa pondered this for a long moment. 'I would be disappointed, soldier,' he said at last, 'if I thought that you had forgotten our deal. Are we not clear on the terms of the arrangement?'

'You want me and my friends here to train your ragtag rabble into something resembling an army,' Ben said. 'We do our job, Jude stays safe. Or so you promise.'

'I am a man of my word, soldier,' Khosa said, his big hand still resting on the cannon and the cannon still pointing at Ben's heart. 'When I say I will do something, I do it. You can depend on that.'

'The part I'm not clear on is just how long you intend to keep us here,' Ben said. 'One month? Six? We don't make for the easiest hostages to handle.'

'Right,' Jeff said tersely.

'Six months,' Khosa said, with a nonchalant shrug. 'One year. Two. As long as it takes, soldier. But I advise you, I am not a patient man. I expect results quickly.'

Ben stared at him. 'You haven't thought this through, have you, Khosa? You're too lost in your own little fantasy world. People will be looking for us. The kind of people you don't want to deal with.'

'There is nothing I cannot deal with,' Khosa said. 'You will learn this, if you have not learned it already. I have the power to do whatever I choose. If I am satisfied that you are doing a good job, perhaps I will choose to extend our deal for another ten years. It is, how do you say? An open-ended contract.' Khosa chuckled at his own joke.

In Ben's mind, he stepped up to the desk. Snatched the model cannon from under Khosa's hand and weighed it in his own. A solid cast-iron lump, plenty of heft to it. Plenty of damage when he smashed it down with all his might on the top of Khosa's head, cracking open the man's skull. And plenty more when he kept on hammering until the African's brains were pulped all over the polished mahogany.

And then all it would take would be one brief phone call from Dizolele or any of the rest, and somewhere out there a gun would be pressing at Jude's temple and the order would be given.

'He dies, you die,' was all Ben could say.

Khosa gave him the demon smile.

'Rest well tonight, soldier. My men will show you to your accommodation, which I trust you will find satisfactory. Eat and drink all you want. Tomorrow you begin your duties.' He stood. 'And now, if you will excuse me, I have a diamond to sell.'

Chapter 5

While Ben and the others were en route with Khosa's convoy, Jude Arundel had been heading towards his own unknown destination.

The conversation in the back of the Mercedes limousine had been every bit as uncomfortable as the ride over endless miles of potholes and ruts. Jude was sandwiched between the tall, dapper César Masango, the man who called himself General Khosa's political attaché, and another well-dressed though somewhat less elegant African who went by the name of Promise. If Masango looked like a rich lawyer, Promise looked like an enforcer for a gangster operation. The muscles, dark glasses and Uzi submachine gun contributed significantly to the effect.

Jude kept stealing glances at the gun. A pressed-steel box with a stubby barrel. Very compact. Ideal for close-up and personal killing. The kind of killing that could be done in the back seat of a car with no danger of hurting anyone but the intended victim. Just perfect.

'This is your new companion Promise Okereke,' was how Masango had introduced him. 'You will be seeing a lot of him, my young friend. From now on, he will never be far away from you. Like your guardian angel, there to keep you from getting into trouble.'

'That's very considerate of you,' Jude said. He was determined not to show the slightest weakness or emotion to his captors. The deaths of his friends Condor and Hercules had shaken him badly and his own predicament was terrifying. But outwardly he remained cool, almost flippant in his defiance.

Masango pointed at Promise. 'Do not try to speak to him, because he will not reply. Promise, show him why you will not reply.'

Promise opened his mouth. Jude didn't really want to see, but it was hard to miss. The space between Promise's lower teeth was a big purple-red hole of flesh and veins where his tongue used to be. If Jude's stomach hadn't been empty already, he might well have distributed its contents over his lap, making the rest of the journey even more pleasurable.

'I don't suppose he was born like that,' Jude said when he'd collected himself.

Masango shook his head. 'The man who did this to him is called Louis Khosa,' he explained. 'The brother of my friend and associate Jean-Pierre Khosa. If you are afraid of Jean-Pierre, you would be much more afraid of his brother. Louis is a very terrible man.'

'What a charming family,' Jude said. 'Are there any more of them? Just so I know.'

'One day soon, Louis Khosa will be dead. Only one man can kill him.'

'Let me guess. His dear brother.'

'That is right. And that is why Promise is so loyal to Jean-Pierre, and to me. He is not called Promise because he keeps his promises. He cannot make any. But he always keeps mine. And I promise you, my young friend, if you try to escape or resist us in any way, there will be no second chance for you. You will die a death that you cannot imagine.'

'Thanks for the tip,' Jude said. 'So am I allowed to ask where you arseholes are taking me, or would that constitute resistance?'

Masango's face was stony. 'To a place where you will be safe and well looked after, as long as you behave yourself. I hope for your sake that you will not forget that advice.'

'Oh, I wouldn't dream of giving you any trouble,' Jude said. And while the Uzi was only a couple of feet away, he wasn't being entirely sarcastic. He thought about his father. In this situation, he was certain, Ben wouldn't waste any time getting the gun out of Promise's hand. Probably breaking a few fingers in the process, but Promise wouldn't have a chance to feel much pain or even cry out, because he'd be dead a second later, quickly followed by César Masango. Or maybe Ben would just break Masango's arms and keep him alive to extract information from him. However he played it, Ben would have got out of this. He wouldn't have sat here like an idiot, letting himself be taken off somewhere nobody would ever find him.

But then, as Jude reflected bitterly, he was not his father.

The Mercedes drove through the night, pausing for the silent driver to refuel the tank from a couple of jerrycans stored in the boot. Jude was allowed a bathroom break behind a roadside bush, with his guardian angel hovering watchfully nearby. Before they set off again, Masango offered a floppy sandwich from a plastic wrapper, a half-melted chocolate bar and a bottle of warm Pepsi. The kind of stuff you'd give a twelve-year-old. Jude wanted to throw them angrily into the bushes, but then recalled Ben's advice: *eat when you can, drink when you can, sleep when you can.* If he couldn't fight like his father, then at least he could manage those.

He polished the food off in resentful silence, then got

back in the car, folded his arms, sank down low in the soft plush seat, and pretended to fall asleep just as a 'fuck you' signal of defiance to Masango.

As he lay there with his eyes closed, he kept wondering what was happening to him. One thing was clear enough – he was a hostage. They were planning on isolating him as far away as possible from Ben, Jeff and the others, so that his friends had no way to find him. He would be imprisoned in some totally inaccessible shithole, a cellar maybe, or a dug-out pit in the ground with a truck parked over the top of it. He'd seen that in a movie and the idea appalled him.

If he was a hostage, it meant there was a deal going on. Jude had already figured that much out, from the moment Khosa had started keeping him under separate guard back in Somalia. Hostages were leverage, either for money or some other kind of trade. Nobody was going to pay money for Jude, at least not while Ben and Jeff were Khosa's prisoners too. Even if they hadn't been, Jude didn't think he was worth much for ransom. No, it wasn't about money. It had to mean that Khosa wanted something else from Ben. But what?

Genuine sleep came eventually, and when Jude awoke it was daylight outside. He expected them to arrive soon. But the drive went on, and on. Another fuel stop. Another floppy sandwich. More interminable miles along empty dirt roads, nothing but trees and bushes to look at all day long. How big was this damn country?

It was evening by the time they arrived at the military checkpoint. Men with guns appeared in the headlights. The Mercedes slowed. Masango rolled down the window and a soldier with a red beret and a bad harelip peered through before waving them on. Jude saw lots of lights and men with guns, and a big wire fence with a metal gate opening to let

45

them pass, then yet more soldiers and fences as the car was ushered through what seemed like more layers of security than surrounded the US president's country retreat at Camp David. Jude hadn't known what to expect, but certainly nothing as elaborate and organised as this.

The Mercedes whisked him onwards, away from the checkpoint and along a narrower, bumpier dirt track that wound past earth-moving machinery and piles of dirt and rock as large as hills. Garbage was everywhere. A bonfire was burning, sending embers like fireflies into the night air and casting flickering orange shadows across a patch of empty ground to a row of makeshift wooden shacks. Jude saw movement in the firelight and realised there were people over there: some who looked like soldiers, and more who didn't. A crowd of them, thin, bent, ragged Africans, men and women, being herded at gunpoint towards the shacks. The way they shuffled along, their bare feet dragging on the ground, they looked ready to collapse from exhaustion. Even in this light Jude could see that their clothes were in tatters and caked with filth.

Who were they? Jude wanted to ask, but then another sight killed the words in his mouth before they could come out.

Planted in the ground on the far side of the shacks, dimly bathed in the fire's dancing light, stood a thick wooden post. The wood was all burnt and blackened, wrapped around with chains. Three blackened skeletons were held with their backs to the post. The burnt debris around the base of the post was still gently smouldering.

Jude felt sick. This was what these animals were doing here, burning people at the stake. He sensed that César Masango was looking at him.

'What is this place?' Jude managed to say. The defiance was all gone from his voice now.

'Your new home,' Masango said. 'Oh, do not worry. You will not be joining the slaves. Here is where you will live, behind these gates.' He pointed ahead. The Mercedes was arriving at another gate inset in another fence, this one built out of galvanised sheet-metal like a high grey wall streaked with dirt and rust in the light of the car's headlights. The gate was heavily chained and padlocked. As the Mercedes pulled up, Promise Okereke got out of the back. He swung the rear passenger door lightly shut and walked towards the gates, taking a key from his pocket. He stopped at the gate; then with his back to the car, brightly lit by the headlamps, he started to undo the padlock. The Uzi submachine gun was dangling from his shoulder.

Jude's heart began to race at the crazy idea that nothing but Promise's empty seat now separated him from the unlocked rear passenger door. All he had to do was make a scramble for it before Masango could stop him, fling the door open and run like hell. For the first time since Khosa had captured them on the ocean, there was a real possibility of escape. A window of opportunity that wouldn't last more than a few seconds, forcing him to make a very quick decision. Could he manage to disappear into the darkness before Promise turned round and opened fire on him? How would he get past the rest of the gates, and the soldiers?

Ben wouldn't be worried about the risk. Ben would go for it.

Jude was suddenly boiling with adrenalin and his muscles were winding up tight as mandolin strings. He was ready. He had to do it. One chance, now or never.

Then Jude felt something hard poke against his ribs. Masango had a small pistol pressed into his side.

'Jean-Pierre told me you have *changarawe*,' Masango said.

47

It was the only word of Swahili that Jude understood. It meant 'guts'.

'But there is bravery, and then there is foolishness. You have already been warned once, my young friend. Do not even think about it again.'

Jude sank back into the seat, defeated and furious with himself for being so cowardly. He wished Masango would just shoot him and be done with it. In the beam of the headlights, Promise was opening the tall sheet-metal gate. The driver eased the car through it and then paused while Promise closed and relocked the gate and got back in. The Mercedes purred on. The area within the metal fence wasn't large, maybe eighty yards across, a roughly square compound made out of beaten earth and empty apart from four green metal prefab huts that stood planted in a row a few metres apart at its centre.

The car stopped again. The driver kept the engine running. Masango climbed out, stretching his muscles after the long journey. 'Come,' he said to Jude. Jude got cautiously out of the car, looking around him. Promise got out from the other door, with the Uzi in one hand and a long flashlight in the other, which he shone first in Jude's face and then at the huts.

'This one here is yours,' Masango said to Jude. 'It has been specially prepared for our important new guest.' He pointed in the direction of the torch beam at a hut on the end of the row. It was bolted together out of sections of the same galvanised sheet metal as the fence. There was a single tiny window, no glass, barred with flat aluminium bars riveted to the outside. The metal door, equipped with bolts top and bottom as well as a hasp and a thick padlock, hung ajar. The hut was pitch dark inside.

Promise took hold of Jude's arm and pushed him into

the hut, lighting the way with the torch. The compound evidently didn't stretch to electric power. The floor was the same compacted earth and reminded Jude of the derelict building in Somalia where Khosa's men had murdered his shipmate and friend Steve Maisky, otherwise known as Condor.

But this was no execution room, and no such gruesome fate awaited Jude here. Not yet. The hut was designed for another, very obvious, purpose. Its sheet metal sections had been assembled around an inner steel cage, a cube welded together out of tubular bars, maybe eight feet long by eight wide by eight high.

The cage was serious business, the kind of solid affair that would have served for keeping dangerous animals inside. It was probably strong enough to contain a silverback gorilla. At one side was a mattress and a chair. In the opposite corner, two buckets. One empty, to use as a toilet, the other half full of water.

'You shouldn't have gone to so much trouble,' Jude said. 'This kind of luxury is much more than I have at home.'

'You will be brought two meals a day,' Masango said. 'If you cause trouble, there will be no food until you learn to behave yourself. If you are good, there will be special privileges, like a magazine to read, and a blanket.'

'Any chance of a pool table?' Jude said. 'A decent laptop with Wi-Fi connection would be handy, too.'

'Guards come and go during the day and night,' Masango told him. 'But Promise will be close by you at all times, and bring your meals. He will also report any instances of unco-operative behaviour back to General Khosa and myself.'

'How's he going to do that, with no tongue?'

Masango looked stern in the torchlight. 'Lock him up,' he ordered Promise. Promise pulled open the cage door, grabbed Jude and shoved him inside. The heavy door shut with a final-sounding hollow clang that Jude didn't like at all. Promise slid home the four bolts that fastened it, and clicked a padlock through each in turn. He rattled them to test they were secure, then stepped away.

Jude clasped the bars. They were cold and dreadfully rigid-feeling. 'Let me tell you something, Masango,' he said in a calm, serious tone. 'You people are making the biggest mistake of your lives if you think this whole thing isn't going to backfire on you. I'm getting out of here, and when I do, you're in deep shit.'

'Goodbye, White Meat,' Masango said. Khosa had called him by the same name. They'd obviously been talking about him, which wasn't a comforting thought. Masango walked out of the hut, followed by Promise, and Jude was left alone in the darkness. He heard the hasp close and the snick of the outer padlock. As if it was even necessary.

Jude stood clutching the bars, listening. Footsteps on the stony ground; Masango speaking to someone, either Promise or the driver, in Swahili. Then the car door slamming; the smooth engine revving, tyres crunching as it rolled away.

Then all that remained was absolute silence, except for the thudding of Jude's heart.

He stood there for a long time afterwards, until finally he groped his way across the cage and lay down on the damp-smelling mattress. He closed his eyes. He wondered whether Promise had gone with Masango or stayed behind, and then wondered what the other three huts were for. If Promise had stayed behind, maybe one hut was the guard house. Were there other captives inside the other two?

Jude sighed, trying to relax. He let his mind wander. For some reason, the next person to drift into his thoughts was Helen. He fingered the little name bead bracelet he still wore around his left wrist, even though they'd split up months ago, and tried to picture her pretty, elfin face. He wondered what she'd been doing since then, and where she was at this moment. Somewhere safe and cosy, he hoped. Not locked in a cage in the middle of Africa, that was for sure.

Then he replayed his cocky parting shot to Masango. What a thing to say. How cool was that? It made him chuckle for a moment, but only a moment.

'Who are you trying to kid?' he muttered to himself out loud. 'You're the one in deep shit.'

Chapter 6

Ben and the other three spent their first night in Khosa City in a poky fourth-floor room of the hotel that had been fitted with makeshift bunks, like a dorm for soldiers to kip in, and a far cry from the opulence of the General's suite high above them. The windows had been nailed shut and barred on the outside, presumably to prevent certain guests from escaping. At least it had a bathroom of its own, with a hot shower that actually worked and felt like a small piece of heaven as they took turns cleaning themselves up after the long, hot, and dusty journey. All except Gerber, who shuffled wordlessly to the nearest bunk and clambered in fully dressed with his boots on and his back to the room, ignoring all attempts to rouse him.

'He's got to snap out of this state,' Jeff whispered to Ben. 'You know what's going to happen if he doesn't.'

Ben did know. Either Gerber would spiral into a depression from which he might never resurface, or Khosa would simply decide he was of no use to him, and sign the death warrant.

The next morning at six, the door was unlocked and a pair of Khosa's militia infantrymen marched into the room, accompanied by an older man in his mid or late thirties whose authoritative demeanour, if not his uniform, marked him as their superior officer.

Ben had already been awake for an hour by then. He'd managed to chase the blackness of his mood away by forcing a hundred press-ups out of himself, followed by a hundred sit-ups and a thorough inspection of their room and the view from the window. He'd taken another long, hot shower, then changed into the clean khaki T-shirt and combat trousers from the pile of clothing that had been left for them. Tuesday had just finished in the bathroom and Jeff was lounging on his bunk with his hands clasped behind his head and a whimsical look on his face. Gerber appeared to be asleep, in the same position he'd curled into the night before. Ben had in fact checked earlier to make sure he wasn't dead.

'I am Captain Xulu!' the officer barked at them. The troopers stood either side of him, holding their AKs in a sloppy rendition of the high-ready position that would have been something to rectify, if Ben had had any real intention of helping to train Khosa's army. The last thing the world needed was an effective fighting force with a rabid psychopath like Khosa at its helm.

Ben stepped towards Xulu and faced him up close. Xulu was an inch shorter, at around five-ten, and paunchy. He was like a smaller, fatter version of his general, without the ferocious facial scarring but doing his best to make up for it by acting tough.

Ben eyed him coldly and said, 'Doesn't this army teach you to salute a superior officer? You're talking to a major.'

Xulu returned the stare with a nasty grin. Every second or third tooth in his mouth was capped with gold. 'You are not in my chain of command, soldier. I take my orders from General Khosa, Colonel Dizolele, and nobody else.' He pursed his lips and added, 'The General thinks you are a great warrior. Me, I think you are just another *muzungu*

53

bastard who thinks he can deceive us. I do not salute *muzungu* shit.'

Ben and Jeff had known each other a long time and could communicate on a level that wasn't quite telepathic, but not far off it. *Might just have to kill this one*, Ben knew Jeff was thinking from the set of his jaw.

Soon, Ben's return glance told Jeff.

Jeff twitched one eyebrow and gave a tiny jerk of his chin, indicating as clearly as if he'd spoken it out loud, *Why wait? Let's pitch the fucker out of the window, snap the necks of these worthless two, take their weapons, and storm the building. You know you want to.*

Ben gave a half-smile. The idea had merit. Its time might come, but that time wasn't now.

The silent conversation between the two men wasn't lost on Tuesday Fletcher, but it went straight over the head of Xulu, who planted his hands on his hips and glared around the room. His disapproving eye settled on Gerber. 'You! Old man! You should stand up when I speak to you!'

'He isn't well,' Ben said. 'Leave him alone.'

'Is he drunk?' Xulu demanded. 'Is he sick? What is wrong with him?' He reached out to grab Gerber's arm and yank him off the bunk.

'He has the simian herpes genitalis virus,' Ben said. 'Caught it from a macaque in Addis Ababa. Very contagious.'

'Makes your bollocks shrivel up and drop off,' Jeff said, pointing downwards. 'And everything else down there with them, if you're really unlucky.'

'Pretty grim,' Tuesday added, pulling a face. 'You can get it just by touching an infected person.'

'We're all vaccinated against it,' Ben said. 'If you're not, I wouldn't get too close.'

'But the infection only lasts a little while,' Jeff concluded. 'He'll be fine by tomorrow.'

Evidently not much of a doctor, Xulu had quickly pulled back his arm and now stepped away from Gerber's bunk with a disconcerted frown. 'Very well. He is excused duty for today.'

'And what duty might that be?' Ben asked.

The nasty gold smile. 'You will soon find out. Come with me.'

Three more soldiers awaited downstairs in the lobby, to escort them to the armoured personnel carrier parked in the street in front of the hotel. Ben was able to get a better look at the six-wheeled APC in daylight and recognised it as a Chinese Type 92. Essentially it was a small tank, except it was fully amphibious. Hardware like it wasn't cheap to come by, even in central Africa where military-grade weapons of all shapes and sizes could be had for a few dollars.

'I wonder what surprises are in store for us today,' Jeff mused as they walked from the entrance. The sun was already hot, burning a hole in the early morning clouds over the city.

'Surprises are foolish things,' Tuesday replied. 'The pleasure is not enhanced, and the inconvenience is often considerable.' He caught Jeff's look and shrugged. 'It's from *Emma*.'

'Who the hell's Emma?'

'You know, Jane Austen?'

Jeff looked blank. 'Sounds like you know some strange women.'

But Tuesday was right about the pleasure not being enhanced as the three of them were made to clamber inside the stuffy, baking-hot interior of the APC. The three-man crew was already in place and the additional five soldiers, plus Xulu, plus their three charges, made twelve people crammed in like herrings in a cask. 'Anybody farts in here,' Jeff muttered, 'and he's dead meat.'

Captain Xulu sat near the front and gave orders to the crew as the hatch was slammed down above them and the heavy vehicle got moving. From his cramped fold-down seat in the back, Ben was able to peer out through a bullet-proof-glass porthole. The sight of the empty city streets rolling by was even more surreal in daylight than when they'd first arrived. 'There's no way Khosa built this place,' he said, voicing his thoughts from last night in a low tone that only Tuesday and Jeff would hear. 'His resources don't stretch this far, nothing like it. And if they did, he'd have spent the money on building a proper military base.'

'Then again,' Jeff said. 'Khosa's as loony as a shithouse rat. If anyone's capable of it, he is.'

'He might be loony, but he's also got a plan. I don't see how this place fits with it.'

'If he didn't build it, then who did?' Tuesday asked.

Ben shook his head. 'And whoever did, why would they let him take the place over? You don't create something like this and leave it empty with just a bunch of crazies with guns running around the streets. There's got to be an angle.'

Tuesday thought about it. 'What if a property developer built it as an investment, and then Khosa and his boys just muscled in and took it from him? For all you know, the poor sod's buried in the hotel gardens.'

'Do you know what the average Congolese makes per year?' Ben said. 'Six hundred dollars. These people couldn't afford a broom cupboard in this place. What kind of luxury property development can possibly pay off in one of the world's poorest nations?'

The APC rumbled on through the deserted city, using the

whole road as there was absolutely no traffic. For a full twenty minutes they saw not a single motor vehicle or sign of life except for a pair of hyenas that had slipped through the perimeter and were running through the streets foraging for scraps. The turret machine-gunner decided it would be fun to have a pop at them, and for a few seconds the shell of the vehicle was filled with the deafening hammer-drill noise of sustained fully automatic fire. From the laughter of the crew, Ben guessed they must have hit something; then as the APC rumbled on he saw the carcass of one of the animals lying in a blood pool in the road. The other had fled.

'Great shooting, boys,' Jeff said. 'Bet that made them feel like real soldiers.'

The blocks thinned out as the edge of the city gave way to a less developed construction zone with earth and cranes everywhere. Soon afterwards, Captain Xulu gave the order to stop, and the APC juddered to a halt. The hatch was flipped open and the soldiers started scrambling out, yelling at their three passengers to do the same. As Ben pushed his head and shoulders out of the hatch he saw the huge building in whose shade they had pulled up. It was the half-built sports stadium that Khosa had mentioned. Until now, Ben hadn't known whether the General was even being serious.

They were at the far western edge of the city, with nothing except razed jungle and some airport buildings between them and the distant perimeter fence Ben could just about make out through the growing heat haze. The sun was climbing higher in the pale sky, the air buzzing with insects and growing chokingly humid as the temperature rose. Ben's shirt was sticking to him within moments. All twelve of them got out of the APC, leaving it empty. Which was something trained troops would never do, but Ben wasn't inclined to say so to Xulu. Sloppy was good, as far as he was concerned.

They entered the stadium through a deep concrete arch, like a semicircular tunnel that was cool and dank. Xulu strutted imperiously in front and the soldiers cautiously brought up the rear as though they believed that the three foreigners were about to bolt. The emptiness around them was almost tangible. Such a desolate and abandoned-feeling space would normally have been scrawled all over with graffiti and strewn with the litter of vagrants and kids, but everything was strangely immaculate and untouched. It was as if barely a living soul had ever set foot here.

The echoing passage opened up into a vast empty arena, oval in shape. Around its outside edge the auditorium was steeply banked like an amphitheatre. The arena itself might eventually become a sports field or race track, but was as yet nothing but a waste ground of patchy yellowed grass and prickly weeds. Ben felt very small in the big open space, and as nervous as a gladiator stepping out to meet his fate. It wouldn't have surprised him if Khosa were planning on staging a few bloodbaths in this arena for the entertainment of his troops.

But not today. Today, something else awaited him. Something he couldn't have expected. In retrospect, it would come to make perfect sense.

Chapter 7

Following Captain Xulu towards the centre of the arena, Ben observed a large circular area of rough grass in the middle of the field that had been squashed flat. He'd seen enough helicopter LZs in his life to recognise the after-effects of a powerful downdraught from some type of serious load-bearing transport chopper coming in to land. He knew it had to be a big one, because the cargo it had dropped in the middle of the stadium was a substantial quantity of crates. Piles upon piles of them, stacked messily on the ground and waiting to be unpacked or loaded onto trucks. Now Ben was beginning to understand what Xulu had meant by their duty for that day.

The captain marched up to the nearest stack of crates and jabbed a finger at it, turning to Ben. 'This is your first task as military advisor to General Khosa. You are to inspect the contents of this shipment and ensure that everything is in order.'

'What is it, fresh socks and underwear for the troops?' Jeff said. 'By the stink of them, I'd say it hasn't come too soon.'

Xulu ignored him with contempt. 'The General wishes for everything to be itemised and logged. You will report any problems to me.'

'And where will you be?' Ben asked.

'Over there, where I can see you,' Xulu said, motioning towards the middle section of the auditorium, where some rows of seats were shaded by the overhang of the half-finished roof.

'So he gets to sit on his chubby arse and watch while we sweat in the sun,' Jeff muttered. 'How jolly nice.'

They were given a claw hammer and a couple of short crowbars to open the crates with. Now that the foreigners were so dangerously armed, the soldiers kept their rifles pointed and retreated to a distance that was far enough to be safe while close enough to watch every move they made. Even in his craziest moments, Ben didn't think he'd have tried to take on eight trigger-happy Kalashnikov-toting militiamen with nothing more than a piece of bent forged steel in his hand. But it was strangely satisfying to know that they feared him. Tactical advantages always start with the enemy being afraid of you.

'Let's get to work,' he said to Jeff and Tuesday.

A quick inspection of the crates revealed sixteen untidy stacks of between a dozen and fifteen boxes of varying size each, plus many more dumped any-old-how on the grass – adding up to over two hundred and fifty of the things to open and check. They were nailed together out of roughly-sawn pine slats and stencilled in black paint with consignment numbers and Chinese character symbols, rope handles at each end. And they were heavy, the larger ones requiring two people to lift. It was hard to say without the means to weigh it properly, but Ben's estimate was around ten tons of freight sitting there in front of them, more or less equivalent to the payload of a Chinook or some other variety of heavy-lift cargo helicopter.

Chinese stencilled lettering. A Chinese armoured personnel carrier. Even before they'd levered open the first box, Ben had a hunch what they'd find inside. It wasn't underwear for the troops, and that was for sure. And it wasn't antique furniture for Khosa's luxury command post, either.

They started with the smaller boxes and worked their way up. As the lids came off, their faces grew grimmer.

Half of the smallest boxes contained six semiautomatic pistols of the type issued to the Republic of China military as the QSZ-92, brand-new and gleaming under their sheen of preservative oil, while the other half were packed with the 5.8mm bottlenecked cartridges to feed them with. But wars weren't won with pistols. In the crates of the next size up, they found dozens of brand-new examples of what the Republic of China's military brass termed *Wēishēng Cōngfēng*, literally 'silenced assault gun'. The British and US military would have called them bullpup submachine guns, and in the hands of Khosa's army they'd have called them trouble. More crates were stuffed with spare fifty-round magazines for them, and large quantities of the 9mm ammo they were chambered to fire.

'A bunch of ratty old AK-47s is one thing,' Tuesday sighed. 'This stuff is going to take these idiots to the next level.'

'And we're helping it happen,' Ben said through gritted teeth.

The bigger the crates, the more destructive the weapons inside. The QBZ-95 rifle was a grown-up version of the more compact submachine guns, this time chambered for the standard 5.56mm NATO round of which copious quantities nestled in more boxes. The PK machine gun was China's answer to the classic British General Purpose Machine Gun or GPMG, lovingly referred to by generations of soldiers as the 'gimpy'. It was only natural, after all, to love something that could cut a car in half, level trees and demolish brick walls all day long without a misfire.

But the firepower of the PK was outdone by the W-85 heavy machine gun, the People's Army's rendition of the venerable fifty-calibre M2 Browning heavy machine gun that had adorned armoured vehicles, fighting aircraft and naval vessels from the Thirties to the present day and been used in every single human conflict of any scale during that long period. There was little that could resist it – and the same was just as true of the Chinese version, built around a Soviet-designed 12.7mm cartridge that, if anything, packed just a little more punch than John M. Browning's trusty old fifty-cal. If you wanted to tear apart a fortified position from a mile or two away and an artillery strike or air assault was out of the question, these monsters would do the job in fine style, especially if you used the optional explosive-tipped round. And if you wanted a lighter bolt-action rifle chambered for the same carrot-sized cartridge that you could use to vaporize individual human targets too far away for the naked eye to see, that requirement was catered for by the AMR-2 sniper rifle. Ben found six of them packed in one of the cases, complete with five-round magazines and long-range mil-dot tactical scopes. They were almost identical in practical terms to the anti-materiel rifles that Tuesday had trained to use as a British army sniper. Nobody needed to tell him what mischief they were capable of inflicting. His jaw fell slowly open when he saw them.

Just about the only thing that could escape unriddled from the power of such weapons was the almost impenetrable skin of a modern main battle tank. But the shipment of arms had that contingency thoughtfully covered, too. The longest, heaviest crates contained enough HJ-10 armour-piercing anti-tank missiles, the Chinese equivalent of the American Hellfire surface-to-air or surface-to-surface rocket, to take out an entire battalion. The launch systems were in a separate freight container.

'This is not good, guys,' Jeff said. 'Not good at all.'

'Funny,' Ben said. 'I was thinking the same thing.'

'I'll tell you something else that's funny,' Jeff said. 'If these fuckers were Muslim jihadists, you'd have security services the world over shitting bricks at the thought that this little lot might fall into their hands. There'd probably be a satellite right overhead as we speak, and a dozen CIA spooks goggling at us live on the big screen in Langley, Virginia. But because Khosa's just your regular African warlord nutcase who's really only a threat to a bunch of other Africans, nobody's going to give a rat's arse. He's got carte blanche to run his fucked-up little kingdom out here any way he likes and do whatever he pleases. How's that for a joke?'

'Hilarious. Then why'm I not rolling on the floor pissing my pants laughing?' Tuesday said.

By the time they'd prised open every single crate and the ground was covered with lids and packing materials, the arsenal had grown to include a trio of fearsome Hua Qing belt-driven rotary 'miniguns', a useful quantity of grenades, several mortars and two flamethrowers. Down to the last nut, bolt, and bullet, the entire consignment had come direct from China.

'Our friends in the east,' was how Colonel Dizolele had described the senders of the shipment. Finally, one or two pieces of the puzzle were coming together. But that wasn't what was uppermost in Ben's mind at this moment, as he debated two possible options.

The first was the matter of how easily he might be able to slip a weapon onto his person unnoticed, for future use in aiding their escape from this damn place. One of the pistols would be best. There would be the difficulty of getting it loaded, as shoving loose twenty cartridges from an ammo crate into a magazine couldn't be done quickly or discreetly enough while being watched. The soldiers, and especially Xulu, were scrutinising everything the three of them did, most likely suspicious about the very thing that Ben was thinking of. Any false moves, and they might just decide to shoot him. Which wasn't going to help Jude's situation.

The second thought hovering in Ben's mind was the notion of sabotage. Whatever kind of business arrangement existed between Khosa and his friends in the east, it was unthinkable that such a lethal shipment could be allowed to enter into the man's possession. Ben wasn't about to forget the horrors that Khosa had already inflicted with just a handful of scuffed, battered old assault rifles and a few rusty old machetes. Give him state-of-the-art ordnance like this, and there was no telling what he'd be capable of.

But disabling ten tons of weaponry wasn't a quick and easy prospect. For a few moments Ben played with the insane idea that a loose grenade dropped into the wrong box could set off a fireworks display that would wreck most of the stadium and be seen and heard for miles. Goodbye shipment. But goodbye Ben, Jeff, and Tuesday too. Maybe that wasn't such a good plan.

With the boxes opened, the job was only just beginning. The sun grew meltingly hot as, for the next three hours, Ben and his companions checked and itemised every single piece of ordnance in the shipment.

'That's the last one,' Jeff said, tossing a rifle back into its crate.

'I'm done,' Tuesday said. He'd been checking the ammo supply for obvious duds such as dented cases or badly seated heads. Sadly, every round he'd examined had been shipshape and ready for business.

'Only question now is, when's the delivery of tanks and fighter jets due to arrive?' Jeff said.

'Don't joke about it,' Ben told him. 'That could be our next job.'

'Even if it's not, Khosa's still got enough toys here to kick off a pretty decent little war.'

'But who against?' Tuesday said.

'This is Africa, old son,' Jeff told him. 'There's never any shortage of folks to attack. Military rivals to overthrow, civilians to slaughter, other races to exterminate. It's what people do all over the world, always have, but here it's the national sport.'

Xulu had left the comfort of the shade and was strutting towards them, sipping from a bottle of water in one hand and carrying a radio handset in the other.

'You have done good work this morning, soldier,' he said to Ben, smacking his lips after a long drink. He didn't offer any of it to them.

'Delighted to be of service. I hope you didn't strain yourself with too much rest back there.'

Xulu held up the radio. 'We have been called back to headquarters. The General wishes to see you.'

'To inform us what our next duty of the day is?' Ben said. 'Maybe he'll have us spend the afternoon drilling some sense into your so-called troops. Starting with teaching them to tell their right hand from their left, and their arse from a rocket crater in the ground. You might want to join in. Might learn something.'

Xulu's gold teeth glinted in the sunlight. 'No, soldier. He wishes to see just you, alone. You are invited to lunch.'

Chapter 8

Just what it was about the idea of Ben having lunch with Khosa that Xulu found so amusing, Ben didn't want to dwell on. Maybe the General had special plans. Maybe it was also lunchtime for another poor starving lion captured by the soldiers, or a cageful of Rhodesian Ridgeback hounds that Khosa kept out back somewhere, and he'd decided to have Ben served up as the main course. When it came to murdering prisoners, the man was as inventive as he was unpredictable.

So it was with a degree of trepidation that, on their return to the Khosa City Dorchester, Ben let himself be escorted to the top floor and shown inside the luxurious command post. His guards closed him in and left.

There was no sign of Ben's gracious host in the palatial suite's living room. After a moment's hesitation, he headed for another door and found himself in an enormous dining room with a table that could have seated twenty people. No sign of places set for lunch. No sign of Khosa, either.

Ben went on exploring. Beyond the dining room, he discovered a narrow hallway with more rooms off it. He silently cracked open a door to his right, peered through the gap and saw it was a bathroom the size of his whole safe-house apartment in Paris, all marble and gilt and mirrors everywhere. The toilet, sink, and bath were pink with gold-plated taps. Ben pulled a face as if he'd drunk vinegar, closed the door and tried another, only to find a walk-in wardrobe even bigger than the bathroom but empty of clothes except for Khosa's uniform jacket and trousers hanging neatly from a rail.

The third door was a bedroom.

Like the rest of the suite it was richly decorated in silks and fine wood, but it appeared that Khosa had added some personal touches. Like the leopardskin covering on the enormous sofa on which the man himself was sprawled with his head lolling backwards and his legs splayed out in front of him.

The General was either asleep or unconscious. The sheets of the giant four-poster that dominated the room behind him were rumpled and looked as if he hadn't long since got up. He was wearing a burgundy silk dressing gown, crocodile cowboy boots, and a gunbelt with the ever-present .44 Magnum Colt Anaconda revolver strapped to his side. Ben wondered if he wore the gun in bed at night.

Khosa had obviously been enjoying a late, liquid breakfast. A half-empty, unlabelled bottle of some kind of pale liquor rested on the coffee table in front of him, next to an empty crystal wineglass and a carved ebony ashtray in which the stub of a Cohiba Gran Corona stood crumpled, nose-down, like a crashed plane. The room stank of stale cigar smoke. Khosa's eyes were closed, but they snapped sharply open as Ben stepped into the room, instantly focused on him. The General made no attempt to get up.

'So you accepted my invitation, soldier,' he said, as though there had been any choice in the matter. His voice betrayed no trace of drunkenness.

'You'll forgive me if I didn't get time to change into something a little smarter,' Ben said.

'Oh, this is not a formal occasion. I very much enjoyed our last conversation. I thought it time that we talked some more.'

That conversation had been back at Khosa's forward operating base in Somalia. They'd discussed war, strategy, the General's grand future plans, and the fact that he'd cottoned onto the father–son relationship between Ben and Jude. Ben had had more pleasant conversations.

'Where's Jude?'

'I told you, soldier. He is in a safe place and being very well looked after. There is no need for you to worry about him.'

'I want to talk to him.'

'That is not possible. You will have to accept my word on this. Do you not trust me, soldier? Do you not yet believe that what I say I will do, I always do?'

Ben made no reply. He did believe it. Khosa could invariably be taken at his word, and that was precisely what worried Ben the most.

Khosa straightened up and waved towards an armchair across the coffee table. 'Come and sit down. I want you to talk to me.'

'I don't have a lot to say to you.'

'Oh, that is not true. There is so much I can learn from a great warrior from the British army.'

'So that you can get better at killing people? Looks to me as if you're pretty adept at that already.'

Khosa found that highly amusing, and laughed loudly. 'Ah, soldier, you never tire of teasing me. You are a very impudent fellow. But as you know, I admire your frankness. Nobody else speaks to me the way you do. It is refreshing to have such open discussions, man to man.' He reached forwards for the bottle and poured himself another glass of whatever was in it. After knocking down half the glass in a single gulp, he offered the bottle to Ben. 'Would you like some Kotiko? Try it, soldier. It is made from palm trees. Very strong. I have many more bottles. Get yourself a glass from the cabinet.'

Ben glanced at the bottle and visualised himself smashing it over the edge of the table and slitting Khosa's throat with the jagged end. 'It's a little early in the day for me,' he lied.

Khosa shrugged, took another gulp, and refilled the glass once more. 'As I was saying,' he resumed, 'there is much I can learn from a man of your experience. You see, I believe strongly in education. Education is something lacking here in my country, and this is very sad. There is no end to learning, not even for the wisest or strongest leader. This is why I read. Military strategists tell us, "The general who wins the battle makes many calculations in his temple before the battle is fought. The general who loses makes but few calculations beforehand."'

Ben recognised the quotation from Sun Tzu's *Art of War*. Khosa loved to show off his erudition. First it had been history and Greek mythology. Now it was ancient military tactical wisdom from the fifth century bc.

'So you're preparing for battle, are you?' Ben asked.

Khosa smiled, his facial scars crinkling like horror-movie latex. 'Oh yes. A very big battle. I have been waiting for it a long time.'

'And it seems to me that Sun Tzu isn't the only Chinese military expert you've been taking advice from lately. Used to be it was the Russians who did most of the arms trading in Africa.'

'You are referring to the shipment you inspected this morning. I trust everything was to your satisfaction?'

'It's not the goods that trouble me,' Ben said. 'It's their recipient, and what he plans to do with them.'

'The Chinese are a worthwhile ally,' Khosa said. 'They despise us even more than we despise them. But this is acceptable. In business there is no room for friendship. I give to the yellow men what they need. In return, they will help me to achieve my goals. It is – how do you say? – a square deal. One that has suited me well. But things are soon about to change. Thanks to this, I will not need the Chinese for much longer.'

Khosa dipped his fingers into the bulging pocket of his dressing gown and took out his precious diamond. Its uncut faces caught the light from the window and reflected it into Khosa's face, casting a diaphanous glow over his nightmare features. Dozens of millions of dollars' worth of gemstone. Maybe hundreds of millions, for all Ben knew. And Khosa was carrying it around in his pocket as though it was a handful of change. He weighed the enormous glittering rock on his outstretched palm, gazing at it for a moment in rapt admiration.

Ben found it hard to take his own eyes off the thing. It was as big as the Chinese hand grenades he'd inspected that morning. And in its own way, it was infinitely more deadly. Ben had as little knowledge of its history or origin as he had of its value. He only knew that people had already died for it. And the dying wasn't over yet.

'It is not by chance that this diamond has come to me,' Khosa said, still gazing at it. 'To possess it was my destiny, all along. I have always known that, one day, it would find me. Now nothing will stand in my way. I will build the greatest army in all of Africa and avenge the wrong that was done to me by my brother.'

Chapter 9

Ben was surprised by the mention of a brother. It seemed strange that a man like this could have anything as normal as a family. That would imply that he'd been born of a human mother, and had a childhood, and once been something other than a murdering lunatic.

'Nothing like fraternal love,' he said to Khosa. 'So what did he do to piss you off so much? Build a bigger tinpot militia than yours? Pin more gold medals out of a Christmas cracker on his chest? Slaughter and kidnap more people than you? That must have been tough on the ego.'

Khosa's face darkened. For a moment, Ben thought he'd pushed him too far, and that the African was about to explode in rage, rip the .44 Magnum from its holster and start blasting. Instead, Khosa drained the last of his Kotiko, then frowned at the empty bottle. He heaved his large frame up out of the sofa. Ben thought he looked a touch unsteady from the effects of the alcohol. He watched him walk over to the drinks cabinet, bend down and take another bottle from the cupboard. Khosa twisted out the stopper as he carried the bottle back to the sofa, then threw himself heavily back down and helped himself to another brimming glass of the stuff.

It looked as though Khosa was content to extend his liquid

breakfast into a liquid lunch. Nothing had been said about food – not that Ben would have eaten a bite at this man's table, if he'd been dying of hunger.

'My brother's name is Louis,' Khosa said. 'We were close once, but he became my enemy. Louis is governor of Luhaka. Do you know Luhaka, soldier?'

'Not intimately,' Ben replied. 'It's a province that straddles the Congo River a few hundred miles from the capital. Some way north and east of here, I'd say, wherever here is.'

Khosa nodded. 'A little more than one hundred kilometres to the north-east of us. Very good, soldier. You have an impressive knowledge of my country. But you do not know its people as well I do, or its rulers. My brother lives like a pig in his palace in Kambale, doing as he pleases. While his people starve he plays tennis in his country club, protected by armed guards. He is a terrible man.'

The tone was all confiding now, but Ben refused to let himself be drawn in. 'Obviously not a common family trait,' he said. 'Considering how well you turned out.'

'I know you think I am bad, soldier, and that you hate me very much.'

'Where did you get that idea?'

'But I am the nice one of the two brothers,' Khosa said, with his scarred face distorted into a wide grin as though he found the idea highly amusing. Then the grin dropped and he looked extremely serious again. 'My men love me, soldier. One day, all the people of this country will love me as well. This is what Louis wants for himself, but you cannot put a gun to the head of your people and expect them to love you. It does not work that way.'

This, from the same man who not so very long ago had been shooting his own men at random while in a tantrum of rage and inspiring their love for him by terrorising them with threats of dismemberment. The benevolent dictator at work.

Khosa drank down another half-glass of Kotiko. He went on, 'Do you know how Louis tried to strengthen his people's love for him?' The palm liquor was beginning to tell on him now, his voice slurring a little.

'Apart from massacring them, you mean,' Ben said.

'He launched a campaign against witchcraft across all of Luhaka. First he ordered his doctors to produce a strong drink made from special herbs. He said that if a normal person drank this potion, it would have no effect on them. But if it was drunk by a person with sorcerer's powers, it would make them sick and dizzy. My brother forced many hundreds of people to drink the potion. He would not drink it himself, because it would have made anybody sick. When the people became ill, they were accused of witchcraft and thrown into prison. My brother ordered them to be burned alive. This is how wicked and corrupt he is. You see? It is as I say: a very terrible man.'

Ben stared at Khosa and wondered whether he'd ever met anybody so unaware of their own nature.

'I have not seen him for many years, but I hear that he wears gold rings on every finger and lightens his skin with a cream. What kind of an African does this? He is jealous of me because as children I was the one with the courage to receive these marks of a warrior.' Khosa touched the mutilated ridges on his face. 'Louis was a coward then, and he is a coward now. I will kill him one day soon.'

Khosa finished his glass and poured another. His posture was beginning to slump and the slur in his voice had thickened a little more.

'I think I will try a taste of that stuff, after all,' Ben said, pointing at the bottle.

73

'Be my guest, soldier. If you like it, I will give you a bottle to take back to your quarters.'

'That's very generous of you, General.' Ben got up and fetched a glass from the drinks cabinet. Settling back in his armchair he poured a half-measure and took a small sip. It wasn't Laphroaig, that was for sure. The palm wine seemed about twice as strong as Ben's favourite single malt scotch. He put the glass down. With any luck, Khosa would just drink himself into a fatal alcoholic coma right there in front of him.

'So that's your plan?' Ben asked. 'To dethrone your brother and become governor of Luhaka Province in his place?'

'No, no. My plans are much greater. It is not just Luhaka Province that is the problem. The Congo is like a rotten fruit. The government is bankrupt and in pieces, with no direction and no love for its unhappy people. In some places, the illiteracy rate among them is total. The biggest employer in the country is the civil service, but the workers must rely on bribery and embezzlement just to make a living.'

It sounded to Ben a lot like modern-day Britain, but he wasn't in the mood to get into a wider discussion.

Khosa went on, 'The poverty is terrible everywhere. Have you ever been poor? I do not think so. You are from Europe, where there is no poverty.'

'None whatsoever,' Ben said.

'You cannot understand,' Khosa insisted, emphasising his point by waving his glass at Ben. 'Do you know what it is to live with nothing in your belly and no clothes on your back? When we were young we lived like animals in the jungle, for years. It was only through war that Louis and I were able to pull ourselves from the dirt.'

The slurring in Khosa's voice was growing more and more noticeable. *You go on like that,* Ben thought. *Just carry right on.*

74

Khosa held up the diamond again, brandishing it as though it were a talisman. 'Thanks to the fortune I will make from this stone, now we will have a chance to build a real country. Luhaka will be only the beginning. After I become governor, all the people of the Congo will come to me. They will give me their strong young men. If I had a hundred thousand fighters, I would be ready to march on Kinshasa and take my place in the Palais de la Nation. Have you ever seen the palace, soldier?'

'I can't say that I have,' Ben replied.

'The president says he has a hundred and twenty thousand soldiers, but this is a lie, like everything else he says. There are more like fifty thousand. It will be easy for me to defeat them. Of course, many of my men will die and we will have much destruction to repair afterwards. But we have a saying in my country: "Where elephants fight, the grass gets trampled."'

At that point in his monologue, Khosa began making strange noises. Ben realised that he was singing. '*One country, one father, one ruler: Khosa! Khosa! Khosa!* That is what they will sing about me, soldier. I can already hear them.'

Another big slurp of Kotiko. 'A strong nation I will make of this country. Like General Amin did for Uganda. How I loved that man. Under my rule, nothing will stop us from becoming a true world power. All my people will benefit from the riches under the soil. They will be happy and united once again. I will build the biggest army Africa has ever seen, and I will pay all my soldiers a hundred dollars a month. The United States president will come to me whenever I summon him. Then with the help of all Africa I will eradicate the Tutsi scum from the land and annex Rwanda as a new province of my republic.'

'You have something personally against the Tutsi, or do you just enjoy killing people?'

'They are treacherous cockroaches and cannot be trusted. Every true African knows this. After the civil war in Rwanda, my country was invaded by a million Tutsi who called themselves refugees when in reality they only wanted to take over all of Zaire. Louis and I, we hunted them. Our death squad killed many, many, many. We called it Operation Insecticide. Sometimes we killed a hundred in a day. We used guns, knives, or ropes to strangle them. Women, children, all cockroaches just the same. But however many we killed, more kept coming.'

Khosa lapsed into a long silence, as if he were replaying the memory of those times inside his head. He guzzled another glassful of Kotiko, refilled it twice more, and knocked it back each time. The second bottle was almost empty now. He closed his eyes, swayed a little, and for a moment Ben thought he would keel over sideways. Khosa slowly opened his eyes, pupils unfocused and his vision clearly swimming. His gaze searched for Ben, found him, and fixed him with a baleful expression.

He whispered, 'When I close my eyes, soldier, I see terrible things. I see bone and rotting flesh and worms. I see a million skulls of people I have killed, looking at me. I hear their voices inside my mind.'

Then Khosa sank back into the sofa and the glass slipped from his fingers.

Ben stood up. He stepped around the edge of the coffee table, bent down and snapped his fingers three times an inch from the African's nose. No reaction. He reached out, grasped the thick muscle of Khosa's shoulder and gave it a shake. He was heavy and hard to move. Ben shook him harder. No response. Khosa was out cold.

Ben's mind began to whirl. Here was this man, this cruel and ruthless and almost certainly insane murderer, Jude's kidnapper, the worst person Ben had ever known in his life, completely helpless and at his mercy. This was an opportunity that wouldn't come again.

But what to do with that opportunity?

The room was full of objects that Ben could have killed Khosa with. He'd been discreetly eyeing them during the conversation. The bottle. The ebony ashtray. Any of the heavy antique lamps would double as a useful club to beat his brains out with. Or else Ben could have used his bare hands, the way he'd been trained, the way he'd last done only a few days earlier when he'd broken Scagnetti's neck. But Scagnetti had been a small, wiry guy, easy to get a grip on. Khosa was a far larger and more powerful man, and nothing about him was predictable. He might not die immediately. He might wake up, and if he did there would be a struggle, possibly a messy one. Ben was certain that the guards who'd escorted him up here to the eighth floor were lurking just outside with their ears to the suite door, ready to burst in and come charging to their general's aid at any sign of trouble.

Once committed, there could be no failure. If Ben was going to kill Khosa, right here, right now, the job had to be done instantly, decisively, and with authority.

There was only one item in the room definitively capable of all three.

Ben thought *fuck it* and reached down Khosa's body to the gunbelt. He unsnapped the retaining strap of the holster and drew out the big Colt Anaconda. Chambered in .44 Remington Magnum, custom-engraved, fitted with a grip made of mammoth ivory. One of a matched pair, much prized by their owner. The other one, Ben had tossed into the Indian Ocean during the battle to regain control of the *Svalgaard Andromeda*.

The revolver was cold and heavy in his hand. He checked the cylinder. He'd have expected someone like Khosa to keep it fully loaded at all times, and he wasn't disappointed.

He stepped back two paces and aimed it at Khosa's head. He cocked the hammer and placed his finger on the trigger.

Chapter 10

Khosa didn't stir. His breathing was slow and deep. Ben stood over him with his finger on the trigger of the gun. He held the revolver in both hands, not just to steady his aim but because the .44 Magnum would kick hard when it went off. Which was a good thing, because every action has an equal and opposite reaction. If a handgun recoils brutally it's because it has launched a very heavy bullet at a very high velocity. In this case, more than enough muzzle energy to blow Khosa's brains all over his nice leopardskin sofa.

It was also going to be extremely loud. Ben wasn't too worried about his eardrums. He knew from experience, repeated many times over, that they'd recover and the high-pitched whine would fade. He was more worried about the shot being heard all over the hotel, across the street and for a wide radius across the deserted city. The moment he squeezed the trigger he'd have to be out of the window and clambering down the nearest fire escape before the guards came rushing in.

Ben squared the sights on Khosa's head with the muzzle at close to point-blank range. He wanted to kill this man more than anything. But it was hard to pull the trigger. The cause of his hesitation wasn't the strange sense of pity that he felt, despite everything, for a man who was obviously deranged and had to die, like putting down a rabid dog. It was the knowledge that by killing him, he would set in motion an irreversible chain reaction. The initial panic and chaos over Khosa's death would buy him a few minutes, maybe half an hour at best. The chain of command would disintegrate, but only temporarily, before Dizolele, or Xulu, or another of Khosa's subordinates picked up a phone or a radio and put the word through to César Masango, the man on whom Jude's fate would then rest.

Which meant Ben would have half an hour at best in which to locate Jude and prevent Masango from killing him in retaliation for Khosa. The odds weren't exactly favourable. When Ben had received the message that Jude was in trouble aboard the MV *Andromeda*, he'd had the GPS coordinates to guide him more or less exactly to Jude's location. Then, distance and time had been far less of an obstacle to rescuing him than the situation he faced now. Jude could be anywhere in the Congo. He could be in Burundi or Uganda or Zambia or Angola. He could be on another continent, for all Ben knew.

Ben's thoughts whirled faster as he stood there pointing the gun and time rushed past him. Maybe there was a better option than killing Khosa. He could kidnap him and hold him hostage, forcing him to reveal Jude's whereabouts and threatening to blow his brains out if Masango touched a hair on his son's head. They could trade: Jude for Khosa. Prisoner exchange at dawn in some remote spot. Any tricks, the General cops it. It sounded good, except for the logistics of dragging a 250-pound comatose body past the guards outside the door, down the lift and into the street in the hope of finding a convenient escape vehicle, all without getting into a knock-down shootout with a small army of soldiers; one six-gun against armoured personnel carriers, heavy machine guns and mortars. And even if Ben did achieve the impossible and get away with his hostage – then what about Jeff, Tuesday, and Lou Gerber?

It would be them or Jude. Ben couldn't save them all. He'd be leaving his friends behind to die, and it wouldn't be a quick and easy death that Khosa's enraged seconds-in-command would inflict on them.

Slowly, Ben lowered the gun. He uncocked the hammer and took his finger off the trigger and let the weapon droop limply at his side.

'Damn,' he said out loud. The moment of opportunity was slipping by him.

Then it was gone. Khosa's inert bulk gave a twitch, followed by a lurch, and he awoke in a panic, as if still half in the grip of some terrible nightmare. His eyes darted and rolled for several seconds before he heaved himself violently off the sofa and crashed forwards into the coffee table, wrecking it and spilling its contents to the floor. Ben could only stand and stare as Khosa reeled back to his feet, staggered sideways several yards and hit the drinks cabinet with his hip, sending an array of wineglasses and a crystal decanter flying. Khosa was screaming and bellowing as if he'd lost what sanity remained to him. Either that, Ben was thinking, or else this was what two bottles of Kotiko on an empty stomach could do to even a sane person. Khosa fell to the floor, beating the carpet with his fists and filling the bedroom with his roaring, braying voice.

Ben had been right about the guards listening at the door for trouble. They burst into the suite and raced towards the sound of their commander's screams. The same two soldiers who had escorted Ben earlier were quickly joined by two more, all of them wearing the same shocked expression as they took in the scene.

By then, Ben had already replaced the revolver in Khosa's gunbelt. He'd moved quickly to the far side of the bedroom and raised his hands to show he was no threat to any of them. The soldiers yelled and pointed their rifles and jabbed and prodded him and fired a thousand questions in Swahili and broken English. What had he done to their illustrious leader? What was happening here? Keeping the other hand raised, Ben pointed at the bottles on the floor and told them the General had drunk something that disagreed with him. He was sick. He needed his doctor.

It took fifteen minutes for the doctor to arrive, by which time another half-dozen soldiers had crowded the suite and more were milling around in the corridor outside. Khosa had long stopped screaming like a mad bull and lapsed back into a comatose state, saliva oozing from his lips and one eye half open. Ben was pinned in a corner of the bedroom by four jumpy soldiers ready to blast him if he moved. He was beginning to worry that if Khosa died, they would accuse him of having poisoned their leader.

Khosa's personal physician was tall and thin and stooped, possibly ninety years of age. He was barefoot and wore a long black robe intricately embroidered in gold thread and a necklace of what Ben at first thought were shrunken human skulls, then realised were those of monkeys. The old man appeared quite calm as he entered the room, took one look at the patient slumped full-length on the floor and strolled over to inspect him.

After a brief examination, the doctor turned, gazed around the room until he spotted the empty bottles still lying where they'd fallen, and in a voice as cracked and dry as parchment asked a soldier to pick one up and bring it to him. After a sniff of the bottle's neck he nodded sagely to himself and then produced a smaller amber bottle from the folds of his robe and trickled a few drops of liquid into the unconscious Khosa's open mouth.

Ben had heard of doctors like this. In French-speaking parts of Africa they called them *féticheurs*. The nearest English translation would be 'witch doctor', a purveyor of magic healing and weird potions of the kind that the patient's brother had apparently tried to purge from his province of Luhaka.

Adolf Hitler had taken military guidance from his astrologer. Tsarina Alexandra had hung on every word of the mystic healer, Rasputin. Jean-Pierre Khosa had his witch doctor. It didn't seem unfitting. With luck, the sorcerer's medicine would finish the job the Kotiko had started, and then nobody could blame Ben for the General's demise.

The old man creaked to his feet, his medical examination of the Supreme Being concluded. 'There is nothing wrong with him,' he declared, in the same hoarse, dry croak. 'He has tired himself and needs to rest.'

'That, and a good dose of lithium,' Ben said.

The witch doctor motioned to the nearest group of soldiers to pick Khosa up and place him on the bed. It took three of them to heave him onto the rumpled four-poster. Khosa was still out for the count. With long, bony hands the witch doctor performed a series of strange gestures over his inert form, rattled his monkey skulls and uttered some sort of incantation in a language Ben had never heard before. Satisfied, he turned away to let his patient sleep off the booze. His wizened gaze scanned the room and fell on Ben. He gave an odd little smile. 'I know who you are. You are the white warrior who has come to help us.'

'I suppose I get pleasure from helping the needy,' Ben said.

'I am Pascal Wakenge,' the old man said. He walked

towards Ben, fixing him with an intense stare. 'You can leave now. There is nothing for you to do,' he told the guards crowded around Ben. The soldiers dispersed and filed out of the bedroom, just a couple of them hovering in the doorway. Evidently, the witch doctor carried some weight of authority around here.

Ben stood up. Wakenge watched every move he made with great fascination. Something in the old man's glittering eyes made Ben's flesh creep. It was easy to understand the sway he would hold over someone who believed in sorcery and witchcraft.

'Jean-Pierre sees much in you,' he said. 'You should not hate him so.'

'Oh, I'm full of human understanding,' Ben replied. 'No hard feelings. He's only trying to do his job, after all.'

'He sees much, but I see more.'

'You do, do you?'

'I see much death in you, white man. You have killed many. And you will kill more. But there is one you wish to kill more than any other. It is your greatest desire to look this man in the eye as you take his life.'

Ben said nothing. He was positive that Wakenge could tell no such thing. The crafty old man was using what he knew to psych Ben out in search of a sign that he could be a threat. Fortune-tellers and other such cranks, at any rate the more successful ones, were often excellent psychologists and extremely devious at winkling out useful information without their victims realising they were being manipulated.

'I'm afraid you must have me confused with someone else,' Ben said. 'I don't want to kill anybody.'

Wakenge went on staring at him for the longest time. Ben returned the eye contact, not wanting to be the first to look away. For a few moments it seemed to have become a battle of wills, one Ben was determined not to lose to this creepy old charlatan.

Then Wakenge said, 'Be warned, white man. You have saved many lost souls in the past. But you should be careful, or you will not be able to save your own.'

Ben gave him a dry smile. 'I'm going to die?'

'Soon,' the old man said.

Chapter 11

It was lunchtime in Kinshasa, too, and the bar at the Grand Hotel in the Presidential district of Gombe was crowded with well-to-do locals, bureaucrats and visiting business executives. It was more or less the most prestigious environment that the capital had to offer, even if the electricity went off several times a day, and César Masango fitted into it well. He was perfectly groomed in a handsomely tailored double-breasted suit of light grey silk, tan leather brogues polished into mirrors, and a Rolex Daytona that was even bigger and glitzier than the model that his friend and business associate, Jean-Pierre Khosa, liked to flash around. None of the corporate types milling around him could have guessed that he'd returned only hours ago from a militarised stronghold deep in the jungle. Any more than they could have guessed what his business was here today in the city.

Masango and his two associates had occupied a corner table by the window, where they sat in silence as Masango scanned the busy street and sipped on an $8 cappuccino. His associates didn't get any, because they weren't paid to eat, drink, or speak on his time unless specifically permitted.

Masango was waiting for Marius Grobler, a fifty-six-year-old white South African who labelled himself a consultant in international import/export but who was in fact a criminal fence specialising in converting dubiously obtained diamonds, gold and other such high-end commodities into untraceable cash. He was effective, discreet, and had been the first name to come up when discussing the various options for selling Jean-Pierre's wonderful new acquisition.

The purchase deal had been brokered on Khosa's behalf by Masango, his political attaché. 'Political attaché' might have been an accurate term, if indeed Khosa had anything much to do with politics – which for the moment he did not, although that didn't deter Khosa's small but rapidly growing legion of followers from viewing César Masango as the man who would one day put their exalted leader in power. While both men believed that day would eventually come (and all the sooner now that Khosa was set to become much richer), for the moment Masango was happy to act as his universal aide, fixer and back-door man. In return for these services, he received more than the General's gratitude and the future promise of a top ministerial job when Khosa grabbed the presidency. For brokering this deal, setting up the meeting with Grobler in Kinshasa and attending to all associated matters, Masango's slice of the diamond sale proceeds would be a lordly five per cent. Which was as generous a percentage as anyone was likely to get from Khosa; in this case, anyhow, it still amounted to a nice little payday for César.

Besides, as only he and Khosa knew, this wouldn't be a one-off payment. Far from it.

Grobler arrived in a shiny X3 BMW, with three large, unsmiling white subordinates who shadowed him like the bodyguards they in fact were as he entered the hotel lobby and was warmly met by César Masango. The South African was carrying a large silver case attached to his left wrist. He was a slight man and clearly struggling with its weight, but not about to entrust such a valuable load to a helper. His manner was gruff and brusque as he and Masango shook hands. His pale-grey eyes darted left and right as if looking for someone. 'I'd understood your client was to meet me in person,' he said, a little nonplussed.

Not missing a beat, Masango smiled and informed him that there had been a slight change of plan, and the meeting was now to be held elsewhere. 'For security reasons,' he explained vaguely. 'I hope you understand. We received reports of a potential confidentiality leak.'

'Not from my side, there isn't,' Grobler snorted. 'I hope your client isn't backing out on me here. I've gone to a great deal of trouble to arrange the funds at such short notice. This isn't the kind of money I normally carry around with me, you know?'

'Please be assured, Mr Grobler,' Masango replied with another charming smile, 'that the meeting will proceed exactly as intended. It will be my pleasure to take you to him. However, unfortunately, also for security reasons, my client stipulates that you attend the meeting alone.'

Grobler didn't take this well. 'These men are my trusted associates. I have no secrets from them.' Which was blatantly untrue, of course. The men were paid thugs with no knowledge of the deal and nothing to think about except how to keep their employer in one piece if things went south. That possibility was an ever-present occupational hazard in Grobler's line of work and he had long since learned to be careful.

'I am sorry,' Masango said. 'I am instructed that if this condition is not met, the meeting is cancelled. My client was very specific on this point. It is, as you say, a deal breaker.'

Grobler quickly considered what he had to lose by missing out, then grunted, 'Very well. But my associates will accompany me to this alternative venue of yours, and wait outside while we do business. Okay?'

Masango shook his head. 'Again, I am afraid that is not possible. Your associates may remain here at the hotel during the meeting. They are welcome to have lunch, at our expense of course. We will return you here once our business is concluded.'

As deeply unhappy as he was to have had the goalposts moved on him, Grobler agreed to the new terms rather than let the deal slip away from him. The asking price set by Masango's anonymous client was, in relative terms, so absurdly low – assuming that the goods were as described, which he would check thoroughly before handing over the money – that the South African stood to rake a fortune from the transaction. He wasn't about to be deterred from such an opportunity. Therefore, doing all he could to hide his anxiety, he instructed his bodyguards to stay put. Lugging his heavy case he followed Masango and his men outside to the black Mercedes Viano six-seater MPV parked behind the Beemer. The solid lump of the Walther automatic nestling concealed under his jacket was something of a solace.

Masango's men climbed into the front of the Mercedes. Masango politely ushered Grobler into the back. Grobler hesitated, then climbed in and sat on the plush leather seat with the case between his feet. The moment they got moving, Masango said, 'I must ask you if you are armed, Mr Grobler. If so, please be so good as to let me have your weapon for a moment. I apologise for this intrusion, but my client is most particular.'

Grobler had no choice but to let Masango have the gun. Masango received it with a gracious smile, dropped out the magazine, emptied the chamber, and returned the empty pistol to him. 'You will have the bullets back later,' he assured him.

They drove for nearly half an hour through the wild Kinshasa traffic, dodging taxis and the yellow buses that ploughed the roads at high speed with little regard for human life. The paramilitary police presence was everywhere, but as no elections were currently taking place no actual tanks were rolling through the streets to quell the usual violent civil disturbances. Like so many African cities Kinshasa was a study in extremes, with great wealth and miserable poverty existing side by side. And it was southwards, away from the tree-lined boulevards, expensive villas, and high-rises towards the poorer districts where the local 'Kinois' lived in varying degrees of tin-roofed squalor on unpaved streets, that Grobler found himself being driven. It wasn't what he'd expected, and he was increasingly restless. 'Where are you taking me?' he kept asking, but Masango just smiled and kept assuring him that they were nearly there.

The car finally pulled up in a suburb of decaying concrete-block homes, where a feral gang of street kids were taking turns at smashing up a derelict car across the street with a sledgehammer. They fled at the approach of the Mercedes, which parked behind an unmarked black panel van in front of a dingy house. 'What the hell is this bloody place?' Grobler demanded. Masango stepped out of the car and motioned for him to follow. Grobler hesitated, thought of the money and swallowed hard. There was no turning back now.

Masango led the way inside the house. Grobler, case in hand, found himself in a room with peeling walls, a single table and chair and two large black men flanking the doorway. Neither of them spoke to him as he walked in, and neither looked like a man with a Jaffa-sized uncut diamond to sell. Odours of mould and rat piss hung thick in the air.

'Okay, so where's your client?' Grobler demanded, working hard to keep his composure. 'You told me he'd be here. What kind of bullshit are you shovelling on me?'

'I am authorised to act as his agent,' Masango said calmly. 'You will be dealing with me.'

'You mean he's not even coming? This is fucked, man. I'm not prepared to do business under these conditions, hear me? Take me back to the hotel. Right away.'

'Mr Grobler, please. Do not make this difficult. Now, I would like to see the money.'

'It's all here,' Grobler said angrily. 'Five million US dollars. But you're not seeing a damned penny of it until I see the diamond. Come on, man. That was the deal.'

'Of course. We will take you to it after we finish counting the payment.'

Grobler stared. His heart was beginning to thud. 'Now wait a minute—'

'Please open the case,' Masango said quietly. When Grobler hesitated just a fraction too long, Masango gave a nod to one of the heavies. The big black man reached under his jacket and pulled out a huge, wide-bladed cleaver. Masango pointed at the chain and cuff securing the case to Grobler's wrist. 'I am sure you would rather open it yourself than have us relieve you of it in a more unpleasant fashion.' He wasn't talking about cutting the chain. Meat and bone were much easier to chop with a single blow.

Blinking sweat from his eyes and in danger of letting go of his bowels, Grobler heaved the case onto the table, turned the combination dials to the number that his panicked mind had almost forgotten, and flipped open the locks. He understood enough to know that the business deal had become a robbery, but at this point he no longer cared about the diamond. The trade was now the money for his life, and he

91

was all too willing to sacrifice five million in order to be able to walk out of here. He'd worry about the crippling financial loss later, once he was home safe with a stiff drink.

The big thug with the knife hovered menacingly while Masango stepped forward to count out the blocks of cash crammed inside. Each was tightly compressed in plastic wrap. He used a pocket knife to slice one open at random and thumbed the banknotes with a practised hand, nodded to himself and examined several more before he seemed satisfied that it was all there.

At last, Masango looked up from the table with a smile to the red-faced Grobler. The South African was dripping sweat. It was staining through his shirt. Masango said, 'Very good. General Khosa thanks you for the donation to his cause.'

It was Khosa himself who had come up with the scheme. He'd begun this enterprise with every intention of selling the diamond on, for an accordingly reduced sum that reflected its nature as a hot item of stolen property. It was only after owning the fabulous object for a couple of days and falling in love with its beauty that he'd realised there was another, much better, way to raise revenue from it. Every criminal diamond fence in Africa would jump at the chance to acquire it at a bargain price, knowing that even as stolen goods they could pass it down the line for a vast profit margin. Its enormous size allowed it to be broken down into a good number of stones that, once cut, would each be unusually large in its own right. Being crooks themselves, they naturally would tell nobody of the wonderful opportunity that had come their way.

Idiots. The lure of the diamond would reel them in, like lambs to the slaughter, one after another. Five million dollars multiplied by the number of greedy fools who would fall for the trick could generate a sum well in excess of what the rock was actually worth, while Khosa still got to keep it for himself. It was the kind of simple, brutal little scam that the General loved.

Of course, once the money had changed hands there was the issue of making sure the fences kept their mouths shut. That was the easy part.

Grobler gaped, too winded with horror to utter a sound, as Masango picked a large empty holdall from the floor by the table and started transferring the money into it. Cramming in the last stack with some difficulty, he zipped the holdall shut and hauled it off the table. Masango then left the room, closing the door behind him. Grobler now found himself alone with Masango's thugs. All four of them were suddenly clutching knives and advancing on him with stone faces.

And now he did let go of his bowels.

'Please,' he croaked, holding out his hands in supplication as he backed away, with nowhere to go. 'Please.'

The four men closed in on him. They made it quick, not out of mercy for their victim but simply because the sooner they got it done, the sooner they would receive their tiny cut of the money.

When they'd finished with Grobler, they sheathed their knives, waited for Masango to unlock the door and then left the house. Moments after the Mercedes and the black van had gone, the street kids returned to continue bashing the derelict car. It would be a long time before anyone found the body inside the empty house. And even when whatever remains the rats had left were discovered, nobody would care. This was Africa, and no one had a deeper understanding of that fact than Jean-Pierre Khosa and his associates.

Chapter 12

It had been a long and difficult night, that first spent inside the cage. With no blanket to pull over himself, Jude curled up on the hard, bare floor mattress and hugged his sides in a futile attempt to keep warm. Sleep came and went. Some kind of night animal was calling in the distance: the plaintive howl and *yip-yip-yip* of a jackal or wild dog. Once Jude thought he heard an entirely different sound, the crying of a woman coming from somewhere closer, but he might have been dreaming.

When morning came and he was awoken by the harsh sunlight streaming in through the single barred window of the hut, it wasn't long before the night chill gave way to murderous heat that ramped up throughout the day until he didn't think he could stand it anymore. The feeble sigh of a breeze coming from the window barely reached him, even if he pressed himself right up against the bars of the cage to get close to it.

With nothing to do but sweat, Jude spent his hours staring at that small rectangle of light and listening intently for movement outside. Sometimes he could hear vehicles come and go, and the sound of boots crunching on the stony ground of the compound, and snatches of conversation that he couldn't understand as the occasional patrol of guards did the rounds of the huts. That told him there must be other prisoners being kept here. Was one of them the woman whose crying he'd thought he'd heard, or had he just imagined it? He listened out for her voice, but didn't hear it again.

The only person Jude saw during all of that first day was Promise. At midday, the hut door was noisily unlocked and the mute jailer came in balancing a tray on one hand; in the other hand was his Uzi submachine gun, which he kept constantly pointed at the prisoner as though Jude could squeeze through the bars and attack him. Promise was cautious that way, it seemed. He laid down the tray and carefully locked the hut door behind him, then waved the gun to indicate he wanted Jude to step back towards the rear of the cage. Promise walked around behind him, grabbed his wrists one after the other and cuffed them together through the bars.

'What do you think I'm going to do, the Ninja death leap?' Jude said. If Promise could have made a reply, he probably wouldn't have. With Jude securely handcuffed and unable to move more than half a step forwards or sideways, the cage door was opened. Still keeping the gun handy, Promise stepped inside and laid down the tray with its contents, a plastic beaker of water and a bowl of food. Next he checked the bucket that had been left for Jude to use as a latrine. Jude hadn't gone anywhere near it. He hated the bucket, and the humiliation of having to use it, and vowed not to until it became absolutely necessary.

Promise then closed, bolted and locked the cage door and walked around to release Jude from his handcuffs. He paused. Jude felt something tug at his left wrist, and twisted his neck to see Promise slip the bead bracelet off him.

'Hey! That's mine! You can't have it! Give it back!'

Promise examined the bracelet as though it was precious jewellery, then tucked it in his pocket and released Jude from the cuffs.

Jude felt violated by the theft. Even though he and Helen had gone their separate ways, that bracelet had seemed like his last connection with the world he'd left behind. He was attached to it. 'It's not worth anything to you,' he protested. 'It's just a bunch of cheap plastic beads. Come on, give it back.'

Promise coolly ignored him. Jude realised it was futile kicking up any more of a fuss over the matter, and gave up. He looked at his first meal in captivity, a small mound of cold rice with a few beans and scraps of meat mixed in. The bowl looked exactly like the pressed-steel feeding dish he'd bought from the local Pets at Home store for his terrier Scruffy, back in England.

'Hey,' he called out to Promise, who was heading back towards the hut door. 'What the hell is this? First you steal my stuff, then you expect me to eat like a dog? Bring me a knife and fork. You hear me?'

Promise seemed to ignore him, and went away. Some time later, he returned with a tablespoon that he tossed through the bars before disappearing again. It was a nasty old piece of cheap tin, but to Jude it seemed a significant victory over his captors to have his demands met, if only halfway. It filled him with energy and lifted his sagging spirits, and he set about tucking into the cold rice concoction with relish, sitting cross-legged on the floor of the cage and smiling to himself as he shovelled the food into his mouth.

These people weren't going to beat him.

The feeling of unease didn't leave Ben for a long time after his encounter with Raphael Wakenge, the witch doctor. The strange old man's last words to him kept ringing in his head as he was taken back to the poky room on the fourth floor.

You have saved many lost souls. As if Wakenge somehow knew about Ben's past, and the people he had helped. As if Ben had 'former kidnap rescue specialist' tattooed across his forehead as a cue for soothsayers and fortune-tellers. There was no way Wakenge could know those things about him, and it was deeply unsettling. Ben had experienced the same peculiar thing with Khosa himself, on a couple of occasions when the man had seemed able to read his thoughts. He still didn't know if that was real or imagined.

Shake it, Ben told himself irritably. You're an idiot if you let yourself be taken in by phony hocus-pocus. He can't read your past, any more than he can predict your death.

When the guards let Ben into the room, he found Jeff and Tuesday sitting at the table in the corner, tucking into a communal bowl of rice stew. Gerber was still in his bunk.

'How was lunch?' Jeff said through a mouthful of food. 'I can only hope it was better than this shit they've brought us.'

'Any of that going?' Ben was content to eat shit, if he could eat it in good company. He pulled up a chair and Jeff let him have his fork, saying he'd had enough. Ben glanced over at the slumped form in the bunk. Jeff shook his head, as if to say that Gerber hadn't moved all morning. Ben sighed. He was becoming increasingly worried that the veteran sailor had shut down and was going to pine away. He'd seen it happen to others.

'What did he want?' Tuesday asked. As he ate, Ben summed up the gist of the conversation with Khosa. Jeff listened to Ben's account and said, 'So in other words, it turns out that the bastard's even more batshit crazy than we reckoned on, and meanwhile we still don't know where they're holding Jude, or what this bloody place is, or how the fuck we're ever going to get out of it. Apart from that, it's all happy days.'

'And Gerber's losing his mind,' Tuesday added sullenly.

'Yeah. That, too. Poor sod.'

'I should have killed Khosa when I had the chance,' Ben muttered. 'I hesitated.'

'Then Jude would have got the chop a minute later. No, mate. You did the right thing.'

'I don't know what the right thing is,' Ben said, shaking his head. 'I'm beginning to think there isn't one.'

An hour later, Captain Xulu was back, with another announcement to make and another task to be completed. 'The soldiers are ready for their training,' he said.

This time, the armoured personnel carrier took them a different route from the hotel, heading east into a construction zone that was anything but deserted, with more people and activity than Ben and the others had yet come across in the strange uninhabited city.

More than that, it was the most extensive building site Ben had ever seen. One block after another was alive with men and machinery, a small army of workers in overalls and hard hats toiling hard and fast amid the heat and dust. Cranes swivelling, mixers mixing, others pouring, diggers pushing vast mounds of earth, trucks rumbling back and forth carrying sand and cement blocks, labourers running with barrows, foremen yelling orders over the noise and barking into radios. For the first time, it was possible to imagine how a whole city could have sprung up in the middle of nowhere. With this kind of intensity, they could have built London in a matter of months.

Ben took in the hectic scene from the porthole window. Not a single head turned towards them as the heavily armed military vehicle rolled by, a stone's throw away. He blinked, thinking he was seeing things. Then turned to Jeff and saw that Jeff had noticed it, too.

'I'm not imagining it, am I?' Jeff said, wide-eyed.

'No, you're not,' Ben said. 'Those building workers are all Chinese. Every man jack of them.'

Chapter 13

A quarter of a mile beyond the edge of the construction zone, the APC juddered to a halt. Xulu ordered everyone out.

They'd stopped at a wide open area of what had once been forest and was now stripped to bare earth, running along the eastern edge of the inner perimeter fence. Another armoured personnel carrier was parked beside them. Next to that was a line of trucks, and beyond the trucks was assembled the biggest crowd Ben had yet seen of Khosa's militia troops. There had to be at least four or five hundred of them, standing around smoking cigarettes and chatting and joking among themselves and waving their weapons around and kicking up clouds of dust from the loose, dry earth of the denuded wasteland.

Captain Xulu strutted towards them, waving his arms and screaming a furious order that seemed to have no effect whatsoever. Colonel Dizolele watched from a distance, leaning against the side of one of the trucks, apparently uninvolved in the proceedings.

'So this is our army,' Tuesday said. 'What a hopeless rabble. And they're only kids, for Christ's sake. The average age must be about sixteen.'

'The more hopeless, the better,' Jeff grunted. 'For us, that is.'

Ben ran his eye across the crowd. They lacked discipline, for sure, and their appearance was a mess of mismatched, cursory nods to military dress with an emphasis on wearing as many bandoliers of ammunition as could be draped around the human body, along with whatever kinds of machetes, knives, and hatchets they'd been able to scavenge along the way. They were the kind of motley crew that gave motley crews a bad name. But appearances were often deceptive. There would be many battle-hardened fighters in their midst, even among the youngest. Kids who had grown up in the most unstable and constantly war-torn region of the globe, who had seen everything, known nothing but conflict and death throughout all their formative years, and in many cases probably killed their first man by the age of twelve. Such kids, when they grew up to be strong and fierce warriors in the sway of a leader they believed in, weren't to be underestimated.

As Ben watched, a large, boxy black SUV came roaring up like a twenty-one-gun salute and pulled to a dramatic halt nearby. The top-model Range Rover Sport was an incongruous sight among all the scuffed and dusty military vehicles. Its vanity plate read khosa1 and its waxed bodywork and black-tinted glass reflected dozens of dazzling little suns. This would be the General's personal ride, then, Ben thought. Every self-respecting tyrannical warlord should have one, or at least until they could afford the bulletproof Rolls Royce.

Jean-Pierre Khosa stepped out of the front passenger seat. He was wearing the crisp uniform that Ben had seen hanging in his wardrobe, his eyes hidden behind mirrored aviator shades. He showed no trace of inebriation, let alone alcohol poisoning. Either he must have the constitution of a rhino, or the witch doctor's elixir had done its work.

Xulu and Dizolele hustled across to their leader's side.

Khosa barely acknowledged them, spotting Ben and striding towards him. 'I call them the Leopards,' he said, motioning grandly in the direction of his assembled troops. 'They are the most elite regiment of my forces. As they are to be the spearhead of the offensive against our enemies, they are to receive the most rigorous training. We will meet here every afternoon for three hours of drill.' He looked at Ben expectantly. 'How do you wish to proceed, soldier?'

The last thing Ben wanted to do was impart any martial ability to Khosa's fighters. He'd already had a taster of how they'd go on to deploy those skills. He couldn't have that on his conscience.

'We need to start by working on their physical conditioning,' he told Khosa.

'They are not in good condition?'

'Frankly? They're an embarrassment to you, General. We wouldn't have allowed such a lack of basic fitness in the regular British army, let alone Special Forces.' Ben pointed. 'Look at that one over there, in the blue T-shirt. He can barely hold up his weapon. He's so out of shape it's a wonder he hasn't died of a heart attack already.'

It wasn't true. The guy Ben had singled out for criticism had fabulous muscle definition and looked as if he could probably run ten miles in full kit and fight a battle at the end of it. But the appeal to Khosa's ego worked like a charm. The General scratched his chin pensively, reflected for a few moments and then declared, 'I see what you mean, soldier. This is very bad. Then it is decided. From now on all my fighters will be subject to the full fitness training that British SAS soldiers receive.'

And so, with Khosa's full endorsement, as the first and only order of the day, Ben and his co-military advisors got the troops running. Weapons were stacked in the trucks, where they could do no harm for the moment. There were grumbles as the men reluctantly removed the ammo belts they loved to drape around themselves. No image-conscious militia fighter could be seen in public without his necklace of shiny Russian 7.62x39mm rifle rounds to show everyone what a big man he was.

'We'll start with a jog around the city,' Ben ordered. 'Let's take it nice and easy to break them in. Say, six miles, nine minutes a mile, back here in just under an hour. The APC can lead the circuit. I'll head up the runners. Jeff?'

'Could do with blowing out the cobwebs,' Jeff said.

'And me,' Tuesday said.

'Think the leg will hold up okay?' Ben asked.

'Don't you worry about my leg,' Tuesday said defensively.

Ben turned to Xulu. 'Care to join us, Captain? Look like you could run off a little weight.'

Xulu sucked in his paunch and replied with a scornful scowl. He clearly had better things to do. Or else perhaps he didn't want to show himself up in front of his men. Rather than risk collapsing in a wheezing heap for all to see, he insisted on riding up front in the armoured personnel carrier.

The APC rumbled off at a pace somewhere between a jog and a run, Xulu glowering back at them from the rear window. Ben and Jeff set off behind it in easy strides and the long column of men followed, with Tuesday acting as drill sergeant to giddy-up any slackers. Ben had always enjoyed running, and took in a ten-miler whenever he could. It felt good to get the heart working and open the airways. Running helped him focus, and at this moment he had a lot of thinking to do.

'You don't really want to whip this lot into shape,' Jeff said, jogging along at his side.

Ben glanced back over his shoulder at the long, winding tail of the column. He could see Tuesday keeping pace at their flank, with no sign of a limp. The reason Tuesday had never made it into the SAS was the serious leg fracture he'd suffered during pre-selection training in the Brecon Beacons, causing him to be invalided out of the forces. He tended to be a little reactive when asked about it. Ben admired the younger man for his toughness and pride, but he sometimes worried that the leg still hurt Tuesday more than he would admit.

'Not in a million years,' Ben replied to Jeff's question.

'So what's the plan?'

'Play for time, play it cool for the moment, let Khosa think we're cooperating, and hope we can figure something out.'

'That's it?'

'That's the best I've come up with so far.'

Ben's other purpose for the six-mile run was to scope out the city, get to know the lay of the land, and start creating a map in his mind. Their route took them back past the huge construction zone and the legion of Chinese workers toiling to knock up streets and buildings as if there were no tomorrow.

'I don't get it,' Jeff said. 'What are they doing here?'

'Nor me,' Ben said. 'Not yet.'

As the troops ran, they spontaneously broke into song. Loud and proud, like US Marines in drill training, but surprisingly melodic and tuneful compared to the macho braying of a hundred beefy Americans.

'Jua limechomoko, wajeshi weee
Kimbia muchaka
Askari eee vita wi yeye
Anasonga corporal, sergeant, platoon commander
Anavaa kombati, boti, kibuyu ya maji'

'The sun is coming out, o soldiers
Go and run
A soldier's life is war
He rises from corporal to sergeant to platoon commander
He wears a uniform, boots and a water flask'

When they got back to the training ground, Khosa and his gleaming Range Rover had gone. So had Colonel Dizolele; and Captain Xulu grasped the opportunity to assume command.

'We are preparing for war,' he told Ben angrily. 'Not training for the Olympics. Enough of this stupid running. It is a waste of time and resources. These men must be taught to kill. This is meant to be your job.'

'Perhaps they'd like a demonstration,' Ben said, looking him in the eye.

Xulu cleared his throat nervously and stepped away, but if he was scared he recovered fast. 'Yes. A demonstration. That is a good idea.' He snapped his fingers, and one of his junior officers hurried to his side. Without taking his eyes off Ben, Xulu barked 'Lieutenant Umutese! How many prisoners do we have in the jail?'

The lieutenant replied instantly, 'Seven deserters that we caught this month, two men who were heard plotting against General Khosa, four Tutsi spies who infiltrated the army, and one man who stole sugar from the food store.'

Xulu nodded. 'Good. Lieutenant, take five men and ride back into town in a truck. Go to the jail and bring me the two traitors and two of the cockroaches. Be quick.' The lieutenant snapped a salute and ran for one of the trucks, waving and yelling at five of the men to come with him.

'He'd better not be doing what I think he is,' Jeff muttered.

Ben said nothing. The sun beat implacably down on his

105

head. He was tired, not from the run. Just tired. He wanted a cigarette. He wanted a drink. He wanted to see Jude again and get him out of this mess and go home.

Twenty minutes later, they found out exactly what Xulu's intentions were, and it was no surprise. The returning truck rolled to a halt in a dust cloud. The lieutenant and his five troopers marched the four miserable prisoners out of the back, fresh from whatever jail they'd been locked up in, and they were paraded in front of Xulu. Their heads were hanging. They knew what was coming. So did Ben, but he was powerless to stop it.

The five hundred troops had reassembled into a milling crowd on the training ground, some weary from the six-mile run, others fresh and ready for another. Their skin was gleaming and their clothes patched with sweat. The buzz of chatter died down as they caught sight of the prisoners being lined up, and anticipation began to mount.

Xulu addressed the men with his chest pouted and his hands clasped behind his back. 'Leopards! You are privileged to fight for General Khosa, our father and the saviour of our beloved country. Many of you have served in battle and killed our enemies. But some of you have not had this honour, like a boy who has not yet been with a woman. If there are fighters here who have not tasted the blood of our enemies for themselves, do not be ashamed. Put up your hands and step forward!'

After a few moments' hesitation and murmur, some fifty men shuffled bashfully from the crowd with their arms raised. Most of them were under twenty, some barely in their teens.

Xulu beamed at them. 'Today, young warriors, is the first day of your advanced military training. You have already shown courage and loyalty. Now you learn to kill.'

At a wave from his captain, Lieutenant Umutese had the prisoners marched across the training ground to the perimeter fence. One of them tried to break away, and made it a few stumbling steps before he was tackled by two soldiers and dragged, kicking and screaming, to join the other condemned men. They flung him against the wire mesh and stepped back.

'These men are your enemies!' Xulu yelled in a voice hoarse with excitement, pointing an accusing finger at the four. 'They have been disloyal to General Khosa! They have plotted against him and planned his assassination! They must die!' He turned his pointing hand towards the fifty or so fighters who had stepped forward, and picked out four of them at random. 'You, you, you and you! Come here. Lieutenant Umutese, give them weapons.'

None of the chosen four members of Khosa's elite regiment could have been more than fifteen years of age. Two of them, one in particular, seemed eager to participate in their blooding. The other two looked much less sure of themselves as AK-47s from the stack of weapons were pressed into their hands.

Xulu thrust his pointing finger back towards the terrified prisoners. His gold teeth glinted in the sun. 'Aim your weapons and kill them!'

Ben had seen enough.

Chapter 14

It didn't matter to Ben that those about to die weren't his friends. He'd seen so much blood spilled already at the hands of Khosa's army that he could stand to see no more – not on his watch, at any rate. And not spilled by children. He strode up to Xulu, pressed a hand to the captain's pointing arm and firmly lowered it.

Xulu stared at him in astonishment. A stunned silence fell over the assembled troops. The only sound was the gibbering of one of the prisoners, who had fallen to his knees by the wire fence. The other three were silent, seemingly accepting of their fate. At least shooting was quicker than being hacked to bits by blunt machetes.

'There aren't going to be any executions in this army,' Ben said to Xulu, quietly, so that the soldiers wouldn't hear. 'Not while I'm the General's military advisor. You made your point. Fun's over. So tell those boys to stand down, nice and easy, and let these poor bastards live.'

Xulu's face was a trembling mask of rage. His eyes boggled at Ben and he could barely talk for indignation. 'You speak to me this way in front of my own men?'

'Is there some other way to speak to a sadistic moron who enjoys watching unarmed men being executed in cold blood?' Ben said. 'Would you understand that better, Xulu?

If so, just let me know and I'll be sure to speak that way instead.'

'I will report this to General Khosa,' Xulu hissed.

'Of course you will. That's the first thing any maggoty little snitch would do. But in the meantime, Khosa's not here to protect you. It's just you and me. So either give that order to stand down, or I'll do it myself. Then I'll explain to Khosa that this isn't how things are done in a proper army.'

The prisoner was still blubbering in terror. The firing squad were still uncertainly aiming their weapons, but with their eyes off the condemned men and turned questioningly towards their captain. Their captain, however, was too busy staring speechlessly at the taller blond-haired white man to give them any direction.

'Can't make a decision?' Ben said. 'You're an unworthy officer, Xulu. You're not fit to captain a fishing boat, let alone a military unit. I'm taking over command here.' He addressed the firing squad and yelled, 'Lower your weapons!' Then repeated it in Swahili, to make the command doubly clear. The youngsters hesitated, but did what they were told.

'I knew,' Xulu said, looking at Ben with narrowed eyes and nodding to himself with quiet triumph, as though he'd been vindicated. 'I was sure of it, and now I know I was right. You are a coward, soldier. You are not a warrior at all. What kind of warrior is afraid of blood?'

Ben looked at him calmly for a second or two. Then he punched him in the mouth, fast and straight.

It wasn't a hard blow. Not enough to take his head off his shoulders, or even to knock him out. But it was enough to mash Xulu's lips against his gold teeth and spray blood all over his chin and the front of his uniform. Xulu went down on his backside and sat there in the dirt, touching a hand to his burst lips and gaping in horror at the red on his fingers. One of his gold teeth had come loose and was lying on the ground next to him.

Jeff and Tuesday were staring at Ben. So much for playing it cool and pretending to be cooperating, Jeff must have been thinking.

'I have no problem whatsoever with blood,' Ben told Xulu. 'If it belongs to the right person. You wanted to see some, there you have it. Now get up on your feet and try to act like a man for a change.'

Xulu struggled upright with a hand clamped to his bleeding mouth. He fired a look of hatred at Ben and beat his inglorious retreat to the armoured personnel carrier, gesticulating at the soldiers and leaving a trail of blood spots on the ground as he went. He disappeared inside the hatch and the vehicle took off with a roar.

'There goes our ride,' Jeff said.

Tuesday watched the APC go off into the distance, back towards the city. 'You've made a friend there, Ben,' he commented. 'He can't get back to the city soon enough, and the second he does he's going straight to Khosa. Just like he said he would.'

'I'm not worried about it,' Ben said, and he meant it. Khosa wasn't going to harm Jude over a minor infraction. For as long as he believed his captives were of use to him, his hostage was too precious a commodity to sacrifice for the likes of Xulu.

Ben's judgement was right, in that respect. But he soon discovered that he'd been wrong not to worry.

A squad of Khosa's personal guard was waiting for them back at the hotel. Stepping down from the truck with Jeff and Tuesday, Ben found himself under arrest. Resistance would have been foolish. With six Chinese submachine guns

110

at his back, he was marched inside the building and taken down a series of corridors to a ground-floor office he hadn't seen before. A male secretary in khakis was one-finger-typing on an antique PC at a corner desk.

Seated behind a larger desk in the middle of the room, hands laid flat in front of him and drumming his fingers on the tabletop, was Khosa. At Khosa's right stood Xulu, with a lower lip crusted in black blood and so swollen that he could hardly manage a twisted leer of satisfaction.

Ben had faced disciplinary proceedings before now. He walked into the room wearing the same brass face he'd worn when grilled by SAS superiors after the Basra affair, among other acts of insubordination that had dotted, and occasionally threatened to mar, his military career. He stopped a foot from the table. There was a chair, but he wasn't invited to sit and remained standing. He looked coolly at Khosa, ignoring Xulu and the rest of the soldiers.

The General got right to the point. 'Captain Xulu has filed a formal complaint against you, soldier. He claims that you disobeyed a direct command, and struck him. Is this true?'

'It's only half true,' Ben said. 'I disobeyed no command. I acted to prevent him from carrying out an order that I considered immoral and unsoldierly. Then I knocked his bloody teeth out. Which I'll do again, as often as necessary, as part of my task to turn this rabble of yours into a proper army. I won't be a party to acts of unwarranted cruelty against unarmed and defenceless prisoners.'

Khosa drummed his fingers some more, pursed his lips, glanced up at Xulu, then let out a heavy sigh. 'I am displeased, soldier. Displeased, and disappointed. You are still new here. I can understand that our methods are unfamiliar to you, but such displays of disobedience are bad for the morale of my men, and cannot be tolerated. Perhaps the punishment I have in mind for you will teach you to show more respect towards your superiors.'

'I don't consider Captain Xulu my superior,' Ben said. 'I consider him a worthless piece of shit who will get what's coming to him too.'

'Then what is needed here, soldier, is a lesson in humility. I hope for your sake that you learn from it. Take him away.'

The soldiers took Ben's arms and wheeled him out of the room and back up the corridor. He could have taken the whole bunch of them down with his bare hands and then used their own weapons on them to make sure they didn't get up again. Instead he bit his tongue and let himself be marched along. He still refused to believe that Khosa would hurt Jude for this. The hurt would be on him alone. They would probably beat him. Fists, sticks, or a whip, he didn't care. He would take their hurt without a word, and when the time was right he would revisit it on them a hundredfold.

They took him outside through a side exit, into a bare brick alleyway where an open-backed Toyota technical was waiting. One of the soldiers produced a black cloth hood, grinning. He rammed it down over Ben's head, and then they bundled him roughly into the back of the pickup truck. He felt the suspension rock as they clambered aboard with him. Then felt the hard kiss of gun muzzles pressing against his chest and head. The engine roared, and the vehicle took off.

If they planned to beat him half to death, they apparently intended to do it somewhere private. Somewhere they didn't want him to see the way to. Twice the vehicle slowed to a crawl, each time Ben heard voices and the clatter of gates. They were taking him outside the perimeter, but he couldn't understand why.

He counted the minutes: at least twenty of them passed by before the vehicle crunched to a halt for the third time, rough hands dragged him out of the back and dumped him on the ground. The soldiers laughed as they kicked and shoved him across what felt like ten or fifteen yards of stony earth. Then one of them whipped the hood from his head, and he caught a glimpse of a large, gaping hole in the ground in front of him before a powerful shove from behind drove him down into it. He fell, slithering, twisting, fingers raking through loose soil for a grip. The hole seemed to swallow him up as he fell deeper and deeper, desperately digging his knees and elbows into its sides to try to slow himself down. For a few instants he thought he was going to keep falling forever; then he hit the solid bottom with a thump that drove the air from his lungs. He blinked dirt out of his eyes, gasping, and looked up at the circle of sky at the mouth of the hole. He'd fallen maybe twenty feet. A couple of faces peered down at him, and he heard laughter.

He got to his knees and groped around him in the semi-darkness. The hole was bottle-shaped, widening out at the bottom with enough room for him to have lain down stretched out if he'd wanted to. The shape of its walls made it impossible to climb out. Try too hard, and you'd only pull down enough earth to bury yourself alive. That was when Ben realised they planned to keep him in here for a while. It wasn't just a hole in the ground. It was a primitive dungeon.

He got to his feet, looked up and heard the sound of an engine that made him think at first that the soldiers were leaving. But then the sound of more voices told him that a second vehicle had arrived. He craned his neck upwards but couldn't see any movement, only the circular window of sky far above him.

Ben involuntarily ducked as a dark shape filled the mouth of the hole and came tumbling down. He pressed his back against the earth wall to avoid whatever it was landing on him. It hit the ground at his feet with a crunch.

It was the dead body of an African. One of the prisoners he'd tried to save from the firing squad.

Three more bodies tumbled down the hole, piling up at the bottom in a grisly heap. All four had had their throats cut, their eyes gouged out and their hands and feet chopped off. Perhaps not in that order.

There was more activity above. Ben caught a glimpse of movement, heard the rev of an engine and saw a dark shadow pass overhead as one of the trucks drove over the mouth of the hole. It kept on going. Ben heard the clink of chains. Something heavy being dragged along the ground, obscuring the circular patch of sky like an eclipse spreading over the face of the sun. It was a steel plate or large manhole cover, and they were towing it into place to close off the mouth of his prison.

Sealing him off. No escape.

Suddenly, the dungeon was plunged into pitch blackness.

And after that, Ben heard nothing more. He was alone with the dead.

Chapter 15

Under a sky heaving with grey clouds, Victor Bronski stepped off the plane at N'Djili Airport, Kinshasa, and surveyed the scene with an air of jaded disapproval. Having travelled to virtually every Third World country in the course of his career, his opinion of the Congo was that someone should invent a Fourth World and plonk the damn place into it, in a class of its own where it belonged. And then toss a nuke in after it. He threw an even more disgusted look upwards, thinking that if the threatening rainclouds did let go, it would only become more unbearably humid. My Christ, what a shitpit.

Bronski was travelling light. His work here should require him to endure no more than a few days, at most. He would get the job done as slickly and efficiently as his reputation promised, deliver the goods and go home with a very fat pay cheque. At fifty-eight, with a quarter century under his belt as a private investigator and another fourteen years before that spent in law enforcement and criminal intelligence, he wasn't someone who left much to chance. All this professionalism, experience, and attention to detail came at an extortionate price, but when your employer was one of America's richest shipping magnates, Eugene Svalgaard, money was bottom of the worry list.

Bronski had no issues with travelling openly to the country in which he intended to conduct criminal business, because he was using false documents in the name of Henry R. Barrington, one of his favourite aliases and one that he felt lent him an air of sophistication. Mr Barrington was smart but casual in nicely pressed chinos, a lightweight blazer, and a white shirt open at the neck with a silk cravat. With a Panama hat on his grizzled, balding head, he looked very much the part of the slightly adventurous American tourist.

Bronski's travelling companion, equipped with an equally convincing and expensively forged passport in the name Josh McKenzie, was a former Navy SEAL called Aaron Hockridge, now working occasional private military contractor jobs from his base in Tucson, Arizona. Aboard the same flight were four more of Hockridge's hand-picked guys, their real identities all disguised. They'd booked individual seats scattered about the plane and made no sign of recognising one another on boarding. They disembarked in the same manner, ignoring one another and passing separately through customs. On the other side, each took a taxicab to the mid-priced hotel in Avenue Rép. du Tchad that was to be their base.

Once Hockridge and the others were checked into their rooms, Bronski phoned Eugene Svalgaard from his own. 'What's the weather there in Knoxville?' he asked, poking a finger through the lopsided blinds to peer down at the chaotic street below.

Pacing the floor of his luxury hotel suite in Mombasa, Kenya, with white beaches and the Indian Ocean in view, almost naked with a dressing gown loose around his short, chubby little body and the air conditioning blasting at full pelt, Eugene Svalgaard replied, 'I'm freezing my ass off while looking forward to a white Christmas. How are you finding Smolensk?'

'This is a real classy joint you booked us into, boss. There are hookers in the hotel lobby and the bed sheets, you don't wanna know. What did I do to deserve this kind of treatment?'

'I'm sure you've had worse. Just cope. Right now I'm really more interested in knowing what progress you're making with our project.'

'I just got here, boss. I'm on it, okay? I'll keep you posted.'

'Every hour. On the hour. I'll be waiting.'

'Take it easy, will you? What happened to trust?'

'Trust my ass. You get this done fast before we miss our chance. No screw-ups.'

'You're hurting my feelings, boss. When did I ever screw up?'

'There's always a first time. Call me the moment you got something to report. And it better be good news.'

'Fat fuck,' Bronski muttered, putting away the phone.

Sixteen hundred miles way on the east coast of Kenya, Eugene Svalgaard slumped on the king-size bed in his luxury suite and stared out of the balcony window at the swath of empty beach, the palm trees and the turquoise ocean beyond. He was a veteran connoisseur of luxury suites all over the world, and he wouldn't have kept a dog in this one. He'd almost exploded when he'd discovered that it didn't come with a private kitchen, chef and other essential staff. But if he had to be in Africa, this was as good a place as any to hole up in, keep his head down and twiddle his thumbs while waiting for Bronski to deliver the goods. The champagne was acceptably chilled, the bathroom roach-free so far, and the ocean view relaxing. Relaxation was what he needed to ease the nagging self-blame over his stupid mistake.

His mistake had a name, one that wouldn't ever be forgotten: Pender, the double-crossing sonofabitch of a shady lowlife ex-mercenary and jewel thief whom Eugene had hired to obtain the Star of Africa diamond for him by whatever means necessary. If Eugene hadn't been so blinded by the power of his lust for that beautiful rock, none of this mess would have happened.

Thank Christ for Victor Bronski. It was only due to Bronski's top-dollar detective skills that they'd been able to trace the diamond's path after it vanished into thin air halfway between Salalah and Mombasa. Following Pender's slimy, disreputable trail to Kenya, Bronski had managed to deduce that the scumbag had been out to screw his boss from the start. To aid him – or at least, that had been the intention – Pender had struck a deal with a man whose reputation was even more gruesome than African luminaries such as General Butt Naked and Joseph Kony of the Lord's Resistance Army. Given what he knew about the Congolese warlord Jean-Pierre Khosa, Bronski was quite confident that Pender was now very much dead; and there were no prizes for guessing who had got their mitts on the hot rock itself.

Now, all Eugene had to do was get it back. Which was a fairly straightforward matter, as he saw it. Knowing what Bronski had told him about this Khosa, the idea of stealing it back was out of the question. Eugene accepted that if he ever wanted to lay his hands on the Star of Africa, he was going to have to pay. He was perfectly willing to write off the trivial $5,000,000 sum he'd wasted on Pender, if he could convince its new owner to part with it for a few dollars more.

That was where Bronski came in. His job was to make contact with Khosa's people and lay an offer on the table that (in Eugene's words) an illiterate drum-banging savage from the Congo jungle couldn't possibly refuse, sealing the deal quickly before anybody else jumped in with a bigger number.

As to exactly how much of an offer he should make, Eugene had spent a while rolling numbers around his head. The figure shouldn't be too high – after all, this was a strictly black market item now, with every cop in Oman and half of Interpol raising hell to find the thing. But the figure shouldn't be too low, either. The deal had to appear dazzling enough that this shit-kicking jungle bunny (again, Eugene's words) would trip over himself in his haste to snap up the cash before the anonymous bidder changed their mind. It had to positively blitzkrieg the negotiating table, eclipsing any chance of another player – of whom Eugene knew there would be many – putting up a bigger number. Eugene needed to show some muscle, seize control of the situation and leave Khosa in no doubt as to who was boss.

To that end, fifty sounded about right. Fifty million bucks was a fair chunk of change, even for the owner of the Svalgaard Line, but given that it represented less than 7.5 per cent of the behemoth $700,000,000 price that the Swiss brokerage agency of Fiedelholz & Goldstein had previously been grasping for on behalf of its original owner, the recently deceased Hussein Al Bu Said in Oman, Eugene was prepared to suck up the cost. The forthcoming insurance payout for his storm-wrecked cargo ship *Svalgaard Andromeda* would go quite a way towards recouping the loss, in any case.

The more Eugene had considered it, the more golden the deal seemed. Okay, so maybe he wouldn't be able to buy that golf course in Scotland. He might have to hold off renewing his Rolls Royce this year. So what? He hated golf anyway, and cars held little appeal for him. His one true passion in this world, even more than money, was diamonds. For a mere $50,000,000, the Great Star of Africa, the holy grail of the diamond world, lost for so long that it had passed into the realms of myth and legend, would at last be his to treasure forever, to adore and fondle every day for the rest of his life and take with him to his grave. He couldn't possess it soon enough. Eugene was dizzy with expectation.

He foresaw little difficulty in executing his plan. If that piece of trash Pender could make contact with Khosa, Bronski could do it twice as easily. The man was a magician. (Damn it all, why hadn't he hired him first time round?) And who wouldn't jump at the chance to become fifty million bucks richer at the click of a mouse? With that kind of cash in the bank, Khosa could do anything he wanted. Declare himself king of the jungle, for all Eugene gave a damn.

For security, it had been agreed to take on extra men, experienced operatives who would watch Bronski's back while the deal was being done. Then, when the funds had been wired to the account of Khosa's choosing, the diamond was safely in Bronski's hands and everyone was happy, Eugene would hop on his Learjet to somewhere reasonably safe like Nairobi or Kampala to take delivery of it personally before flying his beloved trophy home to New York. Nice and easy. What a marvellous, insurmountable moment that would be, the crowning glory of his diamond-collecting career.

Eugene took another gulp of champagne and drifted deeper into his happy daydream.

Chapter 16

Aside from the fear of being murdered at any moment, by the end of his first day in captivity Jude was discovering that his biggest problem was going to be boredom. He was actually starting to look forward to Promise's visits, not for the delicious rice-based concoction his kidnappers were feeding him, but just to have someone to harangue who couldn't talk back, and probably didn't understand a word of what Jude was saying even if he could have responded.

The routine come evening was exactly as before: Promise's entrance was announced by the jangling of keys and rattling of locks, then Jude was made to step to the back of the cage to have his hands cuffed through the bars while the cage door was opened, his empty bowl and cup were removed and replaced with fresh food and water, if fresh was the word.

'Hey, what about a napkin?' Jude called to Promise.

No reply.

'There's got to be a Domino's Pizza place nearby. Can you order me a pepperoni with extra cheese? Get an extra-large and we can share. I won't tell Masango if you won't.'

No reply.

'Sorry I can't offer you a tip for this wonderful service. I seem to have mislaid my wallet.' No reply.

The worst was the bucket. Jude loathed having to be

mucked out like an animal. But at least the bucket's exchange for an empty one made the atmosphere of the hut more pleasant for a while. After Promise had finished his chores and closed him in for the last time that day, Jude sat cross-legged on the floor of the cage and gulped down his food with the tablespoon. Eat when you can, sleep when you can. It was getting dark outside, and he polished off his dinner quickly before he lost the light from the window.

But there had to be more to do than eating, sleeping and passively waiting for tomorrow. With no idea how long he might be kept prisoner in this stinking hut, he was determined not to let his strength ebb and his body start to waste away. He stood up, kicked aside his empty dish, and dropped to the floor on palms and toes to knock out twenty press-ups. Then twenty more, and twenty more again, enough to work up a sweat in the humidity of the hut.

He sprang to his feet and looked up. There was still just enough light coming in to make out the steel bars overhead. The cage roof was about eight feet high. Jude stood five-ten, an inch or so shorter than his father, but it was an easy jump to reach the bars, grab hold and let himself dangle. He hung there for a few moments, letting his muscles and spine stretch out, then crossed his ankles and bent his knees slightly, and pulled himself up until he could kiss the cool steel bars. Up and down. Up and down. Ten vertical raises, a few seconds' rest, then ten more, and again, over and over until he was breathing hard and the sweat dripped down and splashed the cage floor like rain.

On the last raise he kicked his feet up, hooked his toes through the gap between the bars and let go with his hands, now tentatively hanging upside down from his feet. Six months of practice at this, he thought, and maybe he could get a job in a circus. Roll up, roll up, see the Amazing Monkey

Boy in action. Jude laughed at the idea. Laughter made him feel a little better. Or maybe he was already losing his mind. And it was only the second night.

He soon found out that hanging from his feet made for a great stomach workout if he tried to jerk his body back up to reach his toes. He managed it two or three times, but it was hard work. He was panting. The whole cage was rattling with every rep.

Jude stopped and hung there upside down, frowning at the realisation that this was something new. Why was the cage rattling? It had felt solid and immovable before.

He bent his body upwards one more time, grabbed two parallel bars and let his feet drop down, then inched along the bars, one hand at a time, until he'd squirmed his way as far as the corner. It was still rattling like an old iron bed frame. As he wiggled his weight around and swung his legs, he could tell where it was loose. He braced himself against the two adjacent cage walls and let go with one hand so that he could examine the joints.

'Hello,' he muttered to himself. The joints weren't welded, as he'd initially assumed. As he now realised, the cage was bolted together out of sections.

In fact, he reflected as he groped about in the darkness, it was remarkably similar in construction to the dive cages he'd experienced in New Zealand, during his epic and unforgettable holiday spent diving in waters full of large, hungry sharks. The sections of stainless-steel cage had been flat-packed on the deck of the boat. It was Jude's nature to muck in and get his hands dirty, and he'd helped the crew guys bolt it all together. One of them, Nicko, had told him that if you didn't use the exact right size of bolt to match the hole it passed through, it didn't take much vibration and movement to make the structure work itself loose and start flexing at the joints. Not what you wanted to happen, when you were being offered as a potential snack to a thirty-foot Great White.

Jude soon discovered the bolt that had come loose. Maybe the Africans hadn't used the right size for the hole. A torch would have been useful at this moment. Having to rely on feel alone, he fingered the loose bolthead. Its hexagonal faces were smooth to the touch and felt shiny, maybe galvanised or zinc-plated. He thought it felt a little smaller than the bolts that had held the shark cage together. Jude was good at remembering numbers, and recalled that those had needed a thirteen-millimetre spanner to tighten up. But he had no way to measure the size of these bolts, any more than he had anything to use as a spanner to turn them with.

He let himself drop to the floor with a soft thud. His fingers were stiff from all the dangling, and the healing cut on his palm where Scagnetti had gashed him with a knife was sore and sticky, as if it had opened up again. But the pain didn't matter to him as he stood thinking for a long minute.

Then it came to him. Of course! He'd no idea if it would work, but it had to be worth a go.

He went over to his discarded food bowl, hunted around in the darkness and found the tablespoon. It was flimsy metal and easy to bend, but was it strong enough? Would it snap? He folded it into a U, then squeezed the U into a tighter shape, like a hairpin. There was enough springiness to the metal for it to bend without snapping.

'No harm in trying,' he muttered. He clamped the bent spoon in his teeth, then craned his neck upwards to peer at the darkness, bent his knees and sprang up once more. On the first blind attempt his fingers hit the bars painfully, but on the second he got a solid grip and started working his way to the corner where the loose joint was. Like before, he wedged himself into the corner using his feet to brace himself. Taking the bent spoon from his mouth he reached out carefully with it towards the loose bolthead. He was scared the spoon might drop, hit the cage floor and bounce out of reach through the bars, where Promise would find it the following day and know the prisoner had been up to no good. Gripping it tightly, he fumbled and scraped until he'd managed to close the U-shape of the bent spoon like a primitive kind of pincer around the bolthead and squeezed to tighten it against the flats. It seemed to get a purchase. He twisted it, and felt the bolt turn, and a flash of hope went off like a magnesium flare inside his heart.

It took a long time and a lot of impatient twiddling, but eventually he was able to get the bolt loosened enough to undo the rest of the way with his fingers. When it slid out, he tucked it carefully in his pocket.

One down. How many more to go before he could detach the whole roof section of the cage and wriggle out? In darkness, not so easy to judge. But he had all night.

Jude spent the next two hours working as quietly as he could, listening out for the guard patrols that he knew came by occasionally through the night, and praying that the walls of the hut would muffle the metallic clinking and scraping sounds he was making. The cage grew more and more rattly as he hunted out and loosened each successive ceiling bolt in turn, clinging like an ape to the ceiling and gritting his teeth as he worked.

Then, at last, with a silent whoop of triumph, he pocketed the last bolt he needed to remove. He'd left two bolts in place at one end, so that the roof section was hinged like a lid and could be raised and lowered without danger of it falling off altogether with an almighty crash that would be sure to alarm the whole place and bring Promise running over with his Uzi.

At least, that was the theory. When it came to actually raising the lid, it was much heavier than Jude had anticipated and it took him a full thirty minutes to figure out how he could do it, by clamping himself like a limpet to the bars and using his head and shoulders to lift the ceiling up. He managed to get his head out first, then wriggled his upper torso through the gap with the weight of the ceiling panel crushing him; for a moment he began to panic, thinking he was trapped and they'd find him like this tomorrow, stuck like a snared animal. But then he was through, managing to scramble out with only a few bruises.

He let the lid of the cage down as gently as he could, winced as he pinched a couple of fingers, then slithered down the bars on the outside and dropped to the floor.

He was out! It was a thrilling achievement. But he was still locked inside a metal hut with a barred window. He stepped over to it, feeling the coolness of the night air drying the sweat on his face. He gazed out into the night. Nothing but darkness and silence.

The window bars were solid and riveted to the metal frame, but a quick inspection of the seams of the hut itself revealed that they were bolted together like the cage. He still had his improvised spanner, and thought about dismantling the whole hut – but that would take him so long he'd still be at it when Promise came to check on him in the morning. Abandoning that idea, he paced around the inside walls until he realised that the floor was nothing but compacted earth and that maybe he could dig his way out.

That was, if he'd had anything to dig with. The bent spoon wouldn't do him much good there.

But something else might. Jude hurried back to the cage,

slipped an arm through the bars and fetched out his metal food bowl, careful not to let it clatter. Maybe a steel dog dish wasn't a bad thing to have as crockery, after all. A few experimental digs at the earth floor with its rim convinced him that he could do it. He quickly decided that the best place to burrow his way out was directly opposite the door, behind the cage, where the dirt was softest.

With his heart pounding and the sweat running in rivulets, he hacked and chopped and scraped. Working like a madman, in less than half an hour he'd managed to excavate a rathole under the metal wall that he could get his arm through. Twenty more minutes of frenzied digging, and he could poke his head and shoulders out. With a wriggle and a heave, he forced his whole body through the hole.

He was free.

Chapter 17

Jude scrambled to his feet on the other side and brushed the dirt from his hair and hands. Free!

He stood still, barely able to suppress a wild grin as he listened for the footsteps or voices of a lurking security patrol. He could hear nothing, except for the thudding of his own heart and the whisper of the night air. He'd been working in the dark for so many hours that his night vision was sharp and clear. For the first time since he'd been locked up, he was able to see all three of the other huts. He wished he knew which one was the guard hut. It was worrying to imagine Promise lying there so close by, probably just half asleep and ready to spring up at the slightest noise, machine gun at the ready.

But Jude had no intention of rousing him, just as he intended to be long gone by the time Promise got up for his rounds and found the cage empty. All Jude had to do was slip past the armed patrols, make it over two manned perimeter fences topped with razor wire, and then try to figure out where the hell to run to without getting himself shot by soldiers or lost in the middle of the Congo wilderness. But anything was better than being caged.

Jude took a deep breath, steeled himself, then started to make his escape. He ran lightly over the compacted earth, freezing every few steps to listen hard. Still nothing. He ran on, barely making a sound. It reminded him of when he'd been on board the ship, ducking and dodging the pirates as he slipped from deck to deck. The memory made him think of his shipmates who hadn't made it. Mitch, Diesel, poor Park, Condor, Hercules, all of them. Jude's grin fell and he felt suddenly sombre and much more frightened.

In the dim moonlight he could see clear across the compound to the metal fence. Beyond the fence was the terrible place they'd come through in Masango's limo, with the piles of earth and machinery and those poor people cruelly burned at the stake like a scene from hell. He shuddered at the thought that he was going to have to make his way back through it.

Jude was about to make a sprint for the fence when he froze. Two sentries were standing near the metal gates, barely visible in the darkness except for the metallic sheen of their weapons and the glowing red dots of burning cigarettes. He ducked behind the last hut and pressed himself tightly against its side. He'd have to thread his way back through the huts and try to escape from the opposite end of the compound.

Jude's racing thoughts were interrupted by a sound from inside the hut. He tensed, alarmed at first and not sure what he'd heard. Then he heard it again. A female voice, coming from the other side of the tin wall he was leaning against.

It was the same voice he'd heard crying the night before, carried on the wind. All that day he'd wondered about it, undecided whether it had been real or imagined.

But it had been real, after all. She was sobbing softly. It was a heart-rending sound, and he wondered who she was and why they were keeping her prisoner. Just like his hut, hers had a single barred window. It faced away from where the sentries were standing guard. He could slip around the wall of the hut and look inside, and they wouldn't spot him.

Jude moved silently to the window. He didn't want to alarm the woman inside, for fear that she would cry out and draw the sentries' attention or, worse, wake Promise. He tapped gently on the hut wall and whispered, 'Hello?'

The sobbing instantly stopped. He thought he heard a snatch of breath; then rigid silence.

Jude gripped the bars of the window and peered in. It was very dark inside the hut. He blinked and thought he could make out the vertical lines of cage bars, just like his own, gleaming dully in the near-pitch blackness. 'Hello?' he repeated softly. 'Who's there?'

There was such a long pause that he began to wonder if he'd imagined it after all. Then, out of the darkness, came a tiny whisper.

'Who are you?' The voice sounded very scared, and even more suspicious, unsure whether to trust him. The accent was American.

He was afraid to say too much in case his voice carried. 'My name's Jude. They're holding me here. I managed to get out. Are you alone in there? What's your name?'

'Ray,' said the whisper, and for an instant Jude thought the voice must belong to a young boy, maybe a teenager, before he realised that she'd said 'Rae'. Staring hard into the darkness, he could just about make out a slender shape in the middle of the cage. Black hair framing a pale face, out of which gleamed two frightened eyes. She was sitting bolt upright, watching him intently, like a startled deer whose path had crossed with a traveller's in the forest.

'Are they holding you here too?' he whispered.

The pale face gave a quick nod. 'Yes,' she whispered back. 'Why?'

A long pause. Then, 'Don't you know? For the same reason as you. Money. What else? They're holding us for ransom.'

Jude knew that wasn't the reason in his case. But it might be in hers. Four huts. One for Promise, left three. 'Who else is here?' he whispered.

The woman called Rae murmured in reply, 'Craig. They have him too. Have you seen him?'

'No. Is he American? Your relative? Husband?'

'I work for him. We're journalists. We were taken.'

'How long have you been here?'

'Eight days. Maybe nine. I . . . I lost count.'

Jude edged away from the window. The sentries were still standing by the gate. One of them was laughing about something.

'Don't leave me,' said Rae's voice. 'Come back.'

Stepping back to the window, Jude saw the shape inside the cage move. She stood up, clutching the bars and pressing her face through the gap to get as close to him as possible. The fear in her voice had lessened, her tone more urgent as she hissed, 'What are you doing out there?'

'I got out. I'm getting out of here.'

'They'll catch you.'

'Not if I can help it,' he said. He sounded much more confident than he really was.

'Then you have to get me out, too. And Craig.'

'I—'

'Please. You have to help us. If we stay here, we'll die.'

'Oh, shit.' Jude had been so distracted that he hadn't heard the approaching voices until it was almost too late. He glanced breathlessly around the edge of the hut. The sentries were strolling towards the huts for one of their routine patrols.

'I have to go,' he hissed through the window. 'I'm sorry. I have to—'

'Please!'

But there was no time to talk more. He broke away and dashed as fast and as quietly as he could away from the hut, losing himself in the shadows.

He would wait until the sentries passed by, and then he would sprint for the gate and take his chances getting over without being seen. He could do it. He had to believe it was possible.

Or was it?

He sighed. 'Shitbags,' he murmured to himself. 'Bollocks.'

No, of course it wasn't possible. Everything had just changed, now that he knew there were other captives here, locked up in inhuman conditions to face death, or worse.

Jude pictured Rae's frightened face. Heard her voice in his mind, begging for his help. Then he pictured the charred, semi-skeletal bodies left hanging to rot from the post at which they'd been burned alive.

And he knew that he couldn't run away and leave her here.

He was getting out. But he was no longer doing it alone. And not tonight. He needed more time to plan how he was going to get her and her friend Craig away from this awful place.

Unseen by the patrolling sentries, just a shadow flitting through the darkness, Jude made his way back to his hut.

Chapter 18

Eighteen hours after they threw him in the dungeon along with the hacked-up corpses, they came back to release him. The pickup truck came lurching over the rough ground with six of Khosa's soldiers aboard, and pulled up next to the mouth of the hole. In the back of the truck was a coil of sturdy rope, to yank out one thoroughly defeated and humbled white prisoner who had dared to defy their Captain Xulu.

But, like the biblical myrrh-bearers who discovered the empty tomb of Christ, they were in for a shock. The cast-iron plate covering the hole had been moved aside. The mouth of the dungeon shaft was a mess of freshly dug earth. The hole itself appeared to have been completely filled in. And their prisoner was sitting on the ground nearby, relaxing in the fresh morning air as he waited for them. He looked like a wild man, every inch of him from head to toe plastered and smeared with dirt as if he'd crawled through solid ground to reach the surface. This impossible feat terrified them, and the piercing blue eyes that gazed at them out of the mask of mud terrified them even more.

Ben rose to his feet as they stumbled out of the truck and uncertainly pointed their rifles at him. 'Hello, boys. What kept you?'

In fact, he hadn't expected them to return so soon. It had been less than an hour since he'd crawled out of the hole. Just long enough for him to do what he needed. Now that they were back, the message was clear: *Nothing you can do will stop me. No prison will hold me. I am in control. I own you.* And the looks on the soldiers' faces told him that they were reading it loud and clear.

As for the dungeon, it no longer existed. Nothing remained but a grave, at whose deep bottom Ben's dead cellmates had been buried sometime during the long and very busy night. Using a flat piece of stone as his tool, he'd steadily chiselled and scraped at the walls of his dungeon until the dirt was up to his knees. Once he'd stamped it all flat, the floor had been raised about six inches and he was ready to add a new layer. He'd kept at it without a break. After four hours, his gruesome companions were beneath his feet. After twelve, he was more than halfway up the shaft of the hole, where it was narrowest and therefore easiest to fill up. No water, little air. Sweat stinging his eyes and dirt and grit crunching between his teeth as he worked. Five more hours of gruelling work, and he'd finally heaved the iron manhole cover aside and hauled himself out into the sunlight like a revenant.

Escape hadn't been his plan. Not yet. The time for that would come soon enough.

Much more wary of him now than before, the soldiers hooded him and put him in the truck. Thirty minutes later, he was back before General Khosa, dropping bits of dried earth all over the office floor.

'My men are all talking about you, soldier,' Khosa said, leaning back in his chair and puffing thoughtfully on a cigar. On the desk in front of him lay an attaché case with an open handcuff bracelet chained to its handle. Ben wondered if the case contained what he thought it did.

Khosa continued, 'They say you can work miracles. Your appearance tells me that their story is true.'

Ben shrugged. 'Just felt like some fresh air.'

'Then you were not planning on leaving us?'

'Not without my son,' Ben said. 'Or my friends. If you had either, you'd understand.'

'You perplex me, soldier. I hope for your sake that we have seen the end of your rebellious behaviour. Next time, I might have to order my men to pour concrete into the hole. And perhaps your son and your friends could join you. What do you think?'

'I think I'd like a shower, some breakfast and a change of clothes,' Ben said.

'Granted. But first, let me tell you why I decided to release you early from your punishment. I have a new task for you.'

'Teaching your officers how to wipe their own arses? Sorry, not my concern.'

Khosa stood and walked to the window. The office overlooked the flower gardens and the street, where Ben could see some activity taking place. Troops were massing outside, and a line of three heavy transport trucks had parked up in front of the hotel. Something was happening, and whatever it was, Ben didn't like it.

'You say I have no friends, soldier. This is false, as I think you already know. More loyal followers are joining me every day. But when you say I have no children, this is true. I love children. The younger generation of my country are its future.'

'And what a rosy future they have in store,' Ben said.

'I wish to embrace this generation as though they were my own offspring,' Khosa went on, with a grandiose air. 'From all over the nation, I want them to flock to me. I will feed them, clothe them, nurture them as their real parents could never do. Today will see the foundation of a special new division of my army, made up entirely of children.'

'The Khosa Youth,' Ben said. 'That's a novel idea.'

The General swept away from the window and pointed at him with the cigar. 'Yes. That is a very good name. The Khosa Youth. I like it.'

'Seems to me that the average age of your troops is already a bit low,' Ben said. 'Are the old men of fourteen or fifteen not good enough anymore?'

'The younger the better,' Khosa said, puffing a huge cloud of smoke. 'They cost little to feed, take up less room to house, learn fast and are easy to control. But that is not all. A boy of eight can fire a rifle and kill his enemy just as effectively as a fighter twice or three times his age. Even more effectively, as men will hesitate to return fire on one so young, and that hesitation is what costs them their life. All across the country are many thousands of boys aged between eight and twelve who are being denied the chance of glory in my service. It is time that we put a stop to this waste of resources. You, soldier, will have the honour and privilege of helping to gather the first wave of recruits to my new regiment.'

Ben said nothing. He so badly wanted to snap Khosa's neck that his fingers were twitching.

Khosa walked over to a desk where a map had been spread out. 'Here is where we begin,' he declared, prodding the paper. 'There is a school for orphans in a place called Kbali, three hours' drive to the south. The school is run by a French Christian missionary and a dozen or so nuns. My scouts report that there are more than a hundred children there, none older than twelve years. You will accompany a division of soldiers under the command of Captain Xulu. Your orders are to take the orphanage, deal as necessary with any resistance, and bring me these hundred children, so that we can

induct them into the army and begin their training immediately. Is this all clear to you, soldier?'

'Oh, it's clear, all right,' Ben said.

Khosa glanced at the gold ingot on his wrist. 'I am pleased.
And now I must be leaving. I have an important rendezvous
and I do not wish to be late.'

'Your helicopter is waiting, Excellency,' the secretary
informed him.

And so it began. Ben wanted to check in on Jeff and Tuesday,
but it wasn't to be. He was taken directly from Khosa's office
to a waiting Jeep, which whisked him several city blocks to a
large, slab-sided four-storey building on a square he'd never
seen before. He quickly discovered what it was being used for.
From the ground floor up, the whole building had been
subdivided into tiny wood-partitioned rooms that served as
dormitories for Khosa's troops: bunks stacked three high, nine
to a room with barely space to turn around.

Ben was shown to a rudimentary bathroom and given
exactly five minutes to wash off the dried dirt that caked him
all over. When he came out, he was thrown a new uniform
of mismatched combat clothing and then led to a rough-and-
ready canteen with grease-streaked walls and rows of bench
tables, where a scowling African in a filthy apron gave him a
look of disgust and a bowl of boiled chicken mixed in with
some kind of sticky mess made from cassava flour. Ben had
had worse breakfasts. He wolfed it down without tasting it,
a skill he'd learned in his own army, long ago. Three minutes
later, he was marched back outside. The convoy was departing.
They weren't the only ones leaving the city in a hurry. Ben
glanced skywards and saw a chopper flying off into the
distance. Khosa, off to attend to more dirty business.

Ben hoped the helicopter crashed and burned in the
jungle.

The troop transporters were rugged six-wheel-drive Urals with huge knobbly tyres, canvas tie-down canopies and metal benches in the back. The two at the rear of the line were empty, for the purposes of bringing home Khosa's youthful new recruits. Ben was put into the lead truck, crammed in with thirty other men, the only one of them not armed. He received a few suspicious looks from the soldiers, but they quickly ignored him. Through a gap in the canopy Ben caught a glimpse of Captain Xulu strutting towards the front of the truck, sporting a swollen lip that made it look as if he was pouting. Then they were off.

The military convoy rumbled noisily through the streets and across the no-man's land separating the city from the perimeter fences. The gates were already open for them and they streamed through, obscuring the gate guards behind billows of dust. The smooth concrete roadway became a rutted track as the procession of vehicles was swallowed up by the jungle.

For the next three hours the truck swayed and rocked and bumped and lurched. Ben had sat in a hundred army trucks in a dozen countries, though never before as a noncombatant observer. He barely registered the rough ride, the dust and flies, the odour of thirty sweaty troops or the sweltering heat that built and built as midday approached. He slouched back on the bench, leaning against the canvas, closed his eyes and became very still. Outwardly, he might have looked as if he was sleeping. Inwardly, his mind was burning up with thoughts of what he'd seen that day.

The hour he'd spent between escaping from his makeshift dungeon and being picked up by the soldiers hadn't been spent idly. He'd made the most of the opportunity to explore his surroundings alone and unobserved. The hole was situated among scrubland, through which a dirt road snaked roughly southwards away from the city perimeter. That was where Khosa had let it slip that the hydroelectric station that powered the city was located. Ben had spotted it from the top of a thornbush-covered rise, where he'd lain flat and observed some interesting activity.

The hydro plant straddled a wide river. Like the city itself, it was startlingly modern and new: a massive concrete dam holding back countless millions of tons of murky water on its eastern side. On its eastern side, six enormous waterfalls gushed in spectacular torrents of white foam and rainbow-hued spray from sluices in the dam, dropping eighty feet like miniature Victoria Falls before the river continued on its journey east.

It was a seriously impressive installation. Ben couldn't begin to estimate what it must have cost to build. Now more than ever, he was wondering about the strange partnership Khosa seemed to enjoy with his Chinese business associates. Clearly, even more Far Eastern money was being invested into this place than Ben had first realised. But why? He had no idea.

Until he gazed a little further south, past the plant, beyond the far side of the river. That was when the beginnings of understanding began to dawn on him.

The dam was more than just a dam. Its concrete spine doubled as a bridge, with heavily guarded gates at both ends to control vehicles crossing the river. And over the bridge, visible here and there through the thicket of trees that lined the riverside, was a long stretch of security fence that protected what Khosa had described as 'the industrial zone'.

Ben could have done with a pair of powerful binoculars to observe the place in better detail, and take a closer look at the movements of men and machinery that were happening over there. But he saw enough.

They were mining.

Chapter 19

A little more than three hours from the city, the troop convoy arrived at its destination and the soldiers scrambled out of the trucks amid a great deal of yelling and excitement. Captain Xulu strutted and puffed his chest and barked commands that did little to create any kind of order. Ben jumped down from the back of the lead truck, full of apprehension.

The trucks had halted nose to tail on a dirt road shaded from one side by thick forest and flanked on the other by a high stone wall. Beyond dilapidated iron gates that were locked with a chain, a rambling mansion-style residence stood at the end of what had once been a grand driveway. A weathered wooden sign on the wall read ORPHELINAT RELIGIEUX POUR GARÇONS SAINT-BAKANJA. Many years before it had become a Catholic orphanage, back in the colonial heyday of the French Congo, the property might have been the country hideaway of a wealthy merchant, conceived in splendid style with all-around airy verandas, columns and a red-tile hipped roof. Time and decay had taken a heavy toll, though despite its state of disrepair the house retained a certain dignity. The woodwork was badly in need of renovation but freshly painted, and the gardens were well tended. The remote orphanage was a lovingly tended haven of peace and serenity.

Until now.

Nobody was in sight within the orphanage grounds except for a wizened old man of about seventy-five who'd been picking at a patch of weeds by the house. He paused his work to turn and stare at the trucks and soldiers. Even at this distance, Ben could see the whites of his eyes widening in alarm.

'Lieutenant Umutese!' roared Xulu, pointing at the gates. 'I want these gates opened!'

'Very good, Captain,' Umutese replied, snapping a salute and delegating the order to an underling, who immediately scurried to the driver of the lead truck. The driver revved his engine, cranked the big wheels back into gear and the Ural troop transport lumbered towards the orphanage entrance without slowing down for the gates. They were ripped from their rusty old hinges and flattened as the truck rolled through the gateway. Not waiting for further orders the soldiers swarmed in after it, yowling and waving their rifles in glee as they invaded the grounds. The old gardener had frozen stiff as a statue, as though mesmerised by the sight of ninety armed men rushing towards him.

Ben's heart was in his throat. 'What are you going to do to these people?' he asked Xulu.

'We will do what is right,' Xulu said, eyeing Ben with a glint of loathing. 'And what General Khosa commands.' With that, he marched through the smashed, twisted gates after his men. Walking towards the old gardener he shouted, 'You! Yes, you! What is your name? Where are the children?'

The old man was either speechless with terror, or he was brave enough to refuse to answer, or he had no tongue. Either way, he stood there with wide eyes as Xulu strode imperiously up to him, and said nothing.

'I SAID, WHERE ARE THE CHILDREN?' Xulu screamed

at him. When the old man still didn't reply, Xulu tore his pistol from its holster and thrust it towards the old man's face.

The shot went off with a sharp crack. But Xulu's bullet went nowhere near the old man, because the captain was suddenly rolling in the dust, knocked half senseless. His pistol went flying out of his hand. Ben picked it up and stood over him.

'Maybe I didn't make myself clear before, Xulu,' Ben said. 'If you think I'm going to stand by and watch you murder a defenceless bystander, you need to pay more attention to what I say.'

Xulu staggered to his feet. 'That is the second time you have struck me, soldier. There will not be a third time.'

'If there is, you won't be getting up again. You can bet on that.' He tossed the pistol back to Xulu. 'Stick that back in its holster. If I see it come out again, you'll be spitting gold teeth for a week. Clear?'

Quivering with rage, Xulu thrust the weapon in his belt. Then he pointed a shaking finger at Ben and screamed to his soldiers, 'Take him! Take him!'

A bunch of them closed in on Ben all at once. The first one to reach him was carrying a Chinese submachine gun on a sling around his neck. Ben sidestepped him, grabbed the weapon and jerked it so hard that the strap almost broke the soldier's neck and sent him tumbling headlong to the ground, where a hard boot to the temple ensured that he'd stay a while. The second soldier had his legs swept out from under him by a scything kick, and Ben's foot stamping down on his throat to put him out of the game. He wouldn't be needing his AK-47 anymore, so Ben tore it from his fingers and used it to club the third with a smashing blow of its steel butt plate to the face, before the next guy swiftly got

142

the same treatment and went down like an empty suit of clothing with a broken cheekbone. Four down, three seconds.

Then six more were coming at him. Ben's mouth was dry. He couldn't fight them all. But he could do some damage before they took him down. Plenty of damage. That was for sure.

The shot that rang out was from Xulu's pistol, back in his hand now that he was safely surrounded by his men. Ben felt the bullet pass within an inch of his nose. He didn't know if it was a deliberate miss, or whether Xulu was just a bad shot. It didn't matter. He stopped, fists clenched, his legs locked in a low combat crouch. The soldiers formed a tightening ring around him.

'I will kill you, white man!' Xulu screamed, waving the gun. 'I will blow out your brains!'

'Then best get on with it, eh?' Ben said.

Then Ben's vision exploded in a white flash and he felt himself collapse to the ground. Xulu had shot him in the head.

But there had been no shot. Blinded by pain, Ben realised that he'd been clubbed from behind. He clutched his head, tried to get up, but fell back. It felt as if his skull was bursting apart. Flashes and zigzags of lightning danced in front of his eyes. He couldn't see properly. There was a loud rushing in his ears.

Then another hard blow struck him in the jaw and sent him sprawling backwards. Before he blacked out he saw Xulu's towering figure step away from him, grinning down a blurry golden grin.

Ben would never know how long he was unconscious for. Maybe five minutes, maybe thirty. When his eyes fluttered open, his vision was smeared out of focus. The first sensation he registered was the steely taste of blood in his mouth from where Xulu had kicked him. The second was a confused kaleidoscope of noise that took several seconds to come into focus before he realised it was the sound of rattling gunfire and screaming. He blinked his eyes, managed to prop himself up on one elbow where he lay in the dirt, and looked groggily around him at the scene unfolding like a bad dream.

Chapter 20

Nearest to Ben was the old gardener, lying twisted on the ground a few feet away. He was on his belly but his eyes were staring up at the sky. It took Ben a couple of seconds to realise that was because the old man's head was almost completely separated from his body, attached only by a few gruesome strings of tissue where his neck had been chopped.

Closer to the rickety wooden steps that led up to the orphanage's veranda, a group of soldiers was herding terrified nuns out of the building at gunpoint. A large crowd of children had already been corralled into a tight group on the lawn. They were all boys, the youngest ones maybe eight, the oldest approaching their teens, all watching in stunned silence and with a mixture of fear and blank curiosity as the dozen or so nuns were marched roughly down the steps. One tripped and fell. Two soldiers began kicking her in the head and body and she put up her hands to protect her face. They dragged her to her feet and shoved her together with the others. She tried to struggle, so they knocked her back down to the ground and went on kicking her.

Last to be brought out was a reedy white man. He must have been eighty or more, dressed like a priest. The missionary, Ben guessed. When he saw what the soldiers were doing to the fallen nun, the priest gave a yell of rage and shook free of the two soldiers clutching his arms to go running to her aid. He hadn't made it four steps before they unslung their rifles and shot him in the back. He collapsed on his face, arms outflung. Some of the nuns were screaming, others bowed their heads and prayed. Many of the children were crying and howling. Nobody tried to go to him.

Ben was still seeing double from the blow to the head, and his face felt numb and hot where Xulu had kicked him. He felt his jaw to check it wasn't broken, and ran his tongue around the inside of his mouth to feel for loose teeth. He couldn't feel any, but he could taste blood. He spat red. Then three soldiers walked up to him, one put his weapon to Ben's head and the other two yanked him to his feet.

Captain Xulu grinned and pointed and said, 'I want him to watch.'

Ben wanted to close his eyes, but he couldn't close his ears. It was ninety men against one. He'd done all he could to stop them. Now he was powerless to do anything but stand there as the horror unfolded in front of him.

The children were made to watch, too.

First the soldiers held the nuns at gunpoint until the whole building had been swept from top to bottom for anyone hiding. Then Xulu ordered for the nuns to be stripped. The soldiers set enthusiastically about their task, beating and stamping and punching the twelve women into coercion.

While they worked, Xulu turned to the children and began lecturing them about the ills of religious indoctrination. 'We are here to liberate you in the name of General Jean-Pierre Khosa of the Congo Freedom Army!' he yelled. 'You are the lucky ones! You have a new father now, in our saviour General Khosa. Millions of boys would envy you, for you have been chosen to fight for our leader and share in the great victories to come. He will protect you and give you great powers, and in return you will protect him from his enemies. This is how you will repay his kindness to you.'

Xulu waved an arm behind him at the dead priest and the nuns, now being dumped naked on the ground like sacks of flour. 'Forget these wicked people,' he commanded the children. 'All they have done is fill your heads with ignorance and lies. For this, we have been sent to punish them. They are no longer your family. The army is your family now. It will teach you many important lessons. Do you understand? Say "Yes, Captain Xulu!"'

A rippling mutter of 'Yes, Captain Xulu,' came from the crowd of children. Some were still crying.

Xulu folded his arms and tossed his head proudly. 'The army is good, but you will learn that you can die at any moment. How many of you have seen a person die? Show your hands!'

A few shaky hands went up. Ben wasn't surprised. Many of these kids had probably witnessed their entire families being gunned or hacked to death, right in front of them.

'How many of you have killed a person?' Xulu was improvising on the same script he'd used back at the training ground, the previous day. Except this time, there was nothing Ben could do to prevent it from playing out. This time, Xulu would have his way.

'How many? Put up your hands! Do not be afraid!'

There was no show of hands. Xulu scanned the crowd, nodded with satisfaction and said, 'Then, children, today is the beginning of your re-education!'

Xulu held out an open hand. His best gofer, Lieutenant Umutese, immediately ran up to him clutching a shiny black automatic weapon. Ben's fuzzy vision had focused enough by now for him to recognise it as one of the Chinese QBZ

147

assault rifles that he had personally unpacked from their crates just the previous morning. It seemed like weeks ago.

Xulu snatched the gun from Umutese without looking at him. He held it up in the air for all the children to get a good look at. 'This will be your weapon! It is very expensive and very precious. You will learn to treat it with love and learn to use it well. This gun can do many things. First, let me show you how it can be used in close combat, face to face with your enemy. Lieutenant!'

Umutese didn't need to be told what to do. Ben was beginning to realise that the whole sickening routine had been planned out from the start. Umutese barked an order at the soldiers standing over the naked bodies of the nuns. They instantly grabbed three of the women, hauled them to their feet and shoved them up against the railing of the veranda. The women made no attempt to struggle. All three stood quietly, eyes to the ground, muttering prayers under their breath.

Ben's heart went out to them for their courage and dignity. He was so sorry for what he knew was about to happen.

Xulu walked up to within less than ten yards of the women and flipped the fire selector on his weapon to fully automatic. At that range, he didn't need to aim. He fired from the hip, in a raking left-to-right arc that blasted splinters from the railing and cut the women down in a crumpled heap. They died without a sound.

At least it was over for them. Some of the children covered their eyes, some just went on quietly crying, others just stared in shocked amazement.

'You see how easy it is,' Xulu told them. 'And how lucky you are to belong to such a well-equipped army. Now, next I will show you how this rifle can also be used for precision marksmanship at long range.'

On cue, Umutese had the men drag another of the poor nuns to her feet and frogmarched forty yards along the side of the building, to where a gnarly, spreading tree stood alone in the grounds. The soldiers slammed her against the trunk and backed hurriedly away, pointing at her to stay still. The woman looked unsteady on her feet, but didn't move or try to run.

Ben closed his eyes and said his own prayer that Xulu would do this quickly and properly.

Xulu strutted to where he had a clear line of fire. He took his time bracing his feet, then brought the butt of the gun into the crook of his shoulder and lowered his eye to the sights and took aim at the target. The woman still didn't move. The muzzle of the rifle wavered in a sloppy circle and then spat white flame as Xulu pressed the trigger. The woman's right hip burst apart in a spray of blood. She screamed and fell.

'There is something wrong with this gun,' Xulu said angrily. 'It does not shoot straight. Bring me another one!'

The victim was shoved back into position against the tree while Umutese quickly fetched a replacement weapon for his captain. This time, Xulu stepped forward another fifteen yards to shorten the range before he fired again. Ben was thankful that the second bullet hit the woman square in the chest and killed her instantly. Her body slumped to the foot of the tree.

'Sometimes you will not have a gun,' Xulu lectured the children. 'This is when you must use a blade.' He drew out his own machete from its sheath and held it up for them to see. 'This was not made for cutting crops! It is a fine weapon. Look what we did to that old man. I will give you another demonstration of what you can do with it.'

One of the remaining eight nuns was dragged across the

grass for the demonstration. She was a young black woman, perhaps twenty-five. Her eyes remained firmly closed but her lips never stopped moving until her last breath. Xulu grasped a fistful of her tight, short hair, raised the blade and brought it down with a *thwack*. It took several clumsy blows before he finally severed her head from her shoulders, and her body slumped at his feet, her arms and legs twitching.

Xulu held the head up in his bloody hand. 'Here is another important lesson you must learn,' he shouted at the children. 'It is that you must also learn discipline. You will take beatings, as this is the only way you can become strong soldiers. Lieutenant, bring me the whip.' As Umutese scurried off to obey the command, Xulu lobbed the head into the crowd of children as if it were a football.

'Whoever brings me this head will not be whipped! Everyone else will be beaten!'

There was a brief scrum, after which a stocky ten-year-old in red shorts and a frayed blue T-shirt stepped forward with the head in his hands. Xulu by now had the whip in his, a flexible sjambok made of rhino leather, an instrument that in the colonial Congo had been called a *chicote*. Ben had heard of men being flogged to death with such things.

The whipping of the rest of the children took a long time. Xulu waded in among them, thrashing left and right with cruel ferocity until he was glowing with sweat and many of the boys were bleeding and howling in pain. The soldiers leaned on their rifles and seemed highly entertained by the spectacle.

Ben didn't want to see any more, but there was still more to come. Once Xulu had sated himself with the children, he ordered for the seven remaining nuns to be put to death. The soldiers used their bayonets. The bodies were left where they lay in the bloody, trampled grass.

'Now we will load these recruits on the trucks and return to base,' Xulu ordered with a wave. 'General Khosa will be pleased with what we have brought him.'

'What about the building?' Umutese wanted to know. 'Should we loot it? There may be some valuables.'

'We do not need their junk,' Xulu said. 'Burn it.'

Of the four men Ben had injured, one was walking wounded and the other three had to be carried out. Xulu shook his head at the casualties and then turned to Ben with a twisted smile, showing the new gap in his teeth. 'As for you, soldier, you will soon answer for your actions. If simple punishment is not enough to teach you good behaviour, the General will know what to do with you.'

'Keep on smiling,' Ben said to him. 'For as long as you can. Make the most of it, Xulu, because I guarantee you won't be smiling for very long. That's a promise.'

'A promise from a dead man,' Xulu laughed, and the soldiers laughed with him.

The children were marched to the two empty trucks at the rear of the convoy and crammed aboard the cargo flat-beds, fifty or more to a truck, with guards to watch over them. The rest of the troops took their places in the three lead trucks, Ben among them, with never fewer than half a dozen guns pointing at him. Doors slammed, engines grumbled into life and the convoy set off for its three-hour journey home.

The last thing Ben saw of the once-peaceful haven of the Orphelinat Saint-Bakanja was the leaping flames and column of black smoke rising into the sky above the trees.

Chapter 21

Back at the city, the dusty trucks lined up outside the barracks building, which would soon need to expand into neighbouring buildings to house Khosa's rapidly growing forces. As Ben disembarked from the lead truck, soldiers grabbed him and put him in the back of a Jeep with Xulu up front and his lieutenant at the wheel. Umutese sped recklessly through the empty streets to the hotel, where a belligerent and fuming Xulu led the way to Khosa's administrative office on the ground floor.

Khosa's secretary informed them that the General had not yet returned from his business meeting. Xulu looked bitter. Ben couldn't tell which upset the captain more, the disappointment of not being lauded by his beloved commander over the successful mission, or the frustration at not seeing the white troublemaker get what was coming to him.

'This is not the end of the matter,' Xulu warned him as they returned to the Jeep. 'But first we have work to do. Hurry! Hurry!'

Ben felt like hitting him again, just for the pleasure of parting him from a few more of his gold teeth. *In for a penny*, he thought. Then he thought of Jude, and kept his fists to himself.

The Jeep hustled back to the barracks building, which was swarming with soldiers inside and out. But not every face there was hostile. 'Ben!' called a familiar voice as his guards walked him inside, and he turned to see Jeff and Tuesday standing there under the suspicious eye of their own trio of guards. Gerber was with them, the first time since their arrival in the city that Ben had seen the old sailor on his feet and looking less than cadaverous. As pleased as he was to see them all again, Ben was barely able to manage a smile.

Jeff caught his expression. His eyes dropped a few inches and he frowned at the damage on Ben's face. 'You look like you've taken a couple of knocks, mate. What happened out there? You've been gone hours. We were worried.'

Ben touched his bruised jaw. 'Others had it worse,' was all he could bring himself to say.

'Any news about Jude?' Jeff seemed almost too nervous to ask.

Ben shook his head. Jeff's lips tightened and his brow furrowed into deep lines.

'Look who's back in the land of the living,' Tuesday said, clapping Gerber on the shoulder.

'I wanted to say I'm sorry,' Gerber said, 'for letting you guys down. Things just got too much for me, Condor and Hercules and all. I needed some time to myself. Feel a damn sight better if we could get out of this mess, though. And I'm worried as hell about Jude. I love that kid like he was my own, you know?'

Ben felt a surge of sadness and warmth. 'I appreciate that, Lou. Thanks. It's good to see you on your feet.'

'Old Marines never die,' Jeff said. 'They just get tougher. Right?'

'Yeah, right,' Gerber said. 'I guess.'

'Hurry! Hurry!' Xulu barked at them, a man on a mission. The guards prodded and shoved the four through a maze of plywood-sheet corridors that led all the way through the building and back outside to a wide concrete courtyard shaded on three sides with awnings. Some thirty or forty more soldiers were gathered there, standing haphazardly to attention in the presence of Colonel Raphael Dizolele. In full regalia with a peaked cap and gold braid plastered all over, Dizolele was proudly admiring the large crowd of children assembled at the far side of the courtyard: some fifty boys, about half of the orphans harvested that day. A number of the children bore the visible marks from Xulu's whip. All of them had had their heads shaved. They shuffled uncertainly, gazing around in bewilderment at their new surroundings. Most of them had probably never seen a city before, let alone one occupied solely by armed troops.

'Who are all these kids?' Tuesday asked in astonishment.

'There are more,' Ben said quietly, and Tuesday just looked at him.

'They are our new conscripts,' Dizolele proudly announced. 'Now you will begin their training.'

'We're not primary-school teachers,' Jeff said. 'What kind of a joke is this?'

'Silence!' Xulu yelled. 'You will show respect!'

Jeff snorted. 'To who? Him? You? Now *that*'s a joke.'

Xulu shot Jeff a look of contempt, but he had more important things on his mind. He stepped up to Dizolele with an accusing finger pointed Ben's way. 'Colonel, I have a serious matter to report. It concerns that man. He is a dangerous traitor who causes nothing but trouble. I do not believe he can be trusted to train our troops. Today he attempted to divert the operation. He severely injured a number of my men.'

Jeff grinned at Ben, as if to say, *Nice job*.

'This is very bad,' Dizolele said, looking sternly at Ben. 'But we will consider the matter later, when the General returns. Captain, you will carry on with the initiation of the new recruits.'

'Yes, sir!'

Xulu had never looked as happy as he did strutting up and down in front of the crowd of children. His lapdog Umutese hovered nearby, standing beside a folding metal table on which some items had been laid out. There was a small zippered bag, a basketball, and a short-barrelled Smith & Wesson revolver. After what he'd already seen that day, Ben didn't even like to imagine what their purpose was.

He soon found out. At a snap of Xulu's fingers, Umutese scuttled over to him with the bag. Xulu reached inside it like a magician about to pull a rabbit from a hat, and with a flourish produced a cutthroat razor and a sachet of white powder.

Jeff stared at Ben with raised eyebrows. Tuesday's eyes were boggling in alarm.

Next, Xulu pointed to a lanky boy of about eleven at the front of the crowd. 'You, boy,' he yelled. 'Come here. Do not be frightened.' The boy glanced at his friends and then stepped forward, looking deeply apprehensive. Xulu laid a hand on his shoulder. 'What is your name?'

'Asikiwe,' the boy replied in a small voice.

'Asikiwe, you will be a brave and fierce soldier.' Xulu quickly slashed a two-inch-long cut in the boy's temple with the razor. Asikiwe yelped in pain. Umutese held him tight as the blood trickled down his face. Xulu razored open the sachet, licked a finger, dipped it into the white powder and then dabbed a generous quantity into the cut with his moist fingertip.

What in hell's name are they doing? said Jeff's speechless expression.

The effect on the boy was so rapid that there was no doubt in Ben's mind that the white powder could be anything but pure cocaine. Within moments, Asikiwe was reeling and his eyes were floating out of focus. Xulu let him go and pointed to another boy in the crowd. 'You are next! Come here!'

And on, and on. By the time the last boy had been cut, the first few to receive the treatment were well under the influence of the drug. It was a deeply disturbing sight.

Xulu was beaming. 'If you are to become soldiers, I want to see how well you can fight! Attack whoever is nearest to you! Hit hard! Anyone who does not fight with all his heart will be whipped!'

The change in these placid, frightened children was startling and horrifying. The first blow landed quickly and produced a ripple effect that soon had all the boys pummelling one another like a feral pack, out of their minds and completely uninhibited in their ferocity. Their yells filled the courtyard. Bloody noses and burst lips started breaking out everywhere. Several boys fell and were trampled by the bare feet of their comrades.

'I can't watch this,' Gerber muttered.

'STOP!' Xulu screamed, and the fighting petered out almost as quickly as it had started. He snapped his fingers again, and this time Umutese brought him the basketball from the nearby table. 'We have played this game before,' Xulu said to the children, holding the ball up. 'But you did not play it well. Let us try again. This ball is the head of your enemy. Whoever brings it back to me will be spared a beating. The rest of you will be punished for your failure!' He tossed the ball among them.

Ben could only be thankful that it wasn't a real head this time. But that was all that was good about the game. The wildest rugby match ever played by big, powerful men couldn't have compared with the brutality that ensued. Eventually, the victorious boy emerged with bloody knuckles and one eye swollen shut.

'This boy will have food tonight!' Xulu yelled, grasping the winner's shoulder. 'The rest will go hungry! Then you will learn the importance of victory!'

Just then, the thud of a passing helicopter made them all look up. Xulu shot a glance in Ben's direction and grinned a nasty grin to himself. Khosa was back. Unfinished business would soon be attended to.

But the bizarre hazing of the child recruits wasn't over yet. 'You!' Xulu shouted, pointing at a younger boy of about eight. His grimy white vest was spotted with blood and his eyes were rolling. 'What is your name?' Xulu demanded. The boy took a few seconds to register the question and remember the answer. 'Mani.'

'Tell me, Mani. Do you want to eat tomorrow?'

A nod.

'Then you must pass this test,' Xulu said.

Ben and Jeff exchanged another worried glance. Ben was prepared for the worst. The crowd of children, intoxicated with blood and violence, was ready for anything.

'Who are your enemies?' Xulu shouted at Mani. The boy looked blank.

'Your enemies are who we tell you they are! Say it!'

Mani mumbled incoherently.

'What do we do with our enemies?' Xulu yelled, his nose an inch from the boy's. 'Spill their blood! Say it! All of you! SPILL THEIR BLOOD!'

Slowly at first, quickly building in volume, the children

all began to chant it. 'SPILL THEIR BLOOD! SPILL THEIR BLOOD!' The same awful chorus that was still ringing in Ben's ears from the massacre of the village during their journey to the Congo.

'This is sick,' Tuesday said loudly.

And it was about to get sicker.

Chapter 22

At a sharp command from Umutese, the soldiers brought in a young girl of about fourteen, so frightened that she seemed to shrivel at the sight of Xulu and so many men all staring at her. She was the first female of any age that Ben had seen in the city. Perhaps a captive from one of the villages Khosa had raided, kept here as a servant, or worse.

The soldiers shoved her into the middle of the courtyard and stepped quickly back. Xulu unholstered his pistol and thrust it into Mani's hands. As the boy stood there uncertainly holding the weapon, Xulu bent down and bellowed close to his ear, pointing at the girl.

'This cockroach bitch is your enemy! Why? Because I say she is. And what will you do? Spill her miserable blood! Obey your commander! You are a soldier now. Spill her blood for General Khosa!'

Mani had no real idea of what he was doing. His big round eyes were swimming and out of focus. As if in a trance, he raised the weapon in his small fist. Xulu steadied the gun barrel for him.

'We can't let this happen,' Tuesday said in a desperate voice.

Ben said nothing. He could taste blood in his mouth again, because his teeth were clenched so hard. *Just keep thinking of Jude. Don't do anything stupid. You couldn't save her, anyway.* Gerber was standing with his head bowed and his trembling fists balled at his sides. 'No, no, no,' Jeff muttered, shaking his head.

With Xulu doing the aiming for him, Mani's small finger squeezed the trigger and he shot the girl. She fell in a heap.

Jeff covered his face. 'Oh, Christ.' Tuesday looked ashen. Gerber had his eyes grimly shut.

Ben felt so ashamed of himself.

Xulu took the gun from Mani, who was standing staring with glazed eyes at the body on the ground as if trying to make sense of what had just happened. Next Xulu had all the boys line up near the body, and daubed each of their foreheads in turn with the dead girl's blood, making a sign on their brow that looked like an inverted cross.

'Now you are protected,' he declared with a triumphant grin. 'The power of your Lord Khosa is in your bodies. When your enemies see that they cannot kill you, they will drop their weapons and run!'

Lord Khosa.

'Do you believe me? Say it! Yes, Captain Xulu!'

The boys chorused, 'YES, CAPTAIN XULU!'

'It is true,' Xulu assured them. 'I will show you. Lieutenant!' The ever-ready Umutese now brought his captain the snubby revolver from the table. Xulu aimed it into the crowd of children and let off six loud shots.

At which point Ben almost did something stupid, before he understood what was happening. Some of the boys flinched at the gunfire, the rest just stood there in a state of apparent detachment. But none of them appeared to have been hurt. The trickery was obvious, at least to those who could see through it.

Xulu ejected the empty cases from the revolver, reloaded

six more loose rounds and fired them off, straight into the faces of the entranced children. Still no blood, no screaming, nobody falling over or clutching at their ripped flesh.

Xulu tossed the smoking revolver back to Umutese. 'You see?' he said with a laugh to the children, spreading his arms wide like a prophet. 'The bullets cannot harm you! You are invincible! Your Lord Khosa has protected you!'

Ben looked at the spent shells of the harmless blank cartridges rolling on the ground. Then stared at the crumpled body of the girl, her blood leaking in a trail over the uneven concrete. Was it possible to reach a point where you were completely unmoved by the sight of an innocent's death? He knew with a certainty beyond anything that if he stayed in this place much longer, he would either go mad or die.

At that moment, none other than Lord Khosa himself made his sweeping entrance. The soldiers near the doorway stepped back in deference as he strode into the courtyard. A cry went up, as though the miracle the troops had just witnessed – evidently not in on the scam, Ben thought – had reinforced their belief in their commander's divine powers. 'KHOSA! KHOSA! KHOSA!'

The General was puffing on a fresh cigar and looked very pleased with himself. He didn't so much as glance at the girl's corpse as he walked past. Scanning the battered faces and torn, bloodied clothing of the fifty drugged children, he seemed delighted by what he saw. With a gracious wave of his hand he silenced the chants of the soldiers.

'Captain Xulu,' he boomed. 'May I congratulate you on an outstanding mission. You are now promoted to major, and Lieutenant Umutese will fill the rank of captain in your place. I trust that everything is going well with the training?'

'Very well, Excellency,' Xulu replied, actually squirming

with smugness for a moment before his expression darkened. 'But there is something—'

Not to be outdone by a subordinate, not even a freshly promoted major, Colonel Dizolele stepped up to his leader and interrupted, pointing at Ben. 'General, there has been another problem with this man.'

The beaming smile left Khosa's face. 'What is it this time?'

Dizolele said, 'Major Xulu reports that he attempted to prevent the recruitment mission.'

Khosa turned slowly to set his implacable gaze on the offender. Xulu and Dizolele followed his eye to scowl in unison at Ben as they stood shoulder to shoulder with their general.

All close together. All lined up in a row.

Perfect positioning.

But what happened next took Ben as much by surprise as anyone.

Nobody had been paying much attention to Lou Gerber. He seemed to have shrunk into the background and was staring into space with the empty eyes of a zombie, as though the scenes they'd all just witnessed had tipped him quietly back into the semi-catatonic state that he'd only just recovered from.

But now Gerber exploded with the unbearable weight of pressure that had been building inside him all this time. His body went taut. A strange light filled his eyes and he bared his teeth. Then, with a roar of uncontained fury, all of his decades-old Marine Corps training flooding back in a single rushing crazy impulse, he drove an elbow backwards into the stomach of the soldier standing next to him, then smashed a chopping downward blow into the nape of the man's neck as he doubled up.

Not even Ben could have moved fast enough to stop him.

Gerber ripped the QBZ assault weapon from the soldier's grasp. He raised the rifle and pointed it straight at Khosa and squeezed the trigger.

But not before multiple bullet strikes caught him from several angles at once. Ben saw Gerber's jacket flutter as the soldiers' gunfire punched into his chest and ribs. At the same instant as Gerber let off a burst of rounds from the QBZ, his weapon jerked with the impact, skewing his aim. Then the old Marine was tumbling backwards with his face contorted in pain. The soldiers went on pumping rounds into him as he hit the concrete.

Gerber's aim had been skewed, but only by a matter of inches. To Khosa's right, Xulu collapsed to the ground with a strangled shriek that came out as a gurgle as blood sprayed from his ripped throat. To Khosa's left, Dizolele tottered and fell, clutching his shattered thigh. Khosa stood perfectly still, apparently quite calm and still puffing on his cigar. If he'd been so much as grazed by a single bullet, the General didn't appear to have noticed.

Amid the chaos, the panic-stricken soldiers rushed towards Gerber, emptying their magazines and hammering dozens of rounds into his fallen body. Gerber was already dead, but he hadn't gone down alone. Xulu thrashed on the ground for a second or two, clawing at his throat, then went limp. Dizolele was screaming in agony as he tried to stem the bleeding from his leg. A piece of red meat the size of a steak was hanging out of his torn trousers.

Khosa's unruffled gaze swivelled back towards Ben. His wide-set eyes seemed to bore deep inside Ben's mind, as if to say, *This is your doing, soldier.*

There was blood everywhere. The crowd of children had scattered all over the courtyard. The boy called Mani was standing very still, his face a blank of total sensory overload.

Soldiers rushed back and forth. Umutese ran to Khosa, daring to check him all over for bullet wounds, then issuing orders to the men to hurry their leader away to safety. A team of four gathered up the writhing, agonised Colonel Dizolele and carried him away, leaving a blood trail over the concrete. Ben, Jeff, and Tuesday were encircled by two dozen rifles.

With Dizolele gone, a hushed silence fell over the court-yard. Ben and the others were too stunned to speak. Unsure what to do with them, the soldiers jabbed and prodded them inside the building to a kitchen, and shut them inside an empty steel walk-in meat locker that, thankfully, was not switched on.

Nothing more would happen for several hours.

Not until after nightfall, when the retribution began.

Chapter 23

The previous day

When Victor Bronski had assured his boss that he was on it, he'd meant what he said. For an investigator of his experience, his wily ways, his extensive contacts and the kind of resources that Eugene Svalgaard's limitless millions made available, it hadn't been too hard for Bronski to find the right contact. It was simply what Bronski did. No big deal. You want the best, you pays your money and you give the Lee Penders of this world a wide berth. That stupid greedy shitbird Svalgaard had learned his lesson. As for Bronski, he just wanted to get the job done and jump on the first flight out of this dead rat's ass of a place.

As it turned out, none of the underworld sleazebags in Kinshasa could say – or were too afraid to disclose – where the feared warlord Jean-Pierre Khosa might be located in person. But for a few thousand dollars a cellphone number for his 'political attaché' (whatever the fuck that means, Bronski thought) was coughed up shortly before midnight, just a matter of hours since the team had touched down on Congolese soil. The word on the street was that nobody was in deeper with Khosa than César Masango. Which sounded to Bronski like a good place to start, assuming that Khosa still had the diamond. Svalgaard was making that assumption. Victor Bronski never assumed anything – except that nothing was safe and nobody in the world could be trusted.

Sipping on a minibar whisky at 12.30 a.m. in his hotel room, he dialled the number. There was no answer, but then Bronski expected such a man to be every bit as cautious as himself.

'Mr Masango, my name is Walter Reynolds. I represent a client who is in the market to acquire a certain item, one we have good reason to believe is in the possession of a business associate of yours. My client is willing to make a discreet and speedy cash purchase at a price far above the current market value that the said item, due to present circumstances, can be expected to fetch. We are confident that this is the best offer you will receive. If you would like to meet to find out the specifics, call this number. Please be aware that our offer is good for twelve hours only and is dependent on our satisfactory inspection of the goods prior to payment by wire transfer. At precisely noon-thirty tomorrow, the deal comes off the table and you will not hear from us again. I'll be expecting your call.'

Bronski sat by the phone for much of the night and slept little, but he never needed more than four hours' sleep as a rule. Masango didn't call. Bronski waited calmly. Masango didn't call. Bronski used his second phone to check on the team and make sure they were ready to roll at a moment's notice.

Masango didn't call. After five in the morning, Bronski gave up waiting and napped for a while. He was up two hours later, dressed and back to waiting. Then, at 9.03 a.m., his phone finally buzzed. By that time, he was downstairs in the hotel bar drinking coffee with Aaron Hockridge, the ex-SEAL.

'Mr Reynolds?' said a clipped, educated-sounding African voice.

Bronski signalled Hockridge, who put down his coffee and looked instantly ready for battle. Ex-SEALs were like that.

'This is Reynolds,' Bronski said.

'We would like to discuss the details of your offer. Please be in the lobby of the Kempinski Hotel Fleuve Congo at precisely ten a.m. for further instructions.' Then the voice hung up.

'You're on,' Bronski said to Hockridge. Hockridge called the others.

If Bronski had said 'You're on' and not 'We're on', it was for a reason. He didn't intend to be present at the meeting in person, but would instead do the face-to-face via mobile Skype while Hockridge and two members of the team, Doug Weller and Carl Addington, met Masango in the flesh. Weller was a former Delta Force operative, there mainly to back up Hockridge if things got hairy. Addington was a diamond expert, with an employment history that included leading wholesale houses in London, Paris and Durban. Bronski would cut the deal to Masango via a laptop screen; then if all was agreeable he was authorised to set up an immediate wire transfer of the funds into the account of Masango's choice.

Needless to say, not a cent would change hands until the goods had been thoroughly examined and given the nod by Addington. Hockridge would then take charge of the diamond, keeping it securely on his person until he passed it to Bronski.

Unknown to Hockridge, Bronski had taken the extra precaution of having two more guys posted to the ex-SEAL's home town of Tucson to keep tabs on his wife Pam and their teenage kids Johnny and Mary-Kate. In the event that Hockridge, once in possession of the rock, should happen to fall victim to the same kinds of temptations to which the hapless Pender had succumbed, Bronski's guys had orders to move in and take the entire Hockridge family hostage. Similar arrangements were in place with regard to Weller and Addington. You never knew. And if all went according to plan, neither would they.

At exactly 9.45 a.m. Hockridge, Addington, and Weller exited their hire car – the paperwork filled out in a false name – and walked into the lobby of the Kempinski Hotel Fleuve Congo. Hockridge was carrying a metal case that was empty except for a compact laptop equipped with Skype mobile. Addington was carrying a similar case containing the tools of his trade, the most important of which were a three-lens jeweller's magnifying loupe and a portable diamond scope used to examine a stone's complex anatomy and ascertain its carat value. Weller was empty-handed, but packing a forty-calibre Glock pistol in a concealed waist holster plus a diminutive .380 Beretta backup piece strapped to his right ankle.

Victor Bronski was sitting behind the wheel of a plain panel van a block away, eating a pot of yogurt while watching and listening on a laptop remotely hooked up to the powerful transmitting microphone and miniature camera that Hockridge had been fitted with.

Precisely fourteen minutes after the three entered the five-star hotel lobby, they were met by a tall and expensively tailored African with an attaché case cuffed to his left wrist and two large wary-looking men in dark suits hovering in the background, who introduced himself as César Masango. He was eloquent and polite, affable and open, but insistent on the terms of the meeting – which his client stipulated must take place at a secret and secure location well away from prying eyes.

Masango and his bodyguards escorted Hockridge, Addington, and Weller outside to where a black seven-seater Mercedes Viano MPV was parked at the kerbside. The body-guards got into the front. Inside the vehicle, Masango graciously insisted on relieving the three men of any firearms they might be carrying, and Weller made a show of grudg-ingly giving up his Glock. Hockridge was all smiles and understanding. Business was business, no hard feelings, and all that.

A block away, Victor Bronski started the van and switched to GPS tracking. The device hidden in Hockridge's case emitted a signal that appeared as a pulsing red dot on his screen. As his guys began to move, Bronski followed, hanging far enough back to be invisible but close enough to stay in mike and camera range.

Bronski wasn't too surprised when the Mercedes's desti-nation turned out to be a less-than-palatial residence on an unpaved street in one of the poorest areas of the city. Khosa and Masango might be scummy criminal lowlifes about to become outrageously rich, but they were still scummy crim-inal lowlifes. Bronski wondered with a dark smile what the diamond guy, Addington, must be making of all this. It wasn't Tiffany's, and that was for sure.

The meeting took place in a room with draped windows, a bare table, and four chairs. Masango's men stood by while he took a seat at one side of the table facing Hockridge, Addington, and Weller, with the attaché case neatly perched on his lap. Hockridge took the computer from his own case and set it up on the table with the screen angled towards Masango. He explained that his business associate, Mr Reynolds, was sorry he couldn't be there to make the offer in person but had been called away on other business, hence the need for the technology.

'What a wonderful modern world we live in,' Masango said with a smile.

Parked a few streets away, Bronski had a black drape hung behind him so that Masango couldn't tell he was conducting the meeting from the back of a panel van. When the Skype connection was made, Masango's face appeared on his screen in a larger and clearer image than the one that was being simultaneously transmitted by Hockridge's hidden camera.

With a stone face Bronski briefly introduced himself and then cut to the chase. 'My client is a very rich man, Mr Masango. He wants to settle this deal as quickly as possible. Accordingly, he has authorised me to offer you a generous price for the item. It is non-negotiable. If you accept, subject to verification of the item by Mr Addington here, the funds can be wired within the hour to the account or accounts of your choosing. Are these terms acceptable to you, in principle?'

'I have not yet heard what is being offered,' Masango said pleasantly.

'My client will pay fifty million dollars,' Bronski said, in a tone completely devoid of emotion. He watched Masango's reaction carefully. If Masango was blown away by such a gigantic sum, he was extremely good at not showing it. He pursed his lips and touched his fingertips together, appearing to be deep in thought. 'This is much less than it is worth,' he said after consideration. 'We estimate its market value to be in nine figures.'

You greedy sonofabitch, Bronski thought. 'Under the circumstances, my client could have offered far less. As I say, that figure is not open to negotiation. Do we have a deal, yes or no?'

Masango frowned, considered for a few moments more, then slowly nodded and his expression softened. 'Very well. My associate will accept the deal.'

No shit he'll accept, Bronski thought. 'Okay. Now please show us the goods.'

Masango placed the attaché case on the table, opened it, and now it was Bronski's turn to have to hide his reaction. It was hard to believe that the diaphanous, fist-sized monster lighting up the room from within the case's velvet lining was real. He tried not to blink or swallow. 'Mr Addington would now like to examine the item,' he said.

'Certainly.'

Bronski asked Hockridge to turn the laptop so he could watch the evaluation. Addington was sweating and there was a slight tremor in his fingers as he carried out his inspection. With $50 million riding on his decision, the biggest bloody diamond he'd ever seen or even heard of in his hands and Bronski's slate-hard narrowed eyes watching his every move, he had every right to be a little flustered.

'Well?' Hockridge asked impatiently.

'Don't rush me,' Addington snapped. 'Unless you want to shell out fifty million for a worthless chunk of zircon?'

'Fine, fine,' Hockridge relented.

'I can assure you, gentlemen, the diamond is real,' Masango said smoothly.

'Nonetheless, you won't mind if we take just a little longer to check,' Bronski said.

Addington irritably resumed his examination, sweating even more profusely. Finally, he carefully returned the diamond to its case, puffed his cheeks, wiped beads of perspiration from his brow, turned to the screen and pronounced, 'It's genuine, all right. It's—' He seemed to want to say more, but the look in Bronski's eyes checked him.

'Then everything seems to be in order,' Bronski said. 'You have yourself a deal, Mr Masango.'

'My client would like the funds wired to this account,' Masango said, taking a slip of paper from his breast pocket and sliding it across the table to Hockridge. 'There is also an email address to which we would like the transaction confirmation to be copied.'

Hockridge angled the laptop towards himself and read the figures out to Bronski, while at his end Bronski dialled up the secure website and entered the passcodes Svalgaard had entrusted him with. It took a few moments to penetrate the heavy security system, after which Bronski entered the recipient account details and keyed in the transfer amount of a five and seven zeroes. A window flashed up onscreen instructing him to verify the transaction.

For just the smallest moment, Bronski baulked. What the hell. It wasn't his money. He clicked the button and watched as fifty million bucks started winging its irretrievable way through cyberspace towards the offshore coffers of General Jean-Pierre Khosa, about to become one of the richest warlords in Africa. All the more reason for getting the hell out of this country ASAP, Bronski thought.

Then they waited. Thirty minutes later, Bronski's computer pinged to tell him the transaction had been confirmed by the bank. The funds had cleared. Per instructions, he copied the notification email to Masango, and asked Hockridge to turn the laptop back around.

Masango was sitting with a quiet smile as he received the email on his phone. His henchmen lurked at opposite sides of Bronski's screen, arms folded and serious.

'Congratulations,' Bronski said to Masango, and pointed at the cuff attaching the case to the man's left wrist. 'I think you can take that off now. You won't be needing it anymore.'

Masango raised his eyebrows. 'I do not think that will be necessary, Mr Reynolds. I must ensure the diamond's safe return to my client.'

It took a couple of seconds for the African's words to hit home. Bronski stared at the screen. 'Say *what*?'

'Thank you for your cooperation,' Masango said. 'It has been a pleasure doing business with you. Regrettably, the diamond is no longer for sale. Please assure your client that his money will be put to very good use, and thank him for his donation to our cause.'

For the very first time in his long professional life, Bronski was speechless.

Then Masango's two bodyguards stepped closer into the frame, each pulled a micro-sized submachine gun out from under his jacket, and before the unseen Weller had had time to yank the concealed backup .380 Beretta from his ankle holster, they sprayed the table with gunfire.

Bronski's computer screen went black.

Chapter 24

The meat locker was dark, cramped, and airless, with a floor space roughly five feet square that gave the three of them just enough room to sit and wait it out. Ben could see the dimming green glow of Jeff's watch dial. It was nearly midnight. They'd long since given up trying to find a way out. The locker was solid steel and securely bolted shut from the outside.

'Look on the bright side, guys,' Jeff said. 'At least we're not getting frozen like a Tesco turkey.'

'Might starve to death if they don't let us out of here sooner or later, though,' Tuesday observed.

'You worry too much,' Jeff replied, but he couldn't quite conceal the apprehension in his own voice.

'Tell you what else I'm worried about,' Tuesday said. 'I hate to say it, but I'm busting for a crap. We've been cooped up in here for hours and I don't know how much longer I can hold it.'

'Don't stand on ceremony. We promise not to look.'

'It's not the looking that concerns me.'

'We've had worse,' Jeff muttered.

Tuesday shifted about in discomfort, but he was determined to hold it. 'You think he just snapped, or what?' he asked, changing the subject.

'Gerber?' Jeff said. 'Who can blame the guy for cracking up? Not me.'

'It was suicide,' Ben said, and the other two fell silent. 'It's obvious. I think he knew there was no other way out for him. He wanted a quick end, and he got it.'

'Jesus,' Tuesday said after a long pause.

Nobody spoke again. Another hour passed.

And then the soldiers came.

The bright light flooding in from the kitchen made them blink as the steel door swung open and guns pointed at them. Umutese, intent on filling Xulu's shoes as the new captain, snapped orders to the six-strong unit of men he'd brought to release the prisoners.

'The General wants this one,' he said, pointing a pistol at Ben. 'Bring him.'

'What about these two?'

'Bring them as well. They can watch.'

The soldiers marched them from the kitchen and outside into the cold night, where a whole assembly was waiting. Braziers burned fiercely in front of the barracks building, throwing long dancing shadows and flickering firelight over the square and the parked trucks and Jeeps. Many more soldiers had gathered – a hundred, two hundred, it was hard to tell. The bonfires shone in their eyes and glittered off their weapons. A strange hush of anticipation seemed to fall over the square as Ben, Jeff, and Tuesday were brought out. Whatever the soldiers had crowded here to witness, Ben didn't have a good feeling about it and he could sense that his friends shared his trepidation.

General Khosa flicked the stub of a cigar into the flames of a brazier and stepped towards them. His scarred face looked even more monstrous and inhuman in the firelight.

'You have tested my tolerance once too many times,' he

said to Ben in a booming voice that carried across the square. 'Everyone knows that I am a reasonable man. I have given you every chance to honour your promise of loyalty, yet you continue to betray me and now my patience is at an end. I know that today's assassination attempt was your plan. You should have known that it would fail. Bullets cannot kill me. But *you*, soldier, you are mortal. And now it is time for your punishment.'

Something told Ben that this time, they weren't going to be content with just dropping him in a hole in the ground.

Khosa nodded to Umutese. Eight, ten, twelve pairs of hands grabbed Jeff and Tuesday by the arms and hauled them away from Ben. 'You're fucking nuts, Khosa!' Jeff yelled, but he was silenced by a punch.

Ben was shoved towards the middle of the square. The crowd circled him. He lost sight of Jeff and Tuesday. Hostile faces stared at him from all around. Some of the soldiers were grinning in amusement, as if they just couldn't wait for the entertainment to begin. Others glowered at Ben in fear and hatred.

At the square's centre they had erected a wooden gallows, a thick vertical post with a braced horizontal beam from whose end dangled a noose. Ben's mouth went dry when he saw it. This was it. There was no way out this time.

They're going to hang me, he thought. Fine. Then let them. He'd show them what it was like to die with dignity. It would be over fast.

But Khosa had no intention of finishing him off so quickly. The General drew out a fresh cigar and lit it with a burning stick from one of the braziers. Then motioned to a group of his men and said, 'Make him bleed.'

Ben stood his ground as ten men closed around him in a circle. It was his instinct to fight back, and four of them were rolling on the concrete before the first solid blow caught him on the side of the face and made him stagger. He went to strike back but his arms were pinned to his sides and a hard punch rammed him in the stomach. He could take a punch, but not the multiple kicks to the head and body that followed quickly afterwards as he doubled up. Then he was on his knees, and the blows started raining down on him so fast that he couldn't resist them.

The beating went on for a long time. After several minutes, Ben's vision was blurred and he could barely hear the roars of the crowd. He spat blood, tried to get up but fell back down. One thing he welcomed: that his body was so keyed up with pain and adrenalin that he could barely feel the blows any longer.

'String him up,' Khosa ordered.

The soldiers dragged him to the gallows. He lay there at the foot of the thick wooden post, weakly trying to get up but too dizzy to raise himself off the ground. One of them yanked the noose down over the beam so that it hung down low, and stood over him with the coils of rope in his fists and a broad grin on his face.

'Get it done,' Ben mumbled. He wasn't afraid of dying. Every man dies; it was just a question of when and how. And if his time was up, so be it. His one deep regret was that he could no longer be there to help his friends, and that Jude would be on his own. But they would survive. He believed that. He couldn't afford not to believe it.

He waited for the noose to be fastened around his neck. Instead, the man with the rope stepped over him and looped it around his ankles. Ben tried to kick at him, but he had little strength left. The soldiers laughed as they tugged on the rope and took up the slack; next, Ben felt his legs rise into the air, and the excruciating pain as he was lifted clear of the ground and dangled from his feet. The concrete dropped away from beneath him, yard by jerking yard. He began to spin, flailing with his arms to try to latch hold of something to steady himself, but finding nothing but empty air. The faces of the crowd were a whirling upside-down blur. His ears roared as all the blood went to his head. The rope bit and gnawed into his ankles.

Then hands reached out to stop him from spinning, and he dangled there with his head five feet off the ground, swaying gently to and fro as an upside-down khaki-clad figure walked up to him. It was Umutese. He was clutching a machete.

The African pressed the edge of the blade to the white man's throat, then drew it sharply away in a backswing, as if building up the momentum to hack off his head. But that would have been too easy – and besides, the General had not yet given the command.

'Are you afraid, white bastard?' Umutese yelled into the bloodied face dangling in front of him. When there was no reaction he yelled more loudly, 'You should be! We are going to cut off your arms and legs and make you crawl like a snake! Then we will chop off your head and the children will play football with it!'

But the white man just hung there, staring at him with the dancing flames reflected in his eyes and in the red pool that was gathering beneath him in a steady drip. Umutese poked him a few times with the blunt tip of the blade, then gave up trying to get a reaction. He spat in disgust and stepped back.

Next, at Khosa's command, the crowd pulled away. Two soldiers climbed into a pickup truck and fired up the engine, revving it loudly. The headlights blazed into the face of the dangling prisoner. Khosa signalled calmly and the truck reversed a few metres; then the driver whacked it into first gear and hit the gas. The truck's knobbled tyres spun and dug into the concrete and sent it lurching towards Ben with a scream of revs. The driver clutched the wheel and grinned maniacally, intent on ramming the dangling target, its bumper and front grille crunching into flesh and bone like a living punchbag. Ten feet short of the impact, the driver slammed on the brakes and the truck squealed to a halt an arm's reach from Ben's face.

Ben didn't even flinch, or blink at the dazzling headlights.

'Again,' Khosa commanded.

The truck reversed slowly back to its starting line. Once more, the revs piled on and it flew forwards with a roar. This time, it screeched to a slithering halt just inches away, in a game of chicken intended to provoke at least some kind of reaction out of their victim. If they wanted him to die, they also wanted him to die scared.

Jeff and Tuesday watched helplessly from a distance with guns to their heads as the spectacle unfolded. 'He won't break,' Tuesday said through clenched teeth. His eyes were bulging and wet. 'No matter what. He won't give the bastards that satisfaction.'

Jeff shook his head. 'I don't know if he's even conscious anymore, mate.'

'They're going to kill him, aren't they?'

'And then us,' Jeff said sadly. 'Yeah, looks that way.'

'I'm not afraid to die,' Tuesday said.

'Nor me,' Jeff said. 'But I hope they are.'

Chapter 25

Jude had whiled away the entire day just waiting to be able to escape again once nightfall came. On his return to the cage the previous night, he'd covered his tracks with great care – first making sure that no footprints were visible in the dirt outside his hut, then painstakingly filling in the hole under the wall once he was back inside, packing it with loose earth that made his escape route invisible at a glance but quicker and easier to dig back out for his next sortie.

The real test had been Promise. When the silent guard had made his appointed rounds that day, carrying the dreaded Uzi submachine gun as always, Jude had been terrified that he'd spot something was different about the hut, or the cage, or both. But Promise had carried out his mealtime and slop duties without suspecting what his prisoner had been up to. Jude pretended to have fallen into a subdued, withdrawn state, sitting cross-legged on the cage floor and staring into space, rocking mutely from side to side and not appearing to notice his visitor.

The instant Promise left, Jude was on his feet, pacing, planning, listening, waiting, fighting to contain his impatience. He'd tried to jam his head far enough through the cage bars and crane his neck to be able to see Rae's hut through the window, but the angle was impossible.

The passing of the long hours had been brain-numbingly sluggish, though the slowness was easier to bear knowing that he had a purpose now. He'd downed his bland meals and dozed sporadically, tracked the arc of the sun by the shadows on the hut wall, and managed to bide his time without going crazy until, at last, night fell.

Jude did nothing until he was certain it must be approaching 1 a.m., when the stillness was absolute, Promise was sure to be tucked up in his hut and the compound guards were lazy with sleepiness.

Then Jude got to work. He scrambled out of the cage more methodically and efficiently than the previous night, with his bent spoon in his pocket. He hit the floor soundlessly, reached through the bars for his food dish, crept over to the patch of loose earth by the wall and began to dig. Soon he was running free in the coolness of the night, dizzy with liberation, heart thumping at the thrill of the risk and excited at the prospect of seeing Rae again. As he retraced his steps towards her hut, he came across a small object on the ground – a matchbox that one of the guards must have dropped on their rounds. He pocketed the matches and hurried on.

When he tapped softly at the bars of her window, she was waiting for him. 'Is that you?' came a tiny whisper from the darkness.

'It's me. Brought you some fish and chips. I hope you like them with salt and vinegar.'

'You're crazy,' she hissed. 'And keep your voice down!'

'Hold on.' Jude hunted around the bottom of her hut wall, then finding a loose spot he dug his way in. He was getting pretty good at it now. Rae gasped in amazement as he crawled inside her hut, shaking loose dirt out of his hair. 'I can't believe you got out.'

'Take a good look,' he whispered. 'I'm real, all right.' He pulled the matches from his pocket, struck one and held it up. The flickering flame glinted off the bars of her cage and cast their vertical shadows on the hut wall. She moved closer, clasping the bars with slender fingers, and he saw her face clearly for the first time. Her skin was the colour of dark honey in the dim light, and her long hair was so jet black that it gleamed. Jude thought she was the most beautiful sight he'd ever seen, but he kept that opinion to himself in case it might sound weird. 'Where are you from?' he whispered.

'Chicago. But my family's from Taiwan. Blow that match out, before they see the light!'

Jude snuffed the flame. 'Relax. I'll have you out of here in no time. Well, maybe not quite that fast. I don't have much of a toolkit to get these bolts undone.'

'What about Craig?'

'Craig too,' Jude whispered. 'Do you know which hut he's in?'

'Two more. One's the guard hut. The problem is that it could be either of them. If I knew where they put Craig, that would make things a lot easier.

'We were blindfolded when they brought us here. All I know is that he's never answered when I tried to call his name.'

Then he could be anywhere, Jude thought. Or dead. 'We'll find him,' he promised, sounding as optimistic as he could. He grabbed hold of the cage bars and started scrambling up them.

'What are you doing?'

'Trust me, through the top is the quickest way out. You'll need to climb up while I lift the roof. Can you manage that?'

'I'll try. Please hurry.'

Jude made it to the roof of the cage and crawled across it, the bars digging painfully into his knees. He could see her dark shape a few feet below him. Groping about by feel, he found the corner bolts he was looking for and took the bent spoon from his pocket. *Here we go*, he thought. It might take a while, but if no guards appeared and his improvised spanner managed to hold out without snapping in two, they might actually pull this off.

Rae moved directly below where he was spread out on the cage roof, and drew herself up as close to him as possible so they could talk. 'Try not to make so much noise,' she chided him as he worked.

'It's called metal and it kind of clinks and clanks,' he whispered back. 'Not a lot I can do about that.'

'I'm just worried, that's all. So what's your story?'

'You really want to know?'

'I haven't talked to anyone in nearly ten days, except to yell at the guards. You've no idea how good it is to hear a friendly voice.'

Jude had the fork clamped to a bolthead and slowly twisted it, feeling it rotate. Yes! It was coming loose. 'I don't know exactly why I'm here,' he whispered. 'I don't think they're holding me for ransom. Who'd pay? My folks are dead anyway. I think I'm here because of my dad. They're using him for something, and using me to keep him on the hook.'

'I thought you said your parents were dead.'

'They are. Well, kind of. It's a long story.' Jude paused. 'What about you? You said you and this Craig guy were reporters or something.'

'Investigative journalists. I'm kind of his assistant. Photographer, researcher, proofreader, guardian angel, dogsbody.'

'You were here for work?'

'Chasing a story,' she murmured. 'A big one. We were trying to get back to the airfield near Bukavu when they picked us up and brought us here. They took my passport, everything. They won't have wasted any time finding out who my family is and extorting money out of them.'

'Why, are you the president's niece or something?'

'Never mind that,' she whispered back, a little testily. 'Let's just say that, right now, their money's the only thing keeping me alive. Most of the folks they kidnap are poor people. When the families can't pay any more, they just murder the victims. Khosa and his crony Masango have been running their nasty little scam for years. Anywhere but here, they'd have been banged up in jail for it long ago. But hey, this is Africa, right? Where life is cheap and nobody gives a shit.'

Jude had the first bolthead worked almost loose. He paused to let some weight off his knees. 'You know about Khosa?' he whispered down to her, surprised at the mention of the name.

'Are you kidding? I've spent most of the last year finding out all there is to know about that bastard. He's the reason we came to Africa.'

Chapter 26

Jude gazed down through the bars at Rae's slender shadow inside the cage. He could just about make out the pale oval of her face looking up at him. 'I don't understand,' he whispered. 'He's your big story? He's just another warlord.'

'He's a little more than that. You have no idea how deep this goes. Not many people realise it yet, but Khosa's on track to rule this whole country one day, with a little help from his friends. Do you know who his brother is?'

'I knew he had one,' Jude said, appalled by what she was telling him. 'Louis Khosa. Masango told me they don't get on.'

'*Governor* Louis Khosa. The autocratic dictator of Luhaka Province. To say they don't get on is putting it mildly. But they were close once. Virtually from childhood, they fought together for Joseph Kony and the LRA. Then, after the Rwandan genocide when hundreds of thousands of Tutsi refugees flooded over the border into what was then Zaire, the Khosa brothers ran with Hutu death squads hunting them all through the eastern provinces around Goma. They murdered thousands of men, women and children. After a few years, killing wasn't enough for them anymore. They started seeing the potential to become rich and powerful, and they had the skills to achieve it.'

185

With just one bolt removed and the minutes ticking rapidly by, Jude went back to wrestling with the second bolt as she talked. Either the threads had rusted, or whoever had built this particular cage had used nylock nuts; he couldn't tell in the dark, but it was hard work and he was making little progress. The bent spoon was becoming slippery with sweat and he was worried it would snap from the pressure he was exerting on it.

'Louis was always very smart,' Rae went on, in the same low voice. 'He fell in with an Israeli huckster called Gil Mendel, who was buying stakes in government mining interests from behind the front of fake companies set up in the British Virgin Islands. The Congolese Mobutu government was so incompetent and corrupt, Mendel could snap up the mining interests for a fraction of what they were really worth, and then turn around and sell them on the international market for ten times as much, making a fortune in the process. When the government officials found out and tried to reclaim the mining territories by force – that was when the Khosas came in, for a percentage of Mendel's dirty money.'

She paused and moved closer to the window for a moment, listening out for a guard patrol. There was nothing outside but the chirp of insects.

'We're okay,' Jude said. 'Go on talking.' He'd managed to get the second bolt loosened enough to unscrew the rest of the way with his fingers. He wriggled it out of its hole and immediately got to work on the next. A couple more bolts removed, and the top of the cage would start to come free. He was making progress, albeit slowly.

Rae crept back to stand directly below him, looking up. 'Where was I?'

'Khosa and his brother became the muscle for this Mendel bloke.'

'Right. So, the Khosas put together a big militia out of the disparate armed groups from neighbouring states like Burundi, Angola, and Uganda. President Mobutu had always been happy to harbour his neighbours' enemies, but unfortunately for him he hadn't reckoned on the fact that these guys would always work for the highest bidder. It was easy for the Khosas and their mercenary army to keep government forces at bay while Gil Mendel went on making more money for them all.'

'So why did the brothers fall out?' Jude whispered. The third bolt was turning, but only just. His fingers were already going numb. He had to pause more and more frequently to shake some life back into them.

'Louis tried to cheat Jean-Pierre out of millions of dollars of their share,' Rae replied. 'When Jean-Pierre confronted him about it, Louis and his Israeli pals ousted him and almost succeeded in killing him. He's been sore about it ever since.'

'Have to say you can't blame him,' Jude muttered. He was beginning to wonder why Rae was telling him all this, but he was content to let her talk. She had a lovely voice, even when she was whispering.

'Meanwhile, Mendel was backing Louis's campaign to become governor of Luhaka, making an increasingly useful ally out of him. There are a lot of mineral deposits in the region, and more being found all the time. The Israelis wanted in, and Louis Khosa was their ticket. The democratic process was a joke, even by African standards. Louis Khosa literally trampled his way to power. There were all kinds of stories about how he had his soldiers chase opposition witnesses out of the polling stations all across Luhaka, so that his agents could be left alone for hours to stuff all the ballots they wanted. Then when the election result still came out against him, he just used rape, murder, and kidnap campaigns to persuade his opponents to "correct" the result.'

'Sounds pretty much like his brother.'

'He's a pussycat next to his brother. Who, meanwhile, went on the rampage, calling himself a general, gathering a bigger and bigger army around him and conducting his own private wars here and there. He was always looking out to take his revenge on Louis. Better still, to depose him and then move on to bigger things. While Louis had his friends in Israel, Jean-Pierre made alliances with the Chinese who were looking to get in on the mineral boom and were buying land all over the place. It's the curse of the Congo. The poorest nation on earth, with the richest resources on the planet. Diamonds, gold, copper, cobalt, uranium, and lots more. No wonder the place is such a mess.'

'The Chinese?'

'One of the biggest exploiters of minerals in the whole country. They started employing him to look after their private mines. Then the coltan boom started. That's where the real money comes from.'

'I've never heard of it.'

'Not many people have,' she whispered. 'Even though almost everyone in the West uses it. Even fewer people have the slightest idea of the ravages that it causes. Coltan is a short name for something called columbite-tantalite. It's a black metallic ore that's heavily mined and processed to produce the element tantalum, which is used to make tantalum capacitors that are a key constituent of mobile phones, game consoles, digital cameras, computers and all kinds of other consumer electronics. Demand for coltan started soaring in the early 2000s. In the space of twelve months in 2000, its price went from about ten dollars a kilo to nearly four hundred dollars. Now it's even higher. The profit margins are enormous.'

As he finally managed to worm the third bolt out of its hole, Jude wondered again why she was telling him all this. It had to be more than just her desire to talk to someone after so many days in lonely captivity.

'This is your big story,' he whispered, realising. 'This is what you and Craig were investigating.'

'Yes. The Democratic Republic of Congo has about seventy per cent of the world's coltan. It's led to unimaginable suffering here. Any number of militia groups slaughtering each other for dominance, claiming territory and raiding villages so that they can force the people to work as slaves in the illegal mines and live in concentration-camp conditions. The trade is funding war and genocide, just so that folks back home can play computer games and text each other on their smartphones. Lots of the big corporations are secretly involved, but the biggest piece of the pie belongs to China. You wouldn't believe the level of investment the Chinese are pumping into Africa. Kenya, Nigeria, the Congo, all over. They're building highways. Light rail systems. Apartment blocks. Entire cities that are just sitting there, empty, uninhabited, behind wire fences.'

'Come on,' Jude said, feeling in the darkness for the fourth bolt. Once that one was dealt with, he could shuffle across bars to the opposite corner and get started on the next four. 'Why would they do that?'

'Nobody really knows for sure,' she whispered. 'The Chinese government keep that information under incredibly tight wraps. But Craig and I became convinced that in the longer term, they're planning on moving thousands of their own workers in from China to expand their mining operations tenfold, a hundredfold. Gold and diamonds are yesterday's news. It's all about the coltan now.'

'But why is it allowed? Why doesn't anyone stop it?'

'There are restrictions in place under international law, but those are almost impossible to enforce in a country like DRC. Most of these operations are deep in the jungle or the mountains and protected by armed guards, so nobody's been able to get close enough to prove they exist. Meanwhile, there are so many billions being raked in from the illegal trade that the big corporations are able to influence both the politicians and the local authorities to turn a blind eye. Not that it takes much to do that. It's the usual African story – nobody really cares that much about who suffers or dies here. The UN could theoretically step in but they don't do a thing, just like they stood by and did nothing during the Rwandan genocide. They couldn't protect the millions of Tutsi refugees, any more than they could act to disarm the Hutu militias that were hacking them apart in the streets, the schools, the hospitals, and all over the countryside. Aid workers were reduced to going around scattering lime on the piles of dead bodies. Humanitarian missions are just a fig leaf.'

'Slow down,' Jude said. 'This is too much for me to get my head around.'

'That's the very reason why things are the way they are in central Africa,' Rae whispered, speaking more and more urgently as if she badly needed to tell him as much as she could. 'It's all just too complicated, and always has been. Going all the way back through the history of all the wars here, the Western media have never been able to get a handle on this place. There are no clear-cut goodies and baddies. It's not reducible to an easy morality story, like Nazis murdering Jews. The public aren't even aware it's happening. And so on it goes, with these bastards stealing all they can, for as long as they can get away with it, regardless of the human cost.'

'And Khosa?'

'The Congo is in such turmoil politically that the Chinese are loath to get too openly involved yet. For now, they're content to stand back and cultivate local allies to protect their interests, keeping them well supplied with money and guns. That's where Khosa comes in. His army is the fastest-growing military force in the country, thanks to his new backers. In return, he acts as their guard dog.'

'Guarding what?'

'What Craig and I uncovered is probably the most extensive illegal coltan mining complex in central Africa, deep in thick jungle. Just across the river there's an army of Chinese workers building what looks to be a whole new city, a really major project that's completely encircled by high wire fences and soldiers. Khosa's soldiers. He's using it as a military base, tucked away in the middle of the jungle where nobody can get to him.'

'It's unbelievable.'

'It is, but Craig and I had the evidence to prove it. We spent three days living rough in the bush and sneaking around the perimeter of the complex with long-range lenses, taking hundreds of photos of the mines, the slave labour camps, the hydro plant on the river that feeds the city, the Chinese construction crews going in and out on the new purpose-built highway, and even some shots of the security fence around the city, with the high-rise buildings and cranes plainly visible in the distance. We were nearly caught taking those, but we got them. Those photos would have been the basis of the biggest exposé of the illegal coltan trade ever. We'd have blown the lid off the whole thing and finally forced governments to act. We were trying to escape with the evidence when Khosa's soldiers picked us up. I guess we weren't as careful not to get spotted as I thought.'

Jude sensed that whatever Rae was building up to, she was almost at the punchline. He paused, looking down at her through the bars.

'Now do you understand why I'm telling you all this?' she said, speaking more loudly now as her sense of urgency took over. 'Craig and I are the only two people in the world who can prove the link between Khosa, the illegal coltan operation, and the Chinese. Right now, I don't know if Craig's alive, or dead, or what. If they've killed him already, that leaves just me, and frankly I'm beginning to doubt that I'll ever see home again either. Even if I did make it out of here, we're in the middle of nowhere with Khosa's men all over the place. Anything could happen to me. I've seen what they do to people, and I can well imagine what they'll do to a woman. Let's be realistic. My chances are slim. But *you* might make it. Someone has to get out and tell the world what Craig and I found here.'

Jude hadn't expected this, and the surprise almost knocked him off the top of the cage. 'You mean me? I'm not a journalist,' he protested. 'I wouldn't have the first idea what to say to people.'

'Tell them the truth,' she said. 'They'll listen. They'll send more investigators down here. Sooner or later, it'll all be exposed and then at least Craig and I won't have died for nothing.'

'Stop talking that way.'

'I'm serious. I've given it a lot of thought.'

'So am I,' he said. 'You're not going to die, because I'm going to get you out, okay? You have to trust me.'

'Then hurry.'

'I am hurrying.'

She seemed about to say something else, then broke off with a sudden gasp and whirled towards the window, pressing up against the side of the cage to see. 'Did you hear that?'

Jude froze and listened. He had heard it, and now he heard it again. The sound from outside was unmistakably that of the clang and creak of the compound's metal gates being unlocked and swung open. The rev of engines grew louder as several vehicles drove in through the open gates. Next, bright lights glared through the hut window and swept across the opposite wall like a search beacon.

Jude was caught in the beam and crouched there for a split second, blinking and startled. Then he quickly scrambled down from the cage, barking his shins on the metal edges. He ignored the pain and rushed across to peer cautiously out of the window.

What he saw wasn't encouraging. Half a dozen pairs of headlights dazzled him as a line of vehicles surged across the compound, straight towards the huts. Straight towards him and Rae.

Jude ducked his head down below the window and whirled around towards Rae. Her face was lit up by the headlights and there was pure terror in her eyes. Jude knew his own expression must look just the same.

'I think we're caught,' he said.

Chapter 27

At last, Khosa gave the signal to his men to stop the beating. He didn't want Ben Hope to die just yet. For all his insubordinate ways, this man could still be useful to him, at least for the moment. He simply needed to be broken in, like taming a wild animal to the will of its new master. Khosa had allowed his soldiers to take the punishment to within an inch of killing the man, though in his not-inconsiderable experience there were very few who could have taken such a beating and still survive.

Just to make certain they hadn't overplayed it, Khosa summoned the witch doctor, Pascal Wakenge, to come and check the unconscious white man's vital signs. Wakenge arrived on the scene in his robes and monkey-skull necklace, gravely tested the pulse of the limp, bloodied form hanging at the end of the rope and offered his learned medical opinion that the white man wouldn't die before dawn. As an additional temporary insurance, Wakenge rattled his skulls and softly chanted an incantation or two that would keep the evil spirits from stealing away his soul during the night, when it was most vulnerable.

Now that the fun was over, the soldiers reluctantly dispersed in search of something else to do, which amounted to little in a city with no bars or prostitutes. Most would return to their dormitories to sit up late, drinking Kotiko and smoking hashish or chewing khat and laughing about the fun they'd had with the white soldier. None of them thought it likely that there'd be any training taking place tomorrow.

'Shall we cut him down, General?' Umutese asked as Khosa was climbing back into the black Range Rover to be whisked back to the comfort of his suite.

'Let him hang there until the morning,' Khosa said. 'He is protected now. Death cannot touch him until I say so.'

'Very good, General.'

'Cut him down at dawn and take him to the prison. There will be a surprise for him there.' Khosa smiled. 'His real punishment is still to come.'

Moments after the beating had come to a merciful end, Jeff and Tuesday had been put in a Jeep and driven back to the hotel, where they were locked inside their fourth-floor room that now had two empty bunks. Jeff slumped on the edge of his bunk with his head in his hands while Tuesday listened with his ear pressed against the door. 'Sound like at least four guards out there,' he said.

'Or six, or ten, I'll bet,' Jeff muttered without looking up. 'They've got us stitched up like a kipper.'

Tuesday moved away from the door and started pacing agitatedly up and down the width of the small bunk-room. 'We have to do something. It can't go on like this.'

'What do you suggest?' Jeff said, still not looking up. 'We're stuck, mate.'

Tuesday paused and looked at Jeff. A strange little smile came over his face and he patted the pocket of his combat jacket. 'Maybe not that stuck,' he said slyly.

Now Jeff did look up, and noticed the bulge in Tuesday's

pocket that hadn't been there before. Tuesday reached inside and showed Jeff what he'd been hiding in there.

Jeff's eyebrows shot up. 'Bloody hell. Where'd you get that?'

'Lifted it off one of those clowns while they were all too busy gawking at our friend getting beaten half to death,' Tuesday said. 'It's an old Russian F-1 frag grenade.'

'No kidding. I might have seen one or two of those before.'

Tuesday weighed the grenade in his hand. 'Now, the way I see it, we have a couple of choices open to us here. We can use this to blow the door down and take out the guards on the other side of it, in which case we'll probably catch half the shrap when the bloody thing goes off in this tiny room. Which doesn't strike me as a great plan. Alternatively, we can use it to stir things up a bit outside and create a diversion.'

Jeff stared as Tuesday went to the window and peered out at the bars bolted to the wall outside. 'Just as I thought, it'll fit between those bars no problem. We pop it out of the window, it goes bang in the street, all hell breaks loose, Khosa thinks there's an attack kicking off or another assassination attempt or whatever, and in twenty seconds flat everyone's running about like a headless chicken and we're the last thing on their minds. In the meantime we bust out of here, take a Jeep, go and cut Ben down, pray he's still breathing, and get the hell out of Dodge before anyone's the wiser.'

'Just like that,' Jeff grunted.

'Pretty much, yeah.'

'You forgot one minor detail. Jude. Wherever they're keeping him, he stays alive for exactly as long as we toe the line. We make a move, especially that kind of a move, they'll cut his throat in a second.'

Tuesday nodded. 'I agree, there's that risk. But let's be totally realistic here, Jeff. I hate to say it, but we don't actually know for sure that Jude's even still alive. These bastards will murder anyone at the drop of a hat, and they don't exactly play by the rules. You trust them to keep a bargain?'

'Of course I don't. But what if he *is* alive, mate? We can't be sure he isn't.'

'One thing we can be sure of,' Tuesday said. 'All three of us are leaving this place feet first if you and I don't act, and soon. And nor is Jude. If he isn't dead already, he will be the moment they decide he's become surplus to requirements.'

Jeff shook his head. 'I still don't like it. It's taking a big fucking chance. I got Jude into this whole mess. I'm not going to be responsible for him getting offed. Not when there's still a choice.'

'What choice is there? Jude's best chance is that we get out of here and try and find him before they pull the plug on him. Maybe one of the guards will know where he's being held.'

'Doubtful.'

'Okay, then, we could kidnap Khosa and take him with us as a hostage.'

'Are you serious? They'd shoot us to pieces before we got within twenty feet of the bastard,' Jeff said. He paused, and his eyes brightened as an idea came to him. 'But, on the other hand . . .'

'What?'

'There's Dizolele. A senior officer like him is more likely to know where Jude is. Gerber put him in the hospital, and with a hole that size in his leg he won't be coming out anytime soon. I'll bet we can find him easy enough.'

'Can we get him to talk?'

'Thirty seconds,' Jeff said. 'And he'll tell us where he keeps his stash of ladies' underwear. No problem there. But it's still going to be awful tight.'

'You know it's our best bet, Jeff. What's the alternative? I'd rather die trying than not try at all. And I'm pretty certain Ben would say the same thing.'

Jeff snorted. 'You're as mad as he is.'

'Who dares wins,' Tuesday said.

Jeff's face was drawn and lined with worry. After a long pause he heaved a sigh and said, 'I hate to say it, but I think you're right.'

'Course I am.'

'Screw it, let's do it. Not now, though. We wait until four in the morning. Best time for a surprise attack.'

They turned off the lights and sat in the darkened room, counting down the minutes as both thought about Ben out there, bleeding at the end of a rope. At exactly 4 a.m., Jeff said, 'You still up for this?'

'Eager beaver,' Tuesday replied, his eyes shining in the darkness.

'Then let's give these bastards a wake-up call.'

Tuesday used his elbow to smash the window glass. He pulled the pin from the grenade, squeezed his arm through the bars outside the broken window and tossed the grenade as far as he could into the street below.

'Show time,' he said.

Chapter 28

They ducked away from the window milliseconds before the violent explosion shattered the still of the night. The response was exactly as Tuesday had predicted. Within seconds, soldiers from Khosa's personal guard were rushing out of the hotel, firing off shots at the unseen attackers. A Jeep had caught fire across the street, billowing smoke. Moments later, the first armoured car came screeching onto the scene with its machine guns at the ready, quickly followed by another. Troops spilled out and ran in all directions.

'Look at them go,' Jeff said with a smile. 'It's total anarchy down there.'

'Looks like our cue,' Tuesday said.

The flimsy bunk-room door didn't take much breaking down. The corridor outside it was empty, just as anticipated. Jeff and Tuesday sprinted through the hotel, found a fire exit staircase leading downwards and within sixty seconds were bursting out of a ground-floor doorway that opened onto a side alley. Chaos was still raging all around the front of the hotel. The burning Jeep had exploded in a blast even more violent than the grenade, scattering blazing wreckage all across the street.

'All we need now is a vehicle,' Jeff said.

'What about that one?' Tuesday pointed at the hulking

black shadow of the Range Rover parked at the side of the hotel. 'That'll piss off the generalissimo even more, when he finds out we nicked his wheels.'

'You cheeky sod. I love it.'

khosa 1 was unlocked, as befitting a man of his fearsome status, and the keys were still in the ignition. Better still, a submachine gun and QBZ rifle complete with sheathed bayonet lay on the back seat, both loaded. The bayonet would come in handy to cut the rope. Both men hoped they wouldn't need to use the guns.

The inside of the Range Rover smelled of leather and cigars. The dashboard lights and instruments lit up brighter than the flight deck of a jumbo as Jeff twisted the key and the engine burst into life with a rasping twelve-cylinder roar. Where the grid of the city should have appeared on the built-in sat nav, the screen showed only a blank, unmapped nothingness with their GPS coordinates in one corner. Jeff hit the gas hard and the SUV took off like a spurred stallion.

As they sped away from the hotel, Jeff glanced in the rear-view mirror at the scenes of mayhem they were leaving behind. If any of the panicking soldiers spotted Khosa's vehicle taking off at high speed, they would assume for now that the General was escaping to safety. That might buy a little time. Jeff powered the car through the empty streets, driving like a wild man.

'That way. Next left,' Tuesday said, pointing ahead. The dying braziers of the square came into view up ahead, then the makeshift gallows.

'He's still there. He's not moving.'

Jeff screeched to a halt. They leaped out and ran to where Ben's limp body hung upside down from the wooden beam.

'He's alive,' Jeff said, feeling Ben's pulse. 'Mate, can you hear me? Ben?'

Tuesday reached inside the Range Rover to detach the bayonet from the rifle, then clambered up onto the gallows and used the sharp blade to slash the rope. Jeff held Ben tightly in his arms and caught his falling weight as the rope parted. Tuesday jumped back down to the ground. 'Jesus, he's a mess,' he breathed, staring down at Ben's bloody form.

Jeff said, 'He'll be okay. Take his ankles and help me carry him to the car.'

'Then we head for the hospital and grab Dizolele.'

'And a big bag of salt,' Jeff said with a snarl. 'For me to rub into his wounded leg if the bastard won't talk.'

They had carried the still-unconscious Ben just halfway to the Range Rover when floodlights burst into life and the whole square was suddenly lit up like day. Soldiers swarmed from the barracks building. More burst out of hiding from behind another building across the street.

'It's a trap!' Jeff yelled as shots cracked off and bullets flew overhead. 'Hurry!' They made it to the vehicle and with grunts of effort managed to heave Ben into the back. Tuesday slammed the rear hatch. The enemy force that had appeared out of nowhere was overwhelming. More shots rang out. A side window of the Range Rover exploded from a bullet strike and showered Tuesday with glass fragments as he kept his head down and raced for the driver's door. Jeff was just a couple of yards further away from the vehicle, but a couple of yards made all the difference with eighty soldiers bearing down on him at full pelt, screaming and brandishing their automatic weapons. 'Get out of here!' he bellowed at Tuesday.

Tuesday knew that if he hesitated or looked back even for a second, neither of them was going to get away. He had no choice but to leave Jeff standing there, and regret it later. The Range Rover spun its wheels and fishtailed away in a cloud of burning rubber smoke with the driver's door flapping.

Alone, Jeff could do nothing as the soldiers flooded towards him from both sides of the street. He was taken – but at least Tuesday was getting away. He launched himself at a soldier who was firing at the escaping Range Rover. He managed to slap the gun down before a rifle butt caught him in the back and slammed him to the ground. More shots blasted out at the vehicle, punching holes in its bodywork and smashing the back window. Captain Umutese had appeared on the scene and was yelling at them to cease fire, cease fire! The white soldier was not to be killed!

Tuesday glanced wildly back out of the shattered rear windscreen as he screamed away with his foot hard to the floor. He saw Jeff being taken by the soldiers, and knocked to the ground; then a street corner was flashing towards him and he sawed at the wheel and went skidding around it on four locked wheels. His heart was pounding like crazy. 'Hold on, Ben,' he yelled over the roar of the engine. 'I'm getting you out of here!'

It had been an ambush. The rescue attempt was badly compromised, but maybe there was still a chance of escape before a whole fleet of Jeeps and armoured cars came tearing after them. Tuesday gritted his teeth and gripped the wheel, driving like he'd never driven before. Buildings flashed by in a tunnelled blur. Nothing looked even faintly familiar and he was beginning to panic, thinking he was lost in the maze of streets.

Then he caught sight of a park on the left that he recognised from the inward journey in the truck, and shortly after that the Range Rover's headlights were blazing off the fast-approaching construction plant machinery at the edge of the city and he knew he was on the right road out of here.

Moments later, Tuesday was speeding along the smooth, broad stretch of highway that separated the city from the first perimeter fence. His rear-view mirror was empty. He'd given them the slip, but he still had the heavily guarded gates to deal with. He swallowed and pressed his foot down harder.

When the gate guards saw their leader's personal Range Rover bearing down on them and obviously in a great hurry, they rushed to open the gates in time for it to speed through. They were used to seeing their commander come and go at all kinds of odd times. Though it was highly unusual for him to be travelling without an armed escort, it wasn't their duty to ask questions.

It was only when the vehicle hurtled past them through the open gates and some of the soldiers noticed the smashed glass and bullet-holed tailgate that they understood that something was wrong. One of them pointed in alarm and began to jabber to his comrades that the single visible occupant he'd glimpsed through the Range Rover's broken windows was definitely not General Khosa. Realising their mistake in letting it escape, they quickly got on the radio to warn the outer gate that a vehicle was attempting an unauthorised exit. At the other end, the guards muscled up their defences around the gate and got ready to intercept the speeding car with a wall of gunfire that nothing could possibly get through.

It never got there.

The soldiers would find the abandoned vehicle minutes later, left on a dirt slope at the side of the road somewhere in the no-man's land between the inner and outer perimeters. In the back they discovered a loaded submachine gun and a semi-conscious, battered white man whom they instantly took to be an escaping prisoner, and swiftly recaptured. The unidentified young black driver had vanished into the night.

Chapter 29

Ben was slowly coming to as the soldiers slung him into the back of a technical and delivered him back to the city. As consciousness returned, with it came the pain. There wasn't much of him that didn't hurt so badly that the nerves screamed in protest at every movement and every bump of the pickup truck's suspension. It was almost a relief when the jarring trip ended and he was grabbed and thrust into prison.

Khosa's jail block was a crude basement beneath the barracks building. Crude, but effective. The walls were solid, the doors were sheet steel and the only window in Ben's tiny cell was twelve feet above the floor and barely large enough for a monkey to scramble through. Let alone a monkey with multiple contusions over just about every square inch of flesh on its body.

Ben knew he wasn't going anywhere.

The first thing he did was to check himself over for serious damage. He was no stranger to hurt. The last time he'd taken such a thrashing had been at the hands of a bunch of sadistic prison guards in Indonesia. Even that was nothing next to the joyful memory of the roughest phase of SAS training, where the lucky candidates who'd already managed to endure weeks of hell on earth were manhunted through forests and hills, inevitably caught, hooded and knocked about fairly brutally to make them divulge their name, rank and serial number. It was called RTI, Resistance to Interrogation training. Ben had actually evaded capture the first three times they'd tried it on him – a regimental record that to his knowledge was still unbroken. The fourth time he hadn't been as fortunate, although his interrogators had got nothing out of him.

What you took away from those experiences was the knowledge of where your personal limitations lay; Ben had learned that to physically break him, you'd have to kill him. Then wake him up and kill him again. It was a valuable lesson, earned the hard way.

Khosa's men hadn't done any lasting damage, as far as Ben could tell from his painful self-examination. His nose wasn't broken and none of his teeth felt loose. He'd be spectacularly black and blue for a while, and it would take a few days for the swellings across his cheekbones and jawline to go down. But he'd mend in time, and be fully functional again long before then. He lay on the wooden bench that was the only form of bedding in the cell, and gazed up at the ceiling, trying to relax his aching body.

His mind, though, would not relax. Jumbled fragments of half-memory told him that something bad had just happened to Jeff and Tuesday. He'd only vaguely registered being cut down from the rope, but he'd have recognised those voices anywhere. There had been a commotion. Shots fired, then lots of shaking around in the back of a truck. A rescue attempt, one that touched him with gratitude to the deepest core, but thwarted for some reason. Where were his friends now?

The stars were fading in the small rectangle of dark sky above him. The first glimmers of a dawn the colour of blood were threading in from the east. He closed his eyes, alone and weary and in pain. And desperately thirsty. His lips were cut and parched, and his throat was so dry he could barely swallow.

He'd had worse.

But the worst of all, by a long shot, was still to come.

Ben's eyes opened at the sound of his cell door opening. He raised himself painfully up on one elbow and blinked as harsh torchlight shone in his face. Two guards entered his cell, one carrying a dish and a sloshing bucket, the other pointing a rifle as though he seriously expected Ben to try something on. They weren't alone. The broad, tall figure that stepped into the cell with them was instantly recognisable.

'I have brought you some food and water, soldier,' Khosa said. 'Do not tell me I am not fair and considerate, even towards a man who has shown me nothing but disrespect.'

'Where are Jeff and Tuesday?' Ben asked. His voice was just a croak.

'Your friends, unlike you, are very loyal. They would risk death to save you. Such courage is to be honoured. This is the only reason I have decided to spare the white one from execution. He is in a cell down the hall. We have not hurt him very much. As for the black boy, my men will find him soon enough. If he is as clever as he is brave, he will come quietly. If not, perhaps they will have to kill him.'

Ben smiled despite the pain in his broken lips. They were alive, for now at least. That piece of news was more important to him at this moment than his dignity. The slosh of the water bucket was more than he could bear. He rolled off the bench and went to drink thirstily from it.

Then recoiled with a loud yell at the thing in the water.

Sunk to the bottom of the bucket, palely illuminated in the torchlight, was a human hand.

It had been hacked off by a cleaver or a machete, leaving about four inches of wrist and a nub of bone. But it wasn't the sight of a severed body part that brought out Ben's involuntary cry of horror. It was the bead bracelet looped around the stub of the wrist. A bead bracelet that Ben had seen before, lettered to spell the name 'Helen'.

Ben kicked out at the bucket, spilling its contents across the floor. The hand flopped out and fell on its back, fingers curled into a claw like the legs of a huge dead spider. It was colourless and puffy, the flesh swollen and macerated from being immersed in the water. He didn't recognise it. But how well did he know his own son's hand?

Ben's eyes filled with tears that stung the raw bruises on his cheeks like acid. He looked up at Khosa in pure hatred. 'What have you done to him?'

'He is alive. That is all you need to know. And he still has one hand, two feet and his head. For the moment. Perhaps you will reflect on this before you commit any further acts of insubordination. I hope you appreciate that your punishment could have been much worse. You have only my good grace to thank for this act of mercy. The next time I will not be as lenient. Even my benevolence has its limits.'

Ben was silent. He was slumped on his knees on the wet floor, shaking badly and fighting a tide of nausea.

Khosa's awful scarred face frowned sternly down at him. 'Have you nothing to say?'

Ben couldn't find the words. After a long silence, he mumbled, 'Thank you.'

'I would like to hear more conviction in your voice.'

'Thank you,' Ben repeated more firmly. He closed his eyes, unable to stare at Jude's hand for a moment longer.

Khosa gave a broad smile. 'You are welcome. Can I now expect to see an improvement in your attitude?'

Ben nodded, eyes still closed.

'Excellent. It is a shame that we have these difficulties, soldier, but I am pleased that we are making progress at last. Now that we understand each other much better, I will arrange for your immediate release. Your friend Dekker is hereby pardoned for his actions, and will be freed also. Let this be an end to the matter.'

Khosa swept from the cell. On his way out he said to a guard, 'Bring the hand. It will make a nice treat for the dogs.'

Chapter 30

The dawn light had stained the jungle to the colour of blood. Tuesday didn't know where to run; he just had to keep moving to stay ahead of the search parties that would be sweeping the whole area for him by now.

He moved quickly and cautiously through the thick foliage, clutching the rifle he'd taken from the abandoned Range Rover in front of him like a spear with the point of its bayonet leading the way. Every step could put him on a buried landmine; behind every huge, drooping leaf and frond might lurk an enemy. Heavy dewdrops spattered on him like rain from the trees as he went, soaking his clothes and running down his face.

While Tuesday worried about losing himself entirely in the thick forest, it was a relief to know that he was no longer trapped in the no-man's land between the inner and outer perimeters circling the city. In many places the terrain had been too exposed to get close to the outer fence without risking being spotted, but some areas had been reclaimed by vegetation that grew thickly all the way up to the wire.

Lying flat on his belly in the undergrowth at the foot of the most shielded section of fence he'd managed to find, he'd detached the bayonet from the rifle and got to work. The bayonet was a Chinese copy of the Russian AKM model, with a slot in its seven-inch blade that mated to a lug on its metal scabbard to turn it into a scissoring wire-cutter. He'd used the device to snip a hole in the mesh big enough to crawl through, then concealed the hole with bits of branch to cover his tracks. By his rough estimate, he was at least a couple of kilometres from the gate and the road. If he kept his head down and his ears and eyes open, he thought he stood a decent chance of slipping away without getting caught.

Beyond that, he had no idea, no plan, no shred of a strategy in mind. As a soldier he'd only ever worked as part of a structured unit, carrying out someone else's orders. He wasn't like the Special Forces guys who could thread their way through the most trackless wilderness, live off the land right under the noses of superior hostile forces and leave not a bent blade of grass to give away their presence to the enemy. He'd never operated alone on deadly ground, and now he felt hopelessly naked and vulnerable.

Much worse, he was doubly distraught over having left Jeff behind in the city, then having abandoned Ben in the vehicle. He had to tell himself that in both cases, he'd had no choice. Without a doubt, the inner perimeter guards had made him and raised the alarm; there was no way he'd have been able to make it past the outer gates without getting both himself and Ben shot to pieces, and no way that he could outpace a whole unit of soldiers on foot carrying an unconscious comrade over his shoulders. Khosa's troops would have caught up with them within minutes, and killed them both.

What now? As he traced a random path through the forest, Tuesday fought back his emotions and tried desperately to think of his next move. Somehow, he had to go back there and help Ben and Jeff.

He had the gun. It wasn't exactly the kind of top-flight

sniper's tool that the British army had taught him to deploy with extreme long-range precision – but it was a usable enough piece of kit, and the thirty-round magazine was full. By the time it was empty, either he'd have done the right thing by his friends, or he'd be dead. Survival meant little to him in any case, if it involved walking away and leaving them to their fate.

Tuesday slowed to a halt and stood very still, clutching the rifle, eyes darting left and right to peer through the thicket of moist, dripping greenery that surrounded and loomed over him on all sides, straining his ears past the jungle soundtrack of squawking birds and the unbroken chirp and hum of a billion insects to listen out for the enemy's presence. He heard nothing that made him suspect he was being followed. The only human sound he could detect was the rapid thudding of his own heart.

Then the snap of a twig made him jump and whirl around, fully expecting a horde of Khosa's men to attack, and ready to fight for his life.

Too late. The twin black circles of a double-barrelled shotgun zeroed in on him out of the bushes.

Only a man who had spent his whole life in the jungle could have crept up on him in such total silence. And it wasn't a soldier. The African pointing the gun at Tuesday was a big, powerful-looking man, bare-chested and bare-footed. His trousers were ragged and filthy, his muscular torso and arms striped with thorn scratches. Dawn shadows partially obscured his face, but Tuesday could see the hard glimmer of his eyes, the look of determination that told him the man wouldn't hesitate to shoot.

Tuesday had no time to react.

The boom of the shotgun at close range was stunning. Tuesday sprawled backwards, but it wasn't the impact of the

211

blast that knocked him down. It was the violent flinch reflex as his nervous system anticipated devastating destruction. Unharmed and in total confusion, he clawed his way out of the bushes he'd become tangled in and stared up at the African who, apparently, hadn't just shot him after all.

'He was going to spit at you,' the man said, lowering the smoking gun and pointing a finger at the ground nearby.

Tuesday looked and saw the torn, limp shape of a large snake coiled up just a few feet away. He knew little about snakes, but it looked like a dangerous one.

'If the spitting cobra gets you in the eye, the poison will make you go blind,' the African said. He stepped closer, and a shaft of crimson light shining through the trees fell across his face. He held out a big hand to help Tuesday up to his feet. Tuesday was a good three inches shorter and much more lightly built. The man hauled him upright as though he weighed nothing.

Tuesday was about to thank him for killing the snake, when he suddenly realised with amazement that he'd seen this man before. 'Hold on, I know you. You're . . . Sizwe. We met you on our way here.'

So much had happened since the fraught journey to the Congo that it seemed like an eternity ago, when in fact only a few days had gone by. The thought flashed through Tuesday's mind that maybe it was more that he didn't *want* to remember.

The man nodded. 'I know you, too. You were there when the soldiers destroyed my village and killed my family. My brother Uwase and my friends, Rusanganwa, Ntwali, Mugabo, and Gasimba, we were meant to kill you. And you were meant to kill us. But we did not kill each other. It was Khosa who killed them all. My brother, my friends, my wife, my son. That is why I am here.'

212

That was what it all came down to, with such brutal simplicity – the basic primal equation of *you kill me / I kill you*. Sizwe's matter-of-fact tone and stoic expression belied the raw grief and raging desire for revenge that Tuesday could sense were boiling inside him.

Tuesday stared at him. 'You followed the convoy? All the way across the border from Rwanda?'

Sizwe nodded. 'I watched the trucks leave, and I chased them for many hours. They did not see me. When my body became too tired to run fast, I followed the tracks of their wheels. I came to a village. They said the trucks had come this way but did not stop. I told the people that they were lucky that Khosa did not stop in their village. I told them what he did to our people. I told them I must keep following the trucks, and what I must do when I find them. A man there felt sorry when he heard my story. He let me have his motorcycle and this gun, as trade for the watch your friend gave to me. But the motorcycle soon ran out of gasoline and I had no money for more. So I kept running. Now I am here.'

Tuesday remembered how Ben had donated his Omega diver's watch as a goodwill gesture to Sizwe and his fellow Rwandan villagers. That had been before Khosa had characteristically decided to slaughter them all, raze the whole place to the ground and leave behind nothing but a nightmare of hacked body parts and burning huts in his wake. Sizwe had been the sole survivor of the massacre.

'We must move on,' Sizwe said, glancing at the bushes. 'The noise of the gun will draw the soldiers.'

'You know about the city?' Tuesday said as he followed Sizwe at a trot through the trees. Despite his size, the man could move with the speed and agility of an antelope.

'Yes. I have been watching them. Something is happening.'

'My friends Ben and Jeff are in there,' Tuesday said. 'Khosa has them prisoner. I managed to escape, but they're in serious trouble.'

'Ben is a good man,' Sizwe said. 'He tried to save my family. I could not blame him for what happened to them.'

'I'm afraid that Khosa's going to kill him, and Jeff too. Unless I do something. But I don't know what. There are so many of them.'

'Then I must help,' Sizwe said. 'And we will kill Khosa together.'

Chapter 31

Earlier

'I think we're caught,' Jude said, turning away in panic from the window as the glare of headlights and revving of engines drew rapidly closer.

'Hide,' Rae hissed frantically from inside the cage. 'Don't let them see you. Maybe you can still get away.'

'Not without you,' Jude said. 'I'm staying.'

'Don't be stupid, Jude! You have to run! Run! Get out of here!'

But there was nowhere to run to, even if Jude had wanted to. He dared to steal another quick glance through the window. There were five vehicles speeding across the compound towards the huts. Four were jacked-up pickup trucks with all kinds of ancillary grille and roof bar lights that dazzled him as he looked. The fifth, bringing up the rear, looked to be a conventional sedan, long and wide and much lower than the others. Like an executive car, or a limousine.

César Masango.

No place to run. And not enough time to finish unbolting Rae's cage and get her out. They'd be here any second. Throwing open the door of the hut. Crashing inside with

215

weapons loaded and cocked. Catching the would-be escapees red-handed. Jude sank down the wall, screwed his eyes shut and tried desperately to think of a way out of this. *Think!*

Rae pleaded with her eyes. Her fists clutched the cage bars. 'Jude!'

'I told you, I'm not going anywhere without you,' he said.

'They'll kill you if they catch you here.'

'Bollocks to them.'

'You hardly know me. I won't let you die for me.'

'Right now, you're all I've got,' he said, and he'd never meant anything with more sincerity in his life.

Outside, the vehicles skidded to a halt one after the other on the loose dirt. Their stationary headlights blazed through the hut window above Jude's head. He heard doors slamming, footsteps running, a confusion of voices. The elongated sedan was Masango's black Mercedes, all right. Jude would have recognised that car anywhere. The man was back. And that couldn't mean anything other than bad news.

Jude was resolved not to hide. He would sit quietly and wait for them to come bursting into the hut. If he was caught, he was caught – even if he didn't understand how or why it had happened. He'd tried his best, and failed, but at least he'd tried. He would tell them that Rae had had nothing to do with this. He'd do all he could to protect her. Then he would take whatever punishment they had to dish out, and he'd spit in their faces as they did it.

Half a minute ticked by, the longest of his life. Then a whole minute had passed, and still the men hadn't come storming into the hut to unleash a world of hurt on them both.

Jude opened his eyes. Maybe . . . just maybe . . .

. . . He and Rae weren't caught after all.

'Stay down!' she rasped at him. But he couldn't resist.

216

Slowly, cautiously, hardly daring even to breathe, he straightened up on jelly legs and risked another tiny peek out of the window.

Whatever was happening out there, Jude was becoming increasingly certain that it had nothing to do with the two of them. A whole crowd of people was milling outside one of the other huts, just a stone's throw away. One of them was César Masango, every bit as gangster-chic as before in a three-piece suit that shimmered in the lights. Also present was Promise, carrying his Uzi slung from his shoulder. Jude couldn't tell if Promise had been in one of the vehicles or come out to greet their arrival.

What were they doing? As Jude stared, unable to tear himself away, he saw one of the armed guards hop onto the back of a pickup and grab hold of a large, obviously heavy object that he started dragging off the truck's flatbed. Another came to help him. In the bright lights Jude realised that it was a wooden block, a section of trunk sawn top and bottom, maybe three feet long. As the two men heaved it down to the ground, another was setting up a kerosene burner, like a kind of stove, next to the hut. Masango stood by, waiting. Promise was at his side, the pair of them looking very serious and purposeful as they watched the kerosene burner being lit. Meanwhile, the wooden block was down on the ground and being rolled over to them. Jude blinked and went on watching in bewilderment.

'What's happening out there?' Rae asked urgently. 'Speak to me, for Chrissakes.'

'I don't know. It's weird.'

But he was beginning to understand that something ugly was in the offing. Very ugly, and very nasty. That didn't come as a huge surprise.

One of the Africans had taken out a long, glittering thing

that Jude realised with a chill was a machete. The man was inspecting it, running his fingers up and down the blade as though checking to see how sharp it was. The wooden trunk section had been set up on end, like a chopping block. The kerosene burner was lit nearby, its flame glowing and flickering beneath the iron pot that the guards had hung over it. Whatever was inside the pot quickly began to smoke. Jude sniffed a familiar odour that for some reason evoked a childhood memory of the playground at his primary school in rural Oxfordshire, when maintenance men with shovels and a van used to come to resurface it. It was the smell of hot tar.

'What's that stink?' Rae whispered.

'Hush.'

Promise reached down to his belt, unhooked something that glinted in the light and handed it to Masango. It was a large ring of keys, the one that Promise carried with him on his rounds. Masango stepped up to the door of the hut they were all gathered around, fiddled with the keys until he found the right one, then unlocked the door and walked in. Promise and one of the guards followed him inside. The rest stood by, clutching their weapons.

At least now Jude knew which of the other two wasn't the guard hut.

'They're not here for us,' Jude whispered over his shoulder to Rae, now that he was completely sure.

'What are they doing? What's happening now?'

'I can't see them. Oh, wait. Here they come. They're bringing someone out with them.'

He was a white man. Promise had him by the scruff of the neck and was physically pulling him from the hut. He was dirty and dishevelled and looked exactly like a man who had been cooped up like an animal in a cage for quite a few days.

Whoever the poor bastard was, Jude thought, it didn't take much to see that he was reluctant to be brought out. He was kicking and struggling and doing all he could to prevent himself from being dragged across the dirt towards the chopping block.

Jude swallowed hard and told himself, *Get ready for this.* 'What does Craig look like?' he asked Rae, with all the calmness he could put into his tone.

'He's forty-eight. Tall, thin, glasses, greying hair, wears it kind of long. Why?'

Then it was just as well that Rae couldn't see what was going on, Jude thought. He wasn't sure he wanted to either, but he couldn't look away. Promise dragged the prisoner up to the block and let him go. Munro's hair was sticking out in all directions and his glasses had been knocked askew. The eyes behind the lenses were crazed with fear.

'Please! Don't do this!' he screamed hoarsely. 'I'll give you anything! I'll give you everything I own if you'll just let me go!'

Rae heard the cries, recognised her colleague's voice, and began rattling the bars of her cage as though she could have torn them apart. 'What are they doing to him? Jude! Tell me!'

'Keep your voice down,' Jude said. 'Take your hands off the bars, and clamp them over your ears. Hard as you can. Do it *now*, Rae.'

She hesitated, staring at him with all kinds of emotions etched into her face. Then she took her hands off the bars and pressed them hard over her ears as he'd said. She closed her eyes and bowed her head.

The guards simply laughed at Munro's terrorised pleas. 'It is just business,' Jude heard Masango say. 'The General's orders.'

Then the inevitable horror unfolded in front of Jude's eyes. Munro wasn't a strong man. He was a desk guy, a city guy, not a fighter. It took only one guard to pin him down and another to seize his left wrist and stretch his arm out over the top of the wooden block. A third, the one with the machete, took up his position in the middle. He did a couple of practice swings to judge the fall of the blade, like a golfer about to let rip from the first tee. Then his face hardened, he raised the machete above his head and accelerated it hard downwards. The steel struck flesh and then wood, with a dreadful crunch that Jude wished he'd never heard before and certainly never wanted to hear again.

Rae pressed her hands harder against her ears and cringed.

There was a terrible wailing scream, followed by another as the guards dipped the amputated stump of a forearm into the hot tar to cauterise the jetting wound. The fact that they'd gone to so much trouble meant that they had no intention of killing Munro – not that night, at any rate. But Munro was in no state to think that logically. He rolled and thrashed on the ground for a few moments, squealing inhumanly. Then he did the worst thing. He scrambled to his feet and tried to get away, and the guards levelled their weapons and cut off his escape to nowhere with a rattling blast of gunfire. Munro stopped in his tracks and arched over backwards as the bullets slammed into his spine. He collapsed into the dirt and lay still under the lights of the vehicles.

Rae's clasped palms over her ears couldn't block out the sound of gunfire. She clamped them over her mouth to stifle the scream that, if the guards had heard it, would have brought them all running. Jude met her eyes with an urgent glare and pressed his finger to his lips.

Outside, the guards shuffled over to the body and nudged

him a couple of times with their feet, looking as though they were disappointed that he'd died so quickly. For reasons that Jude couldn't yet understand, Masango seemed more interested in the severed hand. He walked up to where it lay on the ground, bent down and picked it up by its little finger and held it at arm's length so as not to get any blood on his expensive suit. Carrying it like a dead starfish that a beachcomber might have stumbled upon at low tide, he took it back to his car, where he dropped it into a plastic bag the driver gave him.

The guards gathered up the rest of Munro and slung his body onto the flatbed of one of the trucks. Promise and Masango exchanged a few brief words, and then Promise turned and walked away towards his own hut. Nobody had even glanced in the direction of Rae's.

The Mercedes was the first to leave, followed by the trucks, a line of burning red taillights receding into the night. The gates closed behind them, and then the compound was still and dark once more.

Rae was in pieces. Jude held her hand for a while and did what he could to comfort her, but he had more pressing matters on his mind. 'We're getting out of this madhouse,' he promised her. She retreated to a corner of the cage and sobbed quietly while he clambered up on top of it and resumed his attack on the bolts with renewed vigour.

An hour later, they were running free.

Chapter 32

The compound was all quiet now, but the light and noise and the awful screaming of the victim still hung over the still night air like the echo of a bad dream. Rae would have to revisit her grief over Munro's death later; right now, there was no time to stop and reflect as Jude and Rae stole away through the darkness. Rae stumbled on one of the tyre ruts that the vehicles had left in the soft earth. Jude caught her arm to stop her falling. He found himself not wanting to let go of her.

Fortune seemed to have blessed their timing. For some reason, the guards had all disappeared – perhaps to help dispose of Munro's body, Jude thought, though he didn b share that with Rae. The two of them followed the tyre tracks to the gate. Jude risked striking another match to give them a little light, cradling the flame in the cup of his hand and shining its small glow up and down the gate to look for a way out. Like the fence either side it was nothing but smooth steel, twelve feet high at least, and offering no kind of hand-holds to climb up it. But the flickering match revealed that the ground underneath the bottom edge of the gate was just as dry and crumbly as the stuff around the huts. The compound had obviously never been intended to house loose captives, only caged ones, and for two slender people who didn't mind getting their clothes even filthier than they already were, it was little problem scrambling underneath the gate. They scraped and hollowed their way out like dogs escaping from a pound, and sprang to their feet on the other side, breathing hard with nerves and excitement.

It was Jude's first glimpse beyond the gate since his arrival, but everything had looked very different passing through in Masango's car. It was a desolate place even in darkness. The dirt road that led up to the compound snaked away between great mounds of weed-tufted earth and scattered huts, rotting metal buildings standing here and there among the garbage and disused machinery. There was nobody in sight.

'Come on,' he said, and wanted to take her hand, but fought the urge.

They ran on, neither one sure which way to go. Rae was several inches shorter than Jude, slightly built and fast on her feet. Suddenly pausing, she gazed around her as if she'd realised something. 'I've seen this place before,' she said in a low voice.

'You've been here before?'

'I've photographed it. From the outside, during the daytime. This is part of Khosa's slave labour camp, where they keep the coltan workers. They ferry them back and forth in trucks between here and the mining complex. Which, if my bearings are right, is just a little distance that way, to the south.' She pointed in that direction, then looked back at Jude. 'I know I'm right about this. We got so many images, I could piece the whole layout together in my sleep. The river's over that way, and the hydro station, and the city on the far side. The whole thing is encircled by one giant fence, which we're going to have to try and find our way through.'

'Meaning we're still well and truly trapped,' Jude sighed,

remembering the layers of security Masango's car had passed through on the way in.

'And meaning that we're sitting right next to Khosa's military base,' Rae added. 'His whole army stationed just next door isn't going to make our escape any easier.'

Jude glumly agreed, but then realised what else it meant. If Khosa was using Ben against his will for whatever purpose, then logic implied that Khosa would want to keep Ben close by. Then, if what Rae was saying was right and Khosa's base was just over there across the river, it occurred to Jude that there was a strong possibility that Ben might be there too.

The revelation stunned him. All this time, he'd assumed they were being kept some vast distance apart. Splitting them up into different vehicles and taking them by two completely different routes had just been a trick to make them think so.

And that suddenly changed everything for Jude.

'Forget the perimeter fence,' he said to Rae. 'I have to get to the city.'

Her eyes shone with concern as she gazed at him in the darkness. 'Haven't you been listening to me? That's the last place you need to be right now. I thought the idea was to get away from this hellhole, not deeper into it.'

Jude shook his head vehemently. 'I know. But my dad's in that city. Or at least, I'm pretty sure he might be.'

'Then God help him,' she said. 'Because you sure can't. Nobody can.'

'You don't understand. It's not him who needs our help. We're the ones who need him.'

'You're not making sense, Jude. If he's in there, he's Khosa's prisoner. Which puts him in a way worse situation than we are right now. I'm sorry, and I understand how you must feel, but to try to go in there after him is insane.'

'There's no choice,' Jude said. 'He's the only one who could get us all out of here alive.'

She looked at him dubiously. 'What is he, Superman?'

Jude chewed over his reply for a moment. 'Fact is, I don't really know all that much. He doesn't talk about himself, or the things he's done. He was in the military. Special Forces.'

'Oh please, spare me the bullshit,' she said, rolling her eyes. 'If I had a dime for every asshole I've met who thinks he's Rambo . . .'

'I know how it sounds,' Jude protested. 'I'd probably think that way too. But I swear it's not bullshit, okay?'

'Right, sure, if you say so.'

'Look, I don't expect you to believe me, and you don't have to come with me. But this changes everything. If he's here somewhere, I have to find him. Go your own way, if that's what you want.'

'Where else do you suggest I go?' she whispered angrily. 'If you're serious about this, then of course I have to tag along. No matter how lunatic an idea it might seem to me, apparently I don't get a say in the matter.'

'You won't regret it,' Jude said. 'Trust me.'

'You said that before.'

He studied her face, trying to read her expression. 'Having second thoughts?'

'Meaning would I prefer to be back in that cage? No way. I'd kill myself first.'

'Then let's go,' he said.

They hurried along the dirt road, sticking to the side and ducking behind the dilapidated buildings that lined its edge. Jude dreaded returning to the spot where the burnings of the workers had taken place, for his own sake but even more for Rae's. He kept her attention diverted from the horrific sight by whispering to her as they ran. So far, they hadn't seen a single other living soul in the place.

'Get down!' he hissed as a blaze of lights suddenly appeared over the brow of an incline in the road ahead. They just had time to scurry behind a mound of earth before what looked like an entire fleet of vehicles came roaring over the rise and came bearing down the hill towards them.

Leading the speeding procession was Masango's long, low Mercedes, ahead of a lengthy tail of armed pickup trucks and sundry four-wheel-drives that were all loaded with grim-looking soldiers. Masango himself was at the wheel of the limousine.

'Did you see who I saw in the passenger seat?' Rae whispered in Jude's ear.

Jude nodded. He didn't need to say the name.

Khosa. He'd have recognised that face anywhere. He saw it every night, in his dreams.

'I don't know what,' Rae said, shaking her head. 'But something's happening and I don't like it. Three days Craig and I watched this place, and we never saw so many soldiers the entire time. Now they're marching through here as if the Marines had landed. And for Khosa to make an appearance in person, that has to mean something.' Her voice trailed off for a moment or two; then her face set with determination and she said, 'It's no good. I can't walk away. I have to know what he's up to.'

Jude stared at her. 'But you said—'

'I wanted to get away from this hellhole. I know. But this could be important, Jude. I mean, imagine if Chen was here, in the flesh, for a meeting with Khosa.'

'Who's Chen?'

'The minister in charge of overseeing African mining operations. Not that there's ever been any proof of his actual hands-on involvement. Nobody's been able to put him at the scene of a real-life coltan mine. Or it might not be that. It could be all kinds of things. They could be closing down the operation, for all I know. Or relocating the whole damn thing to some other place. If they do that, I'll never be able to find them again and all our work has been for nothing. Whatever's going on here tonight, I can't just turn my back. Please. Craig died for this.'

'Thirty minutes,' Jude said, relenting. 'That's how long we give it. If we don't find out anything in that time, we get out of here and we don't look back. Agreed?'

She nodded. 'Deal.'

The last of the vehicles had already disappeared down the road. Jude and Rae slipped out from behind the earth mound and doubled back the way they'd come, following the dust that still hung in the air. Before the road reached the gates of the hut compound, it forked off to the left. Judging from the fresh tracks, that was the way they'd gone.

'They're heading towards the mines,' Rae said.

Chapter 33

The dust was settling on the row of parked vehicles by the time Jude and Rae clambered onto a flat rock at the top of a slope overlooking the main mineshaft entrance. They'd covered the last few hundred yards off-road, darting from cover to cover, working their way upwards onto higher ground.

The moment he took in the scene below, Jude wanted to double back. Now he understood why the rest of the labour camp seemed so deserted; it was because everyone was here. Whether all these extra soldiers had been stationed outside the mine due to Khosa's unexpected visit, he couldn't say. But there were at least sixty of them, all heavily armed, milling around the mine entrance. The shaft looked like the mouth of a cave tunnelling into the rock, one festooned with tons of scaffolding and massive iron railings and danger signs illegible with rust. Heavy plant machinery was everywhere. Trucks were coming and going every moment as the troops hurried back and forth. The whole scene was brightly illuminated by floodlights on masts. The only thing Jude couldn't see was any sign of Khosa and Masango, aside from the dust-streaked Mercedes sitting empty among the hubbub.

As they watched, Rae wondering how the hell they could ever get inside and Jude wondering whether he'd taken leave of his senses in agreeing to this madness, a battered freight lorry rumbled to a halt under the glare of the floodlights. Soldiers jumped out of the front as more strode purposefully to the rear and flung open the tailgate to unload the truck-load of mine workers, perhaps fifty or sixty souls, who were crammed into the back. The ragged slaves were made to disembark amid a lot of aggressive, pointless shouting and pointing of guns. This must be the night shift arriving for duty, Jude thought.

To him, the concept of slaves was something that belonged to a darker, historical past. But here they were, young and old, male and female, some so skinny that they looked like walking skeletons under their tattered clothes. They hadn't even started their shift yet, and already many of them seemed ready to collapse with exhaustion. Even the more energetic and least malnourished-looking poor devils moved in a kind of shuffling gait, eyes locked down towards the ground, never daring to meet the impassive gaze of the guards who drove them from the truck like a herd of cattle. The slower ones were made to pick up their pace with whips and clubs.

Rae leaned close enough to Jude for him to feel her hair on his face. She whispered, 'They'll send them deep under-ground, into pitch blackness, to hack at the rock with blunt shovels and picks. The ones who are too weak to lift tools are made to sift through the rubble with their bare hands, looking for coltan. If they slow down or collapse, they're either left down there to rot or brought up to the surface to be made an example of.'

'It's medieval,' Jude said.

'It's Africa,' she replied. 'And it's profitable. Wherever you find wealth and opportunity on this continent, you'll find misery, exploitation, and suffering.'

'Someone needs to do something to stop this.'

'Then let's do something,' she said. And before he could stop her, she was up on her feet and scrambling down the slope on the soldiers' blind side of the truck. Jude cursed at her recklessness, and went after her.

One of the slave women had dropped a dirty rag that was probably once a headscarf. Rae scooped it up off the ground as she passed the truck and quickly wrapped it around her head to cover her long black hair and most of her face. A guard yelled at her for lagging behind. She fell in with the crowd of slaves, matching their shuffling gait and slumped body posture.

'This can't really be happening,' Jude thought. Horribly aware of how he must stand out, and certain that the guards would rumble him at any instant, he hustled in among the crowd. In a heart-stopping moment one of the soldiers actually looked right at him and then moved on. Jude realised that his face, clothes, and hair were all so caked with dirt from his escapades that night that, at a careless glance, he could blend in.

He kept his head down and focused on shuffling at enough of an accelerated zombie-gait to enable him to catch up with Rae. He tugged at her elbow and hissed furiously in her ear, 'Are you out of your mind?'

'Got us in, didn't I?' she whispered back with a crazy grin.

What kind of woman is this I've met? Jude asked himself.

The yells and cracking of whips began to resonate with echo as the slaves made their way into the dark, rough tunnel dimly lit every twenty paces by liquid fuel lanterns that emitted a guttering stink and belched smoke. A hundred or so yards into the shaft, someone stumbled and fell. The guards instantly waded in, clubs at the ready. Someone else let out a wail. In the commotion, Jude yanked Rae to one side while the soldiers were distracted. 'We can't do anything for them,' he whispered, and pointed at the side tunnel whose entrance he'd spotted in the murk. 'This way!' Checking that none of the guards had noticed them pull away from the crowd, he plucked a lantern off the craggy wall and kept its light hidden with his body.

'Where do you think it goes?' she whispered as they ducked through the narrow opening in the rock.

'Who cares? Come on!'

The tunnel was a third of the width of the main shaft, and wound and snaked much more steeply downwards. The echo of the crowd and the guards was soon out of earshot behind them. Jude lit the way by the paltry yellow glow of the lantern. It gave off choking fumes that smelled as if it was running on diesel oil. He had visions of them suffocating down here, or else of the tunnel narrowing to a stop and their having to retrace their steps, only to run into more guards. 'Might have been a mistake,' he admitted.

'We can't turn back now.'

They pressed on. One thing was for sure, they were no longer in a manmade tunnel. The natural fissure was leading them deeper below ground.

Just as Jude's fears seemed about to come true and he was on the tip of saying, 'It's a dead end,' the way ahead opened up radically and they saw that their cave shaft had rejoined some kind of much larger space. Jude twiddled the knob on the lantern to unwind a few more millimetres of wick and brighten the flame. By its flicker they could see the phosphorescent glitter of mineral deposits buried in the rock, the great jagged stalagmites jutting up from the floor and stalactites hanging in spikes overhead, like giant fangs and tusks inside the mouth of some vast creature that had swallowed them whole. It was like a scene from another world. Nobody might have set foot here in fifty thousand years.

Jude soon realised that wasn't the case.

'What's that stink?' Rae whispered.

He could smell it too, a foul sweetish odour like rotting fruit. 'I don't know,' he whispered back. 'Bats, maybe.'

'Bats? Are you nuts?'

'Bats, rats, how the hell do I know? It's nasty, whatever it is.'

It was Rae who produced the first dry crunching, crackling sound as they made their uncertain way through the shadowy gloom. 'I think I stood on something,' she muttered. 'Shine the light, will you?'

Jude was about to lower the lantern when he felt the brittle *snap* of something giving way under his own heel, like the crisp, thin ice of a frozen puddle on a wintry walk in the countryside. Somewhere, a million light years away, it was November in the familiar surroundings of rural Oxfordshire. Oh, to be there and not here!

Jude shone the lantern down at their feet and saw the crunched fragments of what had once been somebody's head. Then he swept the light a little left, then right, and realised that it wasn't just a couple of skulls that littered the floor of the cavern. 'There are bloody dozens of them,' he gasped, horrified.

'No,' Rae said, taking the lantern from him and raising it high, turning in a circle as she did it. 'There are *hundreds* of skulls, Jude. They're everywhere.'

Empty eye sockets stared at them, and lipless teeth grinned at them from all around. Skulls were crammed into crevices in the rock, piled in heaps on the floor. Many of them had still-recognizable faces, not yet decomposed all the way to bare bone, wearing hideous distorted expressions of terror and pain. Semi-skeletal corpses were impaled here and there on stalagmites, many of them still shrouded in tatters of clothing.

It was an open grave. The stink suddenly seemed fifty times worse, knowing what was causing it. 'We have to get out of here,' Jude muttered, choking up.

'God, I wish I had my camera.'

He was about to say something else when she suddenly gripped his hand and squeezed it so tightly that it hurt. 'Shhh!' He listened, and heard what she'd heard. Voices. It sounded like two men talking, but their words were muffled and distant.

'Look,' she murmured, pointing. Up ahead, the cavern twisted around to the right. There was a soft glow of light shining from around the corner.

Jude took the lantern from her hand and quickly twiddled the knob to lower the wick all the way down. The lantern sputtered and died, leaving them in total darkness except for the strange glow up ahead. Jude took Rae's hand again, and the two of them crept towards the sound of the voices, treading tentatively so as not to crunch any more skulls underfoot.

When they reached the corner, they were in for another surprise. The cavern narrowed sharply to a natural fissure no more than about three feet across; it was from there that the light was shining. Hardly daring to breathe, Jude and Rae moved towards the fissure and peered through.

Beyond it was a room, but it was like no room either of them had ever seen, or could have even imagined. It was a large chamber carved from solid rock deep under the ground, roughly square in shape, with a high ceiling that echoed the conversation of the two men inside, now clearly audible.

The strange light was coming from scores of candles that

had been placed inside human skulls, making them glow like lanterns and shining from their eye sockets and open jaws. Fixed with iron clamps to the two walls that Jude could see, and perhaps the other two that he couldn't, stood a pair of bleached-white skeletons which had been grotesquely wired up to clutch burning torches in their bony hands.

At the chamber's centre was a broad stone slab raised on a plinth. The surface and sides of the slab were mottled with a dark stain that was black in places, brownish-purple in others, running down the craggy stone in dried rivulets. There was little doubt what had created the staining.

Neither of the two men inside the chamber was visible through the fissure, but Jude recognised both voices instantly.

They were those of Jean-Pierre Khosa and César Masango.

Chapter 34

'It has been a very good month,' Khosa was saying, his deep, rich voice resonating around the chamber. 'Did I not always tell you, César, that I would make us both rich?'

'You are a little bit richer than me, Jean-Pierre,' Masango replied jokingly.

'What is this? Are you telling me that I should have given you all of the fifty million dollars?' Khosa chided him in mock indignation, and both men laughed out loud.

Jude's eyes met with Rae's in the glow of the flames as the astounding figure of $50 million hung in the air. It was bad enough that a man like Khosa could get hold of that kind of money. The real terror was contemplating what he was liable to do with it.

'Not everybody is as greedy as Nkunda,' Masango went on, serious again. 'That Tutsi cockroach refuses to lower his price for joining us.'

'I have told you, César, that you should not worry about five million. You must spend money to make money, my friend. Nkunda may be a cockroach, but he has many soldiers and until I kill him he will be a useful ally. With his forces joining themselves to ours, we will become so strong that many more commanders will come to us like sheep and thousands of new fighters will join us every day. From Kenya, from Uganda, from Zambia, from Angola. For another twenty million dollars, in one month we can bring together the biggest army you have ever seen. A hundred thousand fighters. Two hundred thousand. With tanks and artillery and strike aircraft. Not even General Amin could have dreamed of such power as we will have at our disposal.'

'The city will not hold them all,' Masango laughed.

'Forget the city,' Khosa said. 'It has served its purpose, but that purpose is coming to an end. I do not trust the yellow men, and I do not need their money any longer. Let them find themselves another security guard to protect their business. My days of helping others make themselves rich are over, and I have business of my own to attend to.'

'Louis?'

'Yes. Louis.'

Khosa had started pacing the floor, and now he was visible through the fissure through which Jude and Rae were peering, holding their breaths. Khosa waved his arms animatedly as his voice continued booming around the echoey chamber. His face was half lit by the flames. Rae shuddered at the sight of him.

The last time Jude had seen the General, he had been clad in full uniform with the red beret pulled tight over his stubbly hair and the massive holstered pistol slapping on his belt. Now, to Jude's amazement and consternation, Khosa wore a plain black robe that draped him from head to toe, like some kind of weird bishop. What was he up to?

'I told you that my time would come before long, César. Now it has arrived, and there is no time to waste. That is why I want you to wire the five million to Nkunda tonight, but only on condition that he can mobilise his troops immediately and meet me on the road to Luhaka at eleven hundred hours tomorrow.'

'You plan the attack so soon?'

'You know me, César. I do not believe in wasting time. Bosco Gatarebe's forces will be with us at first light. Joshua Mikune's men are already here, two thousand of them. In the morning we will march on Luhaka City with seven thousand troops. By evening, my dear brother Louis will have fallen and I will have taken his place.'

'Do you wish for me to come with you?'

'You are a politician, not a soldier, César. After you have wired the money to Nkunda, go home and wait for a telephone call from the new governor of Luhaka Province.'

Masango laughed loudly. 'I am looking forward to making his acquaintance, Jean-Pierre.'

'It will be soon, I can promise you. And this is only the beginning. Once we have achieved this small victory, we will be ready to move on to greater things. Nothing will stand in our way. And best of all, we will still have this!'

Khosa slipped a hand inside his robe and, with a flourish that was almost theatrical, pulled out a large object that caught the firelight with a shimmering sparkle. He held it out on his open palm, admiring it lovingly.

The diamond. The same unbelievable stone that Jude had first seen on board the cargo ship *Andromeda* and reluctantly possessed for a short time, before Khosa had retaken it from him somewhere off the Somali coast. Even though the diamond was so familiar to him, the sight of it still stunned Jude. Rae, of course, had never laid eyes on it, or anything like it, before. Few people ever had. Her mouth fell open with amazement.

'This is our ticket to glory, César,' Khosa marvelled, clutching his fingers tightly around it and shaking it. 'The very moment I first saw it, I knew that my destiny had brought it to me. Thanks to this diamond, I will grow so rich, I will be able to walk into the Palais de la Nation in Kinshasa and buy the presidency without firing a single bullet!'

Both men found this wildly amusing, and their laughter echoed around the macabre chamber. 'Forgive me, but I do not think that is your style, my old friend,' Masango chuckled.

'You are perfectly right, César. It is not my style. I would rather take the city by storm and place the heads of the president and all his cabinet on the fence spikes of the palace for all the people to see. And think of the money I will save!' This was apparently even funnier, and had both of them in stitches for quite some time. Khosa slapped his thigh and rocked and quaked and gasped with mirth. 'Tomorrow will be a day of victory and the beginning of a new era for our country,' he declared when he could speak again. 'But tonight, my friend, tonight is for our pleasure.'

Jude and Rae glanced at each other, both wondering what kind of pleasure Khosa had in mind.

They soon found out.

It started with the entrance of six of the largest and most fearsome-looking soldiers of Khosa's personal guard, a couple of whom Jude remembered from the attack on the *Andromeda* and the journey inland from the Somali coast. Except they, too, had switched their military garb for the same long black robes as Khosa. They appeared from the shadows, as if from nowhere, carrying silver tankards and bottles of some kind of clear liquor. There must be another way into the chamber, Jude realised.

The bottles were set down on the stone slab. Khosa yanked the first stopper and glugged out the drink into generous servings for everyone. 'To the future!' he yelled as they clashed tankards. Jude could see Masango now. His shiny, expensive shoes poked out from under the hem of his robe.

What were they doing?

The soldiers chanted in unison, 'One country, one father, one ruler! Khosa! Khosa!' The first round of drinks rapidly swallowed, Khosa smacked his lips and attacked the next bottle.

'Bring in the slave,' he called.

Rae and Jude looked at one another. *Oh no*, her eyes said. *Not this.*

The African woman was no older than twenty, in a short white cotton dress. She was struggling in the grip of the men who dragged her into the chamber. Khosa and Masango watched with wolfish eyes as she was forced to lie on her back on the stone slab. Several pairs of hands held her writhing body down while her head was lifted and she was made to drink some of the liquor. She choked and spluttered and shook her head wildly, but they held her firmly and forced more of it down her throat. Whatever the stuff was, its intoxicating effect on her was quick. Her cries diminished. Her eyes began to roll.

And then they got started on her. It wasn't the gang rape that Jude and Rae had feared they were about to witness. It was something unimaginably more horrible.

The soldiers all circled the prone body on the slab. Hands reached into the folds of the black robes. The knives came out. Long, thin blades that glittered like liquid flame in the firelight. The quick-fire popping sounds of steel puncturing flesh were horrific in the echoing chamber. *Tchak, tchak, tchaktchaktchak.* Just as fast as her screams died out, the white dress was soaked in blood and it was running off the edges and pooling on the floor.

Khosa stepped forward, clutching something in his big

hands that Jude saw was a jawless human skull with the top of its cranium removed to form a bony chalice. He held the chalice under the edge of the slab until it was filled with thick bubbling blood, and then raised it to his lips and drank. He passed it to Masango. Masango did the same, gulping greedily until red dribbles ran from the corners of his mouth and spotted his robe.

The first part of the ritual was complete. There was more to come. With his eyes half shut, head gravely bowed, Khosa recited the incantation in a solemn monotone:

'*In nomine Dei nostri Satanas, Luciferi Excelsi—*

'*In the name of Satan, ruler of the earth, true God, almighty and ineffable, who hast created man to reflect Thine own image and likeness, I invite the forces of darkness to bestow their infernal power upon me—*

'*Open the gates of Hell to come forth and greet me as your brother. Keep me strong in my faith and service, that I may abide always in Thee, forever and ever—*'

Masango and the others joined in for the final chorus: '*Ave Satanas! Ave Satanas!*'

The woman on the slab was dying, but still faintly stirring. Khosa took up one of the daggers and drove it down into her chest, making her whole body convulse in a violent spasm. Then he tossed away the dagger with a clatter and plunged both hands into the gory wound, ripping and cracking his way deep inside.

Jude closed his eyes and backed dizzily away. But not before he saw Khosa raise the woman's still-beating heart in his bloody hands and rip into it with his teeth.

'*Ave Satanas! Ave Satanas!*

'*Khosa! Khosa! KHOSA!*'

Afterwards, the soldiers left the chamber and disappeared through the unseen doorway. Left alone, Khosa and Masango drank more blood. They daubed it on their faces and splashed it over their heads until their robes were slick with it. They mixed it with the liquor and kept drinking until the bottles were empty and the rivulets dripping from the slab had run dry. By now, the wall torches were burning low and the candles were guttering one by one, gradually swallowing the chamber in deep shadow. Masango was the first to curl up on the floor, completely sated and drunk on blood and alcohol. Khosa stood motionless for a long time with his back to the fissure in the wall, his head slightly bowed, muttering to himself in that deep, low voice words that Jude and Rae couldn't understand. Then, at last, the tall, broad shape in the darkening chamber settled on the floor, his robe pooled around him, and became still.

Jude slipped out of the fissure before Rae could grab his arm. He paused nervously in the middle of the chamber, glancing around him. Then bent down and picked up the dagger that Khosa had dropped on the floor. Its hilt was sticky in Jude's palm. He walked over to Khosa's slumped form, his teeth clenched and ready to do murder.

But even then, despite all that he'd just witnessed, Jude couldn't bring himself to kill a man in cold blood. His father was right. Jude was not that person.

So he took the thing whose loss he knew would hurt Khosa far more than death. The thing whose power this lunatic could not be allowed to possess.

Jude took the diamond.

Oh, so gently, afraid to wake the sleeping maniac, by the glow of the dying light he reached into the folds of Khosa's black robe and found the leather pouch in which the stone was kept. He carefully slipped the diamond into his own pocket, and was about to run when an afterthought came to him. He hunted half blindly around the floor for a few moments until he found a lump of rock that felt about the same size and weight, stuffed it into the pouch and replaced it where he'd found it.

And then he and Rae fled, running like crazy through the cavern, as though they could ever escape the memory of the blood ritual.

Chapter 35

The dawn had ripened into a sunburst of golds and crimsons over the city by time Ben was finally let out of the prison cell, surrounded by a squad of guards. They were eyeing him with extreme suspicion and keeping their distance, as though their dangerous captive might be about to fly at the nearest one with a neck-snapping kick. At this moment Ben wouldn't have swatted a scorpion about to sting him.

Outside, a frenzy of activity was taking place as an excitable, jabbering crowd of armed men massed around a long and rapidly building line of armoured cars, troop transporters and pickup trucks, military transport vehicles queuing up in front of the building. It looked as though some kind of mass mobilisation was taking place.

If Khosa had decided to invade Europe and set himself up as its king, Ben wouldn't have given a damn. As he watched the goings-on with total detachment, he saw Jeff Dekker being led outside with his own escort of wary guards. Jeff's left cheek was mottled from a punch or two. His eyes opened wide in surprise and alarm at the sight of Ben. The soldiers hustled them towards the street, but the two were quickly left alone as the men hurried to join the throng.

'Your face looks like a butcher's shop window,' Jeff said. 'Going to need stitches.'

'I'll survive,' Ben said, so quiet it was almost a whisper.

'Christ, mate, I thought you'd got away.'

'Apparently not,' Ben said.

'Where's Tuesday?'

'He's alive. And running.'

Jeff grinned with relief, but his grin quickly dropped as he understood from Ben's expression that there was grimmer news. 'What?'

Ben could barely even bring himself to say it. Four simple words. A statement of factual information. Just to utter it felt like climbing a mountain. And then throwing himself off its peak.

He said, 'They took Jude's hand.'

Jeff flinched as though he'd been hit by a bullet. His brow crumpled into a thousand anguished frown lines and his lips became a pale razor slash. Ben could see the thought process racing through his head: something like this, you don't take anyone's word for it; which meant that if Ben believed what he'd just told him, he must know for certain; and if he knew for certain, he must have seen some kind of proof; which had to mean—

'They showed it to me,' Ben said. 'I saw it.'

Jeff had gone very pale. He took a step backwards. For a second, he looked as if he was about to fall over with shock. 'I . . . *fuck* . . . I . . . You're sure it was his?'

Denial. Clutching at straws. The way anyone would have responded. Ben had anticipated the question.

'They cut it off as a punishment for what I did,' Ben told him, sounding outwardly as calm as he could force his voice to remain. 'I might as well have cut it off myself.'

'Don't say that, mate. I can't stand hearing you say that.'

'Khosa warned me more than once. I didn't listen to him. I kept pushing. And now . . .'

Ben stared into space, letting his words trail off and unable to say more. When the brain reaches a point where the weight of emotions is too much to bear, it shuts down and becomes numb. Ben was at that point. It felt as though he'd been pumped full of Demerol. He wanted to lie down on the ground and sleep for a thousand years. But the numbness wouldn't last. When it wore off and the true starkness of the reality pierced through, other emotions would take its place and he'd want to stick a pistol in his mouth. But only after he'd finished setting the world ablaze. Soon, he would start to feel his faint, sluggish pulse wind itself up into a rising drumbeat, and the dull fire in his chest slowly grow into white-hot rage, an unstoppable flow of molten lava pushing its way up through the earth's crust, hungry for cataclysmic destruction.

'I told you,' Jeff said. 'He's tough. Tougher than his old man, even. He can survive this. He's alive. You need to focus on that. Ben? Look at me. Do you hear me?'

But Ben was no longer listening. Jeff could see that from the look in his friend's eyes. Jeff knew that look, but he'd never seen it burn so intensely, and he feared what was coming. He decided to keep his mouth shut.

Not that there was time to talk, even if Ben had been in the mood for conversation. The mobilisation, whatever its purpose and wherever its destination, was entering full swing as Khosa's forces appeared to swell right before their eyes. A volume of troops neither of them had seen in the city before seemed to have come flooding in during the night, with more appearing every minute. Khosa's mobile forces were being joined by a steady stream of olive-green trucks, munitions lorries, missile carriers, and an endless procession of stripped-down four-wheel-drive technicals armed with everything from light machine guns to anti-aircraft cannon.

Almost every vehicle was overloaded with clinging bodies. Where there wasn't room to sit or hang on to the sides, they clustered aboard the roofs of trucks and Jeeps. Many of the newcomers were clad in the same kind of quasi-military uniforms that had been cobbled together for Khosa's Leopards and regular fighters. Many more had turned up in civilian clothing, in flip-flops and shorts and brightly coloured T-shirts draped in as many cartridge belts as their wearers could carry. Clutched in virtually every fist, or dangling on a webbing strap from every shoulder, was the ubiquitous AK-47. It would be decades before the gushing flow of modern Chinese military arms into the continent would replace the good old ex-Soviet 'Kalash' as the unofficial symbol of Africa.

Caught up in the crush of bodies were the boys of Khosa's youth regiment, the new recruits mixed together with the older hands and already hard to tell apart. Ben thought he caught a glimpse of eight-year-old Mani as the youngsters were loaded aboard one of the trucks, but then he disappeared from view. Engines grumbled. Diesel fumes belched. Shots were fired in the air, crackling sporadically over the clamour of thousands of men preparing for war. Through the yells and the cheering and the gunfire came the steady chant, 'Luhaka! Luhaka!'

'What's Luhaka?' Jeff asked, having to raise his voice to be heard above the din. Ben could have told him that it was the name of the province of which Khosa's brother Louis was governor. He could have shared his guess that Khosa had decided this was the moment to make his move against his beloved rival sibling. But he said nothing.

If there's going to be war, he was thinking, *then let there be war.*

Just then, the crowds parted and a roar went up as the massive squat shape of a Hummer came growling by. The soldiers dropped their chant and began instead yelling KHOSA! KHOSA! From the passenger window of the Hummer, dark glasses flashing in the sunlight and cigar clamped between his teeth, the General gave them a gracious wave and then passed on.

'Looks like someone got themselves a new motor,' Jeff muttered.

Through the chaos now appeared the strutting figure of Captain Umutese, who within an incredibly short time had transformed himself into a virtual clone of the lamented Xulu. With his predecessor's beret clamped to his head and gold braid on his shoulder he screamed and pointed and delegated duties as though he'd been doing it all his life. He spotted Ben and Jeff in the crowd and his brows beetled. 'You! Get in the truck!' he yelled as he stalked up to them, jabbing an angry finger in the direction of one of the Russian six-wheelers.

'Smoking or non-smoking?' Jeff said. 'Do we get a window seat? I can't travel if I don't get a window seat.'

'Get in the truck!'

Within thirty minutes the war expedition was rolling out of the city. Ben and Jeff sat in the back of the crowded, swaying troop transporter, surrounded by a mixture of uniformed and militia soldiers who were so worked up by the joyful prospect of battle that they scarcely paid any attention at all to the two white men in their midst. Khosa had them all well and truly in his spell. Their eyes shone at the opportunity to fight and die for their beloved leader. As the procession of trucks cleared the perimeter gates and hit the open road, the soldiers burst into song.

> '*Kibonge*
> *Vijana walihamia msituni*
> *Watatu wakufe*
> *Wanne wa pone, waliobaki watajenga nchi*
> *Kibonge!*'

> 'They are strong
> The youths have moved into the jungle
> Even if three die
> Four will remain to build our country
> Strong!'

One of the soldiers sitting near Ben and Jeff had a couple of packs of cigarettes and was sharing a few of them out with his comrades. Ben reached over and tapped him on the shoulder. 'Hey, you,' he said in Swahili, 'you got one of those for me?'

'What do you have to trade?' the soldier asked cagily.

'I won't ram your teeth down your throat and throw you out of the moving truck like a sack of shit,' Ben told him. 'That's what I have to trade. Sound fair?'

Having a face like a boxer's the morning after a bloody title fight can be an intimidating asset. Ben received four cigarettes in return for his promise. He gave two to Jeff without a word, eased one painfully between his cracked lips and kept the other for later, and their new friend obligingly lit up for him. Ben leaned back and sucked the smoke deep into his lungs. It wasn't a Gauloise, and that was for sure, but he'd gladly have smoked dried elephant dung if it helped to take the edge off his mood. It didn't. He smoked it anyway.

'I'm worried about Tuesday,' Jeff said after a while.

Ben said nothing.

'I'm sorry about Jude.'

Ben was silent.

'You okay, mate?'

Ben went on smoking and didn't reply.

The long, dusty line of vehicles rolled on through the morning, as the sun climbed and burned steadily hotter. The dial on Jeff's watch was reading just after eleven when the convoy slowed, then ground to a halt amid a lot of shouting and excitement. 'Some kind of RV,' Jeff said, leaning out of the side to peer forwards. 'Looks like our little war party just got a little bigger.'

'A little bigger' was a typical Dekker understatement. Getting out to stretch his legs, Ben pushed his way up the line towards the front, and glimpsed Khosa for the first time since his release from the prison cell. The General looked jaunty and merry as he jumped down from his Hummer at the head of the line to greet the leader of the forces that had come to join up with them: a small, trim, pigeon-chested commander in mirror shades and a green beret. The strength of troops he'd brought with him more than doubled their fighting capability, complete with an additional four armoured personnel carriers and a pair of towed artillery howitzers on wheeled carriages. By Ben's rough estimate, they were now marching with some six or seven thousand men. It was starting to look like an army.

War was coming, all right.

Bring it on, Ben thought.

The sudden swelling of their forces created more logistical complications while the line reorganised itself before the convoy could move on. The chaos lasted more than twenty minutes, a break that hundreds of the troops took advantage of to jump down from the trucks and relieve themselves in the bushes. It was during that interval that Ben noticed little Mani again.

Buttoned into his badly oversized uniform and weighed down by a bandolier of assault rifle cartridges, the shaven-headed boy bore little physical resemblance to the child that Xulu had captured from the St Bakanja orphanage. Something had changed inside, too. There seemed to be a weight of indescribable sadness hanging from him that no child should ever experience. The AK-47 rifle he'd been issued was far too big for his little hands and short arms, and seemed to have completely baffled him with its alien workings. He'd managed to get a round jammed in the receiver while trying to cock the action, and was vainly wrestling with the weapon to free the trapped cartridge. As Ben approached him, the boy stopped and looked up, seeming not to recognise him for a moment. That was no surprise. Ben was pretty sure his own German shepherd dog, Storm, wouldn't know his master's face right now behind the mask of purple and yellow bruises.

'Let me fix that,' Ben said brusquely. Taking the gun out of the boy's hands, he released the magazine and yanked the bolt briskly to clear the jam. 'It'll work now. Hey, Umutese! Come here!'

Umutese had been strutting past; Ben's sharp command halted him in his tracks, and he stared in astonishment at this white man who only last night had been strung up helplessly before him and now dared to speak to him like an underling.

'If we're going to fight in this army,' Ben told him in a businesslike tone, 'we're going to need weapons. I'm taking this rifle, and I'll have another for my colleague, plus three spare mags each. Any objections?' He didn't wait for a reply. 'Didn't think so. As for the boy here, go and get him some-thing he can handle. Understood? So what are you waiting for, man? Jump to it!' Umutese boggled speechlessly at Ben, then hurried off to obey the stern order.

Jeff had dismounted from the truck and was secretly watching from a distance as Ben dealt with the kid and bossed Umutese. What Jeff observed did nothing to ease the sense of apprehension that had been building in his mind all that morning. A change seemed to have come over Ben since last night, as if a dark cloud had descended on him and had been growing thicker and more ominous with every mile they'd travelled from the city.

In all the years they'd known each other, Jeff had never seen Ben appear so hard and cold. He'd barely spoken a word since the trucks had set off from base. Now he seemed as if he couldn't wait to wade into battle – the dirtier and bloodier the better. It was a look Jeff had seen before, in a lot of crazy trigger-happy nimrods who generally ended up coming to a sticky end. To see it in Ben was deeply worrying. Because when you put a man like Ben Hope into a fight where he cared even less about his own fate than he did about either side winning, what you had was a recipe for serious trouble.

Jeff wasn't a man to show his own feelings too openly. He found it hard to express his gut-wrenching dismay over what Khosa had done to Jude, but that didn't detract from the pain. Whatever Jeff was going through, he knew that the depth of Ben's suffering at this moment must be a thousand times worse. How much pain could a man bear before he finally reached the limit of what his spirit could endure, and began to crack?

Soon afterwards, the redoubled military convoy continued on its way. The choking red dust thrown up off the road by the pounding of a thousand tyres found its way through every crack and into every crevice, until you could feel it crunching between your teeth and rubbing like sand between your skin and clothing. The men aboard the trucks sweated in the airless heat, and smoked, and fiddled with their weapons, and gradually spoke less and less. The atmosphere grew more intense with every mile as they rolled onwards, as if the turning of their wheels was generating a static charge that kept building and building until the whole jungle seemed to vibrate and pulse with it. Birds screeched and exploded from the treetops in flapping flocks that swooped away to safety at the passing of the convoy. Troops of monkeys chittered and howled unseen from high up in the dense canopy, sharing warning signals that could be heard for miles. The sky grew overcast with leaden clouds, threatening thunder.

Onwards and onwards the vehicles rumbled, crossing bridges over small rivers and passing villages. People at the roadside stared. Some waved, but most looked frightened. A young mother gathered her infant and ran away, yelling loudly to alert her fellow villagers.

But the villagers, for once, had nothing to fear. Jean-Pierre Khosa had bigger fish to fry that day as he led his army towards Luhaka, and glory.

Chapter 36

'No! No! NO! I don't care! I want that rock! I don't give a damn what it takes to get it! You hear me, Bronski? I WANT IT!'

Victor Bronski held the phone six inches away from his ear and let the boss's rant run its scalding course. Even Eugene Svalgaard could only scream and rage for so long before he exhausted himself. Bronski had decided to be patient with him, under the circumstances. After all, it wasn't every day you were told that you'd just been rather unsubtly conned out of fifty million bucks by a bunch of gangsters. His employer's reaction was fairly understandable.

At last, Svalgaard settled down from his apoplectic fury and his voice rasped with mere boiling anger. 'I blame you for this, Victor. Jesus Christ, what kind of lame-ass outfit are you running over there? You told me this would be easy. You promised you'd get me that diamond. You told me—'

'I never said it would be easy, boss,' Bronski interrupted, firm but calm. 'Don't recall using that particular word. And I made no promises. Khosa and his associates are not people that any sane person would do business with. What happened was never totally out of the question. Hockridge and Weller both knew the potential risk involved.' And so had Bronski, or he wouldn't have kept himself at a safe distance from the meeting.

'Maybe I should come out there and take care of this goddamn thing myself. In fact, I think I'll do just that. What am I wasting my time for in Kenya anyway? This place sucks ass and I can't stand it anymore. Sit tight and wait for me. I'm coming.'

'Boss—'

'You still have those three guys, right? Shelton, Gasser and what's-his-name?'

'Jungmayr.'

'I'll get six more. Surely we can do this job with ten men? Or eight more, or twenty. I really don't care. I'll hire friggin' Chuck Norris and fly out there with another fifty million dollars and tell this Khosa dickwad that this time, he screws with me, he's gonna regret it.'

Bronski ran his fingers down his face, struggling to keep his patience. 'Get some therapy, boss. You're already fifty million down. Would it be too much to suggest that you cut your losses and walk away at this point?'

'Walk away? Are you out of your mind? That diamond is mine and I'm not leaving Africa without it. Get me?'

'Whatever you say, boss. But don't come to the Congo. If you think Kenya's bad, you really wouldn't like it here. And hang on to your money for now. I'll see if there's another way to deal with this situation.'

'Great. Why don't you do that? And don't call again until you've got something better to tell me.'

That phone conversation was now twenty-two hours old. Since Bronski had broken the news to his employer about the disastrous failure of the deal, he and his remaining team members had been busy. Bronski's first and most obvious step in trying to rescue the situation had been to locate the whereabouts, with a view to tracking the movements, of César Masango.

For a man of Bronski's skill and generous bribery budget, it hadn't been hard to find out his home address: a sprawling nine-bedroom, ten-bathroom villa on a verdant acre plot in the exclusive quarter of Mont Fleury, Ngaliema, on the western side of Kinshasa not far from where the Lukungu River cut through the city. The property was gated and surrounded by a high stone wall that bounded the street, but it was easy enough to mount watch on. Between Bronski in the van and Shelton, Gasser and Jungmayr in two cars, all equipped with serious binoculars and long-range camera lenses, they'd been keeping up a constant visual surveillance for the last sixteen hours. Setting up the phone tap hadn't been too much harder, thanks to the primitive Congolese telephone wiring and a few Radio Shack bits and bobs that were child's play to crocodile-clip into place in the connection box outside the house. Shelton had set off a dog barking ferociously while he was sneaking around the grounds, but the animal thankfully didn't make an appearance and Shelton had made it back to his car unscathed and unseen.

By nine o'clock that morning, all that the surveillance operation had managed to ascertain was that Madame Olive Masango appeared to have spent the previous night alone in the big villa. The black Mercedes E-Class limousine registered to her husband – that information courtesy of more bribes to the appropriate officials – was apparently not at home, while the gold roadster registered in her name sat on the driveway, gleaming in the sunshine. The only visitor the watchers had observed coming or going was a burly grey-haired woman who had driven off in a battered Renault 4 at five thirty the previous afternoon and turned up again this morning at 8 a.m. sharp, presumably a full-time, live-out housekeeper. Olive Masango herself, a handsome and fashionably dressed lady in her early forties, had been glimpsed only a few times as she pottered about the rooms and gardens of the large villa (more often than not nursing what looked like a large gin and tonic, leading Bronski to wonder if she had a problem with the booze) and basked in the comfortable lifestyle that her marriage provided.

Nine thirty: still no sign of César, no telling where he'd gone and when he might return. As time passed, Bronski was debating the pros and cons of kidnapping the good lady, which would have been a simple matter of driving up to the house, snatching her, and bundling her into the back of the van, gagged and bound, to be whisked off to a secure location. Easy pickings; and after what Cesar's thugs had done to Hockridge, Weller, and Addington, Bronski was running a little low on human kindness right now. If she knew anything, there was no question she'd talk. If she knew nothing, she was still a useful hostage, potentially. In such a case, much would depend on which way César's loyalties swung under pressure: in his wife's favour or that of his employer. Bronski suspected it might be the latter, but experience had taught him not to judge too hastily.

Keeping the idea in reserve as a potential Plan B, for now Bronski went on watching and waiting.

Chapter 37

If sneaking into the coltan mine had been fraught with problems, getting out again had proved even trickier. Jude and Rae had managed to retrace their steps back through the boneyard of the cavern and up to where the tunnel joined the main shaft, but for a long time it had looked as though they would make it no further without getting caught. The buzz of activity around the mine entrance had, if anything, grown even more frenetic with soldiers milling around, trucks roaring, lights blazing. There was no way out, and no choice but to hide in the rocky shadows of the narrow side tunnel until the coast cleared.

They'd waited there for hours, huddled together in the darkness. Rae had eventually dozed off, with her head resting on Jude's shoulder. As much as he found the closeness and the touch of her hair against his cheek exciting, Jude was on edge with the constant worry of the diamond in his pocket. The instant Khosa discovered it had been stolen and a lump of rock substituted in its place, he would have the whole place torn apart looking for it. Without any doubt, he would have the thief torn apart too. Dismembered, dissected, and eaten . . .

Jude could hear Khosa's and Masango's laughter. He could see his own heart, still beating, torn from his chest. Khosa's teeth biting into it. Ripping. Gouging. Swallowing.

Jude's eyes flickered open. He realised with a start that he'd been sleeping, though hardly very restfully. He was still pressed uncomfortably against the rocks with Rae's head on his shoulder. She was stirring in her sleep, making small twitching movements as her own unpleasant dreams played out in her mind. Jude peered past the mouth of the tunnel, in the direction of the main shaft, and saw that it was empty. He could hear nothing. The faint light of early morning was shining in from outside.

'Wake up,' he whispered in Rae's ear, and gently prodded her. Her eyes snapped open in alarm and she gasped. 'What's happening?'

'The soldiers have gone,' he murmured.

They crept out of the passage and ventured tentatively up the slope of the shaft, the way they'd come the night before. Emerging into the daylight, they found the mine entrance completely deserted.

'So Khosa wasn't kidding when he said he was marching on Luhaka at first light,' Rae said. 'He really means to attack his brother.'

'Khosa never kids,' Jude said. 'I can tell you that much about the bastard. He's gone, all right. And it looks like he's taken every last scrap of his army along with him. But what happened to all the workers?'

'Locked up somewhere,' Rae said. 'Or killed.'

'They wouldn't kill their own workers, surely. Not all of them.'

'It wouldn't surprise me. Plenty more where they came from.'

The walk through the deserted camp was an unsettling experience. The dirt road was scored with countless fresh tyre tracks where the trucks had sped away at first light or even before. Jude and Rae reached the gates and found them unmanned. They climbed the wire, dropped down to the other side and kept walking towards the bridge, glancing nervously around them every few moments in case of an ambush. Jude kept fingering the diamond in his pocket. A huge part of him bitterly regretted taking it, just the same way he'd felt after he'd stolen it from Pender aboard the ship. It felt like a giant homing beacon that could be seen from space, screaming: 'Here I am!' But so far, they seemed to be getting away clean.

'Are you okay?' he asked.

She nodded, after a pause and a small shudder. 'I'm okay,' she replied, although both of them knew that nobody who witnessed what they had just hours earlier could ever really, truly, be okay – not ever, as long as they lived.

There wasn't a vehicle or a living soul in sight as they made their way along the concrete roadway that spanned the top of the dam. To their right, the early morning sun glittered on the river; to their left, the cascading water powering the hydro plant roared and foamed and filled the air with a vibrant freshness that seemed to help wash away the dark memory of last night.

'That way to the city,' she said, pointing ahead once they'd reached the far riverbank.

'Let's go,' he said, stepping up his pace, but she clasped his arm and held him back. 'Jude—'

'What?'

'I hate to say this, but if Khosa's gone . . .'

'He's taken my dad with him. I know. And Jeff, too. They're not here any more.'

'Jeff? Don't tell me. Another Special Forces warrior friend of yours.'

He ignored the jibe. 'How far away is Luhaka from here?'

She replied, 'Sixty miles, give or take. Further away than

259

it sounds, in the Congo. The transport system isn't exactly state of the art, as you may have noticed.'

'But I can still get there within a few hours,' Jude said. 'There's got to be some kind of vehicle in the city. A truck, a car, anything with wheels and an engine.'

'You want to go to Luhaka,' she said, staring at him as though he were nuts.

'I have to find them.'

The sun was climbing fast in the east, growing warmer by the minute. After half an hour's hot, dusty walk, during which they spoke little, Jude and Rae reached the deserted fence and could see the city buildings beyond.

'If you're sure,' she said.

'Dead sure.' He grabbed the wire and started to climb.

As they reached the outskirts, they met with the first signs of life they'd seen that morning. The construction crews toiling away on the half-built edge of the city gave them a few strange looks as they walked by, then returned to their business. 'Those guys are all Chinese,' Jude muttered. 'Every single one of them.'

Rae smiled with a hint of triumph. 'Told you, didn't I? Khosa's army, the coltan mining operation, the Chinese building a city in the middle of the jungle that no African civilian will ever set foot in. It all fits. This is the proof of everything we've been saying. God, if only Craig could have seen this place close up.' Her smile fell at the thought of Munro, and she was silent for a while as the two of them walked on. Leaving the construction zone behind, they found themselves trekking through the eerie, empty streets of a ghost town.

'This reminds me of one of those zombie movies,' Jude said, looking around him.

'Relax, I don't think we're going to find any zombies here.'

'I wouldn't care, as long as we could find some transport. Not so much as a bloody bicycle, damn it.' He touched the lump in his pocket and gave a bitter chuckle.

She asked, 'What's funny?'

'I was just thinking, this thing I'm carrying could buy us a thousand Ferraris, or all the private jets we wanted to fly anywhere in the world. And we're scratching around looking for any old banger that'll get us out of here.'

'That's no chunk of glass, is it?'

'It certainly is no chunk of glass.'

'Where the hell did it come from? How did you know Khosa had it?'

'Long story,' he said.

'You know what'll happen when he finds out it's gone, don't you? He'll kill you, too.'

'I had to take it,' Jude said defensively.

'I hope you know what you're doing.'

Jude was about to reply, 'Screw the bastard,' when the sound of an engine froze the words in his mouth. Moments later, his search for a vehicle was over.

The problem was, there were three soldiers sitting in it.

The open Jeep came speeding around a corner, raced towards them and screeched to a halt. The driver stayed behind the wheel, but the other two spilled out and aimed their weapons at the pair of intruders walking in the middle of the road.

'Put your hands up! You are not permitted here!'

Rae glowered at them indignantly and snapped, 'How dare you point those guns at us? Don't you know who I am? Lijuan Wu, Assistant Executive Director of the Zyu Industries Corporation that owns this city. So lower those weapons at once, before I report this incident to your superior officer.'

Jude was almost as taken aback by her fierce display of

authority as the soldiers were. Despite her filthy clothes and dishevelled appearance, Rae was suddenly quite believable as a high-flying exec come to check on her company's foreign investment. The Africans hesitated, seemingly unsure as to how to handle a situation so far above their pay grade. The one who appeared to be in charge chewed his lip and then flapped a vague hand in the direction of the battered green military radio set that nestled in the back of the Jeep. 'We will radio Captain Umutese. He will know how to deal with this.'

But just as the soldier was reaching for the radio, he jerked backwards as though he'd been hooked up by a cable to an invisible speeding train. The sound of the gunshot came a fraction of a second later, but he was already dead by then. His body bounced off the side of the Jeep and hit the ground.

Jude hauled Rae back as the firefight erupted. The second soldier dived behind the front wing of the Jeep and rattled off a deafening stream of bullets in a wide arc, unable to see the hidden shooter. But the hidden shooter could see him just fine, and picked him off with a bullet that raked over the top of the Jeep and caught him high in the chest. The soldier let out a yell and staggered back, finger still on the trigger, emptying what was left in his gun's magazine straight through the flimsy metal of the Jeep's bonnet and side before collapsing on his back. The third soldier, still sitting behind the wheel when the shooting began, was trying to scramble away to safety when he too was hit and went down in a sprawling heap.

The shooting stopped. Jude and Rae were painfully exposed in the middle of the street with nowhere to take cover, but it seemed that whoever had killed the soldiers had no interest in gunning them down as well. They stood rooted in the sudden silence, stunned by the suddenness of the attack and the speed with which it had ended.

Just then the shooter appeared, stepping out from between two buildings across the street with a black automatic weapon in his hands and a huge grin plastered across his very familiar face as he started walking towards Jude and Rae.

'Well, look what the cat dragged in,' he laughed.

Chapter 38

Jude's eyes opened wide and his heart jumped. 'Tuesday! Is that you? Christ, it is you!'

Rae said, 'I'm guessing this isn't your father.'

'I can hardly believe it,' Jude cried out as he ran across the street to meet his friend. It had only been days since they'd last seen one another, but so much had happened that it felt as if six months had passed. Jude was even more astonished when Tuesday's bare-chested companion appeared at his side, holding a shotgun.

'This is Sizwe,' Tuesday said. 'Remember him?'

'I'd like you to meet Rae,' Jude said, waving her over. She approached just a little cautiously, eyeing the two strangers and the guns.

Jude was so full of questions that they were all tripping over each other to come out. Why was Tuesday still in the city? What was Sizwe doing there? Had they any news of Ben and Jeff? He knew he'd get all the answers in due course, and more. In the meantime, he had some explaining of his own to do. Pointing at Rae, he said, 'Khosa had the two of us locked up together in a kind of prison camp, just over there, the other side of the river.'

'Jude got me out,' Rae said, smiling at him.

Tuesday blinked. 'You're kidding me. We thought you

must be the other side of the bloody country. All this time, he was keeping you nearby?'

'That's what I thought about you, too,' Jude said. 'They set the whole thing up that way to fool us.'

'This place is even more unbelievable than I'd imagined it to be,' Rae said, almost twitching with excitement to see more.

'You want unbelievable,' Tuesday told her, 'you should check out the Dorchester. That'll blow your socks off.'

Jude blinked. 'The Dorchester?'

'It's just a few blocks over that way,' Tuesday said, pointing down the street. 'Khosa's got his presidential suite on the top floor. And speaking of Khosa, where the hell's he buggered off to in such a hurry? One minute the place was crawling with troops, the next it just emptied itself. I haven't seen that many trucks rolling out since Afghanistan.'

'Luhaka,' Jude said. 'It's a province about sixty miles from here. Khosa's off to attack the capital.'

'His brother is governor there,' Rae filled in. 'It's a military coup.' She said it as though military coups were an everyday fact of life in the Congo – which, in fact, was more or less the case.

'How come you know so much?' Tuesday asked Rae. Jude answered for her, explaining quickly that she was a journalist who'd come to Africa to investigate Khosa's involvement in the illegal mines and the mysterious Chinese city. Tuesday listened intently, absorbing the details as fast as Jude could spill them out. When Jude had finished, Tuesday in turn filled them in on the events that had taken place in Jude's absence. He held back the worst details about the savage beating that Ben had taken, so as not to upset Jude. But there was one piece of news that couldn't be censored out.

'I've got to tell you, Gerber didn't make it. I know you

and he were buddies. I'm really sorry. All I can say is, it was quick.'

Jude's shoulders slumped. 'How . . . how did he die?'

'Like a bloody hero, mate. Tried to shoot Khosa, took out a couple of his officers. A Marine to the last.'

Jude felt a real pang of sadness. Poor Lou. But there was little time for mourning. 'We have to get out of here,' he said. 'If Khosa's taken Ben and Jeff, I've got to find them.'

'With you there,' Tuesday said.

Until that moment, Sizwe had been listening silently. Now he said, 'I am coming too. I have no home to return to, and no life until I have done what I came here to do. Khosa must die. Where he is, I must go.'

'So it's settled,' Tuesday said. 'Luhaka it is.'

Jude turned to look back at the Jeep. Smoke was trickling out from the slots in the radiator grille. The bonnet was riddled like a colander, and there was little point in even opening it to check the state of the engine inside. The Jeep wasn't going anywhere, that was for sure. 'The question is, how do we get there? I haven't seen a single other vehicle in this place.'

'Nor us,' Tuesday said. 'But someone said there's an airport on the west side of the city. Might be something there, even if it's just an old truck.'

Jude remembered the ragtag squadron of military helicopters at Khosa's base in Somalia, and his eyes lit up as an idea struck him. 'When the army set off this morning, did any choppers pass over?'

'Nothing. We were right at the perimeter. We wouldn't have missed them.'

'Then there's a good chance that we'd find at least one at the airport. Can you fly one of those things?'

Tuesday shrugged. 'I had a pal on the army helicopter

course. He showed me a couple of things. I suppose I could give it a go. How hard can it be, eh?'

Rae looked unsure, but Jude was on a roll with excitement at the idea. 'If we could get airborne we could fly to Kinshasa and from there to Luhaka.'

Rae frowned at him. 'Luhaka is to the north-east, Kinshasa is to the south-west. What the hell do you want to go all that distance out of your way for?'

'To get you safely to the US Embassy,' Jude told her. 'You're a kidnapped American citizen held for ransom, with no papers, no money. They can contact your family to say you're safe, and get you home.'

Rae shook her head. 'I'll call home myself, first chance I get,' she said. 'I know how sick with worry they must be. But I'm not going back. Not yet, anyhow.'

'*What?*'

'Don't you see? This place being suddenly empty is a fabulous opportunity for me. The photo equipment and SD cards the soldiers took when Craig and I were captured might still be here somewhere – and if they are I'm going to find them. If not, there's got to be a camera or a phone that I can use to take more pictures of that mine, the city, the whole damn thing. One way or the other, I'm not leaving here without the evidence I came for.'

Jude stared at her. 'You don't give up, do you?'

'I told you, Craig gave his life for this. I can't let him die for nothing.'

Jude hadn't foreseen this at all. He was suddenly torn.

'Go,' she said, touching his arm. 'Get out of here and find your friends. I'll be fine.'

'What if those three weren't the only soldiers Khosa left behind to guard the place while he was gone?'

'And I'm not going to be responsible for slowing you

down,' Rae said resolutely. 'I can take care of myself.'

'Yeah, like when you were kidnapped.'

'You're wasting time discussing this. I'm not changing my mind.'

Tuesday interrupted them. 'Listen, guys, whatever you decide to do, decide it quickly. If this Luhaka is sixty miles away it's going to take them a while to get there, but the clock's ticking. Sizwe and I can't hang around waiting for you.'

'Then I've decided,' Jude said grimly. 'I'm not leaving until she does.'

'Okay, okay,' Rae relented, holding up her hands. 'Compromise. Give me six hours. Just to let me have a chance to do what I need. Then we all leave here together. Agreed?'

Tuesday shook his head. 'No can do, sorry. Two hours, max. That'll give me time to get to the airport and figure out how to fly the bloody chopper. Assuming there is one to fly. If not, we're screwed anyway, and we'll have to come up with a Plan B.'

'I can't do anything in two hours,' Rae said. 'Give me four.'

Tuesday sighed, glanced at Jude, and said, 'You got three. I won't budge on that, okay? Ben and Jeff will be out there in the thick of it sometime in the next few hours. Maybe I can't help them, but I'm damned if I'm missing the chance to try.'

Rae nodded. 'It's a deal. We'll meet you back here three hours from now.' Turning to Jude, she said, 'You didn't have to do this for me, but I appreciate it that you did. Thank you.' She moved close to him, raised herself up on tiptoe and pecked him on the cheek. The kiss froze Jude up like an idiot, and he stood there staring at her.

Tuesday gave them a couple of walkie-talkies that he and

Sizwe had taken from the soldiers they'd run into, and showed them which channel to use. He also had a pistol lifted from one of the bodies, which he offered to Jude. 'Just in case you meet up with any more unwanted company. Can you handle that?'

'Yeah, I can handle it,' Jude said, taking the gun and stuffing it in his belt behind the right hip, the way he'd seen Ben do. 'I think.'

'Good luck, guys,' Tuesday said as he set off at a run, Sizwe jogging after him. 'You've got three hours.'

Still no sign of the black Mercedes as the morning ticked by and the sun bearing down on Mont Fleury threatened to cook Victor Bronski inside the surveillance van. He'd resorted to running the engine for the air con when his phone buzzed. The call was from Gasser, who was with Shelton a quarter of a mile away watching the villa from the other side and probably suffering just as badly as Bronski. Gasser was calling to tell him to tune into the radio. It sounded urgent.

'I'll call you back,' Bronski said.

The local stations were all in French. Bronski quickly dialled up BBC World Service and caught the tail end of the announcement saying: '. . . *the large contingent of rebel troops was sighted this morning advancing within ten kilometres of Luhaka City's western outskirts. Local reports suggest an imminent coup on the governorship of the province; no further details are available at this time but we hope to bring you an update shortly as the situation develops . . .*'

Bronski turned it off and ran the numbers in his head. If someone was about to launch a coup on Louis Khosa, he had a pretty good idea who that someone might be: a certain loving brother with a serious axe to grind, his eyes on political power and a fifty-million-dollar fortune in his pocket.

'Anything to do with us?' said Gasser when Bronski called him back a moment later.

'Could explain why our boy's not home,' Bronski said. 'Stay tuned and let me know where it goes.'

'Copy.'

Then Bronski saw a movement in his wing mirror and said, 'Hold it. Scratch that.'

The black Mercedes purred up the street. The sunlight gleamed dully on paintwork streaked with dust after a long drive out of the city. The car paused as the villa's automatic gates swung open to let it through, then glided up the drive and parked in the shade of the trees next to the gold roadster. The gates swung shut behind it.

Bronski put down the phone and snatched his binocs to see the tall figure of César Masango unfold himself from behind the wheel of the limo and close the door. He was alone, and looked calm and relaxed, if a little stiff from the drive.

Bronski tracked him as he walked to the house. When Masango disappeared inside, Bronski picked the phone up again and said to the waiting Gasser, 'Honey, I'm home.'

'You want to make a move?'

Bronski gritted his teeth. He'd have dearly loved to get out of this hellhole of a van, but he was far too disciplined to let weakness get the better of him. 'Not just yet. Let's hang back a while longer and see what he does next.'

Chapter 39

RFI 1 Afrique was the station playing on the radio inside Jean-Pierre Khosa's Hummer as the spearhead of the convoy roared into the outskirts of Luhaka City. The army's approach was no longer any secret. The news bulletins were buzzing with tense speculation over the imminent outbreak of fresh fighting in an area that had remained relatively peaceful since the last civil war. Lying seven hundred miles from the mouth of the Congo River, with a population of just over 800,000, Luhaka was one of the country's most important inland ports after Kinshasa and a key hub for river and land transportation, marketing and distribution of goods across the nation. Whoever controlled it commanded immense power.

In Luhaka City itself, the rumours that had been escalating all morning had reached fever pitch even before the first vehicles of the invading army came storming through. People were grabbing their children and whatever money or valuables they possessed, and choking the streets in their desperation to get away.

The actual sight of the column of heavily armed vehicles laden with soldiers caused outright panic to spread like wildfire through the outside edges of the city. The first casualties of the attack weren't military ones, but civilians who were too slow or too infirm to keep up with the stampeding crowds and were trampled underfoot.

Anyone who had dared stop to watch as the convoy blasted by might have caught a glimpse of the fearsome scarred face of the General himself through the dusty windscreen of the Hummer that led the charge, stretched out in the passenger seat, boots up on the dash, arm dangling nonchalantly out over the sill, flash of gold catching the sun. Still sated from the diabolical activities of the night before, fire dancing in his eyes behind the mirrored aviator shades, teeth bared in a snarl of happiness as he led his army into battle.

Jean-Pierre Khosa, relaxed and completely at home in his element.

Soon, he wouldn't be the only one.

The long procession of trucks and off-roaders wound its way deeper into the city in a beeline for the governor's mansion at its heart. So far, their approach had met with no resistance whatsoever – but that wouldn't last. Khosa knew that his brother's two-thousand-strong heavily armed personal guard would be deployed to repel the invaders. Louis Khosa wasn't a man to forget his roots, even if he had one foot in politics these days and had exchanged his combat uniform for a sharp suit and tie. Once a warrior, always a warrior. But Jean-Pierre had three times the military force, and he had the hunger to win. Whatever else happened here today, there was no doubt that much blood would be spilled.

It began minutes later, just eight blocks from the governor's residence. The head of the convoy screeched around a corner that had long since emptied itself of fleeing civilians, and found itself speeding into a dead end. The long, broad street ahead that minutes ago had been a colourful buzz of open market stalls selling fruit, fish, and a thousand other goods of all varieties was blockaded from pavement to pavement by a barrier of trucks, Jeeps, heaped sandbags, oil drums, wooden pallets, burning braziers and heavy machine-gun posts whose gunners opened fire the instant the vehicles came into their sights.

The convoy slammed into a wall of bullets that zinged and splatted into metal, glass, and human flesh. The driver at the wheel of Jean-Pierre Khosa's Hummer swerved violently to the left and ploughed a furrow of flying wreckage through an abandoned market stall, sending up a wave of squashed bananas, pumpkins, sweet potatoes, and yams over the front of the vehicle. The driver skidded into a side street and narrowly escaped the barrage of fire from the blockade. A pickup truck managed to squeeze through at its tail, light machine gun blazing, strafing a squad of enemy soldiers attempting to block their path.

Caught out in the open, the rest of the convoy came to a ragged halt in the street and began returning fire on the blockade. The governor's forces defended their position with equal ferocity. During those opening salvos, the air was so thick with metal-jacketed lead that nothing could have lived in the no-man's land between the blockade and the halted convoy. Windows and windscreens and headlights shattered. Cascades of spent shell casings streamed in golden rivers that caught the sunlight and bounced and rolled on the ground. Sparks danced like lightning off the vehicles and metal barriers of the blockade. Grenades popped from launchers and exploded in bright flashes. Vehicles burst into flames, their occupants spilling out left and right. Men screamed and fell and painted the ground with their blood. The stench of cordite quickly filled the air. Among the first casualties of the attacking army was Colonel Raphael Dizolele, sent into combat despite his wounded leg. But there would be many more before the day was over.

The full-on battle had begun.

Several vehicles back down the line, the first that the passengers in Ben and Jeff's truck knew of that first contact with the enemy was when they were violently thrown forwards under braking as the truck skidded to a halt and narrowly missed piling into the one in front of it. From one instant to the next, bullets were zipping holes in the canvas top, punching through the metal of the cab and sides like hot needles through soft butter. A bullet from a fifty-calibre heavy machine gun was a serious projectile, a copper-plated dart half an inch in diameter and as long as your finger. It could shoot through six inches of armour plate or thirteen inches of reinforced concrete, and keep on moving in search of something else to destroy. When it hit a target as delicate and soft-skinned as a human being, it simply tore it apart at the seams on its way through. From a machine gun generating a thousand rounds a minute, it could pulp a platoon of men like diced watermelons within the space of a heartbeat. And when one of the soldiers just a few feet away from Ben in the back of the truck caught one in the upper arm, it blew the limb clear off at the shoulder in a fountain of blood that splashed over his comrades as if a bucketful had been sloshed over them. There was no scream. The shock killed him instantly. But there was plenty of screaming from the others as they fell about in terror.

Jeff glanced at Ben, eyebrows raised. *Here we go*, his look said.

Ben was the only one in the truck not reacting. He barely glanced at the blood, or the shattered body slumping to the floor, and he felt oblivious of the panic and the chaos around him. Jeff's look lingered on him an instant longer, and in that split second Ben could read a thousand anxious thoughts in his friend's eyes. He knew what Jeff was thinking, that he'd flipped, that he was no longer himself.

And Jeff was right. Because when Khosa had hurt Jude

the way he had, he'd cut away a piece of Ben, too, deep in his core. That was the part of him that cared about getting hurt. An unsafe state for Ben himself to be in, but much more unsafe for others.

To let that happen was Khosa's first bad mistake.

Behind them the convoy broke its line as vehicle after vehicle skidded to an urgent halt, filling the street in ragged formation. Officers were barking commands. Soldiers grabbing their weapons. The trucks emptying as everyone scrambled out and hit the ground running through the noise and the heat. Some making it only a few paces before they were cut down and lay where they fell. The familiar chunking clatter of AK-47s interspersed with the rip of submachine guns and the furious roar of the heavy weaponry tearing the street to pieces, drowning out the screams and yells of Jean-Pierre Khosa's fighters in a maelstrom of sound that split the thick humid air. In combat, it only seems loud for the first few moments. The rush of adrenalin as the body's defences and responses amp up to the max very quickly makes you numb to the noise.

Which was something Ben Hope knew all about. His boots touched the ground, and he was immediately at home. As if he'd suddenly found his place here at last. This wasn't Khosa's world any longer. It was his. The violence and gunfire exploding all around him as if in slow motion felt like laughter and sweet music drifting on a summer evening's breeze. His heart rate was no more than sixty beats a minute. His breathing was calm. He was as cool as a stone. The bruises and cuts over his face and body no longer hurt. The weapon in his hands weighed nothing and fitted his body as though he'd been born with it attached to him.

Ben Hope, armed, dangerous, and back in control.

To let that happen was Khosa's second bad mistake.

Chapter 40

Buildings to the left, buildings to the right. Nothing that offered safe cover from the destruction of the heavy machine gunners hunkered down behind the street barricade sixty yards away. But out of sight was better than being mowed down like the bodies already piling up beside the stopped vehicles. Instants after Ben was the last man to jump from the truck, it took a hit from a grenade and burst violently ablaze, belching smoke and flame.

Jeff was making a break for the shelter of a recessed doorway on the right side of the street. Ben followed. Squibs of dust exploded at his heels, chasing him down. He moved fast, but not hurriedly. He reached Jeff in the doorway. The masonry was taking hits, bullets chewing bite-size chunks of stone out of the wall just inches from where they crouched for shelter. Behind them, in front of them, across the street, dozens of Khosa's fighters were doing the same. Some cowering, others ducking around the edge of the disintegrating walls and loosing off bursts of return fire.

'Take your time, eh,' Jeff yelled over the noise as Ben joined him in the nook of the doorway. 'In case you hadn't noticed, mate, we're being shot at here – and you're strolling about like John fucking Wayne!'

The look on Jeff's face made Ben smile. Like an angry

mother chastising a reckless child for skating on thin ice or riding no-hands on his racing bike.

'I can see that,' Ben said. A second grenade hit the burning truck and it exploded, taking out windows and blowing shrapnel like confetti. For a few seconds they were shrouded in blinding smoke.

'So what's the plan, Mr Wayne?' Jeff yelled.

Ben already knew what he wanted Jeff to do. 'Find the boy.'

Jeff blinked. 'What boy?'

'Mani. You know the one I mean. Find him and keep him safe. Get yourselves out of here.'

Jeff stared at him, not understanding. Ben wanted the boy to be safe. He didn't deserve to be in this. But Ben wanted Jeff to be safe, too. Using the wellbeing of the kid was his way of forcing his friend's hand.

Jeff, though, wasn't so easily persuaded. 'What the fuck are you talking about, get myself out? What about you?'

'I have my own plans,' Ben said.

'Like getting yourself killed.'

Ben shrugged. 'I won't be the only one. But not you.'

'No bloody chance, mate. I'm staying right by your side where I can watch your stupid back, like always.'

They ducked deeper into the doorway as a raking line of bullets strafed the wall, clawing brickwork into dust, leaping right and left like a living thing. One of the men taking cover a few yards ahead of them fell back as the side of his head disappeared in a pink mist, and his weapon clattered out of his hands.

Ben moved closer to Jeff and looked long and hard into his friend's worried eyes. 'I need you to do this. Don't make me beg, Jeff.'

Jeff just stared at him, with a kind of desperation in his

expression as he tried to read Ben's thoughts. A terrible realisation filled Jeff's face as he understood. 'Don't tell me – you're going after Khosa?'

'It has to end here.'

'You're a lunatic. There are thousands of the bastards everywhere.'

'Then I guess I'll just have to even the odds a little.'

'You can't kill them all.'

'If Jude's alive,' Ben said, 'tell him that I'm sorry I failed him. Make him understand I had to do this.'

It was goodbye. Ben had nothing more to say. Before Jeff could reply or try to stop him, and before Jeff could see the sadness that suddenly welled up inside him, he slipped out of the doorway and moved quickly back out into the street, using the wall of smoke that was gushing from the ruins of the truck as cover from the gunsights of the governor's soldiers. He didn't look back. Felt the heat of the fire on his face and the sting of the smoke in his eyes as it enveloped him. More gunfire rattled up the street, making it impossible for Jeff to chase after him.

Ben skirted around the rear of the burning truck and reached the opposite pavement, moving fast up the street past the dead and the dying. Bullets snapped past him and kicked craters out of walls. More vehicles were on fire and pumping curtains of black smoke, like a blanket of night through which the enemy's muzzle flashes lit up like burning stars.

But they weren't Ben's enemy. He had only one enemy, along with the men who fought for him, and anyone who stood in Ben's way as he went after him.

You can't kill them all. Jeff's words echoing in his head. Jeff had been right about that. But then, Ben didn't intend to kill them all. Just the ones he saw.

Twenty yards further on, a group of Khosa's men were sheltering behind a Jeep. Its windows were gone and its bodywork was buckled and riddled with holes. All seven men had their backs to him and were firing indiscriminately over the top and around the sides of the wreck, in that way that inexperienced soldiers have of thinking if they build a wall of bullets around them, nothing can touch them. They were wrong.

Ben recognised two of the soldiers. One was the man who had put the rope around his ankles to string him up. The other had been the pickup truck driver who'd enjoyed playing chicken with the prisoner as he'd dangled upside down, bound and helpless.

So Ben shot those two first. Single shots, in rapid succession, two for two, punching out their lungs and hearts before any of them had time to register his presence. Normally, he preferred not to shoot a man in the back; today he didn't give a damn. Their comrades whirled around. One of them was quicker than the others, and Ben shot him third, before he shot numbers four, five, and six, his rifle sights gliding from one target to the next, *bang-bang-bang*, fast and smooth, drilling centre of mass with instant killing power. The seventh man managed to duck down behind the Jeep before Ben could get to him, squeezed off a wild shot from his AK that went a mile wide and then bolted like a frightened rabbit, running straight into incoming fire from the barricade up the street. The governor's forces had saved Ben a bullet.

Collaboration. Your enemy's enemy is your friend, no matter who they are.

Ben filled his combat jacket pockets with spare magazines from the dead men and moved on, slipping from cover to cover, just a ghost in the fog of the burning vehicles. The convoy was a mess, but two armoured cars were slowly advancing and focusing intense fire on the enemy positions, a line of technicals following in their wake spitting fire from their rear-mounted Chinese machine guns.

Ben peered through the smoke of the wreckage and saw the governor's soldiers falling back as Jean-Pierre Khosa's superior numbers wore them down by attrition. In this sort of savage street fighting, there was just no substitute for good old-fashioned brute firepower. Ben could only guess at the number of times General Khosa had fought such engagements before. It didn't matter to Khosa if he left thousands of men and boys dead on the battlefield, as long as he gained his objective. Napoleonic tactics weren't obsolete yet in the age of modern warfare.

The armoured cars rumbled onwards, two abreast in the middle of the road. By the time they reached the blockade, it had been abandoned by the governor's fleeing soldiers. They trampled the remains of the barriers and crushed the bodies of the dead and wounded under their all-terrain tyres, and rolled relentlessly on through. Ben wasn't inclined to tangle with the steel monsters, or the procession of armed technicals that followed in their imposing wake. He was content to let them lead him towards the epicentre of the conflict. Wherever Louis Khosa made his final stand, that was where Ben knew he would find Jean-Pierre.

Chapter 41

But the battle for the streets of Luhaka City was far from being over. Another two blocks further east, the invading forces were being hampered by a rooftop sniper. By the time Ben arrived on the scene he was already causing mayhem and had single-handedly stalled their advance by firing down on them with what Ben realised must be some type of big-bore anti-tank rifle with a supply of incendiary rounds as well as regular armour-piercing ammunition. One armoured car and three technicals vehicles were already blackened wrecks being consumed in an inferno of flame and smoke; many more of them had detoured away up a side street to escape destruction. Dozens of troops were taking cover where they could and firing up at the sniper's elevated position overlooking the street.

He was nested in tight behind sandbags on the top-floor balcony of what had once been a handsome colonial-era townhouse but was now rapidly becoming reduced to a cratered ruin as it was pummelled with gunfire. So far, they hadn't managed to dislodge the sniper, and he was leading them a merry dance. All that was visible of him was his muzzle flash every time he fired, keeping up a steady WHAM – WHAM – WHAM every few seconds that had the soldiers pinned.

Ben smiled and thought, *Good luck to you.* As he watched, a direct hit on the fuel tank of a battered Mitsubishi pickup blasted it apart in a sunburst of igniting gasoline, engulfing a couple of soldiers who were too close and slicing up another with flying shrap. Ben watched them die and felt no trace of pity.

That was when Ben spotted another familiar face. Captain Umutese was commanding the operation against the sniper from the safety of the pavement directly below, where the angle of the wall prevented him from becoming a target. He seemed to have claimed the space for himself and wouldn't allow anyone else to take cover there, as he jabbed fingers and arms in all directions and screamed so loudly he could be heard over the gunfire. At his command, four terrified soldiers were braving the sniper fire while trying to figure out the operation of the Chinese HJ-10 surface-to-air missile whose twin-tube launcher was mounted on the back of a Russian heavy truck. The sniper had been picking them off one by one as if he enjoyed the sport. Every time one was slammed off the flatbed by the force of an incoming round, Umutese was sending in another hapless trooper to take his place. Despite their terror they eventually got the SAM up and running; and now the sniper had taken his last shot.

The blast of the rocket burned brighter than the glaring late-morning sun and shook the street like a five-magnitude earthquake. Umutese seemed only to realise at the last moment that the townhouse walls would come toppling down to bury him where he stood if he didn't get out of the way. He scrambled for safety as the rocket blasted the top floor, obliterating the sniper and taking out much of the roof of the building. Twenty tons of wreckage came down in an avalanche that filled the street with a sandstorm of dust.

The sniper would not be seen or heard again. He'd had

a good innings, but now he was out of the game. *Shame,* Ben thought.

Now it was his turn.

'Umutese!'

Umutese turned at the sound of his name, blinking and squinting through the smoke and the dust to see who had called out to him. Then he saw Ben striding towards him out of the fog. His eyes locked on Ben's face and then flicked downwards to take in the AK in Ben's hands, and he froze.

There are a lot of things you can say to a man you have witnessed taking part in the sadistic slaughter of innocent people, immediately before you mete out the punishment he deserves. *See you in hell. You had it coming. Say hello to St Peter for me. Eat lead, motherfucker.*

But why waste the words?

Ben stepped up to within ten yards of him and hammered a three-shot burst into his chest. Umutese belched a gout of blood that arced from his mouth as he toppled over backwards, arms flailing. One second, and it was over. It seemed like an anticlimax.

Out of the drifting pall of smoke and dust came a gang of Umutese's troopers, alerted by the shot. They should have run in the opposite direction. Ben flipped his fire selector to full-auto, clamped his finger on the trigger and the AK rattled like a road drill as he mowed them down left to right and then engaged the three on the flatbed of the heavy truck. He'd burned through most of his magazine. Ejected it and slapped in another.

More men were emerging from their hiding places, spotting him and moving his way. Ben sidestepped to put the big truck between him and them as cover. A few rifle shots popped his way and bounced harmlessly off the SAM launcher. He popped a couple of shots back at them.

But bigger trouble was looming. The machine-gun turret of the armoured car was swivelling to point at him. Those rounds wouldn't bounce off a granite mountain, and if he didn't do something about it he had about three seconds before the fifty-cal turned him into stewing beef.

In three fast paces Ben reached the truck and vaulted up onto the flatbed. The SAM launcher was still angled upwards on its rotating pivot, pointing at the empty patch of sky where the top floor of the townhouse had been. Ben grabbed the mount with both fists and yanked it around, fifty degrees right and forty degrees down, so that the remaining missile was levelled straight towards the armoured car at point-blank range, and let it rip.

The rocket was midway between the launch tube and the armoured car when Ben threw himself off the flatbed. The explosion slammed him to the ground like a hot wave. The side of the truck shielded him from the worst of the blast, but even as he hit the ground hard, driving the air from his lungs, he had to scramble desperately out of the way as the shockwave from its own missile lifted the truck off its wheels and flipped it like a child's toy halfway across the street, narrowly missing crushing him.

Ben's ears were ringing, his hands were scuffed and bloody from the flying leap, and the hair on the left side of his head was scorched. He struggled to his feet, and took a few moments to get his breath back. The armoured car was a burning shell and nothing at all was left of the soldiers who'd been anywhere close to it. The rest had had enough. Ben saw the figures disappearing through the curtain of smoke. He raised his AK to fire at them, but the barrel had been uselessly bent by the fall. He threw the weapon away and quickly found another in the clawed hands of one of the dead men. He slung it over his shoulder and walked over to the dusty heap that was Umutese's body, kicked it a couple of times to make sure he was properly dead, then bent down to unclip the walkie-talkie handset from his belt, thinking he might be able to locate Khosa by listening in on their radio transmissions.

As an afterthought, he returned to the dead soldiers and relieved one of them of the handheld launcher and a cluster of 40mm grenades he'd been toting through the battleground. The weapon was nothing more than a stubby fat tube connected by a hinge to a rudimentary wooden butt, like a sawn-off shotgun with a single oversized barrel. Ancient, but still pretty damned effective. Ben calmly popped open the breech and slid in a grenade cartridge.

The tower of black smoke from the burning remains of the armoured cars and trucks was blotting out the sun to make the sky look like dusk. The street was half filled with rubble. The place was starting to look like a real war zone. He could tell from the sporadic outbursts of gunfire crackling over the rooftops that the governor's forces had broken and scattered into smaller pockets of resistance here and there. The invading army would mop them up one at a time until, probably no more than a few hours from now, Luhaka would be totally under their control.

That was, if they still had a new governor to put in the old one's place. Ben walked on towards the heart of the city. Looking for more of his enemies to take down.

He didn't have to walk far before he found some. Barely two hundred yards further up the ravaged street, a pair of pickup trucks came skidding around a corner, each carrying four of the militia soldiers who'd joined up with Khosa en route to Luhaka. They looked if they were part of the general rearguard mopping-up operation, scouring the defeated sectors of the city in search of hold-outs to polish off.

Veiled in the dusky light, Ben was nothing more than a silhouetted outline and they flashed right by him. But he had ways of getting their attention. He trained his grenade launcher at the lead truck, tracked it through the sights, and fired just ahead of it like a hunter shooting at a flying bird.

The pickup sped straight into the path of the grenade and caught the impact on its front wing. A flash of bright flame and the truck flipped and rolled, driver and passengers hurled like straw dolls out of its open cab. The second truck swerved to avoid the wreck, then slithered to a halt. Hostile eyes turned back to stare in Ben's direction as he walked towards them, cracking open the launcher and ejecting the smoking spent cartridge. It hit the ground and rolled away. He walked another step. Loaded another grenade and snapped the tube shut.

The pickup driver slammed his gearstick into reverse, hit the gas and spun the vehicle around. It was a heavily modified Toyota Hilux with a thirty-cal Browning mounted on the back, the cab chopped down and spare fuel cans strapped to the bonnet like the Special Ops Land Rovers Ben's SAS unit had deployed in the deserts of the Middle East. The driver crunched it into forward gear and floored the pedal as if he wanted to run Ben down. The rear gunner angled the thirty-cal.

It was just a matter of who pulled the trigger first.

Ben fired from the hip, still walking. The grenade whooshed towards the pickup and smacked into its radiator grille. The Toyota's back wheels bucked up in the air and it turned a somersault as the fuel cans ignited like a bomb and the vehicle was swallowed up in a mushrooming fireball. Ben felt the heat singe his face and ducked back. The Toyota landed belly-up with its wheels still turning. The tyres were on fire. A burning figure of a man struggled free of the wreck and staggered a few paces. Ben let go of the launcher, quickly shouldered his AK, fired twice and dropped him like a sack of washing. He wouldn't let a man burn to death. But that was where his sympathy ended.

Ben took out the second cigarette he'd got from the soldier on the truck. He paused to light it from the flames of a burning tyre and took a long, deep draw. He walked on, the rifle cradled in his arms. Deeper into the war zone. Looking for trouble and ready to cause more.

Ben Hope, evening the odds.

Chapter 42

The governor's forces had been badly outnumbered even before the invading army's arrival. Now they were dwindling by the minute as those troops not prepared to give up their lives defending their governor took to their heels and fled, and the battle for Luhaka became a rout.

To the sound of screams and rattling gunfire, the two hundred men of Jean-Pierre Khosa's advance guard stormed the grounds and buildings of the governor's mansion firing on anybody who attempted to stand in their way, and anyone who tried to escape. The tall spiked iron gates hung mangled from their hinges where the General had ordered them to be rammed through by an armoured personnel carrier. Dead soldiers, invaders and defenders in about equal numbers, littered the front lawns. The somewhat neglected neo-classical façade of the governor's palatial home, with all its yellowed white stone columns and balustrades, was pocked and cratered from small-arms fire, and its dozens of windows were nearly all shot out.

Inside, several of the governor's personal bodyguards lay scattered about the wide entrance hall. Their blood was spread across the marble floor and up the main staircase and adjoining corridors by hundreds of red boot-prints. Gunfire echoed from all around the building as the invaders hunted down and systematically wiped out those who remained. No prisoners were to be taken: General Khosa's orders. Only one resident of the building, the governor himself, was to be left alive for his brother to deal with personally. The dead body of a maid dangled from an upper-floor balcony, shot in the back as she attempted to fling herself to her probable death to the ground below. The butler who had refused to tell the invaders where the governor was hiding had been beheaded, along with all the staff who hadn't managed to get out in time.

Jean-Louis Khosa wasn't a commander to lead from the rear. He had been the first man inside, and the first of his brother's bodyguards to die had been dropped by a bullet from his Colt revolver. Now he swept triumphantly through the residence ahead of a phalanx of his men, surveying his new prize and the spoils of war it would yield. In truth, there was little of value in the place. The Persian rugs now littered with spent cartridge casings were tatty and frayed. Along every wall were empty patches where large gilt-framed paintings had been taken down to auction off. For all that he filled his own pockets from the coffers of his province, Louis Khosa had been living far beyond his means for a long time and the signs of decay were everywhere.

'We will have to redecorate this place after we take power,' the General said to his men, and they laughed. Just then, his cellphone buzzed in his breast pocket. He hesitated a moment before realising what it was, having spent so much of his time recently out of signal range, then fished it out and saw that the caller ID was César Masango.

'Are you calling to receive the news of my victory, César? Then you may be the first to congratulate me, ha, ha, ha!'

Masango didn't sound as though he shared Khosa's

jocular mood. His tone was anxious, even frightened. 'I have been trying to call you, Jean-Pierre. There is a problem.'

'What problem?'

'I received a text message from Promise Okereke. It is the hostages. The American girl and . . . and . . .' Masango hesitated as if he was too afraid to finish. 'The son of the white soldier. They have escaped.'

Khosa gripped the phone so tightly that the plastic casing creaked. 'How could this happen? When did they escape?'

A heavy sigh on the end of the line. 'They were found missing this morning, during Okereke's rounds. I swear I do not know how they managed to get out, Jean-Pierre. I assure you, this is only a temporary setback. They cannot have gone far. We will find them.'

'Yes, you will, César. And this time we really will cut off the boy's hands. Both of them. And the girl's, which we will send to her family with a demand for more money. And, one more thing, César.'

Masango replied hesitantly, 'Yes, Jean-Pierre?'

'I want Okereke blinded as a punishment for his incompetence. Put out his eyes with a hot iron.'

'I will see that it is done, Jean-Pierre.'

The news risked spoiling Khosa's day. He steamed on through his brother's mansion with gnashing teeth and a face like thunder. Moments later, though, there was better news from a wiry soldier in a sergeant's uniform who scurried up to say, '*Mon général*, we have cleared every room and there are no more of the enemy left alive. We found the governor hiding in a bathroom in the servants' quarters.'

'Very good, Sergeant. Take me to him.'

'*Oui, mon général.*'

Louis Khosa was being held at gunpoint in a small storeroom on the top floor. The yellowed paint was peeling off the walls and there was a smell of mildew, but not sharp enough to mask the scent of fear coming off the governor himself. Like his younger sibling he was a large, powerfully built man, but his body posture was slumped in defeat. He was wearing a rumpled white cotton robe that hung open at the chest, as if the attack that morning had caught him unawares and still in bed. Life in the political fast lane.

'Leave us,' the General snapped at his men. The soldiers filed out of the room. Face to face for the first time in years, the brothers stood looking at each other in uneasy silence – though most of the unease was on Louis's side.

The General took off his mirror sunglasses, and his wide-set eyes penetrated deeply into his brother's face. He took in the greying, receding hairline, the sallow complexion, and the paunch that the bathrobe couldn't hide. His brother's use of skin-lightening cream, something Jean-Pierre abominated, didn't extend to his whole body and his bare chest was several shades darker than his face and hands.

'You do not look good, Louis.'

Louis Khosa could barely make eye contact with his brother, especially as he stood now before him, victorious and decked out in all his military finery. 'Let me go, Jean-Pierre. You have beaten me, but let me go. You will never see me again.'

'If I let you go, you will come back with more men and kill me.'

'No. One brother does not kill another.'

Jean-Pierre Khosa laughed. 'That is a good one, coming from the man who would have had me hung and butchered like a pig, for the amusement of his Jew friends. Where is Mendel? I was looking forward to meeting him one last time.'

'Mendel is gone,' Louis Khosa said with a mournful shake

of his head. 'He cheated me and took all the money. Now there is nothing left. I even had to sell my gold rings,' he added, looking at his hands.

Jean-Pierre Khosa rocked his head back, planted his hands on his hips, and filled the little room with his booming laughter. 'The Jew was too clever for you, Louis. Did I not always warn you about him? I told you he was false. I told you he would deceive you and betray you in the end. But you would not listen to me. Me, your own brother, who loved you and looked after you all those years.'

Louis Khosa hung his head and looked pitiful. 'I am sorry, Jean-Pierre.'

'Do you know what is the worst thing about betrayal, Louis? It is to realise that the fault is your own. That allowing yourself to have been deceived is your mistake, because you were too weak and foolish to know you should never have trusted that person. This is how you feel now, Louis. And I understand, because it was how you made me feel when you chose to side with Mendel instead of your own brother.'

'I am sorry, Jean-Pierre,' Louis Khosa repeated, still shaking his head. 'I made a mistake. I ask you to forgive me.'

'Look at me, Louis. What do you see?'

Louis Khosa looked up with red-rimmed, liquid eyes, like a dog waiting to be kicked.

'You see the man who has defeated you,' Jean-Pierre Khosa said. 'I am a leader now, and you are just a follower. I am strong, and you are weak. I am a lion, and you are just a worm. Say it.'

'I am a worm.'

'Say it!'

'I AM A WORM!'

Jean-Pierre Khosa smiled. 'And what do we do to worms,

Louis? What else is there to do to such a pathetic and worthless creature? We squash them. We step on them, and we wipe their remains off our shoe.'

'Please, Jean-Pierre. We are brothers.'

'You broke my heart, Louis,' Jean-Pierre Khosa went on, tapping his own chest with a finger. 'But you also taught me a lesson, and for that I thank you. You taught me never to trust another man, even if he is my own flesh and blood.' He pointed the finger at Louis, his eyes beginning to bulge now as they filled with rage. 'Trust means nothing. That you are my brother means nothing. Flesh and blood are only good for eating. I have lived by this lesson. This is how I have made myself strong. Do you know what I trust, *brother*? I will show you what I trust. I trust this.'

Without breaking eye contact, he moved his right hand to his belt and drew out the big shiny Colt revolver. He held its muzzle under Louis's nose and the man's eyes widened in fear, thinking he was about to be shot.

But Jean-Pierre Khosa wasn't ready to pull the trigger just yet. First, he wanted to show Louis the thing that he knew would crush him even more entirely than a worm squashed under his boot.

'Now let me show you what else I trust, Louis.'

Slowly, savouring every second of these last moments together with the man he had once loved and now hated more than anyone in the world, Jean-Pierre Khosa replaced the revolver in its holster and reached into the pocket where the leather pouch nestled. His fingers closed on it and he took it out, clasping the pouch tightly in his fist, his eyes dancing at the thrill of what was inside. His sacred totem. The symbol of his absolute superiority and undying power to do whatever he desired, for as long as he desired it. Literally, the jewel in his crown.

Louis Khosa could only goggle as Jean-Pierre loosened the drawstring that held the pouch closed. Dipped his fingers inside, closed them with a thrill of excitement around the hard, cold object. With a flourish, he whipped it out for the condemned man to see before he was executed.

And then both men stared as one at the lump of plain grey rock on Jean-Pierre's upturned palm.

Chapter 43

The General blinked, blinked again. He closed his fist around it and then reopened his fingers, as if by some conjuror's trick the worthless rock might have vanished and the diamond reappeared in its place.

It had not.

Jean-Pierre Khosa almost fainted. He actually staggered on his feet. His brother was staring at him in total incomprehension, and the blank look in Louis's eyes was more than Jean-Pierre could stand.

The guards posted outside the door with strict orders to let nobody enter heard the explosion of berserk fury inside the room and exchanged nervous glances, but knew better than to open the door. They had learned that the appropriate response to the General's rages was to let them run their course and pray you didn't become the target of his anger. But this one was like no other fit of rage they'd ever eavesdropped on before. An orgy of destruction seemed to be going on in there, as if a herd of wild rhinos had been let loose in the room and were trampling and smashing everything to pieces. It went on for several minutes before, eventually, it subsided. Not even General Khosa could keep up such a level of sustained superfury without suffering a fatal coronary.

When the peak of his wrath finally burned itself out,

Khosa stood breathless in the wreckage of the room, stared at his bloody hands and then gazed down at the body of his brother on the floor at his feet. Louis's skull was cracked and his brains had been beaten out. Khosa had no recollection of having bludgeoned him to death with the rock, which lay on the floor next to the body, slicked with blood.

But Khosa did recollect other things. Things that left him in no doubt as to who had stolen his beautiful diamond from him.

The miserable thief had stolen it before, from Pender, on the ship. He had wanted it for himself all along. This was why he'd escaped, and taken the American girl with him – just so he could take the diamond for himself! Yes, that was it. Of course it was. The sneaking little *muzungu* rat bastard had somehow managed to take it from him when he wasn't looking. How or when, Khosa had no idea. But he knew it to be so, with absolute certainty.

He would go after him. There would be terrible vengeance. He would make him crawl like a limbless maggot on the ground. He would make him eat his own burnt organs. There would be suffering like no man had ever suffered.

Khosa clenched his bloody fists and screamed. 'WHITE MEAT!! I WILL KILL YOU!!!'

Sixty miles south-west of Luhaka City, the *muzungu* rat bastard thief was getting increasingly worried.

Tuesday had told them Khosa's base was in a building up the street, which seemed a likely place to find Rae's photographic equipment. Tuesday had been right about it blowing their socks off. Neither she nor Jude were prepared for the experience of walking into a deserted luxury hotel in the middle of the Congo jungle. Jude, who had never seen the real London Dorchester, didn't care if this was an exact replica or not. It was weird.

'Probably built for the company top brass,' Rae said as they stared at the marble-floored lobby.

'Like Lijuan Wu?'

'I just made her up. First name that came into my head.'

'Could have fooled me. What about Zyu Industries?'

'Oh, they're real enough, all right. One day you'll be reading all about them and their little schemes in the news. That's if I ever find my stuff. It's the only proof we have.' She didn't look hopeful.

'At least we haven't run into any more soldiers,' Jude said, and touched the pistol in his belt. It felt odd being there. Maybe after about a hundred years of carrying it, he might get used to having a live firearm strapped to his side.

They hurriedly made their way to the top floor, where Tuesday had said Khosa had his quarters. 'He might have stashed the stuff up here somewhere,' Rae said. 'We'll start here and work our way downwards, okay?'

'Tell me exactly what we're looking for.'

'A bunch of silver flight cases, a couple shorter with cameras inside, a couple of longer ones with the telephoto lenses and tripods. It's just the small ones I want. One of them has the memory card in it, with the images of the mines.'

'I'm on it,' Jude said. 'You take this end, I'll check out the other rooms and we'll meet in the middle.'

'Got it.'

It was a busy search, but it was a fruitless one. Khosa's suite contained everything a despotic warlord with a penchant for high living might ever want by way of trinkets and luxuries, but not a single camera and certainly none of the gear his men had confiscated from Rae and Munro. They'd been rummaging through the place for close to an hour when Jude's walkie-talkie squawked, making him jump.

It was Tuesday, saying he'd found what he thought was a viable aircraft and was working on it. The call was an uncomfortable reminder to them that the clock was ticking.

'We're wasting time here,' Rae said, anxiously looking at her watch.

Working their way downwards through the hotel they ransacked laundry rooms, store cupboards, dozens of unused bedrooms, and found nothing. Finally reaching the ground floor, they spent far too long exhaustively searching the nest of passageways that led to the kitchens, the boiler room, and a series of cluttered storerooms.

Rae was almost weeping with frustration. 'It's got to be somewhere!'

Jude would have loved to say something to comfort her, but he couldn't think what. Tuesday hadn't been back in contact. Jude didn't know if that was a good thing or a bad thing. Either way, their three hours were almost up, and his anxiety was mounting. Rae was as focused as a bloodhound on the trail of her precious evidence. He could sense that she wouldn't relent until she found it. Knowing how much it meant to her, he dreaded her reaction if he made a move to tear her away. Yet he couldn't leave her alone in this place, and nor could he give up on Ben and Jeff. It was an impossible situation.

There were now just a few minutes left to resolve it in. Running out of time faster than they were running out of places to search. They'd narrowed it down to a few remaining storerooms and offices on the ground floor, and Rae was digging through boxes and crates and assorted junk like a rescuer searching for survivors in the rubble of an earthquake. Jude was on the verge of saying, 'Come on, Rae, it's no use,' when a bolt of lightning flashed in his mind.

'Captain Umutese,' he said out loud. 'That was his name.'

'Whose name?' Rae asked, glancing up with a frown.

'Khosa's officer. The one the soldiers were about to radio when they caught us back there.'

'So?'

'So they had a long-range radio in their Jeep. They were in touch with the rest of the army.'

Rae didn't understand. Jude didn't have time to explain. The idea was a hell of a long shot, but then so had been the one-in-a-million chance of getting his SOS email through to Jeff Dekker while all hell was breaking loose aboard the *Svalgaard Andromeda*, stranded out in the middle of the Indian Ocean with pirates swarming all over her decks, killing off the crew and dumping bodies in the ocean. Long shots had worked for Jude before, and this one might – just might – work too.

He took the gun from his belt and urgently pressed it into her hand. 'Take this. Stay right here. Lock the door behind me. Anyone tries to get in, you shoot first and ask questions later, all right?'

Rae stared at the gun in her hand, not liking it. She looked up at Jude in alarm. 'Where are you going?'

'I'll be back as quick as I can,' he promised her, and set off at a run out of the building and down the street towards the Jeep.

Chapter 44

On the bullet-scarred corner of Rue Okapi and Avenue Laurent Kabila across the street from what was obviously now the residence of the former governor of Luhaka, an unseen figure watched from a shadowy doorway and counted the soldiers milling around the front of the building opposite.

Finding the spot had been easy – all Ben had had to do was follow the trail of dead men. The doorway he was using for cover belonged to the entrance hall of a large, comfortable townhouse whose owners must have fled at the first sign of trouble. Wisely so, because the house had taken quite a bit of fire during the exchange between the attacking army and the defending forces across the street. Its ground-floor windows were mostly reduced to empty frames, the front door was matchwood and the façade was going to need a lot of stone repairs. The owners had made their escape from the back door, not bothering to close it on their way out, which was how Ben had got inside.

By the time Ben had got here, the show across the street had already been pretty much over. Meanwhile the distant gunfire that had been crackling here and there across the surrounding city blocks had all but died out, dwindling to just the occasional solitary pop. The radio he'd taken from Umutese's body spluttered and fizzed every few seconds, broadcasting snatches of jubilant back-and-forth dialogue in French and Swahili as the troops gained full control of the city. They sounded giddy with happiness at having won.

The outcome of the attack on Luhaka had probably never been much in doubt. But Ben would have advised the winners not to crack open the champagne too soon. Victory had a way of being snatched out from under you at the very last minute. Sometimes, all it took was a determined man with a gun, the skill to use it, and nothing left to lose. And there was one of those standing right across the street.

He took in the scene. What would normally have been a busy main boulevard filled with traffic and people was empty and hushed, as if the entire population of the city had died of plague overnight or suddenly emigrated to Venus. The only vehicles in sight were those Ben could see parked in a ragged formation at the foot of the white stone columns at the entrance to the governor's mansion. One armoured car had led the assault, battering through the gates and soaking up the worst of the gunfire. Behind it was parked Jean-Pierre Khosa's new Hummer, sporting a few bullet holes of its own but relatively undamaged. A motley procession of technicals had followed, with a second armoured car bringing up the rear.

The last stand of the governor's personal guard had been brief but fairly intense, judging from the number of dead attackers strewn about the lawns. Their surviving comrades left outside to guard the entrance were leaning on their weapons, smoking and laughing and generally winding down from the adrenalin-pumped immediate aftermath of battle. Ben counted thirty-four of them, and reckoned there would be at least as many inside the building, if not more.

A lot for one man to go up against alone, but nothing compared to the numbers that would soon start appearing as the hundreds and thousands of troops currently still circling for blocks around, taking out the last scraps of resistance and merrily raping, looting, and pillaging for all they were worth, gradually recongregated around their leader.

As far as Ben was concerned, the time to strike was now.

He weighed up his options, of which he could see just three. The grounds were fenced off from the street by a high iron railing that ran eighty metres both ways up and down Avenue Laurent Kabila. Option A was to slip past the entrance and work his way quickly and quietly along the railing as far as the corner, then creep around the side of the building and look for a convenient way in. Which would be virtually impossible, even for him, to achieve without being seen. He discounted it right away.

Option B was to retrace his steps back a few blocks, find a side street running parallel to Avenue Laurent Kabila that wasn't teeming with soldiers, and track round in a wider flanking manoeuvre to come at his objective from the rear, in the hope that he could slip inside the grounds and either set up a sniper position outside with a good view of the windows, or infiltrate the building.

Option B wasn't much better than Option A, for four reasons: first, the extreme risk of getting nabbed by a street patrol before he even got close; second, the lack of an appropriate sniper weapon capable of picking off a target through a window at anything better than medium range; third, the reliance on pure luck in hoping Khosa would appear at a window in the first place; and fourth, the exposure while crossing the grounds in full view of the rear of the house.

And all of that was even before he got inside and faced the task of tackling an unknown and vastly superior number of opponents without any real firepower of his own.

So, as crazy as it seemed at first glance, Option C was his

best bet. The attack needed to be swift, explosive, and direct, and bold strokes were called for. Option C ticked those boxes just fine. It involved him walking out of his doorway, straight across the street and in through the gate. They'd spot him right away, of course, but before anyone had time to react he'd surprise them with a one-man assault on the entrance, keeping up a steady walking fire and taking down as many men as he needed in order to get inside the rearward armoured car.

That would be Phase One, and he reckoned it was just about feasible if he didn't catch an unlucky bullet.

Phase Two would be where the fun began. Ben ran the scenario through his mind, visualising it frame by vivid frame like a widescreen movie playing in slow motion inside his mind. Jumping in and locking down the hatch behind him. A fury of point-blank gunfire pinging and popping off the armour-plate shell, like being inside a metal drum during a hailstorm. Diving behind the controls, gunning the throttle and rolling straight towards the entrance of the mansion, crushing and battering its way through the vehicles blocking its path and not slowing for the doorway. The thick steel shell of the vehicle smashing past the columns, up the steps and right through the door, bringing down half the wall as it ploughed inside.

Next, Ben visualised himself abandoning the controls and rushing rearwards to grab the tail machine gun and empty it in the direction of the soldiers who tried to storm into the building after him. Piling them up like sandbags all over the front steps. Then clambering up to the main gun turret and turning his attention on the inside of the building, wreaking all kinds of destruction before making his exit back out of the hatch and escaping through the smoke and confusion to go and find Khosa.

Not exactly a subtle kind of strategy. Potentially effective, more than likely a one-way ticket for him. Ben had no problem with that. As long as he achieved what he'd set out to do, he was willing to pay the boatman. Nothing else mattered.

Ben remembered the witch doctor's prediction of his death. Maybe the weird old bastard had been able to see something, after all. Should have put money on it.

He took three deep breaths. His pockets were weighed down with spare ammunition and there was a fresh thirty-round mag clipped into his weapon. Cocked, locked, set to fire, good to go. He wasn't afraid. He would leave that part to his enemies.

He shouldered his rifle, muttered, 'Fuck it,' and stepped out of the doorway to meet whatever was coming.

Except that he hadn't sensed the presence behind him.

'Psst,' said the voice.

Chapter 45

'Psst,' was one of those handy phrases to grab someone's attention when you were about to shoot them.

Ben whirled. Gun up, finger on trigger, eyes wide, heart jolting. He hadn't known many men who could sneak up behind him unnoticed. But this one had. He'd either been inside the house since before Ben arrived, or he'd crept in through the same back door and made his way through to the front in absolute panther-like silence.

'Hello, arsehole. Thought I might find you here.'

Jeff Dekker had his arms folded, his lips pursed into a lopsided sneer, and didn't seem particularly pleased to be reunited with his old pal.

'Jesus Christ,' Ben muttered, lowering the gun.

'No, just little old me. I'm almost impressed you managed to survive this long, gallivanting about this delightful place on your own. Having fun, are we?'

Ben stepped closer to him, back into the shadows of the doorway. The soldiers across the street had noticed nothing.

'What the hell are you doing here?'

'Uh, that would be saving your skin, Major Hope. Intervening just as you were apparently about to do something very moronic, even by your standards. What the bloody hell were you thinking?'

The radio gave another belch of static, followed by a burst of distorted voices saying something Ben didn't catch. He ignored it.

'Don't call me that.'

'What, moronic?'

'Major.'

Jeff frowned at him, then unslung the submachine gun hanging from his shoulder and waved it in the direction of the back door. 'Whatever. Now, if you don't mind, as one shepherd said to the other, I suggest we get the flock out of here. In a couple of minutes' time this place will be crawling with our new friends.'

Ben shook his head. 'I'm not going anywhere. Khosa's still in there.'

Jeff leaned past Ben's shoulder, cocking an eyebrow as he peered across the street. He shook his head. 'Not anymore, he isn't.'

Ben turned and followed Jeff's gaze out of the doorway, just as General Khosa emerged from the mansion and went storming towards his Hummer at the head of a swarm of his soldiers. 'Doesn't look like a happy chappie, does he?' Jeff said. 'For a guy who's just scored a total walkover of a coup and is all set to become the next governor of this shithole. Wonder what's biting him.'

As they watched, Khosa ripped open the passenger door of the Hummer and climbed angrily inside. Moments later it took off with a squeal of tyres while his soldiers piled into the rest of the vehicles, U-turned across the lawns, trampling several of the dead bodies under their wheels, and the whole procession streamed out of the gates with the armoured cars rumbling along in their wake. Going off in a real hurry, as though something serious had come up.

Ben caught a glimpse of Khosa through the window of

the Hummer as it roared past. The driver was punching the gas hard and the engine was revving loudly as they accelerated away, heading west on Avenue Laurent Kabila. The General had a radio handset clamped to his ear and was yelling into it like a crazy man.

One momentary glimpse. One fleeting chance.

Ben slammed the butt of the rifle tight into the crook of his shoulder and tracked the speeding vehicle in his sights. Giving it just enough lead for the figure in the passenger window to travel into the path of his burst of full-auto fire. His finger curled around the trigger, mounting up the pounds of pressure.

His perfect sight picture was jerked away as Jeff grabbed the muzzle of the rifle and jerked it downwards. Seeing the look on Ben's face, Jeff let go as if the barrel were red-hot, and stepped back with both hands raised. 'All right, then. Take the shot, if that's what you want. Get it off your chest. Kill the bastard. But don't look at me when the rest of them turn right round and blow this house apart with us inside.'

It was too late to fire. The line of vehicles was speeding away with the Hummer at its head. And in any case, Ben knew Jeff was right.

But it was painful to let him go like this, with no way of knowing when he'd catch up with the man again. Ben watched his target disappear into the distance. 'Khosa,' he seethed through gritted teeth.

'To hell with Khosa,' Jeff said. 'The fucker won't live long, whether it's our bullet or someone else's that does the job.'

'You don't understand,' Ben said.

'Look at me, Ben.'

Ben looked at him. Jeff's eyes were hard and small, the way they went when he was deadly serious.

'I understand that angry's not the word for how you feel.

307

I feel that way too. That's why we need to back off here. Because angry guys fuck up, and fucking up will get you fucking killed, my friend. You know it's true, because you've seen it happen even more times than I have, to good men who should've known better.'

Ben said nothing.

'So drop it. We'll get the bastard another time – that, I promise you. But for now, this place is gone tits up and we're out of it. Mani's waiting for you.'

'You found him?'

Jeff's rock-hard expression melted into a grin. 'That's not all I found. Bet you can't wait to see.'

Ben was about to reply when the radio gave another popping fizz and a hiss of static that dissolved into the sound of a crackly voice. It was just a nuisance, no longer any use to him, and he went to turn it off.

But then he stopped. Listened. Heard the same voice again, blurting through the traffic. The caller wasn't speaking French or Swahili. He wasn't giving a military call sign to identify himself. He was using real names, which was something no soldier would do over the radio.

The signal was scrambled and kept breaking up. But there was no mistaking that voice.

Chapter 46

'Bloody hell,' Jeff burst out. 'Am I dreaming, or is that—'

Ben held up a hand to silence him.

'*Be . . . pe . . . re you re . . . ing me? This is . . . ude. Over.*' Pause. Then moments later: '*. . . en Hope? If y . . . out there, pl . . . respond . . . This . . . Jude. Ov . . .*'

Ben's hands were suddenly shaking so badly that he could barely press the transmission button. He cleared his throat. 'Copy Lima Charlie—' he began out of habit, which was army radio-speak for 'receiving you loud and clear'. Catching himself, he reverted to non-military language but decided on the spot to use code to identify themselves only by their inverted initials. This was an open channel and anyone could be listening. 'Alpha Juliet, this is Hotel Bravo. Acknowledged. Where are you? What's happening? Over.'

'*I'm . . . city. H . . . with Tuesday . . . coming to find you.*'

'He's at Khosa's base,' Jeff blurted incredulously. 'How the buggery bollocks did he get there?'

Ben closed his eyes. His legs felt suddenly weak under him, and he badly needed to sit down. He could hardly believe he was talking to Jude, and that Jude was alive and safe. 'Alpha Juliet, are you okay? Over.'

Pause. Buzz. Chatter. Then, '*I'm . . . kay.*'

'But your hand—'

Burp. Fizz. '*Wh . . . about it?*'

'They cut it off. The bracelet. I saw it. I—'

The signal seemed to falter for a moment, and Ben was scared he was going to lose it. Then he heard Jude say, '*N . . . mine. Just . . . trick. I'm okay. Not hurt. Com . . . to find you. Over.*'

A trick! Ben was so stunned, his head was spinning. He no longer cared if any number of Khosa's soldiers, even Khosa himself, might be listening in on their conversation. Let them.

'Negative,' he replied, almost yelling into the radio. 'Maintain your position. Do you copy? I repeat, stay put. Do not leave the city. We will come to you. Over.'

'Tell him we'll be with him in thirty,' Jeff said.

Ben looked at him. 'What?'

'Give or take. Trust me. Go on, tell him.'

Not understanding what his friend was talking about, Ben hit the transmission button again and said, 'Hold tight, Alpha Juliet. We'll be with you soon. Repeat, we will be with you soon. Over and out.'

'Let's go,' Jeff said the instant Ben shut down the call. 'I have a Jeep out the back.'

They ran through the house and outside into the sun-blanched heat of the empty street. Jeff's vehicle was a Suzuki four-wheel-drive with a badly buckled front end that looked like recent damage. Its screen was cut down and a light machine gun on a swivel mount pointed between the front seats, overhanging the bonnet. They jumped in, stowing their weapons at their feet where they could get to them fast if needed. Jeff fired up the engine and the acceleration jerked them back in their seats.

Jeff seemed to know where he was going. He swerved out onto the deserted Avenue Laurent Kabila and hung the next right, clipping the corner of the kerb and taking them up an adjoining street that flanked the tree-lined grounds of the governor's residence. The warm wind and the scent of tree blossoms swirled around them in the open cab, mixed with the tang of cordite and burning diesel fuel wafting in from the battle zones all over the city.

'As long as we don't run into too many of our friends,' Jeff yelled over the roar of the engine, 'we should make it all right. Get ready to jump on that LMG, just in case.'

The weapon looked like a relic from World War II. 'Does it work?'

'Ticks away smooth as a sewing machine,' Jeff said.

Ben didn't bother to ask how he knew. He had a more pressing question, one that he couldn't hold back any longer. 'Mind explaining to me how you plan to get back to base in just half an hour?'

Jeff pressed his foot down harder and flashed Ben another of his trademark grins. 'Like I said, I figured I'd find you somewhere around the governor's pad, because that's where both of the Khosa brothers would be. Got myself in a couple of tangles on the way and had to take a bit of a roundabout route. Anyway, while I was hunting about, I came across . . . well, you'll see soon enough.'

They skirted around the back of the mansion and kept going, zigzagging north across the city, swerving now and then to bypass burning vehicles and bodies that lay in their path. A few blocks on from the centre, the roads were mostly unpaved and the buildings looked more like a shanty town. Jeff turned a sharp corner onto a long, straight avenue crowded on both sides with dismal tin-roofed shacks and graffiti-covered concrete huts that looked like bunkers. He suddenly hit the brakes, bringing them to a sliding halt.

'Uh-oh. Company.'

Ben had spotted them at the same instant – a line of trucks and Jeeps speeding towards them, a hundred yards away and approaching fast. They were bristling with so much weaponry that from a distance they looked like giant spiked porcupines.

'Keep going,' he warned Jeff. 'Sudden moves will only draw their attention.'

Jeff wet his lips and eased the Jeep onwards towards the oncoming vehicles. The distance was closing fast. Either the soldiers would open fire on them, or they'd recognise them as the two white men drafted into Khosa's army. Neither was a desirable option. Ben was shifting towards the centre machine gun, ready to act first if trouble kicked off. If it came to a fight, their chances didn't look so great either.

They were just sixty yards away when the approaching vehicles suddenly swerved off at a right angle across a junction. Swaying on their suspension, big wheels biting down hard on the loose road surface, the soldiers packed aboard all clinging on tight. Wherever they were going in such an urgent hurry, the solitary Suzuki was obviously not a priority.

Ben's instinct told him this had to do with the way Khosa had rushed away from the governor's mansion. Nobody would abandon their prize like that, after having gone to such trouble winning it. Something had happened – and whatever it was, it made Ben very uncomfortable.

'Looks like Khosa's pulling a whole bunch of them out,' Jeff said as the last vehicle roared out of sight across the junction. 'Got to be sixty, seventy trucks down there. Maybe a thousand troops.'

'Heading west,' Ben said. 'Same direction we are.'

'You think—?'

'They're returning to base? Possible.'

'But why?'

'I don't know,' Ben said. 'But if they are, we need to get there before they do. Whatever you've got, Jeff, it had better be good.'

Two blocks further north, the cheap housing ended abruptly at the edge of a large compound, several acres of open tarmac surrounded by a high mesh fence topped with razor wire and plastered with stern warning signs.

'This is it,' Jeff said, turning in through a metal gate that had been buckled off its hinges. Now Ben knew what had caused the damage to the front of the Jeep.

As they sped into the compound, Ben realised it was an airfield. Jeff aimed the Jeep towards a cluster of buildings, the largest of which was a metal hangar with some of its green paint flaked away where the lock on the sliding double doors had been shot away.

Jeff screeched to a halt outside, killed the engine, and honked the horn three times, like a signal. 'They're freaked out enough to start shooting at us,' he said to Ben. 'Gunned down by an eight-year-old, after all we've been through. That would be a right pisser, wouldn't it?'

Ben looked at him. 'They?'

'Wasn't going to leave them all behind, was I?'

As the two of them jogged from the Jeep towards the hangar, the small khaki-clad figure of Mani stepped shyly out of a narrow gap in the sliding doors. He was dwarfed by the submachine gun in his little hands. The boy looked solemnly at Ben and Jeff and then glanced back inside the dark interior with a jerk of his chin as if to say, 'It's okay, you can come out.' Five more of Khosa's child soldiers emerged into the sunlight, blinking up at Ben and Jeff with big anxious eyes. A couple of them were Mani's age, the rest a year or two older.

'These were all I could find,' Jeff said, shaking his head.

'I can only hope the rest of the poor little sods managed to lie low somewhere out of harm's way. Here, mate, help me with these doors, will you?'

Behind the doors was Jeff's discovery, a small red and white Cessna Skyhawk single-engined light aircraft. Its silver nose cone gleamed in the sunshine that streamed into the hangar. The official seal of the governor of Luhaka was painted on its side.

'All fuelled up and ready to rock,' Jeff said with a smile. 'The owner obviously didn't manage to get to her in time, or he'd have legged it out of here like a rabbi from a pig roast. Think you can manage not to crash her?'

Ben swung open the flimsy cockpit door and peered inside. He'd flown plenty of small planes in his time, and some bigger ones too. He'd only crashed a couple of them. Once on purpose; and the other hadn't really been his fault. Although his sister Ruth hadn't bought that excuse at the time.

'I count eight of us,' he said. 'This plane's only a four-seater.'

'Oh, I'm so sorry I wasn't able to locate a 747 to accommodate us all in comfort,' Jeff said acerbically. 'They're kids. They'll cram in. So what do you reckon?'

'I can fly it,' Ben said. 'But our destination's a little hazy. Khosa told me Luhaka was about a hundred kilometres north-east of his base. That's not exactly pinpoint navigation.'

'Always looking on the gloomy side,' Jeff complained. 'Then aren't you lucky that someone happens to know the exact GPS coordinates to get there?' He tapped a finger to his brow. 'Memorised them off of the sat nav in Khosa's Range Rover last night. All we have to do is punch in the numbers and Bob's your uncle. Now, is that genius, or what? Don't all rush in to thank me at once.'

314

Mani looked up at Ben, reached up and plucked timidly at his sleeve. He asked in Swahili, 'Are we going home?'

Ben touched the boy's bristly little shaven head. 'You're going to be safe,' he replied. And he could only hope he was telling the truth.

Chapter 47

Pushing hard south-westwards at two thousand feet with the outskirts of Luhaka City a dozen miles behind them and the early afternoon sunlight spangling like a billion stars off the surface of the Congo River to starboard, they saw the dust plume rising up from the twisty dirt road long before they caught sight of the winding train of the military convoy working its way like a procession of little green toys below.

Jeff leaned close to the co-pilot window as they passed over. 'There they go. What do you suppose he's in such a rush to get back for? Forgot to let the cat out?'

Ben eased the yoke back a fraction, lifting them a little higher out of rocket range. There were a lot of trigger-happy idiots down there, and Khosa had an unsettling way of knowing things. He nudged the throttle lever and the airspeed indicator needle edged closer to the red line. They soon left the convoy behind. But it would catch up with them quickly enough later.

One thing he needn't have worried about was the excess payload on board the little Cessna. Two lean, fit men and half a dozen skinny African kids, even with their weapons and ammunition, probably added up to less than the weight of four average-sized affluent Americans. Or one scheming politician and three large bodyguards. The sky was clear and bright, they had more than enough fuel for the short trip, and thanks to Jeff's coordinates the aircraft's GPS was guiding them straight to their destination.

For Mani and the other kids, whose names were Juma, Akia, Fabrice, Sefu and Steve, it was a moment of wonderment being up in the air. The closest any of them had ever come to an aircraft in their lives was to watch them buzzing high overhead, as mysterious and alien to their world as a spacecraft. All six of them pressed against the windows in the back of the cockpit, jostling each other for the best view of the ground below and grinning with excitement as if the terror and confusion of battle were just a faded memory that they could effortlessly bounce back from. Even Mani seemed to have managed to forget, if only for a few short happy moments, what he'd been made to do during their induction training. In their own way, these kids were tougher and more resilient than most adults.

Ben didn't find it quite as easy to leave his troubles behind. He should have been grinning, knowing Jude was safe, but a voice inside his head kept telling him that more trouble, worse trouble, still lay ahead. Worrying made his face hurt. He worked out his tension by abusing the Cessna's throttle, often verging close to the never-exceed speed of 163 knots, which equated to 188 miles per hour, at which velocity the wings began to shake and the whole plane began to feel as if it was starting to come apart at the seams.

'Steady,' Jeff muttered from time to time, one anxious eye hovering over the dials. Ben kept his gaze fixed on the horizon and said nothing.

They flew over hills and vast sweeping valleys of unbroken green jungle canopy. Uplands and mountain ranges loomed in the distance, shrouded in mist. Unmade roads looked like little brown threads through the green, and the great river receding away to the north was a coiling blue python dotted here and there with small fishing boats that drifted lazily on the still water. The miniature figures of people on the higher ground sometimes looked up as the plane passed over, shielding their eyes from the sun. Mani and the other kids waved, but nobody waved back. Ben wondered if the people recognised the plane as an official aircraft. As long as nobody got it into their heads to go fetch an RPG and try to shoot them down, they might actually make it.

Jeff seemed far away, as though he was working over a question in his mind. 'I hate to ask,' he said after a long silence. 'But . . .'

Ben looked at him. 'What?'

'If that wasn't Jude's hand Khosa showed you, then who was the poor sod they lopped it off of?'

What could you say to that?

Thirty-eight minutes after setting off from Luhaka, the GPS was telling them they were close. Ben dropped a thousand feet and spotted the break in the treetops. Soon after that he saw the city, like a bizarre model sprouting up from the middle of the jungle within its fenced-off no-man's land. Beyond the city was the hydro plant spanning the river, and beyond that again lay the desolate wasteland of the industrial zone. From the ground it was screened by jungle. Exposed from above, it looked like a scar.

For Jeff, who had never ventured outside the limits of Khosa's city until today, this was all new. 'What are they doing down there?'

'Mining,' Ben said. 'Gold, diamonds, copper, zinc, who knows. But whatever it is, it's payrolled by someone with a lot bigger reach than Khosa.'

'That would explain a lot,' Jeff agreed. 'Africa, land of opportunity.'

'For everyone except the Africans,' Ben said.

The unfinished airport lay on the far western edge of the city, but Ben didn't intend to touch down there. They came in low and slow, skimming the perimeter fence, their shadow passing over the stripped ground between it and the city like a giant bird's. The construction crews were still hard at work down there. A few of the workers looked up as the Cessna buzzed over.

The street layout was becoming familiar to Ben, and he steered for the centre, watching for landmarks like the barracks building and the replica Dorchester. 'There,' he said to Jeff, pointing out a broad, straight boulevard just a block from the hotel that would serve as a decent landing strip. They did a couple of passes before Ben came in for the final approach, and spotted the figures on the ground running towards the sound of the incoming aircraft. There was Tuesday, waving his arms and grinning a grin that would have been visible from space. With him was a large African man Ben didn't immediately recognise, but thought looked familiar. He was trying to place him when he spotted another figure he had no trouble recognising at all.

At the sight of Jude, Ben's smile busted the scabs on his lips. He hardly noticed the pain.

The Cessna landed smoothly in the middle of the wide boulevard and taxied to a halt. Ben shut down the engine, flung open the hatch and jumped down. Mani and the rest of the kids were peering cautiously from the cockpit windows, obviously scared to come out. Ben didn't want to press them.

'Ben!' Jude ran towards him. His clothes were grimy and Ben thought he looked thin and a little pale; but he knew he must hardly look the picture of health himself. Smiling even more widely, Ben spread his arms to greet him.

Following more slowly behind Jude was a young Oriental woman, about his age or maybe just a little older. She held back and watched with a half-smile as they embraced. Jeff and Tuesday met in the middle of the street and clapped shoulders, the way men do when they don't want to hug each other.

Ben wasn't holding back his emotions. He squeezed Jude tight enough to crack ribs, then stepped back and stared at him with moist eyes. 'You're okay,' he kept saying. 'Thank God you're okay.' He grasped both of Jude's hands and held them out to stare at them, as if he still couldn't quite believe that both of them were still attached. Part of him had never been so happy, but another part had never been so angry that Khosa could have deceived him so cruelly.

'What happened to you?' Jude said, running his eyes over Ben's battered face.

'This? It's nothing. Just a couple of scratches.'

The young Oriental woman stepped up, still giving that half-smile. 'If that's a couple of scratches, I'd hate to see the other guy.'

'The other guy's dead,' Ben said.

'Figures.' The half-smile opened up and Ben noticed how attractive she was. He wondered what she was doing there, and how she and Jude had hooked up.

'This is Rae,' Jude said. 'She's from Chicago.'

'Rae Lee,' she said. 'Photographer, journalist. And hostage, until recently. Jude and I were captives together.'

'Jude got her out,' Tuesday said, wrapping an arm around Jude's shoulders. 'Can you believe they were just a mile or two away, the whole time? Khosa had them in some kind of bloody hostage camp.'

Ben couldn't believe it. 'If only we'd known.'

'That's what I said too,' Tuesday laughed.

'So you must be the war hero I've been hearing so much about,' Rae said. 'Ben, right? I can see the family resemblance. Kind of, under all those bruises. That's got to hurt.'

'She's right,' Jude said anxiously. 'You ought to see a doctor.'

'When I'm shot to pieces and dying,' Ben said, 'then I'll see a doctor.'

'Definitely the war hero,' Rae said, rolling her eyes.

Ben realised he was still gripping Jude's hands as though they might fly away if he released them. Suddenly self-conscious, he let them go, but he could hardly stop looking at them. Jude was looking at them too, and shaking his head as he imagined what it must be like to have one chopped off with a heavy, sharp blade.

'It was Craig's hand Khosa showed you,' Jude explained to Ben, answering the question nobody wanted to ask. 'Craig Munro. Rae's friend. They were keeping him prisoner, too. Khosa had his right hand hacked off so he could pretend it was mine.'

Rae was looking down at the ground, the smile suddenly gone. Ben said to her, 'Your friend, is he—?'

'They killed him,' she said. 'Shot him dead right in front of us.'

'I'm very sorry.'

'He didn't suffer for very long. I guess that's something to be thankful for.'

'When this is over,' Ben told her, 'the people who did all of this are going to pay.'

'Quite a few of them already have,' Jeff put in.

'Not enough,' Ben said.

The African man standing behind Tuesday said, 'Khosa must pay.' It was the first time he'd spoken, and Ben looked at him. Then *looked* at him. He'd been so consumed with relief at seeing Jude again that he hadn't realised that he knew this man.

'Sizwe! What are you—?'

'He's come to help us,' Tuesday said. 'For his family.'

Ben felt a strange chill as he stood face to face with the man to whom he'd promised his wife and children would be safe, only to be forced to watch them all be slaughtered by Khosa's men moments later.

Sizwe must have read the look in Ben's eyes. He took a step closer and touched Ben's arm. 'I do not blame you. You tried to help. Nobody can change what Khosa does. The only way is to kill him. That is why I am here. If you know where he is, take me to him.'

'No need for that,' Jeff said. 'He's on his way.'

Jude's eyeballs bugged out from their sockets. 'Khosa's coming back?'

'Better believe it,' Jeff said. 'And he's not in the best of moods. Someone nicked the jam out of his doughnut, that's for sure.'

Jude and Rae exchanged nervous glances. 'I told you, you shouldn't have taken it,' she said to him. 'I warned you how it would be when he found out it was gone.'

Jude heaved a sigh. He suddenly looked as if a heavy weight was hanging from his neck.

'Taken what?' Ben asked, his heart sinking as he began to fear the worst. Rae wasn't talking about jam doughnuts. Ben said, 'Jude? What did you take?'

Jude gave another deep sigh, then muttered, 'Oh, what the hell,' and dug his hand in his pocket.

It was only then that Ben noticed the telltale bulge, as if Jude was carrying a tennis ball around in his jeans. Ben's heart sank the rest of the way.

Chapter 48

Jude yanked out the leather pouch and rolled the diamond onto the flat of his palm. 'There,' he said, looking at the glittering stone as if it was a turd.

'I'm not even going to ask how you got that,' Ben said. He'd have been happier if Jude had produced a stick of dynamite from his pocket with the fuse lit. 'On second thoughts, I am going to ask.'

'It wasn't hard. Lifted it when he was sleeping.'

'How the hell did you get that close to him?'

'He and Masango knocked themselves out drinking.'

'And other things,' Rae added with a shiver.

Jeff eyed the diamond for a second, then looked up at Jude from under a furrowed brow. 'Wow, clever move, son. No wonder your best friend's racing back here faster than shit through a tin horn. You didn't reckon on him missing his pretty little bauble at any point? Thought maybe he wouldn't mind you borrowing it?'

'What was I supposed to do, let him keep it?' Jude protested. 'You've no idea what kind of power this has given him. He's a total maniac. He worships *the devil*.'

Ben looked at him. 'Now you're talking like a vicar's son.'

'I'm being literal,' Jude said, vigorously shaking his head. 'Khosa and Masango are actual Satanists. We saw them at it. Chanting in Latin. Wearing black robes. Drinking blood. I'm talking human sacrifice. The whole works.'

'Jude's telling the truth,' Rae said. 'We witnessed it together. It was just . . . horrible. They killed a woman and ate her heart.' She shook her head dismally. 'You hear of these things happening. I don't think I ever really believed it.'

Tuesday looked ready to throw up in horror. Jeff cocked an eyebrow at the mention of Satanism, but Ben gave no response. It wouldn't have mattered to him if Khosa was a Jehovah's Witness, a Quaker or prayed to the great god Xenu from outer space. He would still be Khosa. A man's actions, not his beliefs, determined who and what he was. Bad was simply bad, whatever *ism* anyone tagged it with.

'Believe me, we have a pretty good idea what kind of power he has,' Ben told Jude. 'I also know very well what he's capable of doing to get that thing back. You're crazy, you know that?'

'Like father, like son,' Tuesday said, trying to inject some levity if only for his own sake. It didn't work. Father and son both glared at him, and he quickly shut up.

'You'd best pray Khosa doesn't know it was you who pinched it,' Jeff warned Jude, pointing at his heart. 'Or he'll gobble that up for afters.'

'Of course he knows,' Ben said. 'Who took it off him before, on the ship? Who's just escaped? You don't think Khosa can put two and two together? He may be insane and evil and a lot of things besides, but one thing he's not is an idiot.'

'All right, fine. Maybe he does know,' Jude said defiantly. 'But that can't be helped. I did what I thought was the right thing at the time, and I still do. He can't be allowed to have it.'

'Suit yourself. Then what are you going to do with it?'

'You take it,' Jude said, pushing it towards Ben.

'I've told you before, I don't want it,' Ben said.

'But you let me pass it on to you the other time.'

'Yeah, and I should have thrown it in the sea, like I wanted to.'

'Whose is it anyway?' Rae asked. It was the first time she'd been able to get a good look at the diamond close up, and her eyes were fixed on it as though mesmerised.

Jude shrugged. 'The truth? We have no idea. A crook called Pender had it, but we don't know where he stole it from.'

'It's beautiful,' she said.

'It's trouble,' Ben said. 'Everywhere it goes, it leaves a trail of dead men.'

'Sounds like someone else we know,' Jeff said.

Jude shook his head. 'Not anymore. The authorities will know what to do with it. They have databases. If it's been reported stolen, they'll be able to return it to its proper owner.'

'I'm sorry,' Jeff said with a snort. 'Did you just say "the authorities"? In Africa? Are you kidding? That's one way to make it disappear. And some bent police chief will have a nice retirement.'

'Then tell me what to do with the bloody thing,' Jude said irritably.

'How about you wait here for Khosa to return, tell him nicely you're very sorry there was a misunderstanding, and give it back to him? I'm sure he'll be okay about it. Maybe he'll just settle for a kidney.'

Jude went pale. 'That's not funny, Jeff.'

The children distracted them at that moment by emerging from the plane, obviously satisfied that it was safe to come out. They jumped down one by one and clustered shyly in a group, none of them quite confident enough yet to approach the group of adults. Sizwe's hard expression melted when he saw them. Ben noticed the way he was staring at them, particularly little Juma, and knew he was reliving his grief over his dead son, Gatete, all over again. Seeing this big, powerful man struggling not to break down was hard to bear. Ben looked away.

'Who are these kids?' Rae asked, amazed.

'Khosa's boy soldiers,' Ben said. 'The ones we were able to get out of there, thanks to Jeff.'

Tuesday had been frowning at the diamond, and now he was frowning even more at the children. 'That's great. Only . . . what are we going to do with them?'

'Get them out of here, for one thing,' Ben said. 'Before Khosa rolls up with a thousand men.'

Jeff looked at his watch. 'Which won't be long, boys and girls. Sixty-three miles as the crow flies, call it eighty by road. It took a few hours in the other direction, but that was with stopping to RV with some reinforcements en route. Khosa's already well on his way back here with about seventy truck-loads of troops, and he's not stopping to smell the roses. We've been in the air forty minutes and standing around talking for fifteen. Doesn't leave an awful lot of time. So I'd advise that we start thinking about making a sharp exit.'

'That's where we might have a bit of a problem,' Tuesday said. 'I've just spent the last two hours over at what passes for an airport in this place, trying to get one of Khosa's damned choppers up and running. Remember the piece of junk Puma that they used to pick us up from the ocean? It's there, but it's in pieces. Someone's taken the rotors off, and it's not exactly a one-man job to get them back on again, even if you had the right tools, which are missing. As is one of the rotor blades. I searched everywhere, no sign. Then you have the two even shittier Hueys that escorted us from

Somalia. Some half-arsed mechanic's been at one of them, too. Nothing but a dirty great hole where the engine used to be.'

'What about the other one?' Jeff asked, still clinging to hope.

'It's all there, as far as I could tell,' Tuesday said. 'But there's some kind of fuckup in the electrics. Every time you go to fire it up, it goes snap, crackle, pop and smells like burning. Wiring must be shot to shit. Can't say I'm surprised. These crocks have been flying since before I was born.'

'More like since before *us* old guys were,' Jeff grunted, waving a hand at himself and Ben. He shook his head grimly and pointed back at the Skyhawk. 'Not a chance in hell of all of us getting into that. If we rip out the seats and chuck away anything non-essential, we might just about cram a couple extra bodies on board. But not twelve of us. No way we'd ever get off the ground.'

'And there's not a single road-going vehicle left in this whole city,' Tuesday said. 'Khosa took them all, apart from one Jeep, which is scrap now.'

'Then we risk it on foot,' Jude said. 'We can hide in the forest, and make our way to a town.'

'You haven't been in that jungle, Jude,' Tuesday said. 'An army squadron with machetes would take days to hack a mile through it.'

'And there's about a million square miles of it all around us,' Jeff added. 'Trust me, Ben and I have just flown over it. You're not in the Oxfordshire countryside anymore, mate. There *are* no towns, and if there were we'd never get that far. Not with a bunch of kids in tow, and a—'

'A woman,' Rae said angrily. 'That's what you were about to say, wasn't it?'

'Whatever,' Jeff said. 'This is the Congo, not Chicago.'

'I can rough it as much as any man, sweetie pie,' she retorted.

'Don't take it personally,' Jeff said. 'If it was a Special Forces commando unit taking their chances out there in the arsehole of nowhere with a thousand of Khosa's troops hunting them, I'd say the same thing. These bastards are on their home ground. They've been fighting nasty little jungle wars since they weren't much more than his age.' He pointed at Mani, and shook his head again. 'We wouldn't last half a day out there.'

Nobody could doubt that Jeff was making sense. 'Ben?' Tuesday said, and everyone looked at Ben.

'I'm no aircraft mechanic,' Ben said. 'But it looks to me like we have only one option here, and that's for us all to head for the airport and try and fix the chopper with the electrical problem.'

'And if we can't?' Tuesday asked, chewing his lip.

'Then we figure out another way,' Ben said.

Jude was thinking, looking at the plane. 'If you reckon you can fit two more aboard that, then I say do it. Jeff and Ben, get these kids to safety. Tuesday and Sizwe, you go with them.'

'Unless I'm missing something, that leaves two,' Tuesday said, pointing at Jude and Rae.

'We'll be okay,' Jude said. 'We gave them the slip before. We can do it again.'

'And I still need to find my camera gear,' Rae added. 'If it's not here, maybe it's back at the mine compl—'

'Forget it,' Ben interrupted her.

'But it's important,' she protested. 'Without it, I don't have the evidence to prove what's been happening here, and Craig died for nothing.'

'Then he died for nothing,' Ben said. 'Tough shit. He wouldn't be the first.'

Rae looked as if she'd been slapped across the face. Jude flushed. 'You can't mean that.'

'I mean it,' Ben said. 'Nobody else dies. Nobody stays behind.' He aimed a finger at Jude and Rae. 'You're both coming with us, if I have to knock the pair of you out and carry you over my shoulders like two sacks of rice. Understood?'

Jude fell silent.

'To the airport,' Ben said. 'Let's go.'

Chapter 49

The little Cessna couldn't fly a dozen bodies across the city to the airport, but it could serve as a makeshift people carrier. Jude and Rae climbed up onto the port wing, Tuesday and Sizwe perched on the starboard side, and with everyone else crammed inside the cockpit Ben got the engine ticking over at a thousand revs, enough power to taxi them through the streets. He steered awkwardly using the rudder to control the nose wheel and the toe brakes to control the main landing gear, keeping to the middle of the road so as not to snag the wingtips on any corners. It wasn't ideal, but it was quicker than walking.

The airport lay behind wire-mesh fences a few hundred yards beyond the stadium on the western edge of the city. The runway was unfinished and only about half the length it would eventually need to be to land anything much bigger than a single-engined prop. A few prefabricated buildings stood on concrete near the chain-link gates at the western end. The largest of those was a big hangar with steel roller doors locked down to galvanised posts buried deep in the ground.

'What's in there?' Ben asked Tuesday, and Tuesday explained that he hadn't been able to open it. Some fresh gouges and several bullet holes around the locks were evidence of his attempts to break them open using a lump hammer before resorting to his weapon. Nothing doing. Extremely aware of time ticking by, Ben nodded and turned to survey the rest of their options.

Those were exactly as Tuesday had described. Ben recognised the ancient military helicopters from Somalia: the two Bell Iroquois combat choppers and the medium-lift Aérospatiale Puma that had rescued the survivors from the wreck of the *Svalgaard Andromeda* and carried them all to shore. They'd have been safer staying on their raft in the middle of the shark-infested ocean, and not a day had passed since that Ben hadn't wished they'd never got into that damned Puma. Now, he found himself cursing the fact that he couldn't. Its partially dismantled hulk squatted on the hot concrete like a rotting whale on a beach that the gulls had been gradually pecking to pieces, surrounded by grimy old tools and disassembled rusty components, nuts and bolts and gears and springs and brackets and the battered rotor blades themselves – all three out of four of them, seven metres long apiece and showing the signs of extreme wear that had probably accounted for the missing fourth.

'If I was Khosa, I'd get myself a new mechanic,' Jeff commented dryly. 'And maybe shoot the old one while I was at it.'

The first Bell Iroquois was in an even worse state, just as Tuesday had said. Ben couldn't tell whether it was being overhauled or cannibalised for parts – either way, it was scrap. By contrast, the second Iroquois initially looked much more promising, at least on the outside. As a light, fast transport for mobile infantry during Vietnam, the old 'Huey' had been designed to carry twelve troops along with its crew. It would have been the perfect escape for their motley band. But again, just as Tuesday had found out before him, like the rest of Khosa's sad little air force it had fallen prey to the gremlins of long-term neglect, abuse, and inexpert maintenance. Hauling himself behind the controls and flipping all the right switches to initiate the start-up procedure, Ben had to quickly shut everything back down as sparks flew and something began to give off an acrid plastic burning smell. Moments later, a lick of yellow flame appeared from the instrument panel. Ratty old military helicopters in Africa didn't come equipped with foam extinguishers; Ben managed to dig a bit of grimy rag out from under the seat, and used it to beat out the fire before it got a hold on anything seriously flammable.

'Damn it,' he said.

Standing framed in the open cockpit hatch beside him, Tuesday spread his hands. 'I wasn't kidding, was I? Reminds me a little of that old Land Rover you guys have in France. I've checked the main fuses, replaced all the ones I could find from the other Huey, but it's still doing it. Gets a little worse each time. I dare say, you flip that switch again, the whole thing will just go blammo. So unless you have a brilliant idea, looks like we're grounded.'

Ben wasn't getting any brilliant ideas, and he'd meant it when he said he wasn't an aircraft mechanic.

'Probably just as well,' Tuesday said, his worried look dissolving into a sudden cheery grin. 'If it started playing up once we were in the air, we'd be in a right jam. I like to think of these kinds of situations as our guardian angels looking out for us.'

You could always count on Tuesday Fletcher to look on the bright side at a time like this.

Ben jumped out of the helicopter. He could almost hear the wheels turning as Khosa's army grew closer with every passing moment. 'Damn it,' he said again.

Jude and Rae had found a shady spot next to the big hangar and were crouching there together, side by side. Jude was talking to her in a low voice, and she was looking intently at him as he spoke. Ben could see the closeness in their body language. He smiled, watched them a moment longer and then swivelled his gaze a few degrees left towards the hangar's steel shutter door. Locked down tight, while the other buildings had been left open. He couldn't imagine why. Unless there was something in there that Khosa wanted to protect more than a bunch of dead helicopters.

'I want to get in there,' he said.

'It'd take an RPG to bust those locks,' Tuesday told him.

Ben nodded. 'I reckon you're right,' he said.

'And, like, we don't *have* an RPG?' Tuesday said quizzically, watching Ben's face.

Ben said nothing. He swivelled his gaze back away from the hangar, back past where Jude and Rae were still sitting talking, eighty degrees east towards the sports stadium. A few hundred yards away beyond the airport fence, the grey concrete arena walls shimmered in the heat.

Ben said, 'Hm.'

Tuesday blinked and craned his head forward. 'What?'

Ben said, 'I wonder.'

'Me too. I wonder what you're on about.'

'You stay here and keep an eye on the kids,' Ben told him.

'Where are you going?'

'To check something out,' Ben said. 'Jeff, you want to come with me?'

'Anything's better than standing about gawping at this junkyard,' Jeff said.

Without explaining the idea that had come into his mind, Ben led the way at a run out of the airport gates and across the barren, weed-strewn stretch of ground that separated it from the stadium. They skirted the circumference of the high walls until they reached the same shady concrete arch through which Captain Xulu had led them on their first day in the city. They trotted through the coolness of the tunnel and emerged back out into the heat of the sun with the enormous bowl of the arena encircling them.

'What's up?' Jeff asked.

'That is,' Ben said, pointing at a green mountain in the middle of the arena.

It was as he'd thought.

Chapter 50

The mountain in front of them was a large canvas tarpaulin that had been draped over something even larger and weighed down with rocks around its edges to hold it in place and keep off the rain. Ben ran up to it, kicked away one of the rocks and lifted the tarp to peer underneath. Jeff joined him and bent to look as well. 'Well, I'll be buggered. Looks like someone's been doing a spot of shopping.'

'Or had another delivery from their sponsors,' Ben said. 'That's my guess.' They pulled the tarp back further and Ben saw the stencilled Chinese lettering on the wooden crates that were piled fifteen feet high underneath.

'They're not messing about, are they?'

'Must have arrived while we were in Luhaka.' Ben grabbed the rope handles of a crate and dragged it off its pile, letting it crash to the ground at his feet. It broke open. He bent to pull out handfuls of straw packing that protected the grenades inside. He grabbed half a dozen grenades and stuffed them in his pockets. But it wasn't grenades he'd come looking for. Some of the crates were much larger and more interesting.

He turned and looked across the expanse of the arena, measuring it up and running numbers through his mind as he thought out loud, 'Need about nine hundred feet, should be able to do it. Max payload's a little under two and a half thousand pounds. Might need to dump some fuel to lose weight.'

'What are you muttering about?' Jeff asked.

'Come on,' Ben said, and set off running towards the concrete arch. Jeff scratched his head in confusion, then heaved an exasperated sigh and followed.

Fifteen minutes later and a few hundred pounds lighter, the Cessna buzzed over the stadium, dropped sharply down over the banked auditorium and hit the rough grass with a thump and a bounce. Once they were down Ben had to brake hard to slow the plane. He was taking a chance with the landing distance, like he was taking a chance by dumping out most of their fuel.

He taxied the plane round in a wide curve and they stopped with one wing almost touching the mountain of crates. Leaving the engine running he flung open the cockpit door and jumped out, clutching a claw hammer he'd found among the mess of disassembled helicopter parts on the runway. He attacked the piles of crates, shoving the smaller ones out of the way until he identified those he wanted and began prising them open.

The ones containing the RPG launcher and rockets. Working doggedly with the seconds cracking off like gunshots in his head, Ben grabbed the five-foot-long weapon from its box and tossed it to Jeff, who stowed it in the cockpit. That left plenty of room for half a dozen or so of the spear-like 40mm rockets, plus as many kilos of small arms and ammunition as Ben dared to cram on board the plane. Lastly, Ben grabbed a crate full of Kevlar body armour vests he'd found among the pile. Then they were off again, taxiing back in a loop over the rough grass to point the aircraft towards the widest stretch of ground.

'Here goes,' Ben said, and hit the throttle. The roaring Cessna accelerated faster and faster towards the opposite side of the auditorium until it seemed as if they were hurtling towards certain destruction. Just as the look of terror began to spread over Jeff's face Ben yanked the yoke back almost hard enough to rip it from its mounting, and the plane left the ground and skimmed the auditorium. Its undercarriage cleared the wall with inches to spare and Ben climbed to four hundred feet to peel it back round in a smooth arc towards the airport.

'I'm getting too old for this dangerous shit,' Jeff said, eyes closed with a hand clutching his chest.

'Don't be such a cissy, Dekker.'

'I hope you know what to do if I have a bloody heart attack.'

'The heart's a muscle like any other,' Ben said. 'A little bit of excitement can only be good exercise for it.'

Another five minutes later, Ben had everyone cleared out of the way and he was facing the hangar shutter with the Chinese Type 69 rocket-propelled grenade launcher over his shoulder, aiming it towards the doors at an angle to lessen the chances of destroying whatever Khosa was keeping locked up in there. The thick steel would protect it from the explosion. At any rate, that was the plan.

Chances. Sometimes you just had to take them.

Ben said a quick prayer and fired. He felt the recoil of the rocket push him back on his heels, and the heat on his face as the hangar door was engulfed in a fierce bright flash and buckled inwards. Hardly waiting for the flames to subside, Ben dropped the RPG and ran into the smoke, ducking low to slip through the ragged hole that had appeared in the shutter door. The hangar was at least eighty feet deep and well over a hundred feet wide, but the only light came from narrow slotted windows high up in the walls and it was completely blotted out with the dark smoke still belching through the hole in the door, making it hard to see. Jeff joined Ben as he probed his way through the murk. Ben's leg touched against something solid and he put out a hand to feel what it was.

It was the front end of a four-wheel-drive pickup, jacked up on raised suspension and fitted with a light bar across the grille. Ben ran his hand along the crusty paintwork and wondered what a battered old pickup was doing locked inside a hangar. Still, it was transport, and with luck they might just about be able to cram everyone aboard.

It was then that Ben sensed a much larger presence inside the hangar. He looked up and saw the huge shape overhead, slowly becoming more visible as the smoke cleared. He was standing beneath a wing. He traced its line to the long, thick fuselage it was joined to. The aircraft filled most of the hangar.

'Well, I'll be damned,' Jeff breathed, and smiles broke out on both their faces as they gazed up at the hulk of the resting Douglas DC-3 Dakota airliner. The last time they'd seen the big plane had been moments after it had crash-landed with them on board, in remote countryside somewhere near the Rwanda–Congo border.

'They fixed it up,' Jeff muttered in surprise, stepping over to inspect the undercarriage strut that had been wrecked in the forced landing. 'I take back what I said about the mechanic. Someone's been busy.'

Tuesday stepped tentatively inside the hangar, followed by Jude, then Rae, then the kids. Sizwe was the last to enter. He stood behind the clustered children and laid a protective hand on Juma's shoulder, saying nothing.

'I don't believe it!' Tuesday burst out when he saw the

Dakota. 'Now this is what I call cool. Guys, look no further. We just found our ticket out of here.'

'You can fly this?' Rae asked, looking at Ben.

'He can fly anything,' Jude answered for him.

The smoke had almost completely cleared. With the natural exploratory curiosity of an investigative journalist, and with Jude hovering close behind, Rae stepped beneath the Dakota's wing and started making her way deeper inside the hangar. She glanced at the pickup truck parked next to it. Walked on another step. Then froze, and whirled round to gape at the back of the truck. Her shout echoed through the hangar.

'My stuff!'

Jude rushed to her side. She was excitedly clambering onto the cargo bed to examine the aluminium flight cases piled up against the back of the cab. 'It is! It's my equipment!' She dropped to her knees, set one of the cases down in front of her, and popped the catches. 'Oh, boy, this is incredible. Everything's here. It's all here, Jude. This is where they stashed it away.' She couldn't stop smiling.

Jude jumped up onto the truck and hugged her. 'That's fantastic, Rae.'

'Someone's happy, at least,' Ben said in an aside to Jeff.

Jeff raised an eyebrow. 'And someone else has gone el mucho hotto for a pretty face,' he muttered, looking at Jude.

Ben was surprised. 'What? You think?'

'Come on, mate. He practically has his tongue hanging out whenever he gets within five yards of her. And I don't think she minds it one bit, either.'

'So fast?'

'At their age?' Jeff nudged Ben with his elbow and grinned. 'Come on, old timer, let's check out this flying coffin and see if we've got a real chance of getting out of here this time, or just another pig in a poke.'

A Dakota's main hatch was a rectangular panel on the port side of the fuselage, behind the wing. It was open, with a metal ladder propped against it. Ben scrambled up it first. When he reached the top of the ladder, six thirty-calibre muzzles within a cylinder of black metal stared him in the face and he realised that the repairs to the undercarriage weren't all that Khosa's plane mechanic had been busy working on.

And now Ben had the answer to a small mystery that had come to his notice during the attack on Luhaka. He'd vaguely wondered at the time why no use was being made of the three Hua Qing rotary cannons they'd unpacked on their first day in the city. Capable of delivering an incredible rate of fire from their whirling multiple barrels hooked up to a motor drive, they were one of the most potent weapons in any small-arms arsenal. Their absence from the invasion force had seemed to him something of an omission. But now he knew better. Because he'd just found them.

Khosa's mechanic had fashioned a crude but perfectly serviceable mount out of hardened steel plate, welded to the floor and allowing the weapon to be deployed against targets on the ground if the pilot banked the plane over at an angle. The second cannon was poking from a fuselage window a few feet away. The third was fitted neatly into the tail pointing rearwards, so as to present a serious disincentive to any pursuing aircraft.

Cartridge belts lay coiled all over the floor like anacondas. Miles of them. To Ben's practised eye it looked like about twenty-five or thirty thousand rounds all told: enough ammunition to give a decent-sized combat division a really bad day. The pointed bullets were all black-red tipped to denote that they were armour-piercing incendiary rounds. If you were going to punch through the side of a tank, you might as well torch its insides into the bargain.

'I humbly retract everything I said,' Jeff chuckled. 'The crafty bastards have taken a DC-3 and turned it into Puff the Magic Dragon.'

That had been the unofficial nickname for the AC-47 attack/cargo 'Spooky' gunship developed by the US Air Force from the civilian Dakota airliner as an exceptionally effective means of providing close air support to ground troops in Vietnam. By the time they were superseded in '69 by faster, more powerful gunships they'd flown over 150,000 successful combat missions, fired nearly a hundred million rounds and become the scourge of the Viet Cong, who lived in such fear of the 'dragon' that their commanders issued orders not to attack it lest they infuriate the monster. The aircraft's armament of side-firing General Electric mini-guns, of which the Hua Qings were descendants, were operated from a selective trigger on the pilot's yoke.

When Ben and Jeff made their way forward to the cockpit, they found that the same modification had been made to Khosa's plane.

'Why didn't they use it in Luhaka?' Ben wondered out loud.

Jeff shrugged. 'A few passes from old Puff here could flatten half the bloody city. Maybe Khosa didn't want to rip the place up too badly. No point in being governor of a burning heap of rubble, after all.'

'Maybe,' Ben said. 'Or maybe it's just not operational yet. For all we know, it won't fly.'

'Only one way to find out, mate.'

Ben got behind the controls. While the original American AC-47 gunships had been equipped with a special reflector gunsight mounted in the left-hand cockpit window, Khosa's home-brewed variant made do with a crude arrangement of rear-view mirrors bolted to the outside of the canopy for the pilot to be able to direct his fire on targets on the ground and to the rear. Not exactly a precision setup. A little bit of Kentucky windage, a little bit of 'spray and pray', would be the order of the day.

Ben looked around him. Everything in the cockpit was sheet metal and rivets. Spartan and functional, the way he liked it. Better still, whoever had last sat in the pilot's seat had left a pack of African Tumbaco cigarettes tucked behind the yoke, with a disposable lighter slipped inside.

Ben lit one up. Once again, it wasn't a Gauloise, but any port in a storm. Blowing smoke, he flipped some of the clunky old-fashioned switches and instrument lights came on. Nothing went snap, crackle, or pop. No flames started licking out from behind the dials.

'So far, so good,' Jeff said, then looked up and pointed through the cockpit window. 'Now all we need to do is find a way to open that shutter door.'

Ben puffed some more smoke. 'I don't think that's going to be a problem. They didn't make these old planes out of recycled Coke tins.'

Jeff looked at him. 'You're going to ram your way out, aren't you, you mad bastard.'

'Whatever works,' Ben said. He glanced up at the afternoon sky. The sun was beginning its slow descent in the west. 'What time is it?'

'Time we got out of here,' Jeff replied. 'They must be getting close by now.'

But Jeff was wrong. Khosa wasn't getting close.

Khosa had already arrived at the city.

Chapter 51

'They are not here, General.'

The convoy had come to a halt, filling the main drag with a ragged line of dusty vehicles that tailed almost all the way back to the construction zone on its eastern side. The smell of hot metal and diesel fumes was rich in the air, along with the sounds of running boots and spluttering radios and barked commands as over a thousand soldiers were deployed into units that hurried here and there, spreading out in a wide circle and scouring every street, alley, and building. Within minutes, the sentries posted to guard the city in their absence had been found dead, presumed murdered by the escaped prisoners. The soldiers were under orders to bring both the American woman and the yellow-haired boy to the General for interrogation. It was whispered that the wicked foreigners had stolen something of great, great importance, though the rumour was vague. Whatever the nature of the crime, the soldiers were confident that its perpetrators would be suitably punished – and they couldn't wait to watch.

Jean-Pierre Khosa stood beside his Hummer at the head of the line. His revolver was drawn and cocked in his fist. The wide-set eyes behind the mirrored shades scanned the surrounding buildings, their windows and doorways and rooftops, for any sign of movement. He sensed their presence nearby. He could feel them. He could almost smell the blood in their veins and hear their hearts beating. They would not remain beating for long, once his property was returned to him.

The General appeared calm, but as everyone who knew him understood, sometimes it was when he was at his most calm that he was also at his most volatile. He didn't seem to have heard the soldier who'd reported back to him after the initial search of the area. Nervously, the soldier cleared his throat and repeated himself. 'General, the city is empty. The escaped prisoners are no longer here.'

Khosa slowly turned to look at him, expressionless and inscrutable. He shook his head, and replied with absolute certainty, 'No, Sergeant, they are here. Search again. Every inch of the city. Every crack and hole. Then search the mines. The river. The forest. They are not far away, and you *will* find them.'

Or heads will roll. Literally. The subtext wasn't in any way lost on the sergeant, who had seen enough heads literally rolling before now to take it seriously.

'Where is Pascal Wakenge? Where is my doctor?' Khosa demanded.

'With the convoy, General, as you ordered.'

'Bring him to me.'

The sergeant snapped a salute and ran to carry out the command. Moments later, he returned with the witch doctor, who looked a little bulkier than usual as he was wearing body armour under his robe. Wakenge had accompanied the Luhaka invasion force in a Land Rover near the front of the column, as Khosa liked to keep him on hand for his superhuman powers. Being known to be completely impervious to bullets, the old man's safety in the midst of battle had not been considered a concern. Strangely, though, Wakenge did seem most relieved to be back in the relative safety of the city. Nobody seemed to have noticed the Kevlar padding around his torso.

'*Oui, mon fils?*' Only the witch doctor could be allowed to call Khosa 'my son'.

Khosa explained that he wanted Wakenge to use his magic to find the person who had stolen his most precious belonging from him. Wakenge hesitated for the briefest moment and then nodded sagely. He screwed his eyes shut with a look of intense concentration, so that his old face wrinkled up like a walnut as he shook his monkey skulls and chanted softly to himself in a language he alone understood. Khosa watched him with rapt attention. This went on for a good half-minute. Wakenge opened one eye to a slit, saw the General was watching him, closed it again, and continued his strange chant a while longer. Some kinds of magic took longer than others.

But before old Wakenge was able to finish working his wonders, Khosa interrupted him by suddenly reaching out and grasping his skinny arm in a powerful fist.

'What is it, *mon fils*?' Wakenge looked alarmed. Had his patient, pupil and protégé rumbled him at last?

Khosa took off his dark glasses and stared at the old man with bulging eyes. 'I can hear them,' he hissed.

Wakenge's tension melted. He could hear nothing himself, being rather deaf in one ear. 'This is good, Jean-Pierre. You are learning well.'

'No, I mean I can *hear* them,' Khosa said. He held up a hand. 'Can you not hear it?' He stood very still, listening. Then bellowed at the sergeant, 'Tell those men to be quiet!'

The sergeant shouted orders at the troops. A hush fell over the street. Soldiers glanced at one another in confusion and began crowding around their leader as he stood like a statue, his scarred face locked in concentration. Whatever he could hear, it was no surprise to them that he was alone. His incredible powers of auditory perception were, after all, part of his legend, like his ability to read your thoughts and predict the future.

But then the sound grew a little louder and became audible to ordinary human ears. The soldiers could hear it, too. And if old Pascal Wakenge hadn't been slightly deaf, he also would have been able to detect the distant familiar drone emanating over the rooftops from the western edge of the city.

A sound like no other. The unmistakable low-pitched rumble and chattering clatter of a large, old-fashioned propeller aircraft warming up its twin nine-cylinder air-cooled radial piston engines and taxiing into position as it prepared for takeoff.

Khosa snapped his eyes open and turned to his troops.

'The airport!' he shouted. 'They are at the airport! Hurry!'

Chapter 52

The roar of the Dakota's engines inside the enclosed space of the hangar was even louder than the cyclone that had capsized the *Svalgaard Andromeda*. The entire building was shaking as if an earthquake had hit it.

All twelve of them were aboard, along with their small cargo. Jeff was in the co-pilot's seat that Khosa had occupied on the flight from Somalia. Tuesday and Sizwe were anxiously hovering at the back of the cockpit. Jude and Rae were sitting in the passenger section with the children and Rae's recovered boxes, all carefully stowed and lashed down to protect their important contents from damage. She kept glancing at them, smiling to herself despite everything that had happened. Jude was smiling, too.

A thrumming vibration filled the bare fuselage, as though the Dakota was alive and quivering with eagerness to get into action. 'Ready?' Jeff yelled over the roar.

'As ready as we'll ever be,' Ben replied. He flicked his cigarette stub out of the open window. Halfway through the pack of Tumbacos already. They helped. He took a deep breath. The engines were clattering away at five hundred revs. Ben gently increased the throttle speed and eased the plane forwards towards the steel shutter. This was no time for doubts.

Ramming his way out wasn't quite Ben's plan. The aircraft's big rounded nose cone didn't smash violently through the hangar door. It made contact with a kind of shudder that turned into a rending screech of metal, and pushed on relentlessly through as though the shutter had been made of tinfoil. The hinges gave way and the door collapsed outwards under the massive thrust.

The Dakota's nose emerged into the daylight. Its big wheels trampled over the buckled metal. The sunshine flooded inside the cockpit, lighting up the grin that Jeff was giving Ben along with a double thumbs-up. Ben taxied the Dakota out of the hangar and onto a concrete runoff apron that led to the unfinished runway, with the airport gates to their right and a broad rough grassy runoff area to the left, between the runway and the fence. The strip ran parallel with the fence for about a thousand feet before it dissolved into a wasteground of dirt and rocks. No modern airliner would have stood a chance of getting off the ground in so short a distance, but the Dakota hadn't become legendary for no reason. Smooth concrete was a needless luxury for an old warbird that could have taken off in a ploughed field if necessary.

Ben had spent all the time available getting familiar with the controls as best he could. If flying a little Cessna Skyhawk was like driving a Fiat family hatchback, the vintage Dakota was like getting behind the wheel of a Sherman tank. A multitude of dials and gauges clustered around the throttle quadrant at the heart of the instruments, an assortment of levers that looked like white, black, and red golf balls on sticks acting as the prop pitch, power and fuel mixture controls. Below and behind them were various other wheels and levers, each with its specific function.

He ran through his final pre-takeoff checks. Oil pressure, hydraulic pressure, fuel pump pressure, manifold pressure, mixture richness for takeoff, and a dozen other details. He racked his brain for anything he might have forgotten or overlooked, came up blank, thought, *Fuck it, here we go*, and throttled the plane forwards away from the hangar. Jeff was grinning like a gambler as the dice were rolled. Tuesday's eyes were as big as Frisbees. Only Sizwe looked unhappy at the idea of escape. The further away he was from Khosa, the more it delayed his quest for revenge.

Sizwe's disappointment would soon prove to be short-lived.

The Dakota had only just begun its lumbering approach to the start of the runway when the first bullet hit. The shot impacted its belly below the starboard wing opposite where Jude and Rae were sitting, punched its way through the fuselage at an angle and skipped across the floor right by Jude's feet with a metallic yowl that pierced through the engine roar.

For the briefest moment Jude stared, dumbfounded, at the pencil-thin shaft of sunlight poking through a hole in the fuselage opposite him. He opened his mouth to shout out in alarm, but by then all hell was already breaking loose.

The first bullet was like the first raindrop in a thundering deluge. Within an instant they were being strafed by heavy fire up and down their right flank as the plane accelerated towards the runway. From where he sat Ben felt the shudder of every impact through the controls, as if the aircraft was flinching in pain with each fresh wound to its body. He glanced out of the pilot's window and saw the large military convoy storming towards them through the airport gates. A thousand men or more, packed into a stream of vehicles, speeding straight towards them. Muzzle flash bursting from the overcab guns of the jacked-up technicals. Soldiers clustered like bees on the sides of the heavy trucks, clinging on tight with one hand and firing their weapons with the other.

In front was the same black Hummer he'd last seen leading the troops away from the defeated governor's residence in Luhaka. Khosa was back. Right behind him rolled a pair of armoured cars. Their turrets were swivelled straight at the aircraft, ready to blow them off the runway.

Ben gritted his teeth as the bullets kept raking their unarmed right flank. Any second now, a round was going to find its mark and kill someone. Worse still, one of those armoured cars would hit them with an explosive missile and light up their fuel tanks, roasting every man, woman, and child on board in a fiery conflagration.

Jeff was crouched low in the co-pilot's seat. Tuesday was wedged in the hatchway between the cockpit and the cargo section. Sizwe had gone to the children, who were screaming in fear as mayhem erupted all around. Ben twisted round and yelled, 'Everyone down! Jude! The vests!'

Jude had dragged Rae down to the floor and was shielding her with his body. The crate with the Kevlar body armour vests was just a few feet away from him in the cargo bay. He looked up at Ben, understood, and scrambled towards it, keeping his head down as bullets punched holes in the fuselage and burned past him.

Meantime, all Ben could do was increase throttle power and hope the Dakota's tired old engines would respond in time to leave their pursuers behind. The clatter of the propellers picked up a notch but the plane's rate of acceleration seemed agonisingly slow. In the air, it was a formidable dragon, the terror of the sky. On the ground, it was nothing but a big, fat, slow-rolling target, as soft and easy to hit as a pumpkin on a backyard shooting range. The vehicles kept coming on fast, outpacing them easily and pouring fire into them.

Keeping his head down, Jude managed to reach the crate,

ripped the lid away and yanked out the heavy Kevlar vests which he draped over himself as he scrambled back towards Rae. He covered her with one, then flung three more vests to Sizwe to lay over the children. The vests could stop a .44 Magnum or a twelve-gauge slug at point-blank range, but they wouldn't protect anyone from a direct hit by a heavy military round.

At last the plane began to respond. Ben felt the acceleration pressing him into his seat and determination burned brighter in his heart. The airspeed indicator needle flickered up to fifty knots. Everything in the cockpit was vibrating and rattling as though about to fall apart. Sixty knots. He urged the Dakota on harder, wringing every ounce of power out of its straining engines. Maybe more than the plane could take. Only one way to find out.

But now the enemy put their strategy into action as the hunt closed in. Ben glimpsed the black Hummer veering off to one side, letting the others take the lead. The column splitting into a two-forked pincer formation with an armoured car at the head of each. One fork swerved to its right and put on a spurt of speed, intending to race ahead and slice across their starboard bow, blocking the runway ahead to force the Dakota to a halt. The other fork veered left and passed across Ben's rear-view mirror like an express train as it curved around behind them, rounded their tail and started trying to come up their port flank, hanging cautiously back to stay out of the line of the Dakota's side-mounted port guns. One armoured car drawing level with their cockpit on the right, another keeping pace with their tailplane on the left. Not an ideal situation. Ben gripped the yoke and held his breath, waiting for which one would fire first.

The one on the left did. The bright flash filled the port rear-view mirror, followed by a violent shockwave as a missile exploded directly below their wing, making the plane lurch and swerve drunkenly all over the runway and tip over to the right as Ben fought to straighten their line. He realised the enemy were trying to take out the undercarriage. Khosa didn't want to destroy the plane and have to sift through burning wreckage for his prized possession. If he could, he was going to intercept them and take as many of them alive as he could. Then the General's fun would begin as he dissected them slowly, one at a time, watching and smiling as he fondled his diamond.

Ben couldn't let that happen. Not while he was still breathing.

To the aircraft's right, the machine gun on the armoured car spat flame as it aimed for their starboard engine and propeller, missed, and stitched holes up the side of the cockpit. Sparks flashed. Metal flew. Something stung Ben's cheek and he felt wetness there. The Dakota juddered and lost momentum. Ben swore and pressed it on even harder, but not in time to prevent the armoured car to his right and the line of trucks speeding along behind it from cutting in front of the Dakota's nose.

The runway ahead was suddenly blocked. Ben could either ram right into them and risk ripping off a wheel or buckling a propeller, or he could take evasive action. No choice.

Ben heard a cry close behind him and twisted his head to see Tuesday slump over sideways and crumple to the floor. There was blood on his jacket and on the bulkhead next to him. He wasn't moving.

Jeff yelled, 'Tues!'

No response. No time to check how badly Tuesday was hit. Just feet away from ploughing into the armoured car and trucks that were heading him off, Ben slackened off the throttle and slammed on the port landing gear brake. They were going much too fast for crazy taxi manoeuvres. The plane slewed violently to the left as the wheel locked, sending Rae's camera cases and the rest of their cargo tumbling across the floor.

The children were crying and screaming more loudly than ever, despite all Sizwe could do to subdue them. He was using his muscular bulk as a human shield, lying across them and pinning them with his weight with the bulletproof vests sandwiched between them, protecting as much of their little bodies as they could cover.

Jude had managed to haul Rae over behind one of the mini-gun mounts where the hardened steel plate offered more protection from bullet strikes than the flimsy aluminium shell.

Tuesday hadn't moved.

The Dakota came lurching in a wild anticlockwise arc off the runway and hit grass and hard-baked ruts. It was the move the enemy wanted from Ben, diverting the aircraft from taking off. Forty knots. Thirty-five. Even at low speed it was a rough, bone-jarring ride, and Ben just held on tight and prayed the undercarriage would take it as they went bouncing and rocking over the rough ground, the propellers whipping up a storm of dust. A big, lumbering target a hundred feet wide and sixty feet long. The roar was deafening. Muzzle flashes twinkled like Christmas lights from the line of vehicles blocking the runway behind them. They were absorbing so much fire that soon the plane would have more holes in it than solid material.

Ben had to do something fast, or they'd all be dead.

Chapter 53

So Ben did do something.

Because the enemy were playing a reckless game. They might think they had Ben where they wanted him – but now, as the plane's tail end swept away from the runway in an arc, he had the armoured car lined up slam bang in the middle of his rear-view mirror and perfectly positioned for a demonstration of what kind of sting the old Dakota had in its tail. They'd taken a hell of a beating. Now it was their turn to reciprocate.

The gun control attached to the pilot's yoke was a green metal box fitted with two triggers that were nothing more than simple rigged-up electrical switches soldered to two wires that were taped down the length of the stick and disappeared aft to hook up to the electric motor drives for the rotary cannons. A first-year engineering student could have built the simple device. But simple was good, in Ben's book. Each switch had a stuck-on label with a hand-drawn arrow marked on it. One arrow pointed to the left, the other pointed back at Ben and towards the rear of the plane.

Ben figured that the backward-pointing arrow was for the rear gun. He pressed that one.

And suddenly the mild-mannered lumbering old airliner was transformed into a ferocious, death-dealing war machine.

The fuselage filled with thunder as the recoil from the tail gun jolted the Dakota forwards and spent shell casings spewed out of the mini-gun's ejection port like chippings from a wood shredder. Six thousand rounds a minute. A high-powered armour-piercing incendiary bullet firing off every hundredth of a second, so fast that the noise blended together into a continual roaring screech like no other sound on earth. Every fifth cartridge on the belt was a tracer round, with a small pyrotechnic magnesium charge designed to ignite in flight. The laser-like trail they made as they flew towards their targets, brightly visible even in daylight, was designed to help military machine gunners direct their aim.

And Ben's aim was good.

In his mirror he saw the stream of the tracers, like a streak of dragon's breath, engulf the armoured car. The men inside would never know what had hit them as the tank-busting rounds slammed through their plating and erupted in fierce flame. The armoured car instantly erupted in a violent fire-ball that swallowed the trucks either side of it.

Ben kept his finger on the button and brought the plane round in a tighter arc to port, so that his tail slewed in an arc to the right and directed the stream of fiery devastation along the line of vehicles on the runway. At such close range, the Dakota's fire pummelled everything in its path into instant, total ruin. In a heartbeat, it looked as if the runway had taken a direct hit from a fighter squadron dropping napalm bombs. A curtain of fire leaped forty feet into the air and blocked out the sun with black smoke.

The soldiers never stood a chance. It was murder. Sheer, brutal overkill. Ben almost felt bad about it.

Almost.

The noise from the mini-gun was insane. Jude and Rae had their hands over their ears. Ben kept his finger on the fire button and his eye on the rear-view mirror and braked the Dakota's starboard wheel to flip the tail sideways in the other direction. The blazing tongue of fire blazing from the Dakota was like some kind of death ray that obliterated everything in its path. Trucks and pickups erupted in flames. The soldiers trying to escape were mowed down like grass by the awesome power of the dragon.

Ben released the button and the tail gun fell silent. The clattering drone of the engines sounded oddly quiet by comparison. He could hear the children still wailing in terror. Eight seconds of continuous fire, eight hundred rounds expended. The enemy was badly disabled. But still dangerous.

The line of vehicles that had been coming up the Dakota's left flank on the runway was now massed dead ahead of the plane, twenty or thirty of them, as Ben held his line. Bullets splatted the Dakota's nose and punched through the windows, forcing Ben and Jeff to duck in their seats. The second armoured car was swivelling its turret towards them, ready to fire a rocket.

Not if Ben could help it. He veered the plane sharply to the right, its big wheels bouncing over the uneven ground, crashing over ruts. The enemy's fire raked down their port flank as he brought the Dakota around broadside to the barrage.

Until now, the Dakota's twin side-mounted guns hadn't spoken a word. Now the moment had come for them to have their say. Ben's finger went to the trigger box and found the button with the left-pointing arrow.

Ben had been around a lot of weaponry in his life. He'd seen a lot of destruction and death in more war-torn battle zones than he could easily list. But he'd never witnessed anything quite like the carnage of devastation that tore into Khosa's troops as the old gunship delivered its broadside against them. One touch of a button, and he was directing two hundred rounds a second into the enemy's ranks at little more than point-blank range.

A whirlwind of death hit them like a nuclear blast wave. One instant there had been a formidable fighting force of massed military vehicles and heavily armed soldiers doing everything they could to stop the aircraft and slaughter everyone inside it. The next, there was nothing but blazing wreckage and twisted metal and shattered glass and pulped bodies. Escaping trucks swerved, flipped, rolled, exploded. Swarms of shrapnel, blown-off wheels, body parts flew through the air. The armoured car that had been about to fire on them was a carbonised shell with flames belching and roiling from its windows and turret hatch.

Ben released the fire button. The torrent stopped. The Dakota rolled onwards over the rough grass, towards the airport fence. Through the smoke he could see vehicles and running men as the enemy fell back in disarray. He didn't want to know how many he'd killed just now, how many more ghosts would come to haunt his dreams for the rest of his days. He just wanted this to be over.

Jeff had jumped from his seat and was bent over where Tuesday lay bleeding on the floor behind the cockpit. 'He's alive,' Jeff yelled, sounding worried. 'Took a round in the arm. Must've fallen and hit his head.'

The interior of the fuselage was hazy with gunsmoke. Ben twisted in his seat and couldn't see much. 'Jude! Everyone okay back there?'

'We're okay,' came a hoarse voice. 'Nobody's hurt. Just get us out of here!'

Relief thudded through him as Ben taxied the Dakota in a lurching circle, clear of the fence, past the burning wreckage on the runway and back up onto the smoothness of the concrete. Now he had a clear run ahead of him. Less than a thousand feet to take off in, but the old plane could do it. He gunned it hard, bringing the revs and the airspeed indicator back up again. Forty knots. Fifty. Sixty. Seventy. Tail wheel locked to keep them straight. Cowl flaps open to cool the engines under maximum load. Power throttle set. Propeller speed up to 2,500 rpm. The wheels began to skip on the runway. The front of the plane started to feel light.

But the enemy hadn't given up yet. They were regrouping and giving chase one more time, looming larger in the rear-view mirror. The black Hummer was in the lead, tearing after the plane in a frenzy to catch up. Two technicals raced along either side of it, laying down a continuous stream of automatic fire that threatened to shred the Dakota's tail fin and rear flaps.

Ben pressed the button to activate the rear cannon.

Nothing happened.

It couldn't have run out of ammunition. It had to be a breech jam or a dud round that had stopped the mechanism, or a power failure, or damage. The Hummer and its followers kept coming. Ben thought he could see Khosa's furious face screaming at him from behind the Hummer's tinted glass.

The Dakota was now almost at full takeoff speed and the end of the runway was rushing towards them fast. Then the nose lifted and the ground was suddenly falling away beneath them. A few moments ago, Ben hadn't thought they would ever get airborne. He wiped the sweat from his face, and his fingers came away red from the fresh gash he'd barely even felt until now. His shirt was sticking to his back and his whole body ached from tension. Thinking of Tuesday, he yelled over his shoulder, 'Jeff! How is he?'

'I'm all right.' Tuesday's voice was shaky, but the sound of it sent another flood of relief through Ben. Jeff eased their injured friend to a metal bench, helped him peel off his shirt, and examined the damage to his arm. 'Not as bad as it looks. Small-calibre flesh wound. Bullet passed right through.'

The plane climbed. Ben reduced throttle. Levelled off. Checked his settings. The roar of the engines settled to a steady rumbling drone that resonated all through the aircraft. Time to breathe again, at least for a few seconds.

Jude was making his way forward, stepping carefully over the mass of scorched cartridge casings that were rolling all across the floor. He stood framed in the hatch behind the cockpit, ashen-faced and tousle-haired. Rae was behind him, clutching at a rail for support. 'Is it over?' Jude asked. 'Are we getting away?'

'Not quite yet,' Ben said.

'What are you doing?'

'Finishing this,' Ben said. 'Hold on tight.'

He banked the plane around in a curve. The airfield was a miniature model below them. The black Hummer and the cluster of trucks that was all that remained of Khosa's troops had reached the end of the runway and kept going, bouncing like crazy over the rutted ground and sending up plumes of dust. The Hummer barely slowed for the perimeter fence. It crashed on through the wire. Small starbursts of muzzle flash rippled from the machine guns aboard the technicals. Tracer fire arced up at the plane and popped against the fuselage. Ben should have climbed out of range, but instead he kept banking around in a curve with his port wing dipped towards the ground two hundred feet below.

He watched the little vehicles scuttling like beetles. Ben had never deliberately stepped on a beetle in his life. But these ones needed to be crushed flat and ground into the dirt. Which was exactly what he intended to do. It was a fine balancing act getting the small moving targets centred in his mirrors. His finger hovered over the fire button.

Wait for it . . . wait for it . . . *now*.

The drone of the engines was drowned once again by the thunder of the gunship's twin cannons. The spectacular tongue of flame raked the ground like a searchlight. The recoil of the cannons shifted the aircraft's trajectory and Ben had to compensate with small adjustments as he watched the mirrors and tracked the scattering bugs with his stream of fire. Not the most precise gunsighting arrangement, but he was getting the hang of it. 'Good shooting,' Jeff called out as an explosion blossomed like a rose two hundred feet below them. One down. A second truck went into a wild slalom to escape the hurricane of aerial gunfire chasing after it, but in vain as it was pummelled and ripped apart in a flash of flames. 'Got another!' Jude crowed.

'It's not a damned video game,' Rae yelled over the deafening blast. 'People are dying.'

'They have it coming,' Jude yelled in reply. Rae couldn't answer that.

It was the black Hummer Ben wanted. Sizwe was on his feet and steadying himself on the tilted floor to gaze fixedly through one of the porthole windows, clutching little Juma tightly to his side. He wanted the black Hummer, too.

With two of his escort already destroyed and hellfire raining down from the sky on the rest of them, Khosa had turned around and was speeding back towards the airport.

Ben ignored the rest. Let them scatter. He brought the Dakota steeply down and went after the black Hummer.

'Splatter the bastard,' Jeff said, clambering back into the co-pilot's seat. His hands were shiny with Tuesday's blood.

The Hummer raced back down the runway, speeding towards the airport buildings. With no forward-firing guns,

360

Ben could chase him but he couldn't shoot until he was in position. And Khosa knew that. The Hummer was going hell for leather down there. It must have been doing ninety miles an hour down the runway. Now it was reaching the buildings. Swerving left past the mouth of the hangar. Heading for the open airport gates. Skidding out of them and accelerating hard away.

Ben dropped his altitude to a hundred feet. The Dakota roared over the airport buildings, the big hangar, the derelict helicopters. Ahead, the Hummer was swerving and fishtailing all over the road in its wild haste to get away. Khosa's face appeared, looking up at the aircraft from the passenger side window. Just a small dot, the features too far away to be readable, but Ben could feel the hatred in his eyes. And maybe if Khosa had been able to make out Ben's expression from such a distance, he'd have seen something of the same.

'He's heading for the stadium,' Jeff yelled.

Ben nodded. It was what he'd been afraid of, and there was nothing he could do about it.

The Hummer followed the exact same route that Ben and Jeff had taken on foot earlier. It traced the contour of the stadium's curved outer wall until it reached the concrete archway that led through to the arena, darted inside, and disappeared from view.

The Dakota thundered over the stadium, banking to port with its guns poised and Ben's finger resting lightly on the trigger button, ready to press it at the first sign of the black Hummer emerging into the arena. But there was no sign of it. Khosa had stopped and was hiding in the arch.

'Torch it,' Jeff said.

Ben hit the trigger. The gunship lit up the arena, churning the ground, reducing the arsenal of weapons to scrap metal and matchwood, pulverising the auditorium, blowing craters out of the walls and the roof of the concrete arch, laying waste to everything until there was so much fire and smoke rising up it was impossible to see. Ten seconds of sustained fire, then another ten, firing blind into the smoke, the recoil juddering the Dakota so heavily that it was almost stalling.

Ben let go of the trigger.

'He's toast,' Jeff said.

Ben said nothing. He hadn't had enough yet. He flew three more passes over the stadium and resumed his fire, hammering at it as if he wanted to wipe it completely off the face of the planet. This was the man who had taken Jude. This was the man who had inflicted so much pain and suffering on the innocent.

Ben couldn't stop. The guns kept firing until they ran dry and the rotary barrels whirred silently in their housings. He'd expended more than ten thousand rounds of ammunition. The depleted cartridge belts lay limp over the floor like heaps of dead snakes.

Ben went on circling. Looking for movement, seeing only the aftermath of the destruction. What remained down there on the ground, beneath the pall of smoke and flames, must be little more than rubble. Surely nothing could have survived. Not even Jean-Pierre Khosa.

Ben felt Jude's hand on his shoulder.

'It's time to leave,' Jude said. 'It's over, Dad. Let it go.'

Ben nodded. He placed his own hand over Jude's. He couldn't explain the sadness that suddenly came over him at that moment. Like a lead blanket of sorrow and fatigue that made him want to curl up in a corner somewhere. He sighed and blinked the feeling away.

They headed for the wide open sky. Climbing to a thousand feet. Pointing west, into the afternoon sun. Khosa's city lay below them like a ghost town, a column of black smoke still rising from one end, the twist of river and the mining camp beyond on the other. As they left it behind, the emerald green jungle seemed to stretch out to infinity all around, the jagged ridges of hazy mountains floating like a mirage above the horizon in the far distance.

It looked beautiful from up here. You could almost forget what went on down below. Rae and Jude went to a window and linked hands as they gazed down on the scene, seeing it for the very last time.

'You're going home now,' he said to her, and tears came into her eyes, and he held her. Sizwe clutched little Juma as if he were his own son, and cried too.

They thought it was over.

Chapter 54

Alphonse and Serge had been best buddies for nearly fifty years, and for over forty of them had religiously met up at least twice a week to knock golf balls around Brazzaville's only course. After decades of practice neither of them was ready to enter the Africa Open anytime soon, and now that Alphonse's knees had gone bad it was taking them longer to get around all nine holes than it used to.

Alphonse wasn't having a good day today, and their round had dragged on extra late. The light was starting to fade, but at least that spared them from the pain of watching the balls fly into the snake-infested rough. Both men were looking forward to winding up their game and heading across to the club bar for a nice cold beer or two before each went home to their respective dinners and beds.

Serge was shuffling up to tee off on the ninth, a tricky uphill drive that needed to clear the rise ahead, when the two of them suddenly cringed and ducked as a huge roaring thunder filled the air.

At first they thought it was a violent storm descending on them, though there'd been no lightning flash. Then an

364

enormous dark shape came swooping low out of the sky, skimming the trees, its noise and wind almost knocking the two old men flat. Their jaws dropped open in shocked amazement as it blasted overhead, so close they could almost have reached up with their clubs and scraped its great green underbelly. What the hell was an aircraft doing coming in to land on the golf course?

The roaring plane disappeared out of sight over the rise. Alphonse and Serge exchanged stupefied looks, then dropped their clubs and set off as fast as they could after it. It took poor old Alphonse a few minutes to scale the rise, though Serge wasn't much quicker. As veteran members of the club they knew the top of the slope overlooked the fairway of the second hole, a long par five. When they finally reached the summit, gasping for breath, their eyes opened wide at the sight of the landed aircraft three hundred yards away on the second green.

By the time the club manager had been summoned and a party of puzzled staff and members had plucked up the courage to march up the fairway and investigate, all they found inside the abandoned, bullet-riddled aircraft were a pile of weapons whose ammunition had apparently been ditched overboard before landing, a mass of spent shell casings lying all over the floor, and some crates containing photographic equipment.

It was all a bit of a mystery. As was the whereabouts of the plane's occupants, who had long since slipped away into the darkness.

'Do you make a habit of stealing cars?' Rae asked from the back as the crowded vehicle drove through the night.

'It's not a car, it's a Land Rover,' Ben replied.

He and Jeff had found the thirty-year-old twelve-seater

station wagon parked behind what appeared to be the groundsman's hut at the golf club, with the keys left in the ignition. It had been the easiest theft in Ben's long and undistinguished career as a car criminal. 'And we're only borrowing it,' he added.

'Heard that one before,' Jeff said with a grin.

The decision to cross the border into the Republic of Congo had been made in the air as they headed west towards Kinshasa. Jeff's suggestion, based on the fact that ROC was a comparatively more stable country than its neighbour, for what it was worth – even though the capital cities of the two countries lay just a few kilometres apart, within sight of one another across the waters of the Congo River. Nobody had argued with the choice, or with the idea of leaving the Democratic Republic of Congo behind them, never to return. Brazzaville had a US Embassy where Rae could present herself as an American citizen in distress and be flown home to her family. Jude had other plans of his own to set in action.

But first they had to find a place to hole up for the night, and get Tuesday seen to. The bullet wound to his arm was less serious than they'd first feared, but he was in pain and needed medical attention.

The hot, sultry night had fully descended by the time they found an auberge on the edge of a less rundown suburb of the city. The place was run by a woman named Mama Lumumba: four hundred pounds, sixty years old and as formidable as a lioness. They'd done what they could to clean up and divest themselves of obvious military-looking garb before knocking on her door. Nonetheless, one look at Ben and Mama had been ready to slam the door in their faces – but had melted when she saw the half-dozen ragged and hungry-looking children getting out of the Land Rover and agreed to let them have three rooms for the night.

How Ben was going to pay her was something he'd leave until morning to worry about. If they could get to a computer, they could wire some money from the heavily depleted Le Val business account to a local bank and make a cash withdrawal. Then again, this was Africa. Ben expected complications, though none as tough as the prospect of himself, Jude, Jeff, and Tuesday getting home with no passports and without entanglements with ROC officials who, inevitably, would be full of awkward questions about what four foreigners, some more battered than others, were doing in their country without ID or visas in the first place. If they twigged the fact that three of the four had British military backgrounds, the next word out their mouths would be 'mercenary'. And that would bring a ton of trouble.

But there were more immediate concerns to address in the meantime. Their story was that they'd been involved in a car accident out in the bush. When Ben enquired about the chances of finding a doctor this time of night to treat his friend's injured arm, Mama said there was a nice young fellow down the street who used to work at the hospital.

That nice young fellow turned out to be a seventy-something retired doctor named Paul Bakupa who lived alone and, by Congolese standards, in relative comfort in a small bungalow a short walk from the auberge. The old doctor also kept a well-equipped first-aid cabinet. For the offer of 500,000 central African francs – which sounded like a fortune but equated to only about 750 euros – he at first reluctantly agreed to clean, stitch up, and dress Tuesday's arm and dose him with painkillers and antibiotics. While he was at it, he insisted on taking a look at Ben's battered face, which he painfully but gently swabbed with alcohol, sticking plasters here and there before putting three stitches in Ben's split lip.

As he finished working on Ben, Bakupa said softly,

speaking French, 'I understand I'm not intended to ask too many questions, or else you would not have offered to pay me so much money. But I have to say, my curiosity is aroused. A bullet wound is not the kind of injury one would normally associate with a car accident. However, you and your friends do not seem to me like criminals or villainous people. Thus I can only infer that you must have encountered some kind of trouble that was not of your making.'

Ben touched his lip. The stitching felt solid. Bakupa was a good surgeon, and a good man. Someone who could be trusted. He said, 'Have you heard the name Jean-Pierre Khosa?' The numbness from the local anaesthetic made talking difficult.

'I have,' Bakupa said, nodding sagely. 'Some people say that animal will be president of the Democratic Republic one day. The Lord help us all if such a disaster should occur.'

Ben said, 'Unlikely to happen. Unless they have dead men as presidents. That's all I can tell you about the nature of the trouble that my friends and I encountered. Except to say that you'll get none from us. I promise you that.'

A glimmer came into Paul Bakupa's crinkly eyes. 'I see. Then Africa has just become a better place. Say nothing more, *mon jeune ami*. I have heard all I need to know.' He tapped the side of his nose, then glanced at the children. Mani seemed to have attached himself to Ben and was hanging around nearby, while Juma seemed to want to be close to Sizwe. The others were sitting quietly together in a corner. 'What of these children?' the doctor asked Ben with concern.

'Boy soldiers from Khosa's army,' Ben said. 'Demobbed, as of today.'

'What is to become of them?'

'Anything's better than where they were until now,' Ben said. Though the truth was, he had no idea what he was going to do with six young kids.

'God bless them, I hope they will survive,' Bakupa said.

Chapter 55

Perhaps it was all thanks to the prospect of half a million francs, or perhaps it was also partly in celebration of the demise of the hated General Jean-Pierre Khosa – but having finished dispensing his medical services Paul Bakupa insisted that his guests remain a little longer. He provided them all with a hot meal of beans and spicy fried chicken around the small table in the kitchen, every last chilled bottle of Ngok lager in his fridge and cans of Coca-Cola for the children, as well as a badly needed shower ('though I must warn you that the water pressure is erratic at best'). Most welcome of all for Rae, he was happy to let her use his telephone.

It was the most important and emotional phone call of her life. Jude resisted the urge to stay with her in the narrow hallway outside the kitchen as she dialled home to tell her family she was free and safe. There were a lot of tears at both ends of the line. She ended the call by promising them she'd explain everything, and that she'd go to the US Embassy in Brazzaville first thing in the morning.

'I'm deeply in your debt,' Ben said to Bakupa when it was time to leave. 'I'll bring you the money as soon as I can.'

'It was a pleasure helping you, my friend,' Bakupa replied, shaking his hand. Ben could have hugged the guy.

He felt like hugging Mama too, but she'd already gone to bed, leaving the front door open for them. Rae couldn't get over it. 'You wouldn't do that in Chicago.'

'We are Africans,' Sizwe said with a sad smile. 'You are American, you cannot understand. Most people here are so poor, we have nothing to steal. At home in Rwanda, people in my village—' Sizwe was about to say more, but then his eyes clouded and he fell silent.

Ben touched his arm. It had been a hell of a day for Sizwe. He'd witnessed the murderer of his family going up in flames; now, with a bellyful of beer inside him, and no definite future, he was ready to sleep for a week. Ben knew exactly how he felt.

The room arrangements had been decided in advance. The six children were sharing, which for orphanage kids used to thirty to a dorm was a luxury beyond imagining. It had been agreed to let Rae have a room to herself, being the only woman, and for the men to bunk up together next door.

At least, that had been the plan. Ben's eyebrows rose at the sight of Jude disappearing with Rae into her room. The door closed softly behind them.

'It's an outrage,' Tuesday said, grinning at the look on Ben's face. 'It's not proper.'

'See, what did I tell you?' Jeff said, chuckling. 'They couldn't get away fast enough. Love's young dream, eh? Best let them be.'

'More space for us in here,' Tuesday said.

There were just two beds in the cramped room. Ben settled on the floor and lit one of the Tumbacos he'd taken from the plane. Sizwe sat on the floor opposite him.

'Take a bed, Sizwe,' Ben said.

'I have slept on many floors in my life,' Sizwe said.

'Suit yourselves,' Jeff grunted, flopping on one of the beds and turning out the light.

Tuesday recited in the darkness:

> *'He'll never meet*
> *A joy so sweet*
> *In all his noon of fame,*
> *As when first he sung to woman's ear*
> *His soul-felt flame,*
> *And at every close, she blush'd to hear*
> *The one loved name!'*

'What the fuck are you talking about?' Jeff said.

'Love's young dream. That's poetry, that is. Thomas Moore.'

'You're not normal, are you?'

They lapsed back into silence. Ben smoked and thought.

'We killed a thousand men today,' he murmured in the darkness. 'Sweet Jesus. So many.' He didn't realise he was speaking his thoughts out loud until Jeff replied tersely,

'Yeah, well, screw 'em.'

More silence. Ben went on smoking and tried not to listen out for sounds coming from the next room.

'I miss my family,' Sizwe whispered.

Nobody spoke after that.

Whatever the others assumed must be happening in the next room, they were wrong.

Jude and Rae sat for a long time on the edge of the narrow bed, talking in low voices. The only light was from a weak, flickering bulb on the nightstand, and with the sash window open for some air there were moths the size of kestrels soon fluttering about them.

'You'll be going home tomorrow,' Jude said to her. He tried to sound happy about it, but that wasn't easy.

'I guess,' she replied. She'd been subdued since the phone call to her family.

'That's wonderful.'

Rae nodded, though she didn't look happy. 'Yes, it is. But I'll be walking into a nightmare the moment I step off the plane. FBI, CIA, and who knows who else, all waiting to talk to me. Having to go through the whole thing with what happened to Craig, over and over again. This is bound to blow up into some kind of major international shit storm, and I'll be caught up right in the middle of it. And the worst thing is, there's not a shred of solid proof to incriminate Craig's killers. The bastards will get away with it, like always.'

'Khosa's dead,' Jude said. 'I don't call that getting away with it.'

'Maybe. But what about all the others? Khosa wasn't working alone, you know that as well as I do.'

'I know,' Jude said, thinking of César Masango. He shifted uncomfortably and changed the subject. 'But you'll be back with your family, that's what matters most.'

'To tell you the truth, part of me is kind of dreading that as well,' she admitted. 'I'm worried about what they're going to say to me. You know, once we get past all the emotional stuff. I know they must have paid Khosa's cronies a lot of money in ransom for my release. I hate to even think how much, and all lost. I don't know if I can handle that.'

He touched her hand. 'You're worth it.'

'Wait till I tell them about you, though,' she said, turning to him and forcing a smile. 'You'll be their hero for life.'

'The white knight in shining armour,' he said jokingly, and they both laughed softly. 'Maybe I'll get to meet them one day,' he ventured, then was worried he'd said too much.

She paused a beat. 'You'd come to Chicago?'

'I've nowhere much else to go,' he said. 'I had some plans, but that's all done with now. I don't know what I'm going to do.' After a silence, he said, 'What you told me, about the coltan . . .'

'What about it?'

'It made me think about all the things the public don't know about. I mean, how would people feel if they knew there were components inside their mobile phones and tablets that came from a slave mine in Africa where workers are being tortured and murdered every day?'

'If they care,' she said. Reaching into her pocket, she took out the SD card containing the valuable images she and Munro had taken of the mines and the city, and gazed at it. 'Sometimes I wonder if it's all worth it,' she sighed. 'Does anyone back home really give a crap? Africa might as well be another planet.'

He looked at her. 'They do care. And they will. We'll make them listen.'

'What are you saying? That you want to get involved?'

Jude shrugged. 'Maybe. Yeah. I think I would.'

'You think you would?'

'I definitely would. But mostly, I'd just like to see you. Spend some more time.' As he said it, he could feel his face flushing.

'In Chicago?'

'Problem is, I can't afford a plane ticket,' he confessed.

Rae smiled, the smile coming easily now. 'If that's all that's holding you back, it shouldn't be too hard to fix.'

'Tell me about the place,' he said.

They whispered late into the night, sitting close together on the bed, knees touching, reaching out affectionately to one another every so often as they talked, relaxed and happy

374

in each other's company. Whatever the others assumed the two of them were getting up to in there alone in Rae's little room, they had the wrong idea.

But much later, in the depths of the night, when everyone else was asleep and total stillness had fallen over the auberge, things turned out so they were right after all.

Chapter 56

'I told you before what I had in mind.'

'I didn't think you were serious.'

'Why not?'

'Because it's such a ridiculous idea.'

'Then what else can I do?'

'We've been here before, Jude. When you took the damn thing, didn't you have a better plan than this for getting shot of it?'

'Won't you help me out here?'

The argument had been going on all through their breakfast of French toast, scrambled eggs, and café au lait in Mama Lumumba's homely but tiny kitchen, where all twelve of them were crowded around the table. Jude had got up that morning with an unusually rosy glow about him, mysteriously shared by Rae, though both were acting innocent; but ever since the matter of the diamond had been raised, Jude and Ben had been back at loggerheads over what to do with it and the atmosphere had grown tense. Jude was sick to death of carrying the thing around. He certainly didn't want to keep it, however much it was worth, and he could see only one viable option for getting rid of it.

Ben and Jeff were firmly opposed to the idea of handing it over to the police.

'Why don't you let Jude do what he wants with it?' Rae challenged Ben. 'And if he needs your help, why don't you help him?'

Jeff said through a mouthful of egg, 'Because the cops will magic it away faster than . . . Tues, who's that Yank magician we saw on the TV?'

'David Blaine,' Tuesday said.

Jeff nodded. 'Right. Faster than David Blaine.' He made an exploding motion with his hands. '*Poof.* Now you see it, now you don't.'

'But I have to say . . .' Tuesday added, frowning. He was eating with one hand, his bad arm in a sling.

'What?'

Tuesday shrugged his good shoulder. 'At least then it's out of our hair. Who really cares what happens to it, as long as it's gone, and as long as Khosa can't get his mitts on it again?'

'There. See?' Rae said, pointing at Tuesday and looking fiercely at Ben.

'Besides, we don't know for sure that it would just somehow vanish into the system,' Jude said. 'Why are you being so cynical?'

'T.I.A.,' Jeff said. 'This Is Africa.'

Ben looked across the table at Sizwe. 'What do you think?'

'I have no opinion on this,' Sizwe said.

'Three against two,' Rae said, still looking fiercely at Ben.

Ben put up his hands in submission. 'Fine, you win. We'll drive into the city this morning, find the police headquarters, assuming there is one, ask to see whoever's in command and hand the diamond to him. Then it's gone, come what may. Happy?'

'And afterwards we'll take you to the US Embassy and get you sorted out for a flight home,' Jude said, looking at

Rae. The two of them exchanged a lingering gaze that everyone except the children pretended not to notice. Sefu nudged Fabrice with his elbow and flashed a covert grin. Kids.

'And then it's a trip to the nearest bank,' Jeff said. 'Or Mama will nail our bollocks to the wall.'

'You shouldn't use language like that in front of them,' Rae said, pointing at the boys.

'Can't take me anywhere, can you?' Jeff grumbled.

'What is bollocks?' Juma asked, blinking.

The plan started out with just Ben and Jude going to the police on their own, but quickly grew from there. Rae wanted to spend every available moment with Jude before she left, and nobody was about to deny her. Jeff was set on going along as backup. Tuesday, despite being bandaged and on painkillers, insisted on being present when the diamond was finally squared away. Meanwhile Mani, who appeared not to want to leave Ben's side, kicked up a fuss about being left behind, which meant Juma and the others all wanted to be there as well, which in turn meant that Sizwe decided to tag along in order to be close to Juma.

In the end, after helping Mama do the breakfast dishes, the whole motley band of twelve set off into Brazzaville in the stolen Land Rover which, Rae kept reminding Ben, was only borrowed and would have to be returned to the golf club later.

Jeff rolled his eyes at Ben, as if to say, *What a ball buster.* But Ben was liking Rae more all the time. And he could tell from the look on Jude's face that this was more than just some passing fling for him. For just one good thing to have come out of the horror and suffering they'd all been through, was more than Ben could have wished.

A little self-consciously, just after nine o'clock that morning,

Ben parked the stolen vehicle outside the Brazzaville Police HQ in a district called Makalele. The brickwork still bore the scorch marks and bullet craters from the violent riots that had broken out in the ROC capital a few months earlier in protest against alleged fiddling of election results, during which the angry mob had set fire to government buildings. Nobody had bothered to clean up the damage to the outside of the police HQ, just as nobody on the inside paid the slightest attention to the twelve of them as they walked in.

At what appeared to be a reception desk, Jude cleared his throat to get the attention of the somnolent duty officer and asked to speak to whoever was in charge. A conference between several policemen followed, none of whom looked more than about fifteen years old, as if Jude had requested an audience with the president. Finally, one of them said in English, 'You want to see Chief Zandu?'

'If Chief Zandu is the most senior person in the place,' Ben said, 'that's who we want to see.'

'Let me do the talking,' Jude hissed as they followed the juvenile cop up a grubby, stuffy passage into the bowels of the police headquarters.

'Sorry.'

They were shown into Chief Zandu's poky office, which suddenly became badly crowded as they all filed inside. The children were awed to be inside a police station. The office smelled of mildew and ashtrays. The Brazzaville police chief was a small, pear-shaped man in a paramilitary uniform that was wide open at the neck. On the battered desk in front of him lay a report he'd been examining, concerning the unexplained appearance of a severely damaged military cargo gunship on the Brazzaville golf course the night before. He brushed that to one side, leaned back in a tatty chair and eyed them impassively.

That was, until Jude produced the diamond and set it down on the chief's desk for effect. The police chief rocked forward in his chair, planted his elbows on the scarred desktop either side of the diamond and boggled at it.

'What – is – this?' he asked, very slowly.

'Stolen property,' Jude said. 'Which I'm duly handing over to the authorities so that it can be returned to its rightful owner. We think this diamond was taken by thieves somewhere in Africa, though we can't be sure. Maybe in Oman. But it can be traced, can't it? I mean, something like this would have been reported missing, for sure.' Jude glanced around the office, as though a state-of-the-art mainframe computer giving access to all the international crime databases and INTERPOL records of known fugitives and villains across the world might be in evidence somewhere nearby.

'It is plastic,' Zandu said, poking the diamond with a stubby fingertip. 'It cannot be real.'

'I can assure you it's not plastic,' Jude told him.

'Wish it was bloody plastic,' Jeff muttered in the background.

It took a long time to explain the chain of events to the police chief. Jude stuck to a simplified version of the true facts, which centred around the US cargo ship on which he'd been employed as an able seaman before it went down in a storm off the African coast, the theft of the diamond from its presumed original owner by a white American called Pender, and its subsequent theft from Pender by one Jean-Pierre Khosa (at the mention of whose name Chief Zandu showed no flicker of reaction). Now here it was, back out of criminal hands and ready to be reunited with its proper owner, whoever they might be.

Jude kept it simple because he saw it that way. Ben had feared that the police chief's response would be anything but straightforward, and he'd been right. Once Zandu was persuaded that the object on his desk wasn't a fake lump of plastic, he jumped to the opposite conclusion and seemed to imply heavily that, for all he knew, Jude himself had stolen this diamond from its owner and was now trying to worm his way out of the consequences by posing as an innocent tourist. He asked a hundred conflicting questions and made Jude repeat his story any number of times, like some clever interrogator trying to catch his suspect in a stumble. He kept demanding to see Jude's passport, which Jude explained over and over again had been lost at sea: that would be a matter for the British Embassy here in Brazzaville. Jude explained that as a hired hand on a US merchant navy vessel he had been allowed to enter various African countries without a visa. Which didn't explain how he came to be this far inland, but Zandu seemed to have lost interest in pursuing that line of questioning any further, to Ben's relief as he'd been thinking Jude was digging himself in too deep, and the rest of them with him.

Finally, the police chief declared in a severe tone that he would need to pass the matter on to the appropriate authorities, and required Jude to stay in town for a few days in case they needed to question him further.

'No problem,' Jude said cheerfully.

Zandu asked for a contact address, and Jude wrote the name of Mama's place on an official form, signed and dated it. Next, Jude signed a lost property form waiving all claim of ownership, then another form, then another.

'Watch what you're signing,' Ben warned Jude quietly. But Jude would happily have signed away his parents' old house just to be shot of the burden that had been burning a hole in his pocket.

Zandu produced a rubber stamp and proceeded to thump

away at the forms until Jude's signatures and most of the print were obliterated with ink smudges. Then the forms were duly stored away among the midden of paperwork inside the chief's overflowing desk drawer, probably never to see the light of day again.

At that point, they were dismissed. Jude turned, took Rae's hand and walked out of Zandu's office without another glance at the diamond, which the police chief had assured them would go straight into his personal safe pending a thorough investigation.

'I can only hope you didn't just open a great big can of worms there, mate,' Jeff said to Jude as they were escorted from the building.

'I don't care,' Jude replied. 'I'm just glad to be rid of it. It's in good hands now.'

Ben said nothing to that.

When the foreigners were gone, Chief André Zandu sat alone in his office, sipping from the bottle of Johnnie Walker he kept hidden behind an ancient copy of the Congolese Penal Code on his bookshelf and toying with the unbelievable diamond that had just, almost literally, landed in his lap. He took off his cap and scratched in consternation at the greying stubble on his head.

Of course, all that about it being a fake had been bullshit, just like all the crap he'd fired at the kid about him having stolen it. It was just well-practised bluster, meant to confuse and intimidate. Zandu had known what the diamond was the instant he'd laid eyes on it.

The whole Kinshasa–Brazzaville criminal fraternity, with whom the chief was very well acquainted – and through which connections he had been supplementing his meagre police salary for many years – had lately been buzzing with rumours about the sudden appearance of the fabulous stone in neighbouring DRC and the much-feared individual who, according to the same sources, had now laid claim to the diamond and was using it to scam money left and right with a little help from his equally well-known and feared associates.

Until now, Chief Zandu hadn't known whether to believe the rumours. But here was the proof, glittering in his hands. An unimaginable fortune sitting right in front of him. Zandu shut his eyes, and for a few blessed moments he was wafting down Avenue de la Paix in a gold-plated Rolls Royce Corniche convertible with Scarlett Johansson at his side, gazing adoringly at him, the wind in her hair . . .

Whoosh. Back to reality. Zandu knew only an idiot would fall for the temptation that had come his way. Steal from César Masango? Worse still, steal from General Jean-Pierre Khosa? Forget it, man. There wouldn't be a rathole in Africa where they wouldn't find you, drag you out and crucify you, and then your family, and your friends, and everyone you'd ever known. Police chief or no police chief, he knew better than to mess with such lunatics.

But there could be a big reward for a faithful senior official who showed his loyalty to them. This idea made Zandu smile, even as the vision of untold riches crumbled before his eyes. He nodded to himself thoughtfully. Yes, that was it. His only option.

Scarlett would have to do without him.

Zandu heaved a wistful sigh and picked up the phone.

Chapter 57

Victor Bronski was the seasoned veteran of enough stakeouts to harden most sensibilities, but more than forty hours without a break stuck inside this van in this shitty street in this shitty city in this shitty godforsaken country, baking by day and freezing by night, pissing in a bottle and having to use a goddamned portapotty for the other, was getting to be wearisome even for him. At least he was alone in the van. Being forced to share with Gasser, Shelton or Jungmayr, any of them, would probably have ended with him shooting someone.

César Masango hadn't re-emerged from his house the entire time. No phone calls, no activity, nothing. So many times, Bronski had been on the verge of ordering his team to go in, snatch Masango and his wife Olive and whisk them off someplace more private to find out what the man knew about Jean-Pierre Khosa's whereabouts – more precisely, the whereabouts of Eugene Svalgaard's lusted-after diamond. But something kept holding Bronski back from giving the order. He didn't know what, but he trusted his instincts.

Then at 9.42 that morning, those instincts were finally proven correct when Masango received a phone call that woke Bronski out of his boredom like a bucket of ice water. The caller wasn't Khosa, but as Bronski listened in on his earpiece he quickly realised it was the next best thing.

'This is André Zandu over in Brazzaville,' the caller began. 'You know who I am?'

'Of course,' Masango replied hesitantly. 'To what do I owe this unexpected pleasure, Chief Zandu?'

Bronski's eyes narrowed as he clocked that one. *Chief Zandu*. A cop? Go figure.

'Something has come into my possession that I believe concerns you,' Zandu said. 'Something of value.' He paused. 'Very considerable value.'

Masango's voice became flustered. 'I see . . . ah . . . Forgive me, but I don't understand. I mean, how did this item of value come to you? And when, and from whom?'

'From a foreigner,' Zandu said. 'His name is . . .' A rustle of paper. 'Arundel, Jude Arundel.' Zandu spelled it.

Bronski thought he almost heard Masango flinch at the sound of the name. Whoever this Arundel character might be, Bronski had no idea. This was something new. But Masango knew who he was, all right. And there was little doubt in Bronski's mind what item of value was being discussed here.

The trail of the diamond was suddenly glowing red-hot once more.

Except this was an unexpected development, and Bronski didn't care much for surprises. He had assumed that Masango and his buddy Khosa had been holding on to the rock this whole time. Now it sounded like this Arundel guy had somehow got his hands on it. If that information was news to Masango, then Bronski could only suppose that Arundel must have nabbed it from Khosa personally. And recently, explaining why Masango hadn't been kept in the loop.

Dangerous business. Arundel had balls of brass, whoever he was.

'And the diam— the item?' Masango sounded like he was having palpitations.

'I am looking at it right now, here in my office,' Zandu answered coolly.

The incredulity in Masango's voice reached a new pitch. 'You mean he gave it to you? Just like that? He wanted nothing in exchange?'

'No, he walked into my police headquarters forty-five minutes ago, asked to see the chief and told me he wanted to turn it over to the authorities, so that it could be returned to its proper owner. And then he left.'

Bronski couldn't believe his ears any more than Masango could. What kind of fuckin' retard would risk his life to snatch a rock worth upwards of half a billion bucks from a psycho maniac like Jean-Pierre Khosa and then turn it in, gratis, just like that, to the cops? It would be a dumbass enough thing to do even in America, where not quite all cops were just crooks in uniform.

Zandu said, 'Anyway, it is safe here with me for the moment. I have two officers stationed outside my door on guard duty.'

Bronski shook his head. If Zandu knew the real value of what he was holding there in Brazzaville, it would be a hundred officers stationed outside his damn door, with automatic rifles.

'But I think that you or your, ah, *associate* should come and collect it as soon as possible,' Zandu went on. 'I do not want the responsibility of looking after such a thing. And I hope that my assistance in this matter will not go unrecognised.'

'You have my sincere thanks,' Masango said. 'And that of my associate, who will be most appreciative of your loyalty and, ah, honesty . . . Tell me, out of interest, where is Arundel now?'

Zandu replied, 'Staying in town. He is with a party of others. I think one of them is his father. They looked alike. There was a woman with them, too. Young. Dark hair. Attractive.'

'An American woman?'

'I thought she looked Japanese,' Zandu said. 'Or Chinese. Who can tell the difference? They all look the same to me, like *muzungus*. Do you want the address?' He read it out while Masango scribbled it down. Bronski made a note of it as well. Sounded like some low-rent guesthouse.

Masango clearly couldn't wait to put the phone down. 'I must try to find out what is happening. But I assure you, Chief Zandu, we will be in contact with you again very soon. Thank you again and goodbye.'

Click.

The moment the sensational call ended, Bronski got straight on the walkie-talkie to his guys. Gasser was alternating shifts with Shelton in the car parked on the north side of Masango's large walled property. Jungmayr was in the other car, watching the exits a block to the west in case Masango tried to slip off that way.

Bronski said, 'Did you get that?'

Gasser: 'Loud and clear, boss.'

Jungmayr: 'Roger that.'

'Where's Shelton?'

'Having breakfast in some joint across the street.'

'Reel his lazy ass in ASAP and stand by. Things are about to start happening.'

Bronski sat up straight in the front seat of the van and kept watching the house. Moments later, Masango burst from the back door and hurried towards the Mercedes parked under the shade of the trees like a man with soldier ants in his boxer shorts. He opened the car, but didn't get in. Instead he reached inside and brought out a cellphone. Probably a damn burner, Bronski thought, irritated that he wouldn't be able to trace the call or listen in. Although there could be little doubt who Masango was calling, to find out what the hell was going on.

Bronski might not be able to listen, but you could glean a lot about a conversation from just watching. He grabbed his binoculars and focused in on Masango's face.

Masango paced up and down under the trees as he dialled a number, nervous as a beetle in a chicken coop. He waited impatiently for a few rings and then started yakking away like crazy and gesticulating with his free hand. From his body language, it was hard to tell whether he was shitting himself with anxiety or shitting himself with relief. Maybe a mixture of both.

Bronski kept watching. He cursed as Masango, still on the phone, disappeared out of sight behind some tall bushes. When Masango reappeared, he'd finished his call. He jumped straight into his Mercedes, fired it up, K-turned it out from the shade of the trees and took off down his drive in a tearing hurry.

Bronski started the van as the Mercedes streaked past. He pulled out of the parking space and followed. It felt so good to be back in action at long last. 'We're moving,' he said into the radio. 'Shelton there yet?'

'All present and correct, boss.'

'Heading north. Gasser and Shelton, you should see me any moment now. Stay in contact.'

Masango was really shifting. As he weaved through traffic, keeping the Mercedes in sight, Bronski saw Gasser and Shelton's silver Peugeot filter into his rear-view mirror, three cars back. Jungmayr's green Nissan wouldn't be far behind, gunning it to catch up. They were all pros at covert surveillance and would switch positions constantly so that Masango would never spot the tail. In any case, it looked as if the African had other things on his mind.

Bronski expected Masango to continue north and then cut across town to catch the ferry over the river to Brazzaville. Instead, though, the Mercedes led a twisting route eastwards, parallel with the river for several miles until it became obvious to Bronski that they were heading out of town. Where was the sonofabitch going?

Bronski calmly considered his options and then got back on the two-way. 'Gasser, Shelton, Jungmayr, I want you to cross into ROC and sit on the police HQ in Brazzaville until further instructions. I'll stay on Masango and see where he goes.'

He didn't need to give specifics on the best way over the border. His guys would know to avoid the public ferry and rent a private speedboat to take them the quick route, though they had plenty of bribe cash handy and all the right visas already in place in case they got tangled up with immigration bullshit. They'd be in Brazzaville in a couple of hours, tops.

As for Bronski's own destination, he had no clue where Masango was leading him. While the Mercedes sped east-wards out of Kinshasa, Bronski picked up his cellphone and called Eugene Svalgaard.

'Don't get your knickers in a twist just yet, boss, but I think something's happening over here.'

Svalgaard sounded as though the call had caught him napping, but he responded to the news as if he'd been given an intravenous shot of cocaine straight to the brain. 'What kind of something? Is it good news? You have it? Victor? Did you get it?'

'There have been some developments. Not quite sure what

they are exactly, but it looks like your rock just surfaced in Brazzaville.'

'Where the hell's Brazzaville? Doesn't matter. I'm on my way. Meet me there.'

'Hold on—' Bronski began, but Svalgaard had ended the call. When Bronski redialled the call, Svalgaard had turned off his phone. No doubt already floundering out of his hotel and straight for the Learjet.

'Prick,' Bronski muttered.

He followed the Mercedes to a remote private airfield thirty miles east of Kinshasa that was little more than a tongue of cracked concrete in the middle of yellowed brush land. There hadn't been a living soul in sight for the last five miles, which had made tailing Masango difficult and forced Bronski to hang back almost a quarter of a mile, following a dust plume.

It was hot. Felt like rain was coming. He parked the van behind a clump of thorn bushes on a hill overlooking the strip, where he watched Masango get out of the car and stand alone at the side of the empty concrete runway, waiting and looking up at the overcast sky. He checked his phone once, but was probably getting no reception out here.

Masango went on waiting and Bronski went on watching for a little over thirty minutes before the drone of a light aircraft became audible and a speck appeared in the sky, coming in from the east. Soon after, a pearly white eight-seater turboprop touched down and taxied to a halt as Masango ran to meet it.

Out of the plane stepped a large, powerfully built man in military khaki covered with all the gold braid befitting his self-awarded rank, a red beret clamped on his head. The mirrored aviators, the Havana: no question in Bronski's mind who the guy was.

Jean-Pierre Khosa.

The General looked even nastier and more pissed off than he did in the only photo Bronski had seen. Considering that he'd just had his precious diamond filched from him, it wasn't hard to guess the reason for his foul mood. Even Masango looked terrified of the guy.

Khosa was accompanied by five hard-looking men with automatic weapons who posted themselves around the aircraft and scoured the surrounding area like bodyguards on VIP close protection duty while Masango led Khosa to the Mercedes and they got in.

Bronski had no desire to be shot to death by an African warlord's heavies that day, or any day. Having seen enough, he started the van and made his exit.

Chapter 58

Back at Mama's, Ben dropped off Tuesday, Sizwe, and the kids. Tuesday was flagging and in need of another dose of painkillers. In any case, there was no need for the whole gang to accompany Rae to the embassy. The children gathered in the street outside the auberge, and Rae said goodbye to each one in turn with a little hug. Ben waited behind the wheel of the Land Rover.

'Let's go,' he called from the open window.

Now that the time had come, Jude looked as glum as Ben had ever seen him. He'd never seen a more miserable-looking former hostage about to be returned home and safe than Rae, either. The two of them walked to the car as if they were going to the gallows. Jude let go of her hand to open the back door for her. She lifted one foot inside, and then stopped.

'I don't want to go.'

Jude's face lit up with all kinds of conflicting emotions. 'Come on, Rae, please. Don't do this. You have to go.'

'Does it have to be this morning?' she said. 'Can't it be later? Please. Let me stay just a little longer.' She seemed close to tears. She clutched Jude's hand again and clasped it tight against her side, as if she never wanted to let it go. Visibly moved, Jude put his arm around her shoulders. She rested her head on his.

'Oh, Christ, here we go,' Ben heard Jeff mumble, too quietly for Jude and Rae to hear.

Jude looked at Ben. 'Can we put it off until this afternoon?'

Ben paused a beat, then turned off the engine and stepped down from the Land Rover. 'I don't think a few hours will make much difference in the great scheme of things.'

Jude flashed the brightest smile Ben had seen from him in a long time, and quickly led Rae back indoors. Moments later, they disappeared into Rae's room.

'Those two have got it pretty bad, haven't they?' Jeff said, shaking his head.

'Seems that way,' Ben replied.

'Now we've got a bit of time on our hands,' Jeff suggested, 'I say we take a gander around and see if we can't find somewhere with an internet connection so's I can try to wire through some dosh from the bank.'

For years, Ben had been so in the habit of never travelling anywhere without the comfort of a wad of cash in his pocket that it unsettled him deeply to find himself completely penniless in a strange place. The feeling was also an alarming reminder that his financial situation back home was still just as precarious as when he'd left it. He hated having to ask her, but he borrowed a few francs from Mama so he and Jeff would have some basic expenses money in town.

Brazzaville was a relatively small city with a population only a fraction of that of neighbouring Kinshasa. After not too much searching around, Ben and Jeff discovered the Institut Français du Congo in the Place de la République, a small modern culture and arts centre that also featured a busy little internet café. It might have been 1990s technology anywhere else, but here it felt like a lucky find. They bought coffees and commandeered a computer terminal, from which Jeff emailed Le Val's business banking manager in Normandy.

He outlined the situation and the urgent need to wire several thousand euros to a bank in Brazzaville, where some kind of temporary holding account would have to be set up to accept the funds.

Within minutes, the guy in Valognes emailed back to say it was an unusual request but he'd try and see what he could do.

'Best we can manage for now,' Jeff said as they headed back towards Mama's. 'Looks like we'll be toing and froing for the rest of the day checking emails. I'm sure Alex can sort something out for us. What's the matter? You look worried.'

Ben lit up his last Tumbaco. 'Even if we get the cash through without a hitch, once we see Rae off it's not going to be easy for you, me and Tuesday to get out of here with no passports. Jude's okay, but the rest of us are in a fix.'

'Yeah. The joys of civvy street, eh? And it's not like we can turn up at the Brit embassy pretending we had them nicked, either. Seeing as how we got into Africa under the bloody radar in the first place.' Jeff paused, mulling over the problem. 'Okay, try this on for size. We double back to that internet café and email Auguste Kaprisky. Ask him if he'd send the Gulfstream back out to pick us up.' Calling in a favour from the ageing billionaire had been what had got them from France to Somalia so quickly when the news of Jude's situation had first reached them.

'I'd be surprised if Kaprisky knew what email was,' Ben said. 'He rattles around inside that old chateau of his as if he was living in the nineteenth century. It's a miracle he even has a phone. You know his number?'

'What am I, a walking directory?'

'Then it's not much of a plan,' Ben said.

'But the private jet idea works. How else can you zap about from one continent to another without papers?'

'True, but sadly, we don't happen to own one.'

'What about your sister? She's still the big cheese of Steiner Industries, isn't she?'

Ben shook his head. 'Ruth's taken enough risks and losses because of me in the past already. And I don't think she'll ever let me have another company plane, after what happened to the last one.'

'Fair enough. We could always make our way to the coast and see if the four of us can hitch a lift on another Svalgaard Line tanker.'

'I can just see that,' Ben said.

'I suppose the Dakota's out of the equation?'

'I'd say so, Jeff, yes.'

'Then I'm all out of ideas. Why don't you come up with one for a change?'

'Give me time. I'll think of something.'

They'd been away from Mama's for nearly three hours. When they arrived back there, a pair of four-wheel-drive police cruisers and a bulky armoured van were parked outside. The van looked like something for hauling dangerous criminals off to jail in. Three ROC cops in paramilitary uniform and toting assault rifles were guarding the door of the auberge.

'The SWAT team's here for you,' Jeff said. 'Shouldn't have nicked the Land Rover.'

But as they walked past the guards and went inside, it soon became clear that the police were there on other business. With Mama, Jude, Rae, Tuesday, Sizwe, and the kids inside the kitchen were two more armed officers and Chief Zandu. Mama looked nervous, Jude and Rae more so. Tuesday's eyes were flashing warnings at Ben and Jeff. The children were huddled in a corner, watching the cops warily. Zandu was sitting at the table as if he owned the place.

'They arrived half an hour ago,' Jude said.

Zandu didn't get up. 'We have been waiting for you. Where have you been?'

'Sightseeing. What's this about?'

'I want to show you all something,' Zandu said.

'Like the magic disappearing diamond trick?' Jeff said, a little too loudly.

'Then show us,' Ben said.

Zandu shook his head and smiled, apparently not at all bothered by Jeff's comment. 'Not here. You must come with me.'

Ben pointed at Jude. 'If you have more questions to ask him, then you can ask them here.'

Zandu shook his head again, but this time the smile was gone. He stood up. 'No. You must all come with me. Everyone.' He pointed at Mama. 'Except her. She can stay.'

'This is fucking ridiculous,' Jeff laughed. 'We have six kids here. You want to show them too? Is there a new funfair in town or something?'

Jude was giving Ben anxious looks. *What's going on?*

'Whatever this is about,' Ben said to Zandu, 'these people have nothing to do with it. Take me, if you want. Everyone else stays. That, or nothing.'

Zandu nodded at his two officers. The guns pointed at Ben. 'No more talk,' Zandu said. 'We go, now. Quick.'

'And if we refuse?'

'Then I will have you all arrested,' Zandu said simply.

'On what charges?'

'No charges are necessary. I am the chief of police. I can put you all in jail and leave you there for as long as I want. Nobody will ask questions.'

Ben felt anger and anxiety rise up in him, both at once. Now he understood the purpose of the prisoner van outside. He knew that Zandu could be taken at his word.

Ben pointed at Rae. 'What about her? She has an appointment at the US Embassy here in Brazzaville, in less than an hour. People are waiting for her there. If she doesn't turn up, you'll have the American government all over you. Is that what you want?'

But Ben knew even before he'd said it that the bluff was a waste of time. If there was a way out of this, he couldn't see it yet. For the moment, they had no choice but to comply. Zandu was losing patience fast.

'I know,' Jude said to Ben as the twelve were escorted outside at semi-gunpoint. 'You told me so. I shouldn't have gone to the police. It was a terrible mistake. I'm sorry.'

'You lie down with dogs, you rise with fleas,' Jeff said.

'What do they want?'

'I'm not sure. We'll work it out. Don't worry about it,' Ben answered Jude. But he was, more than he was willing to let show.

Zandu's men separated Rae and Jude from the others and put them in the back of the lead police cruiser. They herded the kids into the back of the second, then put Ben and the rest into the back of the van, which was enclosed with sheet metal on the inside, no windows, just metal benches for the prisoners to sit on. Some people had ventured from neighbouring houses to watch the arrest. Others peeked from windows, too afraid to come out. Zandu's men slammed the van doors.

It was a bumpy ride as they set off at speed through the city's unpaved streets. Sizwe was silent. Jeff was muttering a steady stream of obscenities. Sitting on the metal bench next to Ben in the dark interior of the van, Tuesday said, 'Shit, guys, if I'd known this was going to happen I wouldn't have argued in favour of going to the cops. You know that, don't you?'

'It's just harassment,' Ben said. 'They probably want to shake us down to see what other goodies we might be hiding.' Tuesday didn't seem much comforted. Ben didn't blame him.

It was over twenty minutes of jarring and lurching before the van finally stopped. They heard doors opening and boots clumping and voices, and then the back of the van opened, flooding it with sudden bright light.

'This would be the new police HQ,' Jeff said, peering out. 'Very snazzy.'

The large grey concrete-block building they'd stopped outside was some kind of disused warehouse in an empty avenue of derelict industrial storage facilities. A faded sign for Primus beer hung lopsided and rusting above the doorway. It was the kind of place you brought people to shoot them and dispose of the bodies in the river, which Ben could smell nearby. They were somewhere close to the docks. The city's modern high-rises and the landmark of the Namemba Tower seemed far off in the distance.

The police cruisers had pulled up in front of the van. Jude, Rae and the kids were being marched towards the building by the cops. Ben watched the guns. They were cocked and the safeties were off. A sudden move against Zandu's men wouldn't have been a good idea. Ben wanted to say something, but he kept his mouth shut and kept watching. Whatever this was about, and whatever Zandu had in store for them, he'd find out soon enough.

And moments later, when the rest of them were herded at gunpoint into the shady, dank inside of the warehouse, he did.

Because the twelve of them weren't alone in there with Zandu and his men. Several more figures stepped out of the shadows to meet them. Two of them, Ben had seen before.

But he was only looking at one of them. A face he'd thought he'd laid eyes on for the last time.

'If you knew how happy I am to see you again, soldier,' said Jean-Pierre Khosa. Something in the General's clasped hand caught the light from the doorway and sparkled softly.

The sound of Khosa's laughter filled the warehouse.

Chapter 59

'What a surprise,' Ben said. 'I only wish I could share the sentiment.'

Khosa's men fanned out and pointed gleaming automatic weapons at Ben and the group. Rae and Jude pressed together close while the children shrank away in fear. Sizwe placed his big hands protectively over Juma's shoulders and glared at Khosa with pure hatred. Jeff and Tuesday were expressionless, but Ben knew what they were thinking. The same he was: *How do we deal with this without getting us all killed?*

In Khosa's large shadow stood a tall African in a suit, looking more like a city lawyer than a mobster. Ben remembered him from the day Jude was taken from him. Masango, Khosa's so-called political attaché.

Chief Zandu went over and joined Masango, giving Ben a sneer that said, 'Not so cocky now, are you?' while his men joined Khosa's. Five plus five. That added up to far too many.

Khosa slipped out a cigar and lit it, seeming to savour the moment. He exhaled a cloud of smoke like a howitzer. The eyes behind the mirrored lenses watched Ben through the smoke. When he spoke, his deep voice echoed around the empty building.

'What is it you once said to me, soldier? *"I'll still be here a long time after the world has had the pleasure of forgetting that your ugly mug every existed.'"* Khosa chuckled. 'You were right about one thing. I am ugly. These scars I bear make people frightened to look at my face. I am a monster, am I not?'

'I'm sure you've been called worse things,' Ben said. 'All of them true.'

Khosa smiled and went on, 'But for the rest, soldier, you were wrong. Very wrong. You thought you would outlive me. And you tried very hard to make this happen. You have decimated much of my army. All of my trusted officers are dead. But I am still alive, because I was too clever for you. An underground tunnel leads from the place where you would have burned me alive and blown me to pieces. It is no more than a drain, but it enabled me to save myself from your attempts to assassinate me. And now you see, soldier, that you have failed, and that I will not be forgotten as soon as you thought.'

'I admit I was wrong,' Ben said. 'You'll be remembered, all right. The name Khosa will be talked about for a long time to come. Like some other names that people haven't forgotten in a hurry. Hitler, Stalin, Amin.'

'Ah, now you are talking about my hero,' Khosa chided him. 'You should not insult General Amin, the greatest African leader who ever lived. Until me.'

'I know, you modelled yourself on him,' Ben said. 'You emulated him in all kinds of ways. Torturer, mass murderer, cannibal. In some ways maybe you even outdid him. Except you never got to rule your own country. That must be a real disappointment for you, to know in advance that you died before you could achieve your ambition.'

'I think perhaps you are speaking too soon,' Khosa said, wagging a finger at him. 'I am only disappointed for *you*, that you will never live to see me president. I thought about

401

keeping you alive until that day comes, but as you know, I am not a very patient man.'

'Best get on with it, then,' Ben said.

'Nor do I believe in rushing things. We have all day. Before I kill you, soldier, it will give me great pleasure to share with you the entertainment of seeing your friends die first, and then your son. That is, after your son has watched my men have their own kinds of pleasure with his woman there. I see their time in prison together has brought them very close. That is sweet. It will be even sweeter to watch what happens to her.'

'Bastard!' Rae yelled.

Khosa smiled at her. 'Perhaps I am. But one thing I would not stoop to is to force little children to watch a woman raped and butchered like an animal in front of them. I have more scruples than some of my officers have shown in the past. So naturally, it would be the kindest thing to kill the children before you. In any case they are deserters from my army, and the punishment for desertion is death.'

Sizwe pulled himself up to his full muscular height and said, 'I will not live to see more children die.'

'Then it is decided,' Khosa said. 'You are first, cockroach. Then I will kill the children, starting with that one.' He pointed at Mani, then at Juma. 'Or perhaps that one. I do not like the way he is looking at me. Then I will kill the Jamaican, and then Dekker.' Khosa went on pointing at each in turn as he talked, as if he were playing a game of eeny-meeny. His eyes gave a twinkle as he turned to leer at Rae. 'I am looking forward to hearing the American bitch scream. Then it will be you, White Meat.' The finger aimed towards Jude.

'Fuck you, Khosa,' Jude spat.

Khosa smiled at Ben. 'When we get to your turn, soldier,

I do not think you will offer me any resistance. By then you will want to die. You will beg me to end your life. And after you have begged me enough, I will grant your final wish. Perhaps a quick end, perhaps not. I will see how I feel at the time. It is still some hours away.'

Khosa signalled his men. One of them fetched a rolled-up cloth, set it down on the ground and unrolled it to reveal a clutch of machetes that glinted dully in the dim light. The men took a machete each. They slung their rifles over their shoulders and moved in fast to encircle the group of prisoners. One of them angled a blade against Jude's throat. Another jerked Rae away from him and gripped her arm tight with a machete in front of her face.

'In case you try any of your tricks, soldier,' Khosa warned. 'That is a very sharp blade and Mateso is very quick and strong. He will have the boy's head off before you can blink.'

With five guns still pointing their way in the hands of Zandu's cops, Ben didn't need the extra persuasion of a blade at Jude's throat not to try any tricks. He stood very still. His mouth was dry. The seconds were ticking off fast. *Think. Think.*

Stalling for time, Ben said, 'You really have this thing all worked out, don't you?'

'Oh yes. I have given it much thought, believe me.' Khosa laughed again, and the raucous boom of his amusement echoed through the empty building.

'Reckon you missed out a couple of important details,' said a voice behind them.

Khosa's smile fell and he whirled round. Ben slowly turned his head to look back at the doorway, where the voice had come from.

Standing in the doorway was a man with a pistol.

Chapter 60

He was a white man, not tall, not young, but built solid and wearing the dead-eyed look of a jaded veteran who'd survived enough scrapes in his time not to be fazed by a bunch of guns and blades. He spoke with a New York accent. Ben had never seen him before in his life.

'Who are you?' Khosa barked at the stranger.

'Name's Bronski,' the stranger replied. 'Victor Bronski. You know me as Reynolds. Your guy Mr Masango and I did a little business deal together, one that didn't exactly go according to plan. Remember?'

As Bronski talked, three more hard-looking men appeared behind him, all with short-barrelled pump shotguns and the expressions of experienced fighters ready to inflict serious hurt.

'Meet my associates,' Bronski said. 'Mr Shelton, Mr Gasser, and Mr Jungmayr. I'd tell you more about us, but you might shit your pants, and I'm willing to spare you that embarrassment. Just like I'm willing to overlook the matter of what happened to our other associates, Hockridge and Weller. This is all about business, okay?'

'You had better drop your weapons,' Masango said, coming forwards a step with a nervy glance at Khosa. 'Or we will kill all these people.'

Bronski's eyes didn't flicker. 'Not my problem, sorry. We didn't come here for them. We came for the rock. Our property, bought and paid for. Let's have it.'

'Can you count, old man?' Khosa said. 'We have more guns than you.'

'It's what you do with them that matters,' Bronski replied with a faint twitch of a smile. Another man appeared in the doorway behind him. Ben had no idea who he was either. A few years younger than Bronski, but badly out of shape, his blotchy puffed-up face covered in a sheen of sweat below the rim of his Panama hat. With the bulky white suit, its jacket folded over his arm, and the high-dollar shoes and watch, he looked like an actor in a bad movie playing the part of the rich American businessman abroad. Which, Ben quickly realised, was exactly what he was.

'You have something of mine, Khosa!' the fat man yelled. 'I paid you fifty million bucks for it and I want it!'

Khosa held up his clenched fist and slowly unpeeled his fingers. He rotated the diamond so that it caught the light like a disco ball. 'You mean this?'

The fat man's eyes popped at the sight of it. He swallowed, gulped, and for a moment seemed about to have a heart attack. 'That's my diamond. You stole it from Pender, and Pender was working for me. Which makes it mine, you hear me?'

Jude's eyes flashed with recognition as he remembered the voice of the man he'd spoken to on Pender's sat phone aboard the ship. 'He's Eugene Svalgaard. The ship owner.'

'Quiet!' Khosa snapped, his composure slipping for a second. Mateso pressed the blade more tightly against Jude's throat. Ben's fists clenched tight. He'd forgotten to breathe. Rae was struggling in her captor's grip. The children were streaming silent tears, too terrified to sob out loud. Sizwe was still staring at Khosa, his whole body rigid and trembling in a molten fury. Chief Zandu's eyes were flicking left and right. He was slowly edging away as the atmosphere of tension inside the warehouse continued to mount up towards a crescendo that could erupt at any moment.

'Damn right I'm Eugene Svalgaard,' the fat man yelled, pressing past Bronski to point a chubby finger at Khosa. The blotchiness in his cheeks had gone, as his whole face was now flushed bright red with anger. Spittle sprayed out of his mouth as he ranted. 'Me. The one who set this whole goddamned thing up in the first place. The one you oughtta be thanking that you ever laid eyes on that beautiful rock, because if it hadn't been for me, it'd still be locked up a safe in Oman by some hoarding A-rab asshole who didn't even appreciate it. So now you've had your fun, hand it over. A deal's a deal, even for a lowlife piece of shit jungle bunny like you.'

With a slow, easy smile, Khosa folded his fingers back around the diamond and returned it to his pocket. 'You want my diamond, fat man? Then come and take it.'

'I don't think you heard me, Coltrane. That right there is *my* property. *My* diamond. *Mine.*'

'You are both wrong,' said another voice.

Another total stranger stepped out from the shadows at the back of the warehouse. Lean, in his early thirties, with the olive skin and raven hair of an Arab and a dangerous gleam in his eyes. He was dressed all in black, his clothes tightly fitted to his lean frame. The tiny machine pistol in his hand was pointed somewhere midway between Khosa and Svalgaard.

'Jesus Christ!' Svalgaard yelled, waving his arms and half-turning towards Bronski. 'What is this? Who the hell is this guy?'

The Arab man took another steady step into the light. His body movements were calm and stealthy, but the dark eyes were quick and alert. Ben knew the look very well. If

406

Bronski looked like an ex-cop, everything about this man screamed military. And he wasn't alone, either. As he walked slowly towards them all, four more black-clad shapes emerged from the shadows behind him.

Ben now counted thirty-four people inside the warehouse, twenty-four of them with guns. The tension was like electricity in the air, its voltage surging up ever higher and threatening to blow a fuse at any moment. When it did, it was going to be like a bomb exploding within the confines of the building.

'My name?' the Arab said. His voice was as smooth as a quiet ocean beneath whose surface predators swam. 'I am Tarik Al Bu Said. And that diamond belongs to neither of you. It belonged to my brother Hussein.'

Eugene Svalgaard's eyes bulged in his pudgy face. Even Jean-Pierre Khosa seemed to be speechless as he stared at the newcomer.

The gun in Tarik Al Bu Said's hand swivelled to aim directly at Svalgaard.

'And now I know that I am looking at the man who had Hussein murdered for it,' Tarik said. 'Along with his wife Najila, my little niece Salma, and my nephew Chakir. You commissioned the robbery.'

'It's not like it seems,' Svalgaard blustered, now turning from bright red to white. 'You don't understand!'

'It is not complicated. You hired Pender and his accomplices, knowing what was in my brother's safe. You gave them the order to wipe out the family to steal it for you. You did these things, and now it is time for you to pay.'

Svalgaard stumbled backwards, pale, hands raised. In a panic, he tried to get behind Bronski.

Anticipating what was about to happen, Bronski fired first.

Then all hell broke loose.

Chapter 61

The violence lasted only seconds, but within that short explosive burst of time, everything would change.

Bronski's pistol shot was fired in haste and missed Tarik by a couple of inches. Tarik stood his ground and the small automatic weapon in his hands gave a ripsnort and stitched bullets across Bronski's torso and into Svalgaard, who was trying to hide behind him even as they both fell to the ground.

Simultaneously, Tarik's men opened fire on Shelton, Gasser, and Jungmayr, but not before Bronski's men opened fire in return, taking down two of Tarik's men. Caught in the crossfire and not knowing which way to shoot, Zandu's cops started blasting in all directions as Tarik's remaining men sliced into them with automatic fire.

Ben saw his chance and dived for Mateso, at the same instant that Jude lashed back with his heel and twisted out of Mateso's grip to launch himself at Khosa's man holding Rae. Mateso flailed his machete at Ben. Ben ducked the blow that would have sliced his head in half, moved back in while the blade was still scything away from him with its own momentum, trapped Mateso's arm and broke it and then punched out Mateso's throat before the guy could reach for his pistol with his other hand. Ben whipped the pistol from Mateso's belt and shot Masango, who was about to shoot

Jude. Jude had got the better of the man holding Rae. Jeff and Tuesday had launched into the fight, kicking and punching, Tuesday fighting one-handed with a fury that Ben had never seen in him before as they took down Khosa's men.

Having edged his way towards the shadows at the back of the warehouse, Chief Zandu now made a break for it. One of Tarik's men shot him in the back. Jude had knocked his opponent unconscious and was grabbing Rae, flinging her down and pinning her with his body as a shield the way he'd done on the Dakota. The children were howling and running for the door.

In the middle of the melee, Jean-Pierre Khosa had drawn his .44 Magnum from its holster, sighted Ben through the chaos and drew his aim. Their eyes locked. Khosa's face was a twisted mask of pure hate. Ben raised his pistol two-handed and was about to fire when Sizwe body-slammed Khosa like a charging rhinoceros and smashed him to the concrete floor, roaring in demented fury and raining punches hard and fast into his face, throat, and chest. Khosa was a powerful man, but Sizwe's raging onslaught was so overpowering that Khosa could do little to fight back.

A matter of moments. Then it was over, or almost. Ben's ears were singing shrilly from the gunfire. Bodies lay strewn everywhere. Svalgaard, Bronski, and their entire crew were among the dead. So were Masango, the police chief, and all the cops, along with two of Tarik's men. Only a pair of Khosa's thugs were still alive, though badly injured and bleeding out.

Sizwe was still punching Khosa on the floor, out of control. Khosa's face was covered in blood. He tried to reach up and sink his fingers into Sizwe's eyeballs, but Sizwe knocked his arms aside and went on pummelling him. Something fell from Khosa's jacket pocket. The diamond! Khosa saw it rolling away across the floor, and even as he was being beaten half to death he reached out a flailing arm to make a grab for it. His fist closed on empty air.

Sizwe's arms were red to the elbow. He picked up Khosa's fallen revolver and aimed it in Khosa's bloody face. Thumbed back the hammer. Tears streamed down Sizwe's cheeks. The gun began to shake in his hand, until it was wobbling so violently that he could no longer hold his aim.

'I will kill you!' Sizwe screamed.

But Sizwe couldn't do it. Not like this. He threw the gun down, then lashed out one more time with his fist with a howl of agony, spraying blood over the floor. Khosa groaned.

Jude clambered shakily to his feet, clutching Rae's hand. His temple was bleeding from the fight with her attacker. She was safe now, and he'd keep it that way.

Sizwe might not be able to do it, but Ben could. He picked up the fallen revolver and walked over to where Sizwe was kneeling astride Khosa on the floor. 'Move aside, Sizwe.'

'No,' Jude said.

Ben ignored him and took aim at Khosa's head. Khosa just stared up at him through the blood. Ben had no words to say. The heavy revolver was already cocked and all he had to do was pull the trigger. He lined the sights up on Khosa's forehead.

'No!' Jude shouted. He rushed across and pushed the barrel of the gun away from Khosa's head.

'We don't execute people. I'm not that person, and neither are you.'

'But he is,' Ben said, looking down at Khosa. 'That's why he needs to go.'

'Blowing a man's head off when he's beaten isn't justice. We've had this conversation before.'

'And I listened to you, and let him go,' Ben said. 'Look what came of it.'

'Shoot the bastard,' Jeff said.

'Right here,' Tuesday added, jabbing a finger of his good hand at his own brow.

Jude flashed a resentful look at them, then looked back at Ben. 'This is not what we do, Dad. You kill him now, like this, and I will think less of you. I will no longer respect you. I mean that.'

Ben looked at Jude. Then put the gun down and slid it away so that it was out of Khosa's reach. He stepped back.

Jeff picked up the gun.

'Jeff—' Jude warned.

'Keep your hair on,' Jeff growled. 'I won't shoot him unless he tries anything. You lie there nice and still, General, if you know what's good for you. And count your lucky stars that St Jude here's looking out for your human rights.'

Khosa made a kind of gurgling sound and rolled his eyes.

'What are we going to do with him?' Rae said to Jude.

Jude shook his head. 'I don't know.'

Tarik Al Bu Said stepped over a dead cop and knelt down to pick the diamond off the floor. Only now was Ben able to take a good look at the Arab. The ferocious glint in his eyes was gone and he looked as tender as a deer as he gazed mournfully at his brother's diamond.

'I don't understand,' Ben says. 'What happened here? You're more than Hussein Al Bu Said's brother. Who are you?'

Tarik turned his sad gaze on Ben and held it for a long moment. Then he stood and motioned towards the warehouse doorway.

'Come. Let us speak outside.'

411

Chapter 62

They stepped over the dead bodies near the doorway. Tarik paused momentarily to look down at the corpse of the man who had killed his brother. Ben followed him into the dull, hot afternoon sun.

Outside where they could talk away from the others, Tarik turned to Ben. 'I do not know your name.'

'Ben Hope.'

'I am Captain Tarik Al Bu Said of the Sultan's Special Forces, attached to the Cobra counterterror unit. A man must do something for a living, even if he does belong to one of the richest dynastic families in Oman.'

The way the man moved, the way he held himself, Ben wasn't surprised by that information. 'Your people know my people,' he said. 'We trained together, SSF and SAS. I don't believe you and I ever met personally. I've been out of it for a good few years.'

Tarik gave a small smile. 'I knew, the moment I saw you, that there was something. Men of our kind, we always recognise one another. We are like a hidden tribe, united across all nationalities by our creed. Within the wider world, we inhabit a much smaller one, do we not? An underworld world of shadows, of secrets, and of contacts. Without contacts, there is nothing.'

'That's true enough,' Ben said, and thought about his own contacts that had enabled him to save his son's life. The billionaire, Kaprisky. The specialist in Stuttgart, Rudi Weinschlager. Chimp Chalmers, the crooked arms dealer with connections all over Africa.

'I am on compassionate leave following the death of my brother,' Tarik went on. 'I was overseas, though I am not at liberty to say where, when I heard the news, and flew home immediately. But I did not intend to spend that time mourning alone in a room. Instead, I made other plans, and to execute these plans I drew on these contacts of which we speak. As well as some personal ones. My family's money makes anything possible. I would not spare any expense, however great, to find my brother's killer.'

Tarik took out the diamond, weighing it in his hand. 'What do you know of this thing?'

'Very little,' Ben said. 'Only that men will do a lot of bad things to own it.'

'It is the lost half of the Great Star of Africa, sibling of the famous diamond that now makes up part of the British Crown Jewels,' Tarik said. 'It was discovered in 1905, in a private mine in Pretoria. Four thousand carats, the largest stone of its kind ever seen. A legend, since many experts do not believe in its existence, and those who do have heard no more than rumours. The only thing they can agree upon is that, if it did exist, it would be priceless.'

Tarik paused, gazing at it.

'Only a fool would think this way, of course. There is nothing in the world, no matter how valuable, that cannot be reduced to a price. This diamond has been in my family for generations. It was purchased in a secret auction in 1938 by my great-grandfather, Farouk Al Bu Said, may he rest in peace, for the sum of nearly thirty-seven million American dollars. Today its value is over seven hundred million.' Tarik shrugged. 'Just numbers.'

'But big ones,' Ben said.

'Oh, yes. Although, if you had said that to my brother, he would have laughed. He was much too lax about security, and I often told him so. The evening the robbery took place, all three of his security men were absent from their posts because Hussein had given them the night off. One of them, Jermar, was celebrating his fortieth birthday, and they had all gone into Salalah to enjoy themselves.'

Ben raised an eyebrow. 'The same night? A coincidence?'

Tarik motioned with his finger. 'We think alike, you and I. As it turns out, it was not. As I said, in order to hunt my brother's killers I drew on my professional contacts. I assembled a small team of men, the very best. We abducted all three of Hussein's security men. We tortured them.' Tarik Al Bu Said related this quite openly, in a matter-of-fact tone, as though torture was an everyday part of ordinary life. 'Two were innocent, one was not. His name was Riad. He is dead now, of course, and his end was not comfortable. Before he died, he confessed that he had been paid to leak the information that my brother's home would be unguarded that night. The man who paid for that information was an American former soldier of fortune, who went by a number of aliases.'

'Pender,' Ben said. 'I never had the pleasure of meeting him, but my son did. Jude saw him die. Khosa killed him.'

'Pender had vanished by this time,' Tarik continued, 'but through my investigations I was able to trace one of his former criminal associates, not connected with the robbery. We abducted him, also. Under pressure, this man informed us that the word in the street was Pender was believed dead, killed in a business deal that had gone bad. Not long before the robbery, Pender was reported to have boasted to an acquaintance that he had had a meeting in Kenya with an African mercenary leader, with whom he was planning a major job that would make him, Pender, fabulously rich.'

'Khosa.'

'At the time, I did not know his name.'

Now it was all making sense to Ben at last. 'Pender was smuggling the diamond out of Oman down the east African coast, on board an American cargo ship on which my son happened to be a crewman. Pender did a deal with Khosa, whereby he and his men hijacked the vessel posing as Somali pirates. Pender kept the diamond a secret from Khosa, which was a smart move, as far as it went. When Khosa found out, he gave Pender the chop.'

'And the owner of that ship was the man Pender was working for all along,' Tarik said. 'I am sorry I was not able to kill both of them.'

'But how did you track the diamond here?' Ben asked him. 'The trail had gone cold. Khosa wasn't an easy man to locate, even if you'd known who to look for.'

'I suspected that the diamond must still be somewhere in Africa,' Tarik said. 'A very big continent, and to find it I knew I would need to cover every square mile. That is where my family's wealth came in just as useful as my professional contacts. I did not have to worry about what it cost to put the word out to every corrupt police chief in the entire continent, of whom there are many, as well as every diamond handler, every fence, anyone at all who might potentially offer information in return for a very handsome reward. If this stone turned up anywhere, I wanted to know about it. And when it did, my team and I would be ready to move in and strike, faster than a cobra. We stationed ourselves in Kenya, where Pender's meeting with the unknown African had taken place. My personal Cessna Citation X was on permanent standby, day and night. It is the fastest civilian jet plane in the world,' he added with just a hint of pride.

'Chief Zandu was one of your contacts?' That seemed odd to Ben.

Tarik shook his head. 'According to my sources, he could not be trusted. But I had a reliable spy within his department, who overheard Zandu speaking on the telephone with a known criminal across the border called Masango. They were discussing an item of great value that had somehow come into his possession. I understood immediately what that item must be. Within minutes of learning this news, my men and I were flying towards the Republic of Congo. It took only a matter of a few hours to reach Brazzaville. We arrived at the police headquarters just in time to see Zandu driving away with his squad, and we followed them: first to the guesthouse where they arrested you, and then here. We slipped around the rear of the building and entered by a window.'

'I'm glad you turned up when you did,' Ben said. 'It seems that I owe you.'

Tarik shook his head and smiled sadly. 'I am not sure who owes more to whom. From my spy in Zandu's office who overheard his conversation with Masango, I learned that the diamond had been handed in to the authorities by a person named Jude Arundel. You mentioned his name to me a moment ago. He is your son?'

Ben nodded. 'Jude thought he was doing the right thing in handing it in. Maybe, in the end, he was.'

'And how did your son come to have the diamond?'

Ben ran through the events, compressing them into as few words as he could. 'When Khosa attacked Jude's ship, Jude was able to send a distress message. My friends and I

416

flew out and dealt with the situation. Later, the ship was hit by a storm and sank. Khosa had the upper hand then, and he used it to take us prisoner and bring us to the Congo. Not all of us made it. Khosa was holding Jude hostage, but Jude escaped and took the diamond back from him. Khosa came after us to retrieve it, aiming to kill us all as a reprisal. Which was what was about to happen when you turned up.'

'Then I have you, your son, and your friends to thank,' Tarik said after he'd carefully digested Ben's account. 'Not only for having recovered my brother's diamond, but for having led me to his killer. It is I who owe you an enormous debt of gratitude, not the other way around.'

'You saved my son's life,' Ben said. 'And mine.'

'And now I have a new brother,' Tarik said. He thrust out his hand. Ben gripped it, and they shook firmly. Tarik wiped a tear from his eye. 'Do you understand that I can never fully repay you for what you have done for me? Nothing I can do will ever be enough.'

'I think you've done plenty already,' Ben said.

'You are wrong, my friend. Very wrong. For instance, if I understand your story correctly, you did not travel to Africa by normal means?'

'We were in a bit of a hurry,' Ben said. 'A friend lent us his jet.'

'Jets are indeed very useful to have at such times of need. Do you still have it?'

'What I have is what's in my pockets,' Ben said, pulling them out to show they were empty.

'Then, as I see it, you are stranded in Africa with neither papers nor money,' Tarik said. 'How exactly do you propose to return to your own country?'

'Plus we owe one or two people here in Brazzaville for their help,' Ben admitted.

417

'They shall be paid what they are owed, and much more besides. Your friends are my friends, your allies my allies. Tell me who these people are and it shall be taken care of immediately, today.'

In no position to argue on that score, Ben said, 'I appreciate that, Tarik.'

Tarik suddenly looked thoughtful. 'Tell me something. Your son is not one of us. By which I mean, he is no soldier. Am I right?'

'Jude has grown up to be a better man than his father,' Ben said.

'He has scruples, certainly. He does not want this African, Khosa, to die, even though Khosa would have had him butchered and his woman violated. That takes a very strong heart, although I must say such an attitude is a mystery to me.'

'Whatever Jude wants, I have to honour it,' Ben said. 'That's just the way it has to be.'

Tarik nodded and thought. 'This Khosa is not my enemy, and it is not my right to decide what should happen to him. But if you desire, I will dispose of this trash for you.'

'Without killing him,' Ben said.

'If you do not wish for him to die,' Tarik said, 'then it will be so. There are other ways for an evil man to be . . . neutralised.'

'No torture,' Ben said. 'No limb amputations, no blinding, nothing cruel or unusual.'

'What would be the point?' Tarik shook his head. 'He will be left alive and will suffer no pain. You have my word on that. Yet, he will pose no further risk to anyone. That, I also guarantee.'

'Deal,' Ben said, and they shook hands once more.

Tarik looked at his watch. 'Let us go. My men will bring

the vehicle around the front. They are entirely at your disposal, as am I. What is first on the agenda?'

Ben nodded towards the warehouse. 'Bit of a mess in there. You want to leave it that way?'

'It will be taken care of,' Tarik said with a wave, as though he was talking about a spilled cup of coffee. 'There will be no repercussions. In any case, nobody will miss the police chief. I gather he was not popular.'

'Whatever you say. My son and his lady friend would like to spend a little more time together. After that, she needs to be driven to the US Embassy here in Brazzaville, so she can go home to her family.'

'Consider it done.'

'And I have to return some borrowed property to the Brazzaville golf club.'

'You play?'

'Not exactly.' Ben might have added that, even if they could have had a game together, one of the fairways was currently blocked by a large obstacle.

'It is of no importance. And once your business is done here, you will of course accept a ride home on my jet, wherever home is? It will be my pleasure to deliver you safely to your door within a matter of a few hours.'

Again, Ben realised that he had no option but to agree to Tarik's offer. But the situation wasn't so simple. 'There are some other loose ends I need to tie up before I can leave Africa.'

'Loose ends?'

'Seven of them.' Ben pointed again towards the building.

Tarik nodded, understanding. 'The children?'

'They were taken from an orphanage and recruited into Khosa's army.'

'Barbaric. We have seen this so many times. It disgusts me.'

'I have to find a safe place for them,' Ben said. 'And for Sizwe in there. The big man. His family and village in Rwanda were wiped out by Khosa's forces. I have a particular debt to him. Though right now I have no idea what I can do for the poor guy.'

'Would money help Sizwe?'

'Nothing can bring back his family,' Ben said.

'But it would enable him to pick up the pieces and begin a new life. And provide a safe place for these children. A fresh start, for all of them. Somewhere safe, secure, and peaceful.'

'Maybe. But I have no money,' Ben said. 'Certainly not that kind of money.'

Tarik smiled. He wrapped an arm around Ben's shoulders. 'There is something else you ought to know, my friend, which I did not mention to you before.'

And then he mentioned it.

Chapter 63

Two weeks later

Ben stood at the window of the farmhouse kitchen at Le Val and looked out at the November rain. Storm, the German shepherd, sat by his side, his nose an inch from the cold glass, misting it up with his panting. It was obvious from the way the dog kept glancing up with a melancholy kind of frown that he was anxious about something. Ben rubbed the silky fur between Storm's big pointy ears.

'Don't worry. I'm not going anywhere, not for a while. That's a promise. You've got me all to yourself from now on, okay?'

Storm yawned a toothy GSD smile, pressed himself against Ben's leg and seemed reassured, even if he'd heard such promises before.

Jeff had taken Tuesday into Valognes to get the stitches removed from his arm, which was healing well. Ben's own injuries were slowly fading. Soon, he'd be able to look in the mirror without being constantly reminded of what would come to be known as 'the Africa thing'. Since their return neither he, nor Jeff, nor Tuesday had been willing to talk much about the experience. They all just wanted to move on.

That wouldn't be easy. None of those involved would ever

421

deny that the episode would leave an imprint on their lives forever; time would never fully erase some of the memories they'd brought home with them, which Ben knew would haunt his dreams for many years to come.

And yet, as he stood savouring a Gauloise and watching the raindrops trickling down the windowpane, he had to reflect on the positive things that had, in the end, come about as a result of their journey into Jean-Pierre Khosa's kingdom.

It was good to know that Jude was happy again. All four of them had returned to Le Val together, but it hadn't been more than a few days before Jude had packed a bag and run off to Paris to catch a flight to Chicago. He was still there now. Ben hadn't heard from him since his departure and didn't know when he might see him again, but he often thought of Jude and Rae together, and was glad that the relationship seemed to have blossomed into something good for them both. They needed it, after what they'd been through. If they stayed together and anyone asked them how they met, it should make for an interesting tale.

But Jude's and Rae's happiness wasn't all that had come about.

Ben had thought long and hard about whether to accept Tarik Al Bu Said's offer. He could still remember the moment, as clearly as if it had happened minutes ago. A disused warehouse full of dead bodies, in a sordid dockyard in a city Ben never wanted to see again, was a strange setting in which to have your life potentially change forever for the better, and those of others around you.

Tarik had left the subject till last, cleverly fishing to gauge Ben's reaction before he came out with it. Then, putting his arm around Ben's shoulders, he'd told him about the reward that the Al Bu Said family had put up in return for the return of the Star of Africa diamond – more importantly, in return for justice for the men who had murdered Hussein, Najila, Salma, and Chakir. The humble sum of $20 million dollars was, the family felt, due recompense without running the risk of offending anyone's sensibilities by an overly ostentatious display of wealth.

'It is yours,' Tarik told Ben. 'And you will please not do me and my family the dishonour of turning it down.'

If there hadn't been for the others who stood to benefit, Ben would have turned it down, dishonourably or not. But he wasn't alone in this. And so, after a lot of thought, and after they'd seen Rae tearfully fly off to Chicago, Ben and Tarik had shaken hands for the third and last time.

The money had already arrived by the time Ben, Jude, Jeff, and Tuesday had reached Le Val, although it hadn't been until a couple of days later that Ben had told them about it and gathered them around the old pine table in the kitchen, over a bottle or three of wine, to explain to his stunned audience how he intended to divide it up.

Sizwe was still in Brazzaville, living at Mama's and unsure of anything in his immediate future except his desire to adopt Juma as his own son. Ben planned to give Sizwe $5 million with which to build a new life for them both. Another $10 million was to be allocated to a tax-free trust fund Ben had already started setting up, which would provide a comfortable future and education for little Mani, Akia, Sefu, Steve, and Fabrice, in the capable care of Mama Lumumba. $2 million would go to Le Val, to repay the business for the severe financial hit it had taken over the 'Africa thing', and maybe help it expand a little more.

A further million of the reward money was already in another fund Ben had set up for Jude, much to Jude's initial protest and refusal when he heard this news. Jude settled, though, when Ben told him he intended to donate an equal amount to help Rae pursue her crusade against the illegal coltan trade in Africa, on the strict promise that neither she nor Jude would endanger themselves by ever returning to the Congo. Rae already had all the evidence she needed to sink the corporate players involved.

On those terms, Jude grudgingly accepted Ben's deal.

So far, that accounted for nineteen of the twenty million. What of the rest?

Ben didn't want to be rich. Never had been, never would be, never gave it much thought. But with a cushion under him, he would no longer need to sell his place in Paris. It would give him peace of mind, and who didn't want peace of mind?

As for the roving life he'd lived since leaving Le Val in Jeff's hands, drifting around Europe and the wider world getting himself into all manner of scrapes and generally honing his talent for trouble – that was over now. From this moment onwards, all that lay before him was a life of peace and quiet.

Or so Ben liked to tell himself.

Then again, who could ever really predict what the future held?

Epilogue

Six months later
Somewhere in Africa

He stopped what he was doing and paused, as though he had lost track of what his next action should be. Slowly turned his head and fixed his slack gaze on the area of dirt he had missed.

He thought dully to himself, 'Ah.'

Then his hands tightened on the long shaft of the yard brush and he shuffled over a few steps and resumed sweeping. Clouds of dirt blew up and soiled the trouser legs of the torn denim dungarees that were his only clothing, but he did not notice and wouldn't have cared anyway.

A chicken strutted across his path. He paused again and looked at it. Its beady eyes met his, and for a few moments they gazed at one another. The man smiled. He liked the chicken. It was his friend.

He did not know its name, however, just as he struggled to remember his own. Memory didn't come easily to him.

The man went on sweeping. Then a harsh voice called across the yard to tell him that he had missed another bit over there, you stupid bastard. Placidly, he shuffled a few more steps and obeyed his master's command.

It was very hot under the sun. He blinked the sweat out of his eyes and put the broom down for a moment as he rubbed his face, feeling the ridges and bumps that marked his features. He didn't know why he had them. People said he was ugly, and sometimes that hurt his feelings, but most of the time he didn't really take notice. He took off the ragged baseball cap and ran his fingers over his moist scalp. There was a bit on his head that still hurt, where the hair had been shaved away and a tender scar ran across his skull. He had mostly forgotten the doctors who used to come and see him in the hospital, and the bandages that used to cover his head until they were removed. That was before he came here, a distant and irretrievable past that no longer had any relevance.

The chicken strutted away. He smiled as he watched it go. Later, he would get back together with his friend, where they both slept on a bed of straw in the barn. Sometimes, it let him stroke it. Other times it pecked him, which made him sad.

The man cocked his head and put a finger to his mouth. A fresh thought had come to him. His name, remembered now as if appearing through a veil of cobwebs in his brain.

His name was Jean-Pierre.

But he supposed it didn't matter, and so he went back to his sweeping.

If you enjoyed *The Devil's Kingdom*, you'll love

THE TUNNEL

A Ben Hope Short Story
From SCOTT MARIANI

ONE MAN

Christmas Eve, 2004. Ben Hope has quit the SAS, but he's
back in full-blown military mode and embarking on a
deadly one-man operation in the remote winter wilderness of the Scottish Highlands.

ONE MISSION

His target: a man he once respected and loved like a
father. His purpose: to seek out the hidden truth about a
black-ops mission so covert that not even the SAS knew
about it . . . and a secret so shocking that it could never
be revealed to the world.

ONE CHANCE

When you're up against the best in the business, there's
no surrender and no room for compromise. If Ben's
suspicions are proved right, he will have no option but to
kill. That's if his enemies don't get him first.

Turn the page to read it . . .

1

Somewhere in the remote Highlands of Scotland
Christmas Eve, 2004

Just before the last crimson-purple glow of the falling sun dipped behind the mountains and nightfall spread over the glen, the stag appeared suddenly, silently, at the top of the rise. He stood there for a long moment, as still and poised as a statue, his head held nobly aloft and his magnificent twelve-point rack of antlers silhouetted against the streaks of fire in the sky.

The stag surveyed the wintry, bleak wilderness that stretched for miles in all directions. Two centuries since the last Scottish wolf had been hunted to extinction, this was his sanctuary, his only remaining natural predator being humankind. He was an old male, veteran of countless rutting conquests and fights, and age and experience had made him wily enough to avoid the few human beings who ventured up here into the wilderness. Confident that all was well, the stag gave a snort or two and moved on, in his unhurried way. He paused to nibble at a shrub, then disappeared over the next rise and was gone.

The man concealed in the gorse bushes watched the animal stride away over the brow of the hill. The old monarch of the glen had come within eight feet of him without sensing a human presence.

Ben Hope stood up and slowly emerged from his cover, careful not to leave a single broken twig as evidence he'd ever been here. For the last twenty minutes, the thicket of gorse had served him as an observation point from which he, too, had been surveying the unspoilt panorama that seemed to go on forever in all directions.

Unlike the deer, Ben Hope wasn't scanning for predators. Because he was the predator.

But his hunt wasn't for wild quarry. He was here today to stalk a very different and far more dangerous kind of prey. His prey was a man. A man he'd known for a long, long time, whom he'd thought he could count as a loyal comrade, if not a friend. A man who was one of the remote few he'd encountered in his life whom he considered possibly more accomplished in their chosen profession, more skilled, hence more lethal, than Ben himself.

Whether that was still true, time would soon tell.

A chill wind was blowing from the mountains as darkness fell, numbing his face. The icy rain that had lashed the glen all day long had finally cleared, and the moon was bright, dimmed every now and then by dull clouds that threatened to fill the sky and, if the conditions changed and the wind dropped, could signal possible heavy snowfall over the next few hours.

Ben frowned up at the sky and hoped that wouldn't happen. It wasn't the cold that concerned him, or the possibility of getting stranded out here in the middle of nowhere. Rather, it was the near-impossible challenge of moving over snowy terrain without leaving tracks. If tonight's operation went as he thought – and feared – it might, then the repercussions would be swift, harsh and rigorous. The kind of men who would be sent out to scour every inch of ground for miles to search for evidence wouldn't be easy to deceive. They'd be professional trackers with years of experience and exactly the same level of training as his own. Which was the highest level available anywhere on the planet. Ben was all too aware of the resources the opposition could unleash to catch him.

He tightened up the straps of his pack and kept moving. Night came fast this far north and so late in the year. He welcomed the darkness. It was his element and he felt protected by it.

He'd long ago learned to navigate by the stars, but in these conditions of alternating cloud and bright moonlight he opted for the handheld GPS tracking and digital compass unit he carried on his belt. To avoid the single road that cut through the valley, he had selected a route that would fish-hook around the objective for about four miles and take him onto high ground to the northeast, where he would mount his final OP before moving in. Route selection was the first requirement of tactical movement. Night work was slower, but safer. You avoided pre-existing tracks, footpaths and human habitation at all cost. You made maximum use of natural cover, crossed open ground at its narrowest point, and then only after a careful scrutiny of the terrain. Hills were to be contoured some two-thirds up their slopes, in order to keep to the high ground wherever possible and at the same time minimise the risk of being silhouetted against the sky, should the cloud cover suddenly break.

These things had all been instilled so deeply in him that they came as naturally as walking and breathing. But never once, not even in his most sombre dreams, had he ever thought he'd one day find himself using such skills against the very same people who had taught them to him.

He was dressed in black from head to foot. Below the hem of his beanie hat, his face was camouflaged with burnt cork. When the clouds passed over the moon he was nothing more than a moving patch of black on black, invisible even to a fox. From time to time, when the cloud cover parted and the landscape glowed with the moonlight, he instinctively paused to check his background and ensure that he wasn't outlined against the sky or casting a long, moving shadow that would be a giveaway to any potential spotter.

Only by constant vigilance was it possible to move totally undetected, and it was a skill at which he'd excelled since the earliest days of his SAS training. Nobody could see, hear or even smell him coming – literally. He'd left the cigarettes untouched for several days, so that the scent of tobacco smoke and aromatic tar couldn't be carried on the wind to be picked up by a sensitive nose as much as quarter of a mile away. Before setting out he'd washed himself carefully with a neutral and odourless soap, for the same reason. Overcaution wasn't in the SAS vocabulary. On covert missions into hostile enemy territory, where the smallest mistake could spell fatal disaster, even spicy foods had to be avoided for up to a week beforehand, to avoid telltale scents leaking out in your sweat.

And a mission into enemy territory was exactly what Ben was engaged in at this moment. A mission sanctioned, planned and carried out by him alone, and for which he would bear the sole responsibility if he failed, or was taken captive, or was killed. Any of which, when going up against an opponent like this one, was a very possible outcome.

With that in mind, he'd equipped himself as thoroughly as if he were on an official military operation. As carefully, too. The van in which he'd driven up through Scotland could never be traced to his name. The lightweight infra-red binoculars with laser rangefinder were the same model he'd carried on active duty. So were the silenced Browning nine-millimetre semiautomatic pistol strapped to his right thigh and the Heckler & Koch MP5 submachine gun with integral sound suppressor slung around his shoulder. Needless to say, he'd acquired the hardware without leaving any trails. The firepower was no kind of an overcaution, either. Ben would have been surprised if his target wasn't similarly armed. Whatever happened tonight, if blood was spilled it would be done swiftly and quietly.

His preparations hadn't stopped there. The soles of his boots were covered with rough, grippy leather pads that he had taped into place over the rubber to avoid leaving tread marks. The CTT combat tracker team would be able to tell from even the faintest partial print exactly what kind of boot the intruder had been wearing, and he wished to give them not even the smallest shred of evidence. For the same reason, the leather pads would prevent mud from getting into the treads, which might easily get scuffed against a rock and leave a telltale smear. SAS soldiers were taught that nothing could be allowed to leave a trace of their passing whilst on patrol behind enemy lines. If you had to piss, you did it in a special sealed container. If you had to do the other, you carried it with you in a bag inside your pack for the duration of the mission.

Another piece of equipment he'd fielded was a decidedly non-standard item. During the Malayan jungle campaign in the 1950s, one of the tricks employed by Communist guerrillas to evade British Army Ghurkha trackers had been to shoot a poor unsuspecting tiger and use one or more of its severed paws to print pugmarks over their own tracks in soft ground. Ben had obtained the deer's foot a few days earlier, and was using it in the same painstaking fashion, step by step, to obliterate any tracks he left in the dirt. A true deer spoor couldn't be replicated exactly that way, but by the time the trackers came, the prints would have been weathered enough by morning dew, rain and even sunlight to confuse them.

Hours passed. Inch by inch, mile by mile, pausing frequently to look and listen, he worked his way around the objective until, eventually, he reached the north-east point overlooking it from the high ground. There he used the cover of thick bushes to lie flat and scan the surrounding area with his night-vision binoculars, examining it in overlapping strips to study every detail.

The old stone house was all in darkness, except for a single light in a window on the first floor. It was a large and imposing property, all the more so for its remoteness, standing completely alone in the midst of the wilderness.

Based on Ben's knowledge of his target, he didn't expect the man to have company. That of the female variety, at any rate, could be ruled out with almost complete certainty. He was vociferous in his staunch dislike of women generally, partially resulting from, and partially the cause of, the unhappy endings of his four marriages. As for male company, he had no close friends of his own sex either. He was famously independent, curmudgeonly and unsociable, preferring his own solitary company to that of even a dog, let alone the family he'd never had, and was exactly the sort of person who would be inclined to spend Christmas alone up here in the big, rambling house in the middle of nowhere.

Nor did Ben expect the target to be expecting him. Seven years was a long time. Plenty long enough for guards to be dropped, and for guilty men to convince themselves they'd got away with it.

But Ben was being prudent nonetheless. This wasn't a man to be taken lightly, not by him, not by anyone.

434

The target's name was Liam Falconer. He was fifty-six years old, a career officer with three and a half decades of service. The last time Ben had seen him, six years earlier at his retirement ceremony in Hereford, he'd been slender and fit, sandy hair just beginning to turn silver at the temples. There was no reason to suppose he had changed a great deal physically from that day, when Ben had shaken his hand and thanked him sincerely for all he'd done for him. Soon after that, Falconer had moved to Scotland to live in peace and seclusion on his hundred-acre Highland estate and pursue his interests of grouse shooting and salmon fishing. His nearest neighbours, if indeed they had ever spoken to him, would have no idea of his real identity. Even less of an idea of what his job had been until March 1998, or the secret military world he had presided over for almost sixteen years – a world whose scope and true nature most ordinary people could barely begin to understand.

The reality was that men like Falconer never really retired; they just became more deeply, subtly embedded in the system that had formed them. There were always jobs for those kinds of men. Falconer belonged to that rare breed, possessed of a certain skill set and a certain mentality, who were far too precious to be allowed to spend the final decades of their lives gardening or vegetating in front of television sports. Their minds were their real asset, not their ability to jump out of helicopters and run up a mountain in full pack, or engage the enemy in battle, or stalk up to a sentry in absolute silence and unhesitatingly slit their throat with a razor-sharp killing knife. Those physical skills they might once have excelled at were just the very bottom rung of a ladder that went so high, it disappeared into the clouds. Only those who reached the top ever really knew what went on up there.

And Falconer had reached the top, the very top.

Because, prior to his retirement, Brigadier Liam Falconer CBE had been the head of Ben's direct chain of command as the British military's DSF, Director of UK Special Forces.

2

These days, Ben Hope called himself a 'freelance crisis response consultant'. It was a deliberately vague and euphemistic cover-all term for the kind of work he'd drifted into during the six months since quitting the SAS after too many long and brutal years.

The work he did now wasn't any less dangerous, but someone had to do it. With the secrets of his past that still haunted him, his military skills, his flair for languages and his talent for undercover detective work, it hadn't been long before he'd found himself drawn into the world of kidnap and ransom, safeguarding the victims of the billion-dollar business that preyed on innocent people and their loved ones. There was nothing Ben despised more than those who violated and exploited the weak and the defenceless.

Wherever there were people, and wherever those people had money, the kidnap and ransom business flourished. Along with warfare and prostitution, as a trade it was as old as human history itself and showed little sign of ever going away. In the modern age, 'K&R' was expanding at an exponential rate year on year. As a result, his work carried him all over. Europe, North Africa, Central America, the Middle East, all the big hotspots.

Sometimes it didn't take him so far from home. When

the eleven-year-old daughter of a wealthy private cosmetic surgeon had been snatched from an exclusive private girls' school outside London in early October that year and her parents had despaired of getting the kind of help they needed from the police, Ben had been privately contacted via the word-of-mouth networks. After agreeing to meet the girl's father at a discreetly-chosen location, he'd jumped on a plane to London and been hired on the spot to sniff out contacts to trace a certain former nanny to the child who, it was suspected, might have colluded with a certain present boyfriend to snatch the girl as a sure-fire ticket to raising a million or two.

It wouldn't have been the first such case in the world, and it wouldn't be the last. These things happened all the time.

Chasing up leads, Ben had followed the trail to an all-night joint in one of the less salubrious districts of Peckham, where an old pal of the ex-nanny's boyfriend was reported to hang out. Ben's plan was to find him, lean on him a little and find out what he knew, but the guy hadn't shown up.

Ben had been about to leave when he'd spotted the familiar face among the crowd thronging the bar. And the familiar face had spotted him in return. One of those chance events, just a flash in time, that can lead you to places you never could have guessed.

In retrospect, the seedy club was exactly the kind of place one might have expected to run into Jaco Lennox. The ex-Para had passed SAS selection a couple of years after Ben, in 1993, but Ben hadn't known him well. The way the regiment operated, frequently working in small teams deployed overseas for months at a time, it was possible for men from different squadrons to cross paths only seldom. In Jaco Lennox's case, Ben counted it as a blessing that he'd never had to work with the guy. Lennox had a reputation as a rough, brutal troublemaker. It had been said it was hard to tell which he loved most: women, whisky or war. All three had threatened to take him down on numerous occasions. And he was an unmanageable bastard, too. He'd been through more disciplinary scrapes and teetered on the edge of dismissal from the regiment more times than any other trooper Ben knew.

It therefore hadn't come as much of a surprise to hear through the grapevine that Lennox had quit, just a couple of months after Ben himself had left. The circumstances of Lennox's departure from the regiment had been shrouded in the usual military bureaucratic secrecy that usually indicated a little overfondness for the bottle, among other vices. The rumour mill had suggested much the same. It was amazing he'd stuck it for so long.

Ben hadn't intended to stay long in his company that night. He didn't like the guy any more than he enjoyed talking to a drunk, and Jaco was already slurring his words when they grabbed a corner table away from the music and the crowd. Just a quick drink or two was Ben's plan, for old times' sake. Chat, catch up, a few minutes of small talk, nothing too involved: then back to his hotel to work out his next move on the case. But the few minutes became an hour. Then two. By then, Jaco was too drunk to say much more.

Which didn't matter. Because he'd already said plenty.

It hadn't taken Ben long that night to realise that Jaco Lennox was a man struggling under the weight of an enormous burden. It wasn't the drink, the drugs, the STDs or even the debts. He admitted to Ben what Ben could already clearly tell from his bloodshot eyes and pallid, shiny skin: that he hadn't slept properly in weeks, months, even years, from the nightmares that kept him staring at the ceiling all night and haunted him throughout each day. He was falling apart mentally and emotionally. He was no longer fit for war; whisky no longer helped; and women would no longer touch him, other than those who might do so for cash in the hand – and he could no longer afford those.

Which was telling, in itself. Former SAS men could do very well for themselves in the security industries, especially overseas, where tax-free earnings flowed like water for experts with the right credentials. In terms of admitting its owner to an exclusive and top-paid élite, the winged dagger badge was better than the best first-class Oxford University degree. Even the least distinguished ex-soldier bearing that coveted stamp on his CV could, with a little networking, expect to pull down a handsome paycheque for the rest of his working life. But one look at a broken-down babbling wreck like Jaco Lennox, and prospective employers were shying away. He hadn't landed a job since quitting the army.

What it was that made Lennox open up the way he did, Ben would never know for sure. It was obvious he was a man wrestling with a secret that was bursting to get out, but Ben wasn't sure if Lennox's long and detailed confession was moti-vated purely by deep-seated shame and the need to talk to someone, or whether it was just the drink loosening his tongue. Either way, it didn't matter. After years in the SAS, Ben had thought nothing could shock or surprise him any longer.

He was wrong.

The story Jaco Lennox told him was seven years old. It was one everybody in the world already knew. Or thought they did. Very few people would have been willing to even contemplate the reality of the version Lennox revealed to Ben that night. Not even Ben himself.

He didn't really believe it at first. Lennox must be out of his mind, or must have frazzled his brain down to the size

440

of a grape with coke and crystal meth and LSD. Ben worked over a thousand possible explanations, each crazier and more improbable than the last – but he was willing to accept almost anything rather than what Lennox had confessed to him. It was easier to dismiss the whole thing, put it out of his head and get on with the job at hand.

Which was what Ben had duly done, ploughing every ounce of energy he had into tracking the missing girl, following up more leads, kicking down doors and dealing with the situation the only way he knew how, and as only he could.

Two weeks later, the case was happily resolved, the kid was safely back in the arms of her parents, and the ex-nanny who, it turned out, had indeed hatched the plan to kidnap her for ransom had been anonymously delivered into the hands of the police (who hadn't themselves managed to unravel a single lead). The ex-nanny's boyfriend had been less fortunate. Which had been his own choice, and his own undoing. His first mistake had been to get involved in the first place. His second mistake had been not to cut and run before Ben got to him. The exact details of his demise would never be known. Nor would his remains ever be found, except, perhaps, by the fish that lived in one of England's biggest and deepest quarry lakes.

Ben only collected payment for his services from those who could well afford them. With the money in his pocket, no further employment offers to chase up, and the things Jaco Lennox had confessed to him still just an unpleasant question mark in his mind, he'd returned to his rambling home on the windswept west coast of Ireland.

There he'd done what he always did in his downtime: cracked open a fresh bottle of Laphroaig single malt, let himself be fussed and mothered by Winnie, his housekeeper, gone for long lonely walks on the beach and smoked and gazed out at the cold implacable ocean and waited for the next call to rouse him back to action. Sooner or later, usually sooner, there was always another call.

When the call had come, it hadn't been quite what Ben might have expected.

'Did ye hear the news, laddie?' said the familiar gruff voice. No "Hello Ben, how are you doing?" No "It's been a while; what are you up to these days?" But then, his old regimental pal Boonzie McCulloch had always been known for getting right to the point.

'What news?' For all Ben knew, England might have been invaded, or London totally flattened in a nuclear blast. He didn't watch TV, didn't buy any newspapers. Life on the Galway coast got a little isolated at times. That was how Ben liked it.

'Lennox is deid.' Boonzie had long ago retired to live in Italy, but he would take the Glaswegian accent to his grave.

'Jaco Lennox?' As if it could have been anyone else.

'They found the fucker hangin' from a tree in Epping Forest. Topped hisself.'

Ben wasn't entirely surprised to hear it. But he could tell from Boonzie's tone, and the pregnant pause that followed, that there was going to be more to the story. He could almost visualise the knowing look on the grizzled old wardog's whiskery face.

'At least,' Boonzie added cryptically, 'that's what we're told.'

'Meaning what?'

'Meaning, there're certain details left oot. Such as the fact that said stiff managed to cuff his ain haunds behind his back and put two boolits in his heid before he stretched his neck.

442

Looks like our Jaco must've made some bad acquaintances. Guid riddance, if ye ask me. He had it comin' a long time.'

'Would it be too much to ask how you came by this information, Boonzie?'

Another low chuckle. 'Och, let's just say someone in CID owed me a wee favour.' Which was all Ben would ever get out of Boonzie, and he didn't press the matter. Soon afterwards, they hung up the phone. Boonzie went back to his peaceful retirement, and Ben went for another walk on the beach.

For three days afterwards, Ben struggled to reconcile the news of Lennox's sorry end with what the dead man had revealed to him that night in Peckham. There were suicides, and there were 'suicides'. Some more discreet than others. But always for a reason. And when certain people went to certain lengths to make sure certain secrets were kept that way, in Ben's experience it tended to suggest that those secrets were, however unbelievable, however unthinkable, most probably true.

That was why, at dawn on the fourth day, Ben said 'Fuck it' and grabbed his bag and was off again. He couldn't stand it any longer. He needed to find out for himself.

Yet back then in late October, it had all seemed too impossible, too monstrous. Even to him, the man who sometimes couldn't sleep at night because of the things he'd done in the course of what he had once considered his duty, his profession, his calling. 'Queen and country', they called it. He'd often thought about that expression, and had eventually come to decide it was a misnomer, for two reasons. Firstly, Ben very much doubted whether the Queen of England, or for that matter whoever might succeed her, or any modern-day reigning monarch, or for that matter again any ruler figure whose face and name were known to the public, knew half of what really went on in the dirty, bloody world of international politics and the conflicts it gave rise to. Secondly, the unsuspecting public who made up the vast majority of the country knew, or were allowed to know, even less. So, by logical deduction, it was clear that these activities were not carried out either for Queen, or for country, or on their behalf, with their consent or even with their knowledge. They went on purely in order to further the agenda of those few, those invisible and nameless few, who held the only true power – not just on a national level, but a global level.

In his thirty-plus years, many of those spent fighting to protect the interests of those powers, Ben had seen enough, learned enough, deduced enough, to know that the only truths worth knowing in this world were those kept carefully hidden behind a smokescreen. Nothing else was real. Not governments, not elected representatives, not nations, not democracy. Everything the public saw, or was allowed to see, was an illusion.

And everything the public heard, or was allowed to hear, was a lie.

These people even lied to their own.

And so, when it came to information of the kind that Jaco Lennox had spilled to him, it was easy to understand the motive of the secret keepers. Easy to understand why they'd do anything, everything in their power to prevent loose tongues from wagging. The alternative was simply not an option.

Ben could understand it, but he couldn't forgive it. If Lennox's story was true – if even a quarter of it was true – this one went way too far off the scale for that.

Two months and a lot of miles later, Ben now believed he'd covered as many angles and dug up as much evidence as he needed. He was ninety-five percent certain that what he'd uncovered, however disconcerting, was more than just the booze-addled ramblings of a worthless former soldier on the edge of mental breakdown.

That was the reason why he was here tonight, prepared to do whatever it took to press the final truth from a man he had once admired and respected with all his heart.

And then, if Ben's worst fears were proven right, he would have no choice but to kill that man.

3

It was late now. The temperature was dropping fast and frost was forming on the heather as Ben lay hidden in his observation point, scanning every inch of the house and buildings through his binoculars. The single light in the upstairs window stayed on, casting a dull glow across the front yard, but he saw no movement from within. Nothing stirred. The only sound was the low whistle of the night wind across the glen. It was chilling him down steadily, beginning to bite through his clothes, and he knew he'd have to get moving before he started going numb. The first serious sign of hypothermia kicking in was a dulling of the mental faculties. That was something Ben couldn't afford to happen here tonight.

After thirty minutes of observing, Ben finally emerged from his observation point and began the slow, painstaking final approach down the hillside and across the open ground towards the house. From here on in was the time of maximum danger, where he would be the most vulnerable to being spotted. The lie of the land was extremely exposed, not a tree or a bush or a rise behind which he could hide until he reached the stone wall that surrounded the property.

The wall was some fifty yards from the house at its nearest point, forming a wide rectangle that was completely closed off apart from the pillared double gateway in front. A beaten-earth track that served as a driveway led for sixty yards in a straight line right up to the main entrance. There was nothing between the gates and the house except a stone stable block converted into a long, low garage, slightly off to the left, and a barn to the right, both half-lost in shadow. To use either building as cover, he would still have to cross a good stretch of open ground in full view of the house's dark windows. He didn't like it much. If a powerful torch beam or security floodlight should suddenly blaze into life, he'd be caught in it like a lamped rabbit. But his instinct told him that wasn't going to happen. Everything he'd seen so far convinced him that the element of surprise was in his favour.

Ben didn't know it then, but that was a deadly mistake.

He reached the wall ten yards to the left of the gates and skirted along its edge, his footsteps crunching lightly on the frosty grass. He paused at the thick stone gate pillar to check his weaponry one last time before stepping up to the gates.

The black iron bars gleamed dully in the faint glow from the lit-up window sixty yards away. They were unchained. Ben ran his eye up their length, all the way up to the spikes at the top, looking for a security system that would sound off the moment he tried to open them. But there was nothing. He took a deep breath, gently placed a gloved hand against the bars of the left-side gate and gave a push.

The gate swung open a couple of feet, smoothly and silently. It was very much like Liam Falconer to keep his hinges well oiled. And to Ben, it was another small sign that his visit wasn't expected. He stepped through the gap and started walking, very slowly, up the beaten-earth driveway. Fifty yards from the house. Step by step, thinking about tripwires, alarm mines, motion sensors, infra-red security cameras.

Forty-five yards from the house. He paused. Watched. Everything was still. The angles of the roof and the four chimney stacks were darkly silhouetted against the sky, their lines traced here and there by silver moonlight. The single lit upstairs window cast an amber shaft of illumination across the yard. Ben strained his ears for any sound of movement from the house. The scrape of a dark window opening. The cocking of a gun. The bark of a dog.

Nothing. He kept moving. Forty yards from the house. Thirty-five. He was almost level with the side of the garage block to his left. He paused again.

And froze.

He could still neither see nor hear anything except the whisper of the wind and the soft thud of his own heartbeat. But he could smell something.

Cigarette smoke. Just a trace of it on the cold night air. Faint, but unmistakeable.

Unless there had been a dramatic reversal in his habits, Liam Falconer didn't touch tobacco. Wouldn't have the stuff in the house.

With a rush of apprehension, Ben suddenly realised he'd been wrong in assuming that Falconer was alone here tonight. Very wrong. He quickly sidestepped off the drive and ran for cover towards the side of the garage.

And a dark shape charged out of the shadows to meet him.

The knife blade was black and dull and reflected no light, because it was a military killing knife designed for use in fast, brutal covert raids where speed and surprise were essential. Ben sensed it coming as the rushing figure closed in on him. He heard its sharp point whip through the air, slicing towards his throat. He ducked out of its swing, blocked the arm that was holding it and lashed out with his boot. Felt his heel connect in a solid impact. Heard the muted grunt of pain and the crunch of a kneecap.

The attacker went down on his back and a wheezing gasp burst from his mouth as the air was knocked out of him. Ben went straight down after him, pinning the knife arm to the ground and ramming the butt end of his submachine gun hard into the man's face. Then again. He twisted the knife out of the man's gloved hand. Grabbed him by the neck and dragged him a yard along the ground, to where the shaft of light from the house shone past the side of the garage.

The man's face was streaming with blood and his nose and teeth were broken, but at a glance Ben saw he wasn't Liam Falconer. He was twenty years younger, rough-featured, his cheeks mottled from standing outside a long time in the cold on guard duty. He was heavily wrapped up in a military parka and a fur-lined hunter cap. His eyes fluttered, then opened wide and he lunged up at Ben as if to head-butt him. Ben smashed him in the throat with the edge of his left hand, then clamped it over the man's bloody mouth. With his right hand he drove the long, slim blade of the killing knife down hard, punching though the heavy coat, between the man's ribs and deep into his heart. It was over for him.

But it wasn't over for Ben.

The chatter of a silenced machine carbine set to fully-automatic fire was a sound designed to be lost among the ambient noise of a jungle or urban environment. Out here in the dead stillness of the Scottish glens it ripped the night air like the buzz of a chainsaw.

Even as the bullets were still in the air, Ben was moving. He dived away from the dead guard and hit the ground and rolled around the edge of the garage. The bullets thunked into the hard earth and cracked off the wall. Splinters of stone stung his face. He rolled over twice more and then sprang up to his feet just as the dark shape of the shooter appeared around the other side of the garage, fifteen feet away. Ben could see the glint of steel and the flash of his eyes and his feet braced wide apart in a combat stance as he drew his weapon up to fire. Ben was quicker. He had to be. He clamped the butt of the MP5 against his hip and let off a burst that stitched a line diagonally across the man's torso before he could touch his trigger. The shooter let out a grunt and crumpled to the ground like a sack of washing.

Ben felt the wetness cooling on the side of his face from where the flying stone splinters had opened up his cheek. He didn't bother to check the cut, just as he didn't bother to check the second dead man on the ground. He already knew it wouldn't be Falconer, either.

Lights were coming on inside the house as whoever else was inside was alerted by the shooting. Ben wasn't worried about losing the element of surprise, because you couldn't lose what you'd never had to begin with. He realised now that Falconer had been expecting him after all. Ben cursed himself for his stupidity. It had almost cost him his life. It might yet.

Ben thought, *Fuck it*, and sprinted for the front entrance. He shouldered his way in through the door. Light was coming from up a passage beyond the wide entrance hall, gleaming off heavy oak furniture and stone floors. The walls were thick and craggy.

Movement up ahead. A door swinging shut as someone quickly retreated back through the house, too fast for Ben to see his face – but it was a tall, lean man who could have been Liam Falconer. Ben chased after the retreating figure. Heard the loud crack of an unsilenced pistol and ducked as a mirror shattered a foot from his head. He let off another stream of fire at the closing door. The bullets punched through the solid wood.

He kept running. He reached the door and grasped the handle and wrenched it open. The inside of the door was tattered from where the bullets had torn through. Splinters littered the floor; a single spent .45 pistol cartridge casing rolled across the slate flagstones.

Nobody there. Ben paused, heart thumping, senses jangling. The air was heavy with the scent of fresh cordite and the trickle of gunsmoke that oozed from the muzzle of his weapon's silencer.

He thought he heard uneven footsteps racing away, around the corner where the stone-floored passage twisted ninety degrees out of sight. He went after the sound. Framed oil paintings and Scottish broadswords and ancient flintlock fowling pieces and hunting trophies hung on the walls, the mounted antlers throwing spiky shadows down the corridor. Ben reached the bend in the passage and felt something slippery underfoot. He looked down and saw the bright red blood splats glistening on the dark flagstones. There was a trail of it. One or more of his bullets had certainly hit home, but his target was only wounded and still on the move.

Ben spent a second too long looking down at the blood.

Something moved behind him, coming out of the shadows. He whirled round and ducked simultaneously, catching his gun against the wall and letting it drop as the blast of a gunshot filled his ears like a bomb going off. The muzzle of the black combat shotgun was just feet away, swivelling towards him for a second shot as he lunged to grab hold of the weapon's barrel before it could blow his head off. His ears were ringing and he was disorientated from the huge twelve-gauge blast in his ears, but if he didn't move fast he was a dead man.

The struggle was short, intense and vicious. Ben's gloved fist closed on the shotgun. He gripped it tightly and twisted it away from his face and thrust it backwards with all the violence he could muster, trying to unbalance the attacker who'd just almost managed to kill him. The shotgun butt slammed against the man's collarbone and Ben felt the snap resonate through the length of the weapon as it broke. There was no time to turn the gun on his attacker. No time to draw his own pistol, no time to do anything except hurl himself at the guy in a wild exchange of strike, block, strike, block, kick and punch and head-butt and elbow and gouge. Ben's opponent was strong and young and well-trained. It was hand-to-hand brutality in its purest form for several seconds, and it could have gone either way until Ben landed an elbow strike against his enemy's smashed collarbone that produced a sharp scream of agony. The man staggered back a step and Ben hit him with a pincer punch to the throat that collapsed his windpipe. Disabled and choking and clawing at his neck to try to get air that would never come, the man crashed to the floor. Ben grabbed a heavy brass candlestick from a side table and upended it like a short axe and pounded its circular base into the man's skull until he stopped thrashing and became inert.

Ben tossed away the bloody candlestick and leaned against the wall, panting hard. He closed his eyes for a few moments until he got his breath back and his hands stopped shaking. He was numb from all the blows he'd absorbed on his chest and arms, but he knew there'd be plenty of pain in his short-term future. If he lived that long. Falconer was still somewhere in the house.

Ben limped back to retrieve his fallen weapon. He picked up the blood trail again and started following it through the house. Nobody else tried to kill him, for the moment.

The further it went, the more the blood trail thickened. The zigzag of splashes and smears led Ben past doorways and rooms to a downward flight of stone steps. At the bottom of the steps was another door, heavy oak, with ancient iron hinges. A bloody hand was printed on the wood. More smears were on the old iron handle.

Ben opened the door slowly and tentatively, ready to shoot. The steps continued downwards into what he realised was not a basement, as he'd first thought, but a wine cellar, with a bare concrete floor and dim lighting from naked bulbs suspended on their wires from the arched ceiling. Ben descended the steps. The cellar smelled of damp. It was richly stocked with hundreds of bottles stored horizontally on tall wooden racks. A connoisseur's collection, labels faded and mildewed with age, the dark green bottles all dusty and venerable.

The blood trail snaked over the concrete floor, between the wine racks to where it terminated in a spreading pool in a corner. In the middle of the pool, sitting slumped against the wall with his legs splayed out in front of him, his chest heaving, his head lolling on his shoulder with a grimace of pain etched on his lean face, was Brigadier Liam Falconer CBE, former Director of UK Special Forces.

'You shot me,' he breathed.

Ben looked at him. Falconer stared back, his teeth slightly bared, like a trapped wild animal. His right hand fingers were still loosely curled around the handle of his Colt 1911 automatic pistol, but he could no longer raise it. His right arm was broken and useless, the sleeve of his white shirt almost black with blood. His left hand was clamped to the more severe wound in his stomach, the one most of the blood was coming from. Penetrating a solid oak door wiped some velocity off a nine-millimetre bullet. But not enough to prevent it from doing real damage to anyone who might be standing on the other side.

'You're not looking so good, Liam,' Ben said, walking up to him. He kicked the .45 auto from Falconer's hand. It clattered across the concrete floor, far out of the wounded man's reach. Ben stepped back again. Falconer was in serious trouble. But he was also probably one of the hardest men to kill that Ben had ever known. It wouldn't have been a good idea to get too complacent, or too close.

Falconer laughed, then broke into a cough. He spat. The spit came out red. 'Benedict Hope.'

Ben shook his head. 'Come on. You know I hate being called Benedict. By the way, your guard dogs are dead. It's just you and me now.'

'Why are you here, Major?' Falconer tried to move, and his face clouded with pain. He winced.

'Don't call me that either. Just Ben will do fine. And I think you know why I'm here. I came to find out if what I've heard is true.'

Falconer glared up at him through eyes narrowed to slits. 'I have no idea what you're talking about. You broke into my house. You killed my men. What the hell are you playing at, Hope? Is what true?'

'Don't waste time you don't have,' Ben said. 'You should have guessed that Operation Solitaire would catch up with you, sooner or later. You've had seven years to atone for it. Have you?'

'Operation what?'

'You heard me,' Ben said.

'I heard you. I'm not aware of any mission of that name.'

'Then let me be a little more specific, to refresh your memory,' Ben said. 'Twenty-three minutes after midnight on the last day of August, 1997. The Pont de l'Alma road tunnel on the banks of the Seine River, in Paris. I was in Bosnia at that time, chasing down war criminals. Where were you? Did you oversee the operation in person, or did you just run things from a cosy little office somewhere?'

Falconer pressed his left hand more tightly against his stomach. Blood leaked out from between his fingers. He groaned. 'I won't talk.'

'Yes, you will. Because I don't take silence for an answer. And because you're a dying man. If you don't get to a hospital, that bullet in your belly is going to make you bleed to death. You don't have very long, so you'd best get started.'

'Don't be a fool,' Falconer said. 'Do yourself a favour and walk away now. Call me an ambulance on your way out. No reprisals. It's over.'

Ben took another step closer. 'We've gone from "I don't remember" to "no comment" to "let's make a deal". So far, I'm not hearing any hot denials.'

Falconer spat again. Redder this time. 'Would it do me any good?'

'None whatsoever,' Ben said.

'What if I were to plead my case? Lay out the evidence to prove to you that whatever it is you *think* we did, you're making a huge mistake?'

Ben shook his head. 'I'm not here to listen to more evidence, Liam. The official version of events has become a matter of historical record now. If they ever open another inquest, it'll be just the same old rubber stamp job. As far as anyone's concerned, you got away with it. And as for the Increment, they never existed.'

4

The Increment. Inside the secretive walls-within-walls of UK Special Forces, Ben had always believed they were more myth than legend. What the verifiable facts said was . . . nothing. Because nothing about the Increment was, ever had been, or ever would be, verifiable. What the rumours said, and had repeated persistently for years, was that the Increment was the name given to an ultra-covert black ops organisation that worked invisibly under the auspices of the British Ministry of Defence, so low in profile as to be known only to an élite core of individuals. It was whispered that the unit was composed of secretly-selected recruits from the Special Air Service, Special Boat Service and MI6, and existed to fulfil missions of the kind that could quickly and easily be denied by officialdom, in the event of such covert operations becoming compromised.

In short, the Increment was an illegal paramilitary assassination team. Employing only a certain breed of operative, possessed of the necessary qualities above and beyond those of normal Special Forces soldiers. Above and beyond, not in terms of their physical or mental ability, but in terms of their moral flexibility and willingness to accept assignments so dirty that normal men couldn't be asked to carry them out, or trusted not to speak out in protest at what they were being asked to do. For that reason, the very existence of the

Increment was kept hidden even from the closest comrades of the men within it.

That was, if you bought into the rumours. Ben never had, because wild speculation and crazy conspiracy stories had forever buzzed around the closed world of SF like flies trying to land on a foil-wrapped turd.

But now he knew differently.

Falconer coughed. He wiped red from the corner of his mouth. The colour was arterial bright. 'Who said they did exist?' he rasped.

'Jaco Lennox did,' Ben replied. 'He was one of them. You should never have trusted him, Liam. The problem with hiring men of loose morals is that they tend to have large appetites. To keep them happy, you have to pay them a hell of a lot. But the likes of Jaco Lennox don't believe in stashing it away for a rainy day. Once he'd drunk himself into a hole and the money ran out, you should have known that he'd fall apart. He was a loser who was guaranteed to burn out and start blowing his mouth off. If it had been me, I'd have kept a closer watch over him.'

Falconer let out a bitter, resigned-sounding laugh, and his shoulders sagged. 'We had our suspicions. But we couldn't mount constant surveillance. We didn't have the resources.'

Another piece of the puzzle slotted into place in Ben's mind. It was all beginning to make sense.

'I wasn't the only one Lennox blabbed to, was I? Talking to me was what broke the dam. My guess is that soon afterwards, he started making calls. And I'm also guessing that MI6 were listening in. That's when they realised Lennox was going into serious meltdown and drinking heavily. How were they to know who he might talk to next? What if he went to the media? What if some idealistic reporter locked him down and sobered him up and got the whole story out of him? It would have been unsurvivable. He had to be silenced before the worst happened. Another little job for the Increment. How am I doing so far?'

Falconer said nothing. Which was the same as saying everything. Ben knew he was right.

'A drunk like Lennox couldn't have been hard to pick up. The usual method. A dark street, no witnesses. One guy comes up to ask the time. The other steps up behind and puts a bag over the target's head. Then they cuffed and stuffed him into a van, drove him out into Epping Forest, popped two in his head for good measure and then strung him up with his hands still tied. Not the neatest job in the world, was it?'

'I had nothing to do with it,' Falconer protested.

'Of course not. You're retired,' Ben said. 'Now, I'd imagine that before they killed him, they pressed him to find out who he'd already been talking to. I'm guessing he confessed that he'd spilled his guts to someone from the regiment. Hence the guard dogs. You were expecting trouble. But you didn't know who was coming, or else you'd have made damn sure you got to them first. My guess is, the night I met Lennox he was so pissed he couldn't remember afterwards who it was. Am I right?'

Falconer gave a weary sigh. He slowly closed his eyes, then reopened them. Something rattled in his throat. 'We narrowed it down a list of four potential names,' he said, after a beat.

'Was I on the list?'

Falconer nodded. 'We knew that if it was you, you wouldn't take it lightly. A team was dispatched to Ireland to look for you, but you weren't at home.'

'I'm a restless soul,' Ben said. 'What about the other three? You'd better not tell me they've come to any harm.'

'Still watching them,' Falconer said quietly.

'So then you decided to post your guys here and wait. Nice work, Liam. You've got a great big guilty sign hanging around your neck. Just as I thought.'

'You know damn all,' Falconer said, his anger flaring up. 'You're shooting in the dark with only the ravings of a drunken idiot to go on.'

'Not quite,' Ben said. Not taking his eyes off Falconer for a second, he tore open the Velcro fastener of one of the pockets of his black combat jacket. He slipped out a slim package wrapped in waterproof plastic. Inside were four glossy 9x13 photographic prints. He drew one of them out and flicked it into Falconer's lap. Falconer hesitated, then slowly peeled his left hand away from his stomach and reached down to pick it up. When he did it, Ben could see the fresh blood leaking from the bullet hole in his abdomen. Falconer must have been in terrible pain.

The photo was of a white car, a boxy, no-frills hatchback. It was parked on grass with trees in the background. The angle of the shot showed that it had French number plates.

'Fiat Uno,' Ben said. 'Familiar to you?'

Falconer tossed the photo on the floor, where it landed in the pool of blood and started absorbing red. 'I don't remember having seen it before,' he murmured, exhausted from the movement. His energy was steadily ebbing away.

'Neither does its former owner,' Ben said. 'That's because he's been dead for four years. His name was James Andanson. You knew him, didn't you, Liam?'

Falconer stared at Ben but said nothing.

'Need me to jog your memory again?' Ben said. 'Andanson was a photographer. A very successful, very wealthy photographer. Born in England, lived in France. Aged fifty-four when he died. He made his money hounding a lot of silly famous people all over the world to sell his snaps to the press. Personally, why anyone would want to pay to see those kinds of pictures is a mystery. Celebrity gossip never was my thing and I don't read the papers. But I do know that Andanson was in the Pont de l'Alma road tunnel that night. And I also know that he wasn't just your regular lens hound. Once upon a time, or so I've been told, he served a spell in the Territorial SAS. Later on he worked as an informer and freelance agent for MI6 and French Intelligence. Some might even go so far as to claim he was working for the Increment. That sounds about right to me.'

'You're insane, Hope.'

Ben smiled darkly. 'I must be. What a way to spend your Christmas Eve.' He drew another photo from the plastic wrap. It showed another car. This time, a black BMW saloon. It was parked in a clearing in a forest, dappled sunlight filtering through the foliage. The car was a burned-out wreck, sitting on bare rims, its glass streaked with soot, most of the plastic trim shrivelled away to a crisp. The fire had been so hot that it had melted the paint down to the bare metal in places. The forest floor around the car was scorched black.

'Seems like working for the Increment must be a stressful occupation,' Ben said. 'Judging by the suicide rate among its members. Jaco Lennox wasn't the first, was he?'

Again, Ben spun the photo into Falconer's lap. Again, Falconer just gave the picture a momentary glance before he silently discarded it.

Ben said, 'That was the car James Andanson owned at the time he killed himself in May 2000, in woodland near Montpellier, four hundred miles from his home in Nant. Did a pretty thorough job of it, too, just like Jaco Lennox. It took a month for the French police to identify him from dental records. Some people take pills, others slit their veins in the bath, others jump off cliffs or under trains. Seems that our man Andanson drove hundreds of miles into the middle of the sticks, with no ignition keys anywhere on his person or in the car, then doused himself with twenty litres of petrol from jerrycans he'd bought en route. After he'd emptied the lot, he fastened his seatbelt and locked the car doors. Then he shot himself twice in the head, *then* torched the car from the outside, with himself locked in it.' Ben smiled grimly. 'Now that shows some kind of ability, even for a former Territorial SAS guy. Wouldn't you say so, Brigadier?'

'There's no evidence of any of that.'

'Of course not. At least, none that would be admitted to an official investigation. Maybe that's why the coroner decided to write it up as suicide. Or maybe someone just paid him to. We'll never know, will we? I tried to find the coroner who signed off on the body, but it turns out the guy died of cancer last year. Shame. He might have had some interesting things to tell me.'

Ben took out the third photograph and tossed it down for Falconer to see. 'But this guy here had plenty to say.' The photo was of a white male, forties, receding dark hair and sunglasses.

'His name is Christophe Pelât,' Ben said. 'He's a fireman who works in Montpellier, and he and his crew were the first to arrive at the scene of Andanson's burnt-out car. Now he lives in fear. When I tracked him down at his home, he had the strangest notion that I was an assassin come to shoot him. Then when he realised I wasn't, he became a little more amenable. He confirmed that even though the body was heavily charred, to the point of being virtually unrecognisable, he was certain that the victim had been shot at least once in the head, and probably twice.'

'That's all just hearsay and speculation,' Falconer said. He broke into another fit of coughing that doubled him up in agony.

'Maybe so,' Ben said, taking the fourth and final photo from the plastic wrap. 'I wonder what this man would have to tell us about that.' Once more, he tossed the picture at Falconer. Once more, Falconer barely looked at it.

'Actually, he probably wouldn't say too much,' Ben said. 'Not any more. Because guess what? He's dead too. His name was Frédéric Dard. He was a French crime novelist who lived in Switzerland. Famous one, too. Wrote more than three hundred books, sold hundreds of millions of the damn things. I tried to read one of them, on the plane back from France. I thought it was trash, but what do I know?'

'Is there a point to any of this?' Falconer grated. 'I'm bleeding here.'

'Oh, there is,' Ben said. 'As it turns out, Dard wasn't just interested in writing fiction. He and Andanson were friends, and they'd been talking about co-writing a book about what really happened in that tunnel in Paris seven years ago. They were going to blow the lid off the whole thing. Except it never happened, and it never will. Dard died just five weeks after his would-be co-author. Heart attack.' Ben smiled. 'Tell me, Liam. Are the CIA and MI6 boys still using poison to induce fatal cardiac arrest, or have they come up with fancier methods since the Cold War?'

'You're talking rubbish,' Falconer snapped. 'Not a shred of this bullshit is conclusive in any way.'

'You're right,' Ben said. 'The Increment always cover their tracks well. Just like they did that August in Paris. Who's going to remember the traces of white paint on the wreck, from Andanson's Fiat? Nobody who matters. Just like nobody's going to bring up the testimony of the witnesses who claimed they saw a bright flash from inside the tunnel, a second before the accident happened. The real evidence was removed, along with the debris on the road and the CCTV footage that was never recorded because someone turned off the cameras. The rest was all buried under a ton of disinformation. All the carefully-orchestrated grandstanding and finger-pointing. The wild conspiracy theories. The royals did it. The French did it. Terrorists did it. Aliens from outer space did it. The blood samples that may or may not have been fiddled to show the driver was drunk. The debates about whether she was pregnant. All whitewash. All the usual weapons of mass distraction. You dump enough conflicting information on the public, pretty soon everyone's head is spinning so badly that nobody even cares any more. You and your Secret Service pals had it all so neatly sewn up. Nobody would have known anything for sure. Except you left out the one key witness who could sink the lot of you. It was a bad mistake, Liam. You should have had someone put a bullet in Jaco Lennox the morning after Operation Solitaire.'

Falconer was silent for a long time. The blood pool was spreading wider on the floor. The front of his shirt and his trousers were saturated and slick with it.

Finally he breathed, 'Lennox told you everything, didn't he?'

Ben nodded. 'Yes, he did. He told me every last detail of what you all did that night.'

5

Ben related it all back to Falconer as Jaco Lennox had told it to him, leaving out the heaving sighs, the drunken sobbing and the long, vacant pauses that had punctuated his account. Lennox might have been half shot away from booze and sleeplessness, but the facts had all been there, sharp, clear, forever branded into his memory from seven years of torment.

The black Mercedes with its three passengers had left from a rear exit of the Paris Ritz Hotel at twenty minutes after midnight on August 31st, 1997. Its driver, who had been under surveillance by Increment operatives the whole evening, was known to have consumed only a very modest quantity of alcohol that night and was certainly not drunk. That was of no importance to the Increment. The fix was in.

As Lennox had confirmed, the car had been a last-minute replacement from the one originally intended. The reason for the switch had been in order for covert agents to carry out enough subtle sabotage to the brakes for them to fail at speed. In order to ensure that the driver would keep his foot down, the Mercedes was pursued by Increment operatives on motorcycles, posing as paparazzi. One of the motorcycle pillion passengers was in constant radio contact with the driver of a white Fiat Uno that was already hovering on standby close to the entrance to the Pont de l'Alma road tunnel, not far away. The Fiat's driver wasn't alone. Andanson's backseat passenger was another Increment operative, Jaco Lennox.

The Mercedes sped across the Place de la Concorde, then along the river embankment, and at twenty-three minutes past midnight entered the short underpass from which it would never emerge in one piece.

As the larger car approached the mouth of the tunnel, the pursuing motorcycles slackened off their speed and fell back, as prearranged. The white Fiat accelerated into position with the Mercedes coming up fast behind it. Just as the driver of the Mercedes went to overtake, the Fiat suddenly swerved into its path and a blinding white flash of light exploded from its rear window.

Directed-energy weapons known as dazzlers had first been designed for military use, as a so-called 'non-lethal option' with multiple potential applications. They did exactly what their name implied, which was to emit a high-energy flash of light at the precise wavelength most able to cause temporary blindness and disorientation to the target. Versions capable of causing instant permanent blindness had been developed also, and despite being banned by a UN protocol, were still sometimes used. The model issued to Jaco Lennox for Operation Solitaire was a STEALTH optical distraction device with a range of up to a thousand metres, effective even through tinted glass.

From less than a car's length away, it was devastating.

The driver of the Mercedes never stood a chance. Blinded and panicked, his natural instinct was to stamp down hard on the brake; perhaps if it hadn't been for the sabotage done to the braking system beforehand, the car might have been able to scrub off enough speed to prevent such a dreadful crash.

But the Mercedes failed to slow. It glanced off the rear of

the Fiat, which skidded harmlessly to one side and accelerated away as the Mercedes spun wildly out of control. Fractions of a second later, it came to a sickening, crunching halt against one of the tunnel's reinforced concrete roof support pillars.

The rest of the story was history. The operation was a resounding success. The white Fiat and its two occupants would somehow be erased from the official version of events.

'I couldn't believe it to begin with,' Ben said. 'But now you've given me the final proof that I needed, and I know that what Lennox told me was the truth. She was an assassination target for the Increment. The other two who died that night were just collateral damage.'

With all the cards on the table, Falconer knew there was no longer any point in pretending.

'For God's sake, man. What choice did we have? Don't you think, if there had been any other way, we would have jumped at the chance? It's not as if she wasn't warned. MI6 told her over and over again to stop meddling in things she didn't understand. She just wouldn't listen.'

Ben looked at him. 'Is that a yes? I confess? We did it?'

Blood bubbled from between Falconer's teeth and his voice was raspy and thick. 'The woman was a threat. Have you any idea how much it cost the country in loss of revenues when the landmines were banned, thanks to that interfering pea-brained bitch and her little band of do-gooders?'

'And you're still manufacturing them every day,' Ben said. 'Behind phony company fronts in countries that never signed up to the treaty.'

'For Christ's sake, get real. You're a soldier, Hope. You're not a businessman. If we didn't make them, someone else would. It's supply and demand. There's a market. It gets catered to. That's all that matters in the real world.'

'I'm not sure if you even remember what the real world is any more,' Ben said. 'Have you ever seen an African child with both legs blown off at the hip from stepping on a mine? Or blinded with half their face missing, or disembowelled and trying to pack their guts back inside their ripped-open body? I have.'

'Who gives a shit?' Falconer spat, blood splotting down his chin. 'In any case, the landmines were just the beginning. That airhead wasn't going to stop until she'd brought the whole damned UK arms industry to its knees. Your "People's Princess" was nothing more than a liability, pure and simple.'

'I don't care about your politics,' Ben said. 'I don't care who she was. I don't care about her family name or her connections or her money, or what she did or didn't do to make herself a target. I only care about one thing: that you murdered an innocent woman. You're a piece of filth and I'm ashamed that I ever stood up to be counted with you.'

'Who the hell are you to judge, anyway? You never took an innocent life in the line of duty?'

'Some things I did, I'm not proud of,' Ben said. 'Other things, I wouldn't have done at all. You were right never to ask me to join your little hit squad, Liam. Because if I'd had any idea what you were up to behind the scenes, it would be you they'd have had to scrape off the wall. What you did was wrong. It was beyond wrong.'

'Oh, spare me the sanctimonious bullshit,' Falconer sneered. 'That's the privilege of a nobody, who never took responsibility for his actions or made any real decisions. In the big boys' game, doing the right thing is a virtue we can't afford.'

'Who said I was virtuous?' Ben said.

He reached down. Unsnapped the retaining catch of the tactical holster that was double-strapped to his right thigh.

He closed his fingers around the rubber-gripped butt of the nine-millimetre pistol and drew it out. The Browning Hi-Power was stock military issue. The exact same model he'd carried with the SAS. Probably the same model that was still issued to the men from the Increment.

It seemed fitting, somehow.

The Browning was already cocked and locked, with a round in the chamber and thirteen more in the magazine. He wasn't going to need the extra thirteen. He clicked off the safety. Then he pointed the pistol at Falconer.

'You wouldn't bloody dare,' Falconer said. 'Not like this.'

'Didn't you teach us that who dares, wins?'

Ben aimed the Browning at Falconer's head. With the fat tubular silencer attached, the sights were obscured. But that didn't matter at this range. He curled his finger around the trigger. He'd polished and honed the internal mechanism until it had a light, crisp pull of just under four pounds. He had three and a half pounds on it when he paused.

'You were my mentor, Liam,' he said. 'I looked up to you like a father. What happened to you?'

A nerve in Falconer's face started twitching. 'Do you want money? I have over a million pounds cash in the safe upstairs. It's yours if you let me live. You walk away. We say no more about this. Nobody will ever know it was you.'

'No deal.'

'Don't do it, Ben. Please. I'm begging you. Show me mercy.'

'Mercy,' Ben repeated. 'If she had begged you for it, would you have shown her any?'

'You'll never get away with it. They'll hunt you down like a dog.'

'They'll try,' Ben said. 'But they'll fail. I was never here. There won't be a trace for anyone to follow. You taught me well.'

'Don't kid yourself. You're a dead man. You might as well put that gun to your own head.'

'I'm not the one who has it coming,' Ben said.

'We all have it coming,' Falconer said.

'You first,' Ben said. He brought the gun closer to Falconer's forehead.

Falconer's eyes blazed up at him with anger. 'I'm a senior member of the British establishment,' he hissed.

'Then all the more reason,' Ben said. And pulled the trigger.

The silenced pistol's report echoed through the cellar. Blood flew up the wall behind Falconer's head. His body lurched, gave a heave, then keeled over sideways and lay still.

Ben put the pistol back in its holster and turned away from the dead man.

When he stepped outside a few minutes later, the night sky had clouded and snow had started to fall thickly. He looked at his watch and saw it was two minutes after twelve.

Christmas morning, 2004.

The glen was in complete silence, just the soft patter of the spiralling snowflakes layering themselves on the frozen ground. Ben pulled the hem of his hat down tight, zipped his jacket collar up to his chin and started off on the long walk back.

Read on for an *exclusive* extract
from the new Ben Hope adventure by

Scott Mariani

The Babylon Idol

Chapter 1

So many times in the past, when Ben Hope had vowed and declared that his crazy days of running from one adventure to another were over and that he was going to stay put at home for the foreseeable future, for one reason or another it hadn't been long before some new crisis had come barrelling into his life and whisked him off again – the latest in a sorry, never-ending series of broken promises, to himself and to others, that had sometimes made him wonder if he was cursed by fate.

This time, though, he was determined to be true to his word. This was it. Mayhem, violence, war, intrigue, chasing around the world – he was done with the lot of it, once and for all.

It wasn't so much that, as his longtime friend and business partner Jeff Dekker sometimes joked, 'we're getting too old for this shit'. In his early forties, Ben had plenty of life left in him and could still outrun, outtrain and, if necessary, outfight guys half his age. But he'd have been lying if he'd said that the recent African escapade hadn't taken a lot out of him, physically and emotionally. The same went for Jeff, who'd been right there at Ben's side in what had to be the deadliest, most complex and disturbing rescue mission either man had ever experienced, either during their time in British

473

Special Forces or in the years since. Likewise for Tuesday Fletcher, the young ex-trooper who had not long since joined their small staff at the Le Val Tactical Training Centre in rural Normandy but proved himself ten times over to be a stalwart asset to the team and forged bonds of comradeship with Ben and Jeff that could never be broken.

Just nine days had passed since they'd all returned to Le Val, to find a mountain of mail waiting for them. The business was growing by the month, attracting so many bookings from military, law enforcement and private close protection agencies worldwide looking to refine and extend their tactical skillset, that it was hard to keep up with demand. Now that the operation had received a substantial cash injection in the wake of the Africa mission, they were set to grow still further. But all of that had been set aside for a week, as an official Le Val holiday was declared.

Ben had spent that time recuperating. For most people, 'recuperating' might have meant lying in bed, or sitting around idle, licking their wounds and feeling sorry for themselves. For Ben it meant getting back into the punishing exercise routines he'd followed for most of his life. Working back up to a thousand push-ups a day, lifting weights, honing his marksmanship skills on Le Val's pistol and rifle ranges, scaling cliffs and sea-kayaking off the Normandy coast and going for long runs through the wintry countryside with Storm, his favourite of the pack of German Shepherds that patrolled the compound. The harder Ben trained, the more he emptied his mind and the further he left the horrors of Africa behind him.

Jeff Dekker was no slouch either, but he'd used his recuperation time differently. His romance with Chantal Mercier, who taught at the *Ecole Primaire* in the nearby village of Saint-Acaire, had grown more serious over the last months.

In all the years Ben had known Jeff, throughout the never-ending sequence of on-off, part-time, short-term girlfriends whose names were too many to remember, he'd never seen him so committed to a relationship. He was happy for his friend, and Jeff seemed happy too. Even Jeff's French had improved.

Meanwhile, Tuesday Fletcher had taken advantage of the week's holiday to fly home to London to see his parents, Rosco and Shekeia, second-generation immigrants from Jamaica. Tuesday was still recovering from a gunshot wound to the arm, sustained during their flight from the Congo. Ben had no doubt that he'd come up with some white lie to conceal from his parents just how close he'd come to being killed. If anyone could make light of a bullet in the arm, it was the ever-cheerful Tuesday.

The second week back, the three of them had started easing themselves back into business-as-usual mode and begun working their way through the backlog of emails, letters, accounts, orders, bookings, hiring new staff to cope with the expanding Le Val operation, and a hundred other matters that had accumulated during their absence.

That was where Ben found himself at this moment, sitting alone in the prefabricated office building across the yard from the old stone farmhouse. It was an early December morning, and the icy rain that had been drumming on the office building roof since dawn was threatening to turn snowy. The fan heater was blasting waves of warm air that engulfed Ben as he sat at the desk sipping a steaming mug of black coffee. Storm and two more of the guard dogs, Mauser and Luger, appeared to have given themselves the morning off and were curled contentedly at his feet, like a huge hairy black-and-tan rug spread over the floor. Ben didn't have the heart to kick them out into the cold.

From where he sat, through the window he could see the parked minibus that had brought the current crop of trainees to Le Val: eight agents from the French SDAT anti-terror unit anxious to up their game in expectation of more of the troubles that had been rocking Paris in recent times. Tuesday was currently out with them on the six-hundred-metre range, probably all freezing their balls off as he took them through their sniper paces. Trembling hands and numb fingers were no great boon to long-range accuracy. Poor sods. Ben was scheduled to teach a two-hour session that afternoon in the plywood and car tyre-walled construction they called the 'killing house', covering elements of advanced live-fire CQB or close-quarter-battle training that they were unlikely to learn anywhere else. At least they'd be indoors out of the wet. Two more members of the Le Val team who'd be happy to huddle indoors with mugs of coffee were Serge and Adrien, the two ex-French army guys who manned the new gatehouse – the latest addition to the complex – and controlled people coming in and out.

As for Jeff Dekker, Ben wasn't quite sure where he was at that moment. He'd said something about checking the perimeter fence for wind damage; the region had been buffeted by one winter gale after another that week. With the kind of arsenal that Le Val kept locked up in its special armoury vault, and the sort of work that went on within the various sections of the compound, government bureaucracy insisted on the property being ultra-secure. Not that Ben had lately noticed any gangs of Jihadi cutthroats roaming the Normandy countryside in search of military hardware. But rules were rules.

Ben reached for his Gauloises and Zippo lighter, flicked a cigarette from the familiar blue pack, clanged open the lighter and lit up in a cloud of smoke. It suddenly felt even better to be home. Puffing happily away, he reached across the desk for the stack of mail he'd been sifting through. So far it had all been bills, bills, and more bills. But this letter looked different.

'Strange,' he said.

Chapter 2

The letter certainly was unusual. More than the Italian post-mark, Ben was surprised to see the ink-stamped legend ISTITUTO PENITENZIARO BOLLATI on the envelope. He'd heard of the Bollati medium-security prison in Milan, but never been there, could think of no connections the place could have to him, and wouldn't have expected to receive a letter from anyone there. Yet there was no denying his name and address neatly handwritten on the front of the envelope. Above it, the date on the postmark showed that the letter had left Milan while Ben was struggling to survive somewhere in the middle of the Congo jungle.

'Hm,' he said.

At his feet, Storm cocked an ear and glanced up as though to see what the fuss was about, then lost interest and went back to sleep.

Ben took another slurp of scalding coffee and another drag on the Gauloise, then put down his mug and rested the cigarette in the ashtray and picked up the old M4 bayonet that served as a letter-opener in the Le Val office. He carefully slit one end of the envelope, reached inside and was about to draw out the single folded sheet of paper when his phone suddenly came to life and started buzzing on the desk like an upturned bee.

'Got a problem in Sector Nine.' Jeff's voice was barely audible over the crackle of the wind distorting his phone's mic. Sector Nine was what they called part of the east perimeter fence. 'That sodding apple tree Marie-Claire wouldn't ever let me cut down? Well, we won't need to now. Sorry to drag you out here, mate, but I need your help.'

Ben could imagine what had happened. He'd read the letter later. He grabbed his leather jacket from the back of his chair and slipped it on. 'You want to come?' he said to Storm, who instantly sprang to his feet as if it was feeding time. Life was simple when you were a dog.

Outside in the biting wind, the sleet was turning snowier by the minute. Ben pulled up the collar of his jacket and crossed the yard, past the minibus and over to the ancient Land Rover. It was a tool box on wheels, filled with all kinds of junk including a greasy old chainsaw. Storm hopped in the back and found a space for himself while Ben got behind the wheel, and they set off across the yard and down the rutted track between the buildings that ran parallel with the rifle range, skirted the butts and led across the fields towards Sector Nine. He heard the muffled boom of a rifle coming from the range, the ear-splitting report and supersonic crack of the bullet in flight muted by the high earth walls that ran parallel from the firing points to the butts at the far end and prevented any 'flyers' from escaping the range boundaries. Not that such elementary mistakes could happen, under Tuesday's expert supervision. He could splatter grapes all day long at five hundred metres with his modified Remington 700, and he was one of the best instructors Ben had ever seen.

The old tree had been a bone of contention for years. Marie-Claire, the local woman they'd employed since the beginning as an occasional cook, swore by the particular apples it produced as being essential to her mouth-wateringly delicious traditional Normandy apple tart recipe. As popular as her tart was with the parties of hard-worked and hungry trainees at Le Val, Jeff had always griped that the tree was too close to the fence and had argued that they could get perfectly decent apples at the grocer's in Saint-Acaire or the Carrefour in Valognes. It had been an endless and hard-fought debate with neither side giving an inch, while the tree kept growing taller and spreading outwards year on year. Now it looked as if the winter wind had settled the argument for them.

The track wound and snaked through the grounds. To Ben's right, he passed the patch of oak woodland, now bare and gaunt, that in summer completely screened the ruins of the tiny thirteenth-century chapel where he sometimes retreated to sit, and think, and enjoy the silence. To his left, beyond hills and fields and forest, he could see the distant steeple of the church at Saint-Acaire pointing up at the grey sky.

He loved this place, in any season. He couldn't imagine why he'd ever wanted to leave it.

But then, he'd done a lot of things in his life that he couldn't understand why, looking back.

As Ben approached Sector Nine in the Land Rover, he saw Jeff's Ford Ranger over the grassy rise up ahead. Then saw Jeff himself, standing in the diagonal sleet with his arms folded and frowning unhappily at the branches that had become enmeshed in the wire. The whole tree had uprooted and toppled over, flattening a ten-metre section of fence with it. Those ever-lurking Jihadis had only to come running through the gap, and they'd be just a step away from total European domination.

'What did I always say?' Jeff grated, pointing at the fallen tree, as Ben stepped down from the Land Rover. 'What did I always warn that old bat would happen one day? And did she ever listen to a word? Did she buggery.'

'No use crying about it now,' Ben said. He grabbed the chainsaw from the back of the Landy. The dog clambered into the front seat, fogging up the windscreen with his hot breath as he watched the two humans set about dismantling the tree.

Ben started with the smaller branches, trimming them off while Jeff dragged them away and tossed them in a heap to one side. Once the gnarly old trunk was as bare as a telegraph pole, it was time to start chopping it up into sections before the real work of rebuilding the broken fence could begin. By then, the sleet had delivered on its threat to turn snowy. Ben and Jeff took a break, and sat in the Land Rover watching the snow dust the landscape. Ben lit another Gauloise, smoking it slowly, savouring the tranquillity of the moment.

'I love her, you know,' Jeff said, out of the blue after a lengthy pause.

'The old bat?'

'Chantal. I'm in love, mate.'

Ben had never heard his friend say anything like that before. From his lips, it was like Mahatma Gandhi saying how much he loved a good juicy beefsteak.

Jeff shook his head, as though he could hardly believe it himself. 'I mean, I know what it sounds like, and I never thought this would happen to me. But I think she's the one. Christ, I really fucking think so.' He glanced at Ben. There was a look in his eyes something like helplessness.

'Chantal's great,' Ben said, even though he'd only met her briefly a couple of times.

'Yeah, she is.' Jeff swallowed, like a man about to make

a confession. 'Listen. I . . . uh, I asked her to marry me. She said yes. Wanted you to be the first to know.'

Ben masked his complete astonishment and said, 'I'm sure you'll be very happy together.' The subject of marriage wasn't one that was ever discussed between them, given Ben's patchy history in that department. He wasn't well qualified to extol the joys of married life, but it was all he could think of to say right now.

'Thanks, mate.' Jeff smiled, then pointed through the windscreen, obviously keen to change the subject. 'Look at this frigging snow.' It was thickening by the minute, blown about in sheets by the increasing wind.

'No point waiting for it to stop,' Ben said. 'Let's get on.'

The chainsaw buzzed and snorted and kicked in Ben's hands as he sliced the tree into sections, him bending over the prone trunk, Jeff standing at his shoulder waiting to grab each piece as it came loose and toss it into the pile. Ten minutes later, the top half of the tree was next year's firewood logs ready to be loaded on a trailer and split and stacked in the barn.

Two minutes after that, *it* happened.

There was a strong gust of wind, followed immediately by a strange whizzing crack that was only faintly audible over the noise of the saw. At almost the same instant, Ben heard Jeff's strangled cry of shock and pain. He looked quickly around, just in time to see the blood fly. As if in slow motion, like a scarlet ribbon fluttering from Jeff's body, twisting in the air. Jeff doubling up. Falling against him. Collapsing into the trampled grass. Mud and snow and sawdust and more blood. Lots of it, spilling everywhere. Ben yelling Jeff's name. Getting no response. The sudden fear twisting his guts like a pair of icy gripping hands.

In those first confused instants, Ben thought that the

chain had broken and gone spinning off the bar of the saw, hitting Jeff in some kind of freakish accident. In a panic he hit the engine kill switch. The saw instantly stopped, and Ben realised the chain was still intact.

He threw the saw down and fell on his knees by Jeff's slumped body. Jeff wasn't moving. The snow was turning red in a spreading stain under him. Ben yelled his friend's name. Tried to shake him, to roll him over, to understand what was happening. Blood slicked his hands and bubbled up between his fingers. So much blood.

Now Ben was thinking that the spinning chainsaw might have dislodged an old nail or fencing staple buried deep in the tree trunk from long ago, and sent it flying through the air like a deadly piece of shrapnel.

'Jeff!'

Jeff's eyes were closed. His face was white, except where it was spattered red. His jacket and shirt were black and oily with blood. Ben ripped at the material.

And then he saw the gaping bullet wound in Jeff's chest.

Ex-SAS major Ben Hope is looking for peace but his past is about to catch up with him . . .

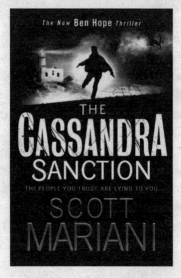

The twelfth book in the exhilarating action adventure thriller series starring ex-SAS major Ben Hope.

Read it now!

**Where ex-SAS major Ben Hope goes,
trouble always follows . . .**

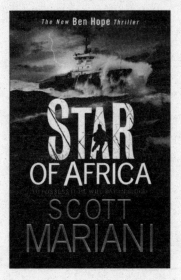

The prequel to *The Devil's Kingdom*.
Read the first part of this sensational two-book
sequence, the biggest and most epic Ben Hope
adventure yet!